A DOG AMONG DIPLOMATS

A Bull Moose Dog Run Mystery

J. F. ENGLERT

A DELL BOOK

A DOG AMONG DIPLOMATS

Published by Bantam Dell
A Division of Random House, Inc.
New York, New York

"Luck," from *The Collected Poems of Langston Hughes,*
copyright © 1994 by the Estate of Langston Hughes. Used courtesy
of Alfred A. Knopf, a division of Random House, Inc.

ISBN 978-0-7394-9589-6

Printed in the United States of America
Published simultaneously in Canada

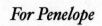

For Penelope

Acknowledgments

J. F. Englert would like to thank Danielle Perez for her fine editorial counsel; everyone at Bantam Dell for their work, both practical and artistic; Susan Stava for her photography; Jamie Block for his music and permission to use his lyrics in the epigraph; Claudia Cross and Marcy Posner at Sterling Lord Literistic for making sure that Randolph found a good home both in the United States and abroad; and Catherine and Dulcie for their kind walk-on into Randolph's world.

The Queen of 5th St.
Holds court in a one-room flat.
The jewels of state in a shoebox,
The Dog's the Diplomat.
And the stars on the ceiling
They change once a year.
Makes her feel like she's touring
Another hemisphere.

—*from "Queen of 5th St."*
by Jamie Block

A
DOG
AMONG
DIPLOMATS

IT'S NOT EVERY DAY THAT a young man clad only in boxer shorts embossed with red hearts dies beneath an opened parachute in a small third-floor room in one of New York's last boardinghouses. It's even rarer that a visual artist, the owner of a Labrador retriever equipped with a generous belly, a fine mind and an admirable temperament, is called to the scene by the police department before the body is even cold. Yet this is exactly what happened just after ten p.m. on a recent mild March night.

I was sitting on my haunches in our cozy apartment on the Upper West Side of Manhattan, looking into the middle distance and allowing a mother lode of Chinese spareribs to settle pleasantly in my gullet. I felt a postdinner nap coming on and was not planning to resist (in this hectic world it is often a struggle to get my twelve-hour sleep quota). Harry, my twenty-something owner, was beginning the third hour of a documentary on the life of Vincent van Gogh, narrated, it seemed, by a narcoleptic whose voice rose at all the wrong moments, as if he had just been poked awake again in the sound booth.

Then the phone rang. My owner had already taken me for my evening Numbers 1 and 2 (shortchanging himself van Gogh's contentious roommateship with Gauguin at Arles) and was loath to be roused from Grandfather Oswald's La-Z-Boy for anything short of an evacuation of Manhattan for the apocalypse. He let the machine pick up, and Imogen's voice filled our living room.

"Leave a message after the beep," she said before trailing off into an uncertain whisper. "Harry, is it a beep?"

The mild but decisive voice of the caller came next.

"Harry, it's Detective Davis. If you're there, pick up. It's important. It involves . . . her."

Harry flew out of his La-Z-Boy recliner and grabbed the phone. My nose could detect the strong waves of hope, excitement and possibility that my owner shed. I wondered if Detective Peter Davis, the lead investigator in Imogen's case, had a breakthrough to report. Our lovely

Imogen, who had rescued me from the pet-store clods and then included Harry in our domestic arrangements, had disappeared over a year before without a word or lead—foul play suspected. I had not yet informed Harry, but I had spotted her once again disappearing into a subway tunnel after the successful—if brutal—conclusion to our last mystery. That investigation had pushed both Harry and me to great extremes of endurance and ingenuity, and the end found us on the verge of an even larger mystery, which promised to span the globe in a conspiratorial and high-stakes web before it brought some resolution to our loss of Imogen. Detective Davis's phone call was the beginning of what would prove to be Act II.

"I'm here," Harry said into the receiver, then listened without a word. He found a pen amid a pile of paintbrushes on the side table and scribbled down an address.

"Okay, Peter. I'll be there in twenty minutes."

My owner hung up the phone, grabbed a light jacket and disappeared through the door and down the stairs without a word to his dog. The peace was shattered—what is peace if it can be broken so easily?—and all prospects of an after-dinner nap seemed to vanish in the face of this fresh anxiety. But fortunately I am built to endure, and soon the soporific magic of the spareribs began to affect me and I closed my eyes for a dreamless snooze.

Let me now share with you the particular facts that mark my existence. I am a Labrador retriever who lives in Manhattan, the isle of my birth, to which I am deeply attached. I am also sentient. Other dogs might be as well, to a greater or lesser degree, but few take pleasure from reading the important works of your human literature or make expansive journeys of imagination as Yours Truly does. I am self-taught, having learned to read from the pages of New York's finest tabloid newspapers laid out for my house-training. The writers, particularly those responsible for headlines, are the unheralded poets of our age (by way of evidence, the *Post*'s sublime: HEADLESS BODY FOUND IN TOPLESS BAR). Lest I lose myself in the sometimes lurid virtues of the tabloid, the main challenge of this Labrador's life is the fact that his prodigious brain—2.3 pounds of smoothly functioning gelatinous gray matter—is trapped within a body as unresponsive to the nuances of thought as a piece of chocolate (a delicacy I am supposed to avoid because my liver cannot handle it). Because of this physical "frozenness," I cannot express in any facial gesture what I am thinking.

Blankness is my trademark, though many humans describe my eyes as "soulful." My tail has a life of its own and wags idiotically even when I am in a black mood. Then there is an involuntary body tremble that my owner frequently mistakes for bladder-based urgency because it jingles the tags on my collar (not that I am ever ungrateful for regular outings to the sidewalks, dog runs or parks of New York). Owners, please never underestimate the importance of liberal access to Numbers 1 and 2 — no need to make us test our house-trained credentials.

Being unable to choose when I can relieve myself and under what conditions is symbolic of the many restrictions in my life. I cannot, for example, simply walk out the front door of our apartment and wander the streets without a human chaperone. For most of my relatively short life (I will be six in November) I have not minded these restrictions. I have had wonderful people to whom I belonged and who belonged to me. I have had my books and a cozy corner in which to discreetly enjoy them, to listen to the wind or the rain on the drainpipe and mull over the wisdom of the classics and the music of words.

But then Imogen disappeared and people died and I needed to apply whatever strengths I had to protecting my owner and learning the truth. Prior to this development I had always steered clear of trying to communicate with humans. As warm as my relations are with Harry, I never trusted the species as a whole. There is always some P. T. Barnum in the woodwork, ready to try to make a buck from the latest animal freak, or, worse still, an overly zealous scientist eager to shave off every inch of a Labrador's fur and snap on the electrodes to prove that we are a higher form of life. No thank you. But despite my reluctance to "shine," the necessities of protecting my owner and solving a mystery required that I construct a bridge between species. I did this by using Harry's favorite cereal, Alpha-Bits, and composing messages from "beyond" out of the friendly little letters. Harry is susceptible to the idea of the paranormal. Ghosts, spirits, communication from beyond now make up part of his worldview. Someday, I hope, this irrational fever will pass, but we all nurse our wounds differently and losing Imogen was a harsh blow. For my part, I stick to reason and those elements of intuition and dog sense that have helped me navigate this life. Perhaps I stick to these things a little too much. The point, though, is that I used Harry's susceptibility as a way to introduce the messages I wrote and make them credible. The messages came from a spirit guide whom I dubbed Holmes. My uncritical owner left the stone unturned and I was never found out, even though near the end I had Holmes indicate that I had been "inspired" and that my owner should follow my lead.

Harry returned to our apartment after three hours, and I awoke from my after-dinner slumber to find him smoking one of his emergency cigarettes as he came through the door. Things were clearly very grim.

Fortunately, my owner often gives voice to his recent experiences and thus keeps his dog well informed. The following is a narrative of what transpired after Harry left our apartment, which I have pieced together from his reiteration of events and information I gathered soon after.

My owner had taken a taxi to the address provided by Detective Davis. He stepped out of the cab to find himself standing before a large redbrick residential building in the East Village. Most of the windows were dark, but one room on the third floor was ablaze with light, and Harry saw figures appear and disappear in the window: a man with a tape measure; someone else in a big white suit with a face mask. It was a forensics team collecting evidence.

"No one in. No one out," a police officer said. He stood between Harry and the entrance to the building.

"Detective Davis told me to come," Harry said.

The policeman stepped aside. Harry climbed a short flight of stairs and, entering through the open front door, found himself in the lobby of what could have been mistaken for a New England bed-and-breakfast if it were not filled with an oddly incongruous bunch of foreign nationals, drag queens and vagrants.

"Wow," Harry muttered as he absorbed the scene.

Rough-and-tumble bachelor-athlete type though Harry may be, even my owner knows that doilies, woven wicker baskets, plastic cornucopias with waxy grapes do not typically belong in the East Village and definitely not with this pirate crew.

"They're the residents," Detective Davis said from the landing of the interior staircase. He spoke loudly, as if he wanted everyone to hear. "Come on upstairs, Harry."

Harry did as he was told and began to climb the several flights of stairs to the third floor.

"Interesting place," Harry said. "What is it?"

"A boardinghouse," Detective Davis said. "Probably one of the last ones in Manhattan. There used to be hundreds, thousands even. Then they turned most of them into SROs—single-resident-occupancy buildings—but not this one. This one is classic Bowery bum."

"Yeah, the people don't really seem to fit," Harry said as they climbed the stairs, occasionally brushing past crime-scene personnel carrying clear plastic bags filled with suspicious-looking contents gathered up above on the third floor. "I mean, there's a complimentary coffee and tea station. There's a fire going in the fireplace. There're Currier and Ives prints on the wall."

"Some of those aren't prints," Detective Davis said in hushed tones. "Let me give you the short version. Ten years ago this place was a dump. A gun cage around reception. Dealers on the stoop. Graffiti all over that wall where the Currier and Ives are now. Then two things happened: the neighborhood started to improve, and the lady who owns the place won the lottery. Instead of doing what most people would with the winnings—buy a villa in Tuscany, sail the world—she decided to renovate the place."

"I got it," Harry concluded. "But she couldn't

get rid of the old tenants. That explains the people downstairs."

"No," Detective Davis said as they arrived at the third floor. "She didn't *want* to get rid of the tenants. She wanted to give them a taste of the good life too. Harry, I think that she is either one of the craziest women on the planet or the happiest. Most of the time I lean toward thinking she's the happiest. After all, only the happiest sort of person would win all of that money and not leave their past behind. Only the happiest sort of person has that kind of peace."

He paused.

"Now let's go look at the corpse."

Detective Davis motioned for the forensics team to clear the room, and two men and one woman in sanitary jumpsuits promptly exited with more bags of evidence. Harry moved as if to cover his nose the way he had seen in detective shows, but Davis intervened.

"No need. There's no smell. If he's been dead more than two hours I'd be surprised. Forensics will tell us soon enough."

Harry stood just inside the room and looked around. At first there was not much to see: a queen-sized bed, a writing desk and desk lamp, a waist-high chest of drawers and two large klieg lights brought by the police to illuminate the

room. Then Harry saw the legs sticking out between the bed and the window. The legs ended
in the white boxer shorts embossed with red
hearts. The rest of the body was covered by a
gently inflated white parachute that draped
from the bed onto the floor like the roof of a
child's tent playhouse.

"You haven't moved it yet?" Harry asked.

"Oh, yeah. We moved it, but I had them put
it back."

"For me?" Harry asked.

"For me," Detective Davis said. "I like to
freeze the scene in my mind. It helps me trace
backward if I know how it all finally ended."

"Sounds like a meditation."

"Only when the bodies don't stink or someone's not shooting a gun at you or swinging a
machete."

"The parachute's strange," Harry observed.

"The parachute's a real winner. The touch of
the poet," Detective Davis said. "He didn't die
falling off his bed. He was strangled with the
parachute cord. He's a strong young man. Very
fit. But there isn't a sign of a struggle. People
don't let themselves get strangled. They kick.
They punch. They scratch. They fight. The only
time they don't is when they aren't conscious to
begin with. Whoever did this first made sure he

wasn't conscious. He was probably drugged. I'd guess chloral hydrate. We found two champagne glasses and a bottle—Schramsberg—the California bubbly Richard Nixon used to toast détente with China in the seventies. It's all being tested now, but I can already tell you what they'll find. Powerful sleeping agent in only one of the glasses and plenty of DNA over everything..."

"I don't get it, Peter. What's this got to do with Imogen?"

Detective Davis motioned toward the dresser, which was bare except for a large photo frame.

"Take a look at those pictures."

The frame contained two photographs, one above the other. Both featured our mistress. The top photograph showed Imogen in a red cocktail dress, smiling broadly. The bottom photograph showed my mistress and Yours Truly, but I will save further description of the picture because it was the top photograph that gripped my owner now. In it, Imogen's arm was around the shoulder of a young man. Her hair was short, as it had been when I had last seen her racing toward the subway.

"My God. It's her," Harry whispered. Harry reached to pick up the frame and hold it close, but Detective Davis stopped him.

"Harry, please don't touch. It's evidence."

"Who's that guy?"

"That guy is *that* guy," Detective Davis said, pointing at the body beneath the parachute. "Beyond that I couldn't tell you. I was hoping that you could tell me."

"I've never seen him before," Harry said. "But Imogen looks so different."

"Short hair," Detective Davis said. "Is that it?"

"I've never seen the dress," Harry said. "It's very un-Imogen. She was a jeans and T-shirt girl."

"So you think the photograph is recent?"

"Excuse me?"

"That it was taken after she disappeared..."

"What?"

Harry could not grasp the meaning of Detective Davis's words, because, as I mentioned above, I had not yet informed him that Imogen was alive. There was no "after she disappeared" for Harry. In Harry's mind, Imogen had no "after" life that did not include him. Harry was of two minds: Imogen was dead, but, because he loved her beyond telling, she never could be. She haunted him but was permanently frozen as the girl who had disappeared one winter's night going to buy bread at Zabar's. I should have conveyed what I knew to Harry,

but, instead, I had decided to approach the revelation of her being alive in my own fashion,
which meant after much careful and literary
reflection. Dante, my Florentine poet guide,
promised no help in this area, since Pinsky's excellent translation was still buried beneath the
daybed in our living room, where Harry had
kicked it by accident on his way from bedroom
to bathroom one drowsy morning. I turned to
Proust and his prodigious work on memory but,
alas, was asleep before the first madeleine. So I
crossed the Channel to the land of Dickens.
Dickens mixes his poetry with practicality, and
his novels, of course, are stock full of people disappearing and popping up again. I began to
work my way through *Great Expectations* in a
small-print, nose-unfriendly paperback edition,
and as Pip and Estella and Miss Havisham rose
up to me from the page and began to play—not
very nicely, those last two—in my imagination, I
realized, once again, something that I have
always known but frequently forget: literature
is not a way to get practical things done. Nor
should it be. It is a destination and occasionally
an escape. When we return to this so-called real
world from the book, it is like stepping back
into time at the exact moment we had left.
We may feel different, but nothing else has

changed. And if we are different, we are different in ways that might be rich, wide and soulful, but not really practical. Go into a great novel or poem looking for the answer to A and you'll get the answer to Z. It will be a good answer. But it will still be the answer to Z, not A.

"Harry, we think Imogen is alive," Detective Davis said in a soft voice. He reached out and rested a hand on my owner's shoulder. "We think that she has been living here for several months."

"In this boardinghouse?" Harry asked.

"In this room," Detective Davis said.

Harry looked the tiny space up and down. His eyes came to rest on the queen-sized bed, with its dingy bedspread and its two mauve pillows undisturbed despite the corpse beside them.

"But I thought this was his room?"

"It was his room . . . and it was her room too."

"They were together?"

Detective Davis nodded.

"A couple?"

"I'm sorry, Harry. They didn't mix much with the people here, but all the inhabitants agreed on that point. They heard things, you know, from behind the door."

"She's alive," Harry said. "Imogen's alive."

Detective Davis was not a man who normally

looked down at the floor in awkward situations, but he did so now.

"Yes. She's alive. That's the good news. The bad news is that they were seen entering the room together tonight and then two people saw her fleeing from this room shortly before the body was discovered."

Again, Harry struggled to digest the information.

"Harry, Imogen is the prime suspect in the murder of the young man beneath that parachute."

INDEED, THE NEWS WAS grim. Very grim. Harry returned to our apartment with four packs of emergency cigarettes crammed into his jacket pockets and a shopping bag filled with enough liquor to stock a weekend party for a drunken English thespian. We would be in for a long night.

My owner was reeling and so was I. Imogen was alive. But who was she exactly? Such strange facts marred the image of my mistress: champagne glasses, one generously marked with thick red lipstick; a photograph of her in party mode, arm draped around a now-dead man with whom she was apparently living while Harry and I endured a yearlong eclipse of her sun; and then the strong possibility (at least, in the eyes of Detective Davis of the NYPD) that Imogen was a murderess. Was she following in Iris, her mother's, homicidal footsteps? Was a bloody gene blooming? Her dog refused to believe this. The surfaces of things can be deceptive. The photograph could be posed. The expression faked. The living arrangement suggestive of other possibilities.

After all, there was that other photograph in the frame. The picture below the one that so disturbed Harry had transmitted a different message to me. This photograph was taken in long-ago, happy days for our family. I was very familiar with it. Imogen had two copies that I knew of: one was still in a frame next to the bed in our apartment, and the other had been on her desk at the Morgan Archives, where she worked. Even if I didn't have a copy close at hand to refresh my memory, I could have recalled all of the elements vividly: the cozy cluster of three figures, the leafy background, the expressions of glee (Imogen), tongue-protruding, damp-snout blankness in the middle (me) and joy (Harry). The photograph had been taken in Central Park on a fine day in May: low humidity, blue skies and squads of tourists wandering about who were more than willing to stop and participate in a "New York moment" by snapping a photograph of two city-dwelling young lovers and their amiable dog. We made a fine trio. It was this photograph that occupied the lower portion of the frame—but with

KARL SCHROEDER

SUN OF SUNS

Virga | BOOK ONE

A TOM DOHERTY ASSOCIATES BOOK **TOR®** NEW YORK

SUN OF SUNS: VIRGA, BOOK ONE

Copyright © 2006 by Karl Schroeder

This book is printed on acid-free paper.

Edited by David G. Hartwell

A Tor Book
Published by Tom Doherty Associates, LLC
175 Fifth Avenue
New York, NY 10010

www.tor.com

Tor® is a registered trademark of Tom Doherty Associates, LLC.

Library of Congress Cataloging-in-Publication Data

Schroeder, Karl, 1962–
    Sun of suns / Karl Schroeder.—1st ed.
        p. cm. — (Virga ; bk. 1)
    "A Tom Doherty Associates book."
    ISBN-13: 978-0-765-31543-4
    ISBN-10: 0-765-31543-2
    I. Title
    PR9199.3.S269S86 2006
    813'.6—dc22   2006005929

First Edition: October 2006

Printed in the United States of America

0 9 8 7 6 5 4 3 2 1

Acknowledgments

As always, I'd like to acknowledge the hard work and good advice of my editor, David Hartwell, as well as Denis Wong at Tor Books; my agent Donald Maass for having the good grace to run with this project when I unexpectedly dropped it in his lap; and of course, Janice and Paige for their patience during my extended periods of impractical musing and daydreaming.

TO THE INDISPENSABLE:

Cory Doctorow, Phyllis Gotlieb, Sally McBride,
David Nickle, Helen Rykens, Sara Simmons,
Michael Skeet, Hugh A. D. Spencer, Dale Sproule,
Allan Weiss, and Theresa Wojtasiewicz

SUN OF SUNS

1

HAYDEN GRIFFIN WAS plucking a fish when the gravity bell rang. The dull clang penetrated even the thick wooden walls of the corporation inn; it was designed to be heard all over town. Hayden paused, frowned, and experimentally let go of the fish. Four tumbling feathers flashed like candle flames in an errant beam of sunlight shooting between the floorboards. The fish landed three feet to his left. Hayden watched the feathers dip in a slow arc to settle next to it.

"A bit early for a spin-up, ain't it?" said Hayden. Miles grunted distractedly. The former soldier, now corporation cook, was busily pouring sauce over a steaming turkey that he'd just rescued from the oven's minor inferno. His bald skull shone in the firelight. "They might need me all the same," continued Hayden. "I better go see."

Miles glanced up. "Your ma left you here," he said. "You been bad again. Pick up the fish."

Hayden leaned back against the table, crossing his arms. He was trying to come up with a reply that didn't sound like whining when the bell rang again, more urgently. "See?" he said. "They need somebody. Nobody in town's as good with the bikes as I am. Anyway, how you gonna boil this fish if the gravity goes?"

"Gravity ain't gonna go, boy," snapped Miles. "It's solid right now."

"Then I better go see what else is up."

"You just want to watch your old lady light the sun," said Miles. "Don't you?"

"Today's just a test. I'll wait for tomorrow, when they light it for real."

"Come on, Miles. I'll be right back."

The cook sighed. "Go, then. Set the bikes going. Then come right back." Hayden bolted for the door and Miles shouted, "Don't leave that fish on the floor!"

As Hayden walked down the hall to the front of the inn another stray beam of sunlight spiked up around the plank floorboards. That was a bad sign; Mom would have to wait for deep cloud cover before lighting the town's new sun, lest the Slipstreamers should see it. Slipstream would never tolerate another sun so close to their own. The project was secret—or it had been. By tomorrow the whole world would know about it.

Hayden walked backward past the well-polished oak bar, waving his lanky arms casually at his side as he said, "Bell rang. Gotta check the bikes." One of the customers smirked doubtfully at him; Mama Fifty glared at him from her post behind the bar. Before she could reply he was out the front door.

A blustery wind was blowing out here as always, even whistling up between the street boards. Sunlight angled around the edges of the street's peaked roof, bars and rectangles of light sliding along the planking and up the walls of the buildings that crammed every available space. The street boards gave like springs under Hayden's feet as he ran up the steep curve of the avenue, which was nearly empty at this time of day.

Gavin Town came to life at dusk, when the workers who slept here flooded back from all six directions, laughing and gossiping. Merchants would unshutter their windows for the night market as the gaslights were lit all along the way. The dance hall would throw open its doors for those with the stamina to take a few turns on the floor. Sometimes Hayden picked up some extra bills by lighting the streetlights himself. He was good with fire, after all.

If he went to work on the bikes Hayden wouldn't be able to see the sun, so he took a detour. Slipping down a narrow alleyway between two tall houses, he came to one of the two outer streets of the town—really little more than a narrow covered walkway. Extensions of houses and shops formed a ceiling, their entrances to the left as he stepped into the way. To the right was an uneven board fence, just a crack open at the top. An occasional shuttered window interrupted the surface of the fence, but Hayden didn't pause at any of them. He was making for an open gallery a quarter of the way up the street.

At moments like this—alone and busy—he either completely forgot himself or drowned in grief. His father's death still weighed on him, though it had been a year now; was it that long since he and his mother had moved here? Mother kept insisting that it was best this way, that if they'd stayed home in Twenty-two Town they would have been surrounded by reminders of Dad all the time. But was that so bad?

His father wouldn't be here to see the lighting of the sun, his wife's completion of his project—their crowning achievement as a family. When Hayden remembered them talking about that, it was his father's voice he remembered, soaring in tones of enthusiasm and hope. Mother would be quieter, but her pride and love came through in the murmurs that came through the bedroom wall and lulled Hayden to sleep at night. To make your own sun! That was how nations were founded. To light a sun was to be remembered forever.

WHEN HAYDEN WAS twelve his parents had taken him on his first visit to Rush. He had complained, because lately he'd come to know that though Slipstream was a great nation, it was not his nation. His friends had jeered at him for visiting the camp of the enemy, though he didn't exactly know why Slipstreamers were bad, or what it meant to be a citizen of Aerie instead.

"That's why we're going," his father had said. "So that you can understand."

"That, and to see what they're wearing in the principalities," said Mother with a grin. Father had glowered at her—an expression his slablike face seemed designed for—but she ignored him.

"You'll love it," she said to Hayden. "We'll bring back stuff to make those pals of yours completely envious."

He'd liked that thought; still, Father's words had stuck with him. He was going to Rush to understand.

And he thought he did understand, the moment that their ship had broached the final wall of cloud and he glimpsed the city for the first time. As light welled up, Hayden flew to a stoutly-barred window with some other kids—there was no centrifuge in this little ship, so everybody was weightless—and shielded his eyes to look at their destination.

The nearby air was full of travelers, some riding bikes, some on prop-driven contraptions powered by pedals, and some kicking their feet to flap huge white wings strapped to their backs. They carried parcels, towed cargos, and in the case of the fan-jets, left behind slowly fading arcs and lines of white contrail to thatch the sky.

Their cylindrical frigate had emerged from the clouds near Slipstream's sun, which it made an inferno of half the sky. Seconds out of the mist and the temperature was already rising in the normally chilly ship's lounge. The other boys were pointing at something and shouting excitedly; Hayden peered in that direction, trying to make out what was casting a seemingly impossible shadow across an entire half of the view. The vast shape was irregular like any of the rocks they had passed on their way here. Where those rocks were usually house-sized and sprouted spidery trees in all directions, this shape was blued with distance and covered with an even carpet of green. It took Hayden a few seconds to realize that it really was a rock, but one that was several miles in diameter.

He gaped at it. Father laughed from the dining basket, woven of wicker, where he perched with Mother. "That's the biggest thing you've ever seen, Hayden. But listen, there's much bigger places. Slipstream is not a major state. Remember that."

"Is that Rush?" Hayden pointed.

Father pulled himself out of the basket and came over. With his broad laborer's shoulders and calloused hands, he bulked much bigger than the kids, who made a place for him next to Hayden. "The asteroid? That's not Rush. It's the source of Slipstream's wealth, though—it and their sun." He leaned on the rail and pointed. "No . . . *That* is Rush."

Maybe it was because he'd never seen anything like it before, but the city simply hadn't registered in Hayden's mind until this moment. After all, the towns of Aerie were seldom more than two hundred yards across, and were simply wheels made of wooden planks lashed together and spoked with rope. You spun up the whole assembly and built houses on the inside surface of the wheel. Simple. And never had he seen more than five or six such wheels in one place.

The dozens of towns that made up Rush gleamed of highly polished metal. They were more cylindrical than ring-shaped, and none was less than five hundred yards in diameter. The most amazing thing was that they were tethered to the forested asteroid in quartets like mobiles; radiating from each cylinder's outer rim were bright sails of gold and red that transformed them from mere towns into gorgeous pinwheels.

"The asteroid's too big to be affected by the wind," said Father. Hayden shifted uncomfortably; Father was not trying to hide the burr of his provincial Aerie accent. "The towns are small enough to get pulled around by gusts. They use the sails to help keep the wheels spun up." This made sense to Hayden, because wind was the result of your moving at a different speed than whatever airmass you were in. Most of the time, objects migrated outward and inward in Virga to the rhythm of slowly circulating rivers of air. You normally only experienced wind at the walls of a town or while flying. Many times, he had folded little propellers of paper and let them out on strings. They'd twirled in the rushing air. So did the towns of Rush, only much more slowly.

Hayden frowned. "If that big rock isn't moving with the air, won't it drift away from the rest of Slipstream?"

"You've hit on the very problem," said Father with a smile. "Slipstream's more migratory than most countries. The Slipstream-ers have to follow their asteroid's orbit within Virga. You can't see from here, but their sun is also tethered to the asteroid. Ten years ago, Slipstream drifted right into Aerie. Before that, we were a smaller and less wealthy nation, being far from the major suns. But we were proud. We controlled our own destiny. Now what are we? Nothing but vassals of Rush."

Hayden barely heard him. He was eagerly staring at the city.

Their ship arrived at midday to find a traffic jam at the axis of one of the biggest cylinders. It took an hour to disembark, but Hayden didn't care. He spent the time watching the heavily built-up inner surface of the town revolve past. He was looking for places to visit. From the axis of the cylinder, where the docks sat like a jumble of big wooden dice, cable-ways radiated away to the other towns that made up the city. One wheel in particular caught his eye—a huge cylinder whose inside seemed to be one single building with bal-conies, coigns and glittering glass-paneled windows festooning it. This cylinder was surrounded by warships, which Hayden had seen in photos but never been close to before. The massive wooden vessels bristled with gun ports, and they trailed smoke and ropes and masts like the spines of fish. They were majestic and fascinating.

"You'll never get there," said Father drily. "That's the pilot's palace." After ages they were finally able to descend the long, curving, covered stairway to the street. Here Hayden had to endure another interminable wait while a man in a uniform examined Father's papers. Hayden was too distracted at the time to really notice his father's falsely jovial manner, or the way his shoulders had slumped with relief when they were finally accepted into the city. But after some walking he turned to Mother and kissed her, saying quietly, "I'll be back soon. Check us into the hotel, but don't wait for me. Go and do some shopping, it'll take your mind off it."

"Where's he going?" Hayden watched as Father disappeared into the crowd.

"It's just business," she said, but she sounded unhappy.

Hayden quickly forgot any misgivings this exchange might have raised. The town was huge and fascinating. Even the gravity felt different—a slower turnover of the inner ear—and there were points where you couldn't see the edges of the place at all. He followed his mother around to various outlets and while she haggled over wholesale paper prices for the newspaper she helped run, Hayden was happy to stare out the shop's windows at the passing crowds.

Gradually, though, he did begin to notice something. Mother was dressed in the layered and colorful garments of the Aerie outer districts and, like Father, made no attempt to hide her accent. Even her black hair and dark eyes marked her as different here in this city of fair-haired, pale-eyed people. Though the shopkeepers weren't actually hostile to Mother, they weren't being very friendly either. Neither were the other kids he saw in the street. Hayden smiled at one or two, but they just turned away.

He could have forgotten these details if not for what happened next. As they approached the hotel late that afternoon—Hayden laden with packages, his mother humming happily—he spotted Father at the hotel entrance, standing with his hands behind his back. Hayden felt his mother clutch his shoulder even as he waved and shouted a hello. It was only then that he noticed the men standing with his father, men in uniform who turned as one at the sound of Hayden's voice.

"Shit," whispered Mother as the policemen converged on her and a very confused Hayden.

The rest of the trip mostly consisted of waiting in various pale-green, bare rooms with his mother, who sat white-faced and silent, not answering any of Hayden's increasingly petulant questions. They didn't go back to the hotel to sleep, but were given a couple of rough cots in a small room in the back of the police station. "Not a cell," said the sergeant who showed them to it. "A courtesy apartment for relatives."

Father had reappeared the next day. He was disheveled, subdued, and had a bruise on his cheek. Mother wept in his arms while Hayden stood nearby, hugging his own chest in confused anger. Later that day they boarded a passenger ship considerably less posh than the one they had arrived on, and Hayden watched the bright pinwheels of Rush recede in the distance, unexplored.

Later Father had explained about the Resistance and the importance of assembling the talent and resources Aerie needed to strike out on its own. Hayden thought he understood, but what mattered was not the politics of it; it was the memory of walking through Rush's crowded streets next to his father, whose hands were bound behind his back.

THE GALLERY WAS just a stretch of street empty of fence, but with a railing you could look over. Mother called it a "braveway";

Miles used the more interesting term "pukesight." Hayden stepped
up to the rail and clutched it with both hands, staring.

A gigantic mountain of cloud wheeled in front of him, nearly
close enough to touch. The new sun must be behind it; the ropes of
the road from Gavin Town to the construction site stabbed the heart
of the cloud and vanished inside it. Hayden was disappointed; if
the sun came on right now he wouldn't see it.

He laughed. Oh, yes he would. Father had impressed it upon him
again and again: when the sun came on, there would be no missing
it. "The clouds for miles around will evaporate—poof," he'd said
with a wave of his fingers. "The temperature will instantly shoot up,
in fact everything within a kilometer is going to catch fire. That's
why the sun is situated so far from any towns. That, and security reasons, of course. And the light . . . Hayden, you have to promise not
to look at it. It's going to be brighter than anything you can imagine.
Up close, it could burn your skin and dazzle you through your
closed eyelids. Never look directly at it, not until we've moved the
town."

The cloud appeared to rotate as Hayden gazed at it; Gavin Town
was a wheel like all towns, after all, and spun to provide its inhabitants with centrifugal gravity. It was the only form of gravity they
would ever know, and it was a precious resource, costly and heavily
taxed. Grant's Chance, the next nearest town, lay a dozen miles beyond the sun site, invisible for now behind cloud.

Cloud was why the Griffins had come here. At the edges of the
zone lit by Slipstream, the air cooled and condensation began. White
mist in all its shapes made a wall here separating the sunlit realm
from the vast empty spaces of winter. This was the frontier. Here you
could hide all manner of things—secret projects, for instance.

The town continued to turn and now sky opened out beyond the
barrier of mist—sky with no limits, either up, down, or to either
side. Two distant suns carved out a sphere of pale air from this end-

less firmament, a volume defined by thousands upon thousands of clouds in all shapes and sizes, most of them tinged with dusk colors of rose and amber. There were ragged streamers indicating currents and rivers of air; puffballs and many-armed star shapes; and many miles away, its outlines blurred by intervening dust and mist, a mushroom head was forming as some current of cold impacted a mass of moist air. Below and above, walls of white blocked any further view, while whatever lay on the other side of the suns was obscured by dazzle and golden detail.

As it radiated through hundreds of miles of air, that light would fade and redden, or be shadowed by the countless clouds and objects comprising the nation of Aerie. If you traveled inward or up to civilized spaces, the light from other distant suns would begin to brighten before you ran out of light from yours; but if you went down or back, you would eventually reach a point where their light was completely obscured. There, a creeping chill took over. In the dark and cold, nothing grew. There began the volumes of winter that made up much of the interior of the planet-sized balloon of air, called Virga, where Hayden lived.

Gavin Town hovered at the very edge of civilization, where the filtered light of distant fires could barely keep crops alive. It wasn't lonely out here, though; above, below, and all about hung the habitations of Man. Three miles up to the left, a farm caught the suns' light: within a net a hundred feet across, the farmer had gathered pulverized rock and soil, and was growing a crop of yellow canola. Each plant clutched its own little ball of mud and they all tumbled about slowly, catching and losing the light in one another's shadow. The highway that passed near the farm was busy, a dozen or more small cars sailing along guided by the rope that was the highway itself. The rope extended off into measureless distance, heading for Rush. Below and to the right, a sphere of water the size of a house shimmered, its surface momentarily ridged by a passing breeze.

Hayden could see a school of wetfish swirling inside the sphere like busy diamonds.

There was way too much to take in with a single glance, so Hayden almost didn't spot the commotion. Motion out of the corner of his eye alerted him; leaning over the railing and sighting left along the curving wall of the town, he saw an unusually dense tangle of contrails. The trails led back in the direction of the sun and as he watched, three gleaming shapes shot out of the cloud and arrowed in the same direction.

Strange.

Just as he was wondering what might be happening, the gravity bell rang again. Hayden pushed himself back from the rail and ran for the main street. It wouldn't do for somebody else to get the bikes running after he'd promised Miles he'd be there.

The stairwell to the gravity engines led off the center of the street. Gravity was a public service and the town fathers had insisted on making its utilities both visible and accessible to everyone. Consequently, Hayden was very surprised when he clattered down the steps into the cold and drafty engine room and found nobody there.

Bike number two still hung from its arm above the open hatchway in the floor. It wasn't a bike in the old gravity-bound sense; the fan-jet was a simple metal barrel, open at both ends, with a fan in one end and an alcohol burner at its center. You spun up the fan with a pair of pedals and then lit the burner, and you were away. Hayden's own bike lay partly disassembled in the corner. He'd been meaning to get it running tonight.

When started and lowered through the hatch, bikes one and two would produce enough thrust to spin Gavin Town back up to a respectable five revolutions per minute. This had to be done once or twice a day so normally the engine room would have somebody in it either working, topping up the bike's tanks, or doing maintenance.

Certainly if the gravity bell rang, somebody would always be here in seconds and the bike operational in under a minute.

The wind whistled through the angled walls of the room. Hayden heard no voices, no running feet.

After a few seconds, though, something else came echoing up through the floor. Somewhere within a mile or two, an irregular popping had started.

It was the unmistakable sound of rifle fire.

A CRACKING ROAR shook the engine room. Hayden dropped to his stomach to look out the floor hatch, just in time to see a bike shoot by just meters below. It flashed Slipstreamer gold. A second later another that gleamed Aerie green followed it. Then the town had curved up and away and there was nothing out there but empty sky. The firing continued, dulled now by the bulk of the town.

Now he heard pounding footsteps and shouting from overhead. Shots rang out from nearby, making Hayden jump. The volleys were erratic, undisciplined, while in the distance he heard a more even, measured response.

As he ran back up the steps something whistled past his ear and hit the wall with a *spang*. Splinters flew and Hayden ducked down to his hands and knees, knowing full well that it wouldn't do any good when this section of the town rotated into full view of whoever was firing. The bullets would come straight up through the decking.

He emerged onto the still-empty street and ran to the right, where he'd heard people firing. A narrow alley led to the town's other outer street. He skidded around the corner to face the braveway—and saw bodies.

Six men had taken up firing positions at the rail. All were now slumped there or sprawled on the planks, their rifles carelessly flung away. The wood of the rail and flooring was splintered in dozens of places. There was blood everywhere.

Something glided into view beyond the railing, and he blinked at it in astonishment. The red and gold sails of a Slipstream warship spun majestically there, not two hundred yards below. Hayden could make out the figures of men moving inside the open hatches of the thing. Beyond it, partly eclipsed, lay another ship, and another. Contrails laced the air between and around them.

Hayden took a step toward the braveway and stopped. He looked at the bodies and at the warships, and took another step.

Something shot past the town and he heard a shout from the empty air outside. Gunshots sounded from below his feet and now a wavering contrail dissipated in the air not ten feet past the railing.

He ran to the braveway and took one of the rifles from the nerveless fingers of its former owner. He vaguely recognized the man as someone who'd visited the inn on occasion.

"What do you think you're doing?" Hayden whirled, to find Miles bearing down on him. The cook's mouth was set in a grim line. "If you poke your head out they're gonna shoot it off."

"But we have to do something!"

Miles shook his head. "It's too late for that. Take it from somebody who's been there. Nothing we can do now except get killed, or wait this out."

"But my mother's at the sun!"

Miles jammed his hands in his pockets and looked away. The sun was the Slipstreamers' target, of course. The secret project had been discovered. If Aerie could field its own sun, it would no longer be dependent on Slipstream for light and heat. Right now, Slipstream could choke out Aerie's agriculture by shading their side of the sun; all the gains that Hayden's nation had made in recent years—admittedly the result of Slipstream patronage—would be lost. But the instant that his parents' sun came on the situation would change. Aerie's neighbors to the up and down, left and right would suddenly find a reason to switch allegiances. Aerie could never defend its sun by itself, but by building it out here, on the edge of darkness, they stood to open up huge volumes of barren air to settlement. That real estate would be a tremendous incentive to their neighbors to intercede. That, at least, had been the plan.

But if the sun were destroyed before it could even be proven to work . . . It didn't matter to Hayden, not right now. All he could think was that his mother was out there, probably at the focus of the attack.

"I'm the best flyer in town," Hayden pointed out. "These guys made good targets 'cause they weren't moving. Right now we need all the riflemen we can get in the air."

Miles shook his head. "Listen, kid," he said, "there's too many Slipstreamers out there to fight. You have to pick your battles. It ain't cowardice to do that. If you throw your life away now, you won't be there to help when the chance comes later on."

"Yeah," said Hayden as he backed away from the braveway.

"Drop the rifle," said Miles.

Hayden spun and raced down the alley, back to the main street. Miles shouted and came after him.

Hayden clattered down the stairs to the engine room, but only realized as he got there that his bike was still in pieces all over the floor. He'd planned to roll it out the open hatch and fire it up when he was in the air. The spin of the town meant he would leave it at over a hundred miles an hour anyway; plenty of airflow to get the thing running, if it had been operable.

He was sitting astride the hoist that held bike number two when

Miles arrived. "What do you think you're doing? Get down!"

Glaring at him, Hayden made another attempt to pull the pins that held the engine to the hoist. "She needs me!"

"She needs you alive! And anyway, how are you gonna steer—"

The pin came loose, and the bike fell. Hayden barely kept his hold on it, and in doing so he dropped the rifle.

Wind burst around him, blinding him and taking his breath away. Fighting it, he managed to wrap his legs around the barrel shape of the bike and used his own body as a fin to turn it so that the engine faced into the airstream. Then he grabbed the handlebars and hit the firing solenoid.

The engine caught under him and suddenly Hayden had a new sense of up and down: down was behind the bike, up ahead of it— and it was all he could do to dangle from its side as it accelerated straight into the nearby cloud.

His nose banged painfully against the bike's saddle. Icy mist roared down his body, threatening to strip his clothes away. A second later he was in clear air again. He squinted up over the nose of the jet, trying to get a sense of where he was.

Glittering arcs of crystal flickered in the light of rocket-trails: Aerie's new sun loomed dead ahead. Jet contrails had spun a thick web around the translucent sphere and its flanks were already holed in several places. Its delicate central machinery could not be replaced; those systems came from the principalities of Candesce, thousands of miles away, and used technologies that no one alive could replicate. Yet two Slipstream cruisers had stopped directly over the sun and were veiling themselves in smoke as they launched broadside after broadside into it.

Mother would have been topping up the fuel preparatory to evacuating her team. Nobody could enter the sun while it was running; you had to give it just enough fuel for its prescribed burn. The engineers had planned a two-minute test for today, providing there was enough cloud to block the light in the direction of Slipstream.

A body tumbled past Hayden, red spheres of blood following it. He noticed abstractly that the man wore the now-banned, green uniform of Aerie. That was all he had time for, because any second now he was going to hit the sun himself.

Bike number two had never been designed to operate in open air. It was a heavy-duty fan-jet, powerful enough to pull the whole town into a faster spin. It had handlebars because they were required by law, not because anybody had ever expected to use them. And it was quickly accelerating to a point where Hayden was going to be ripped off it by the airstream.

He kicked out his legs, using them to turn his whole body in the pounding wind. That in turn ratcheted the handlebars a notch to the left; then another. Inside the bike, vanes turned in the exhaust stream. The bike began—slowly—to bank.

The flashing geodesics of the sun shot past close enough to touch. He had a momentary glimpse of faces, green uniforms, and rifles, and then he looked up past the bike again and saw the formation of Slipstream jets even as he shot straight through them. A few belated shots followed him but he barely heard them over the roar of the engine.

And now dead ahead was another obstacle, a spindle-shaped battleship this time. It flew the bright pennants of a flagship. Behind it was another bank of clouds, then the indigo depths of winter that lurked beyond all civilization.

Hayden couldn't hold on any longer. That was all right, though, he realized. He made sure the jet was aimed directly at the battleship, then pulled up his legs and kicked away from it.

He spun in clear air, weightless again but traveling too fast to breathe the air that tore past his lips. As his vision darkened he turned and saw bike number two impact the side of the battleship, crumpling its hull and spreading a mushroom of flame that lit a name painted on the metal hull: *Arrogance.*

With the last of his strength Hayden went spread-eagle to maximize his wind resistance. The world disappeared in silvery gray as he punched his way into the cloud behind the flagship. A flock of surprised fish flapped away from his plummeting fall. He waited to freeze, lose consciousness from lack of air, or hit something.

None of that happened, though his fingers and toes were going numb as he gradually slowed. The problem now was that he was soon going to be stranded inside a cloud, where nobody could see him. With the din of the battle going on, nobody would hear him either. People had been known to die of thirst after being stranded in empty air. If he'd been thinking, he'd have brought a pair of flapper fins at least.

He was just realizing that anything like that would have been torn off his body by the airstream, when the cloud lit up like the inside of a flame.

He put a hand up and spun away from the light but it was everywhere, diffused through the whole cloud. In seconds a pulse of intense heat welled up and to Hayden's astonishment, the cloud simply vanished, rolling away like a finished dream.

The heat continued to mount. Hayden peered past his fingers, glimpsing a silhouetted shape between him and a blaze of impossible light. The Slipstream battleship was dissolving, the flames enfolding it too dim to be seen next to the light of Aerie's new sun.

Though he was slowing, Hayden was still falling away from the battle. This fact saved his life, as everything else in the vicinity of the sun was immolated in the next few seconds. That wouldn't matter to his mother: she and all the other defenders were already dead, killed in the first seconds of the sun's new light. They must have lit the sun rather than let Slipstream have it as a prize.

The light reached a peak of agony and abruptly faded. Hayden had time to realize that the spherical blur flicking out of the orange afterglow was a shockwave, before it hit him like a wall.

As he blacked out he spun away into the blue-gray infinity of winter, beyond all civilization or hope.

2

THE HEADACHE WASN'T so bad today but Venera Fanning's fingers still sought out the small scar on her jaw as she entered the tiled gallery separating her chambers from the offices of Slipstream's admiralty. A lofty, pillared space, the hall ran almost the entire width of the royal townwheel in Rush; she couldn't avoid traversing it several times a day. Every time she did she relived the endless time after the bullet hit, when she'd lain here on the floor expecting to die. How miserable, how abandoned.

She would never enter the hall alone again. She knew it signaled weakness to everyone around her, but she needed to hear the servant's footsteps behind her here, even if she wouldn't look him in the eye and admit her feelings. The moaning of the wind from outside was the only sound except for her clicking footsteps, and that of the man behind her.

While that damnable hall brought back the memories whenever she entered it, Venera hadn't had the place demolished and replaced as her sisters would have. At least, she would not do that until the pain that radiated up her temples morning, noon, and night was ended. And the doctors merely exchanged their heavy-lidded glances whenever she demanded to know when that would be.

Venera flung back the double doors to the admiralty and was assailed by noise and the smells of tobacco, sweat, and leather. Right in the doorway four pages of mixed gender were rifling a file cabinet, their ceremonial swords thrust out and clashing in unconscious battle. Venera stepped adroitly around them and sidled past two red-faced officers who were bellowing at one another over a limp sheet of paper. She dodged a book trolley, its driver invisible behind the stacks of volumes teetering atop it, and in three more steps she entered the admiralty's antechamber, there to behold the bedlam of an office gearing up for war.

The antechamber was separated into two domains by a low wooden barrier. On the left was a waiting area, bare except for several armchairs reserved for elderly patrons. On the right, rows of polished wooden tables were manned by clerks who processed incoming reports. The clerks passed updates to a small army of pages engaged in rolling steep ladders up and down between the desks. They would periodically stop, crane their necks upward, then one would clamber up a ladder to adjust the height or relative position of one of the models that hung like a frozen flock of fish over the clerks' heads. Two ship's captains and an admiral stood among the clerks, as immobile as if stranded by the hazard of the whizzing ladders.

Venera strolled up to the rail and rapped on it smartly. It took a while before she was noticed, but when she was, a page abandoned his ladder and raced over to bow.

"May I have the key to the ladies' lounge, please?" she asked. The page ducked his head and ran to a nearby cabinet, returning with a large and ornate key.

Venera smiled sweetly at him; the smile slipped as a pulse of agony shot up from her jaw to wrap around her eyes. Turning quickly, she stalked past the crowding couriers and down a rosewood-paneled corridor that led off the far side of the antechamber. At its end stood an oak door carved with bluejays and finches, heavily polished but its silver door-handle tarnished with disuse.

The servant made to follow her as she unlocked the door. "Do you mind?" she asked with a glower. He flushed a deep pink, and only now did Venera really notice him; he was quite young and handsome. But, a servant.

She shut the door in his face and turned. The lounge's floors were smothered in deep crimson carpet, its walls of paneled oak so deeply varnished as to be almost black. There were no windows, only gaslights in peach-colored sconces here and there. While there were enough chairs and benches for a dozen ladies to wait in while others used the two privies, Venera had never encountered another woman here. It seemed she was the only wife in the admiralty who ever visited her husband at work.

"Well?" she said to the three men who awaited her, "what have you learned?"

"It seems you were right," said one. "Capper, show the mistress the photos."

A high-backed chair had been dragged into the center of the room and in it a young man in flying leathers was now weakly rifling through an inner pocket of his jacket. His right leg was thickly bandaged, but blood was seeping through and dripping on the carpet, where it disappeared in the red pile.

"That looks like a main line you've cut there," said Venera with a professional narrowing of the eyes. The youth grinned weakly at her. The second man scowled as he tightened a tourniquet high on the flyer's thigh. The third man watched this all indifferently. He was a mild-looking fellow with a balding head and the slightly pursed lips of someone more used to facing down sheets of paper than other people. When he smiled at all, Venera knew, Lyle Carrier lifted his lips and eyebrows in a manner that suggested bewilderment more than humor. She had decided that this was because other people's emotions were meaningless abstractions to him.

Carrier was a deeply dangerous man. He was as close to a kindred spirit as she'd been able to find in this forsaken country. He was, in fact, the one man Venera could never completely trust. She liked that about him.

The young man hauled a sheaf of prints out of his jacket with a grimace. He held it up for Venera to take, his hand trembling as though it were lead weights he was handing her and not paper. Venera snatched up the pictures eagerly and held them to the light one by one.

"Ah . . ." The fifth photo was the one she'd been waiting to see. It showed a cloudy volume of air filled with spidery wooden dock armatures. Tied up to the docks was a row of stubby metal cylinders bristling with jets. Venera recognized the design: they were heavy cruisers, each bearing dozens of rocket ports and crewed by no less than three hundred men.

"They built the docks in a sargasso, just like you said," said the young spy. "The bottled air let me breathe on the way through. They're pumping oxygen to the work site using these big hoses . . ."

Venera nodded absently. "It was one of your colleagues who discovered that. He saw the pumps being installed outside the sargasso, and put two and two together." She riffled through the rest of the pictures to see if there was a better shot of the cruisers.

"Clearly another secret project," murmured Carrier with prim disapproval. "It seems nobody learned from the lesson we gave Aerie."

"That was eight years ago," said Venera as she held up a picture. "People forget. . . . What's this?"

Capper jerked awake in his chair and with a visible effort, sat up to look. "Ah, that . . . I don't know."

The image showed a misty, dim silhouette partly obscured behind the wheel of a town. The gray spindle shape suggested a ship, but that was impossible: the thing dwarfed the town. Venera held the print up to her nose under one of the gaslights. Now she could see little dots scattered around the gray shape. "What are these specks?"

"Bikes," whispered the spy. "See the contrails?"

Now she did, and with that the picture seemed to open out for a second, like a window. Venera glimpsed a vast chamber of air, walled by cloud and full of dock complexes, towns, and ships. Lurking at its edge was a monstrous whale, a ship so big that it could swallow the pinwheels of Rush.

But it must be a trick of the light. "How big is this thing? Did you get a good look at it? How long were you there?"

"Not long . . ." The spy waved his hand indifferently. "Took another shot . . ."

"He's not going to last if I don't get him to the doctor," said the man who was tending the spy's leg. "He needs blood."

Venera found the other photo and held it up beside the first. They were almost identical, evidently taken seconds apart. The only difference was in the length of some of the contrails.

"It's not enough." Frustration made hot waves of pain radiate up from her jaw and she unconsciously snarled. Venera turned to find only Carrier looking at her; his face expressed nothing, as always. The leather-suited spy was unconscious and his attendant was looking worried.

"Get him out of here," she said, gesturing to the servants' door at the back of the lounge. "We'll need to get a full deposition from him later." Capper was roused enough to lean on the shoulder of his attendant and they staggered out of the room. Venera perched on one of the benches and scowled at Carrier.

"This dispute with the pilot of Mavery is a distraction," she said. "It's intended to draw the bulk of our navy away from Rush. Then, these cruisers and that . . . thing, whatever it is, will invade from Falcon Formation. The Formation must have made a pact of some kind with Mavery."

Carrier nodded. "It seems likely. That is—it seems likely to me, my lady. The difficulty is going to be convincing your husband and the pilot that the threat is real."

"I'll worry about my husband," she said. "But the pilot . . . could be a problem."

"I will of course do whatever is in the best interest of the nation," said Carrier. Venera almost laughed.

"It won't come to that," she said. "All right. Go. I need to take these to my husband."

Carrier raised an eyebrow. "You're going to tell him about the organization?"

"It's time he knew we have extra resources," she said with a shrug. "But I have no intention of revealing our extent just yet . . . or that it's my organization. Nor will I be telling him about you."

Carrier bowed, and retreated to the servants' door. Venera remained standing in the center of the room for a long time after he left.

A thousand miles away, it would be night right now around her father's sun. Doubtless the pilot of Hale would be sleeping uneasily, as he always did under the wrought-iron canopy of his heavily guarded bed. His royal intuition told him that the governing principle of the world was conspiracy—his subjects were conspiring against him, their farm animals conspired against them, and even the very atoms of the air must have some plan or other. It was inconceivable to him that anyone should act from motives of true loyalty or love and he ran the country accordingly. He had raised his three daughters by this theory. Venera had fully expected that she would be disposed of by being married off to some inbred lout; at sixteen she had taken matters into her own hands and extorted a better match from her father. Her first attempt at blackmail had been wildly successful, and had netted her the man of her choice, a young admiral of powerful Slipstream. Of course, Slipstream was moving away from Hale, rapidly enough that by the time she consolidated her position here she would be no threat to the old man.

She hated it here in Rush, Slipstream's capital. The people were friendly, cordial, and blandly superior. Scheming was not in fashion. The young nobles insulted one another directly by pulling hat-feathers or making outrageous accusations in public. They fought their duels immediately, letting no insult fester for more than a day. Everything political was done in bright halls or council chambers and if there were darker entanglements in the shadows, she couldn't find them. Even now, with war approaching, the Pilot of Slipstream refused to beef up the secret service in any way.

It was intolerable. So Venera had taken it upon herself to correct the situation. These photos were the first concrete validation of her own deliberately cultivated paranoia.

She resolutely jammed the pictures into her belt purse—they stuck out conspicuously but who would look?—and left by the front door.

Her servant waited innocently a good yard from the door. Venera was instantly suspicious that he'd been peering through the keyhole. She shot him a nasty look. "I don't believe I've used you before."

"No, ma'am. I'm new."

"You've had a background check, I trust?"

"Yes, ma'am."

"Well, you're going to have another." She stalked back to the admiralty with him following silently.

Bedlam continued in the admiralty antechamber, but it all seemed a bit silly to her now—they were in a fever of anticipation over a tiny border dispute with Mavery, while farther out a much bigger threat loomed. Nobody liked migratory nations, least of all Slipstream. They should be ready for this sort of thing. They should be more professional.

A page jostled Venera and the photos fell out of her purse. She laid a backhanded slap across the boy's head and stooped to grab them—to find that her servant had already picked them up.

He glanced at two that he held, apparently by accident, then did a double-take. Venera wondered whether he'd tripped the page behind her back just so he could do this.

"Give me those!" She snatched them back, noting as she did that it was the mysterious photos of the great, dim gray object that he'd looked at. She decided on the spot to have him arrested on some sort of trumped-up charge as soon as she reached the Fanning estate.

Blazing with anger, Venera elbowed her way through the crowd of couriers and minor functionaries, and took a side exit. Cold air wafted up from the stairs that led up to the cable cars connecting the other towns in this quartet. Fury and cold made her jaw flare with pain so that she wanted to turn and strike the insolent young man. With a great effort she restrained herself, and gradually calmed down. She was pleased at her own forbearance. *I can be a good person*, she reminded herself.

"Fifteen hundred feet," murmured the servant, almost inaudibly.

Venera whirled. He was trailing a few yards behind her, his expression distracted and wondering. "What did you say?" she hissed.

"That ship in the picture . . . was fifteen hundred feet long," he said, looking apologetic.

"How do you know that? Tell me!"

"By the contrails, ma'am."

She stared at him for a few seconds. He was young, certainly, and his high-cheeked face would have seemed innocent but for the weatherbeaten skin that reddened his brow and nose. He had a mop of black hair that fell like a raven's wing across his forehead and his eyes were framed with fine lines in an airman's perpetual squint.

He was either far more cunning than she'd given him credit for, or he was an idiot.

Or, she reluctantly admitted to herself, maybe he really had no idea that she'd met with someone in the ladies' room, and didn't expect a lady like herself to be carrying sensitive information. In which case the photos, to him, were just photos.

"Show me." She fished out the two shots of the behemoth and handed them to him.

Now he looked doubtful. "I can't be sure."

"Just show me how you reached that conclusion!"

He pointed to the first picture. "You see in the near space here, there's a bike passing. That's a standard Gray forty-five, and it's running at optimum speed, which is a hundred twenty-five knots. See the shape of its contrail? It only gets that feathered look under optimum burn. It's passing close by the docks so you can tell . . ." he flipped to the second picture, "that here it's gone about six hundred feet, if that dock is the size it looks to be. It means the second picture was taken about two seconds after the first.

"Now look at the contrails around the big ship. Lady, I can't see any bikes that *aren't* Gray forty-fives in the picture. So if we assume that the ones in the distance are Grays too, and that they're going at optimum speed, then these ones skimming the surface of the big ship have traveled a little less than half its length since the first picture. That makes it a bit over twelve hundred feet long."

"Mother of Virga." Venera stared at the picture, then at him. She noticed now that he was missing the tips of several fingers: frostbite?

She took back the pictures. "You're a flyer."

"Yes, ma'am."

"Then what are you doing working as a body servant in my household?"

"Flying bikes is a dead-end career," he said with a shrug.

They resumed walking. Venera was mulling things over. As they reached the broad clattering galleries of the cable car station, she nodded sharply and said, "Don't tell anybody about these, if you value your job. They're sensitive."

"Yes, ma'am." He looked past her. "Uh-oh."

Venera followed his gaze, and frowned. The long cable car gallery was full of people, all of whom were crowding in a grumbling mass under the rusty cable stays and iron-work beams that formed the chamber's ceiling. Six green cable cars hung swaying and empty in the midst of the throng. "What's the holdup?" she demanded of a nearby naval officer.

"Cable snapped," he said with a sigh. "Wind shear pulled the towns apart and the springs couldn't compensate."

"Don't drown me in details, when will it be fixed?"

"You'd have to ask the cable monkeys, and they're all out there now."

"I have to get to the palace!"

"I'm sure the monkeys sympathize, ma'am."

She was about to erupt in a tirade against the man, when the servant touched her arm. "This way," he murmured.

With a furious hmmph, Venera followed him out of the crowd. He was heading for an innocuous side entrance. "What's down there?" she asked.

"Bike berths," he said as he opened the door to another windy gallery. This one was nearly empty. It curved up and out of sight, its right wall full of small offices with frosted-glass doors, its left wall opening out in a series of floor-to-ceiling arched windows. Beyond the windows was a braveway and then open turning air.

The gallery floor was full of hatches. About half had bikes suspended over them. The place smelled of engine oil, a masculine smell Venera found simultaneously rank and intriguing. Men in coveralls were rebuilding a bike nearby. Its parts were laid out in a neat line across a tarpaulin, their clean order betraying the apparent chaos of the opened chassis.

She was in a place of men; she liked that. "You have your own bike?" she asked the servant.

"Yes. It's right over there." He took a chit to the dock master and traded it in for a key and a worn leather jacket. They went over to the bike and he knelt to unlock the hatch beneath the gently swaying machine.

"Let me guess," she said. "A Gray forty-five?"

He laughed. "Those are work-haulers. This is a racer. It's a Canfield Arrow, Model fourteen. I bought it with my first paycheck from your household."

"There's a passenger seat," she said, suddenly thrilled at the prospect of riding the thing.

He squinted at her. "Have you never flown a bike, lady?"

"No. Does that surprise you?"

"I guess it's always been nice covered taxis for you," he said with a shrug. "Makes sense." He winched open the hatch and she took an apprehensive step back. Venera had no fear of the open air; it was speed that frightened her. Right now the air below the hatch was whipping by at gale force.

"We'll get blown off!"

He shook his head. "The dock master's lowering a shield ahead of the hatch. It'll give us several seconds of slipstream to cruise in. Just hunker down behind me—the windscreen's big—and you'll be fine. Besides, I won't take us flat out, too dangerous inside city limits."

He straddled the bike and held out his hand. Venera suppressed her grin until she was seated behind him. There were foot straps but she had nothing to hold on to with her hands except him. She wrapped her arms tightly around his waist.

He pushed the starter and she felt the engine rumble into life beneath her. Then he said, "All set?" and reached up to unclip the winch.

They fell into the air and for a few seconds the curve of the town's undersurface formed a ceiling. There was the shield, a long tongue of metal hanging down but pulling up quickly. "Head down!" he shouted and she buried her face in his back. Then the engine was roaring to drown all thought, the vibration rattling up through her spine, and they were free in the air between the city cylinders. The wind wasn't tearing her from this man's grasp, so Venera cautiously leaned back and looked around. She gave an involuntary gasp of delight.

Contrails like spikes and ropes stood still in the air around them. Tethers with gay flags on them slung here and there, and everywhere taxies, winged humans, and other bikes shot through the air. The quartet of towns that included the admiralty was already receding behind them; she turned to look back and saw that the cable car system, whose independent loop touched the axle of the vast spinning cylinder, was indeed slack. Men floated in open air around the break, their tools arrayed in constellations about them as they argued over what to do. Venera turned forward again, laughing giddily at the sensation of power that pulled her up and up toward the next quartet.

They passed heavy steel cables and then the broad cross-shaped spokes of a town's pinwheel. Up close the brightly colored sails were torn and patched. In far too little time the bike was rising under another town, the long slot of a jet entrance visible overhead. Venera's flyer expertly inched them into a perfect tangent course, and it seemed as if the town's curving underside simply reached out and settled around them. Her flyer shut down the engine and held up a hook, clipping it to an overhead cable just as they began to fall again. And there they were, hanging in a gallery almost identical to the one they just left. A palace footman ran up and began winching them away from the slot. They had arrived.

Venera dismounted and staggered back a few steps. Her legs had turned to jelly. Her servant swung off the back of the bike as though nothing had just happened. He grinned happily at her. "It's a good beast," he said.

"Well." She cast about for something to say. "I'm glad we're paying you enough that you can afford it."

"Oh, I never said I could afford it."

She frowned, and led the way out of the gallery. From here she knew the stairs and corridors to take to reach Slipstream's strategic command office. Her husband, Admiral Fanning, was tied up in meetings there, but he would see her, she knew. She thought about how much she would tell him regarding her spy network. As little as possible, she decided.

At the entrance to the office she turned and looked frankly at the servant. "This is as far as you can go. Wait down at the docks, you can run me back home the same way you brought me."

He looked disappointed. "Yes, ma'am."

"Hmm. What's your name, anyway?"

"Griffin, ma'am. Hayden Griffin."

"All right. Remember what I said, Griffin. Don't talk about the photos to anyone." She waggled a finger at him, but even though her head was pounding she couldn't summon any anger at the moment. She turned and gestured for the armed palace guard to open the giant teak doors.

As she walked away she thought of the beautiful freedom Griffin must have in those moments when he flew alone. She'd caught a glimpse of it when she rode with him. But entangled as she was in a life of obligation and conspiracy, it could never be hers.

HAYDEN WATCHED HER go in frustration. So close! He'd gotten to within a few yards of his target today. And then to be thwarted at the very entrance to the command center. He eyed the palace guard, but he knew he couldn't take the man and the guard was eyeing him back. Reluctantly, Hayden turned and headed back toward the docks.

He'd nearly blown it picking up those pictures. Obviously he'd underestimated Lady Fanning. He wouldn't do it again. But since he had been assigned to her, he hadn't been able to get anywhere near Fanning himself. If she liked him, though . . .

It was only a matter of time, he decided. Admiral Fanning would come within arm's reach one day soon.

And then Hayden would kill him.

3

A FLOCK OF fish had wandered into the airspace inside Quartet One, Cylinder Two. Disoriented by the city lights spinning around them and caught in the cyclone of air that Rush's rooftops swept up, they foundered lower and lower in a quickening spiral, until with fatal suddenness they shot between the eaves of two close-leaning, gargoyle-coigned apartments. They banged off window and ledge, flagpole and fire escape, to end flapping and dying in a narrow street along which they'd scattered like a blast of buckshot.

Hayden ignored the cheering locals who ran out to scoop up the unexpected windfall. He paced on through the darkened alleys of Rush's night market, noticing nothing, but instinctively avoiding the grifters and thieves who also drifted through the crowds of out-country rubes. He felt slightly nauseated, and twitched at every loud laugh or thud of crate on cement.

The market was stuffed into a warren of small streets. Hayden loved walking through the mobs; even after living here for two years, the very fact that the city comprised more than one cylinder amazed him. The rusting wheels of the city provided gravity for over thirty thousand souls. Throw in the many outlying towns and countless estates that hung in the nearby air like sprays of tossed seed, and the population must push a hundred thousand. The anonymity this afforded was a heady experience for an unhappy young man. Hayden could be with people yet aloof and he liked it this way.

He was dead tired after another long day at the Fanning estate; but if he went back to the boarding house now, he would just pace until his downstairs neighbors complained. He would pull at his hair, and mutter to himself as if he were mad. He didn't want to do that.

He paused to buy a sticky bun at a vendor he favored, and continued on down a twisting run sided with fading clapboard. Slipstream's sun was on its maintenance cycle, and darkness and chill had settled over the city. Here and there in the alleys, homeless people kept barrel fires going and charged a penny or two to anyone who stopped to warm their hands. Hayden sometimes stopped to talk to these men, whose faces he knew only as red sketches lit from below. They could be valuable sources of information, but he never revealed anything about himself to them, least of all his name.

To be so close to his goal and yet be unable to act was intolerable. He walked through the Fanning household like a dutiful servant for hours while his mind raced through scenarios: Fanning walking by distracted in a hallway; Hayden slipping into the Admiralty unnoticed by the omnipresent security police . . . It was all useless. The chances never came, and he was getting desperate.

He'd driven Venera Fanning again today—unnecessarily, for she could easily have taken a cable car. He wondered at her motives in riding with him. When he'd returned to his room he'd discovered that a faint scent of her perfume still hovered on his jacket. It was alluring, as she was with her porcelain complexion—marred only by the scar on her chin—and her hair the color of winter skies. Attractive she might be, but she was also without doubt the most callous human being he'd ever met. And she traded on her beauty.

How strange that she should be the first woman he'd given a ride to since arriving in Rush.

Halfway down the alley was a cul-de-sac. A knife seller had set up his table across its entrance, and had mounted targets on the blank wall at the dead end. Hayden stopped to balance a sleek dart knife on his finger. He held it out facing away from him, then at right angles to that.

"It's good in all the directions of gravity," said the vendor, who in this light was visible only as a black cutout shape with a swath of distant lamplight revealing his beige shirt collar. The black silhouette of an arm rose in an indistinct gesture. "Try it out."

Hayden balanced the knife for a second more, then flipped it and caught it behind the guard fins. He threw it with a single twitch of his wrist and it buried itself in the center of a target with a satisfying thump. The vendor murmured appreciatively.

"That's not our best, you know," he said as he waddled back to retrieve the knife. His mottled hand momentarily became visible as he pulled the knife from the wall. "Try this." Back at the table, he fished in a case and drew out a long arrow shape. Hayden took it from him and turned it over with a professional eye. Triangular cross-section to the blade, guards that doubled as fins for throwing, and a long tang behind that with another fin on its end. Its heft was definitely better than the last one.

He thought of Admiral Fanning and his purpose in coming to this city. With a muttered curse he spun and let fly the knife. It sank dead center in the smallest target.

"Son, you should be in the circus," said the vendor. Hayden heard the admiration in his voice, but it didn't matter. "Say, do you want to hang around a while and throw for the crowd? Could bring in some business."

Hayden shook his head. He wasn't supposed to have skills like knife throwing. "Just dumb luck," he said. "I guess your knives are just so good that even an idiot can hit the bull's-eye with one." Ducking his head and aware of the lameness of his excuse, he backed away and then paced hurriedly down the alley.

"That wasn't smart," said a shadow at his elbow.

Hayden shrugged and kept going. "What's it to you?"

The other fell into step beside him. Hayden glimpsed a tall, rangy figure in the dim light. "Somebody you owe a favor, Hayden."

He stepped away involuntarily. "Who the—"

The man in the shadows laughed and moved into a pale lozenge of candlelight that squeezed out between the cracks of a low window. The profile revealed was of a lean, bald man with bushy eyebrows. "Don'tcha recognize me, Hayden? Last time I saw you, you were dropping out of Gavin Town on a runaway bike!"

"Miles?" Hayden just stood there, painfully aware of how meetings like this were supposed to go: the prodigal and the old soldier, laughing and slapping each other's backs in surprise and delight. They would head for a bar or something, and regale each other with stories of their exploits, only to stagger out again singing at three the next morning. Or so it went. But he'd never much liked Miles, and what did it matter, really, to find out now that one other person had survived the attack on the sun? It didn't change anything.

"What are you doing here?" he asked after the silence between them had stretched too long.

"Looking after you, boy," said the ex-soldier. "You're not happy to see me?"

"It's not that," he said with a shrug. "It's . . . been a long time."

"Well, long or not, I'm here now. What do you say?"

"It's . . . good to see you."

Miles laughed humorlessly. "Right. But you'll be thanking me before long, believe me." He started walking. "Come on. We need to find a place to talk."

Here it came, thought Hayden: the bar, the war stories, the laughing. He hesitated, and Miles sighed heavily. "Kid, I saved your ass today. If it weren't for me, you'd be on your way out of Rush by now with a permanent deport order issued against you."

"I don't believe you."

"Suit yourself." Miles started walking. After a moment Hayden ran after him.

"What do you mean?" he asked.

" 'It's so good to see you, Miles. How are you doing, Miles? How did you survive Gavin Town?' " The ex-soldier glared at Hayden as they crossed a busy and well-lit thoroughfare. "Jeez, you were always a surly little runt, but let me tell you, I'm wondering whether I should have bothered faking the docs for your background check."

"What background check?" He'd had two of them already, he knew, a cursory one when he first applied for Rush residency, and a more thorough check after he answered the call for work at the Fanning residence. It seemed all too plausible that somebody somewhere should want to do more digging—and now he realized who. "Venera Fanning. She had me investigated."

"But not by the legal authorities," said Miles as he ducked into another alley. This one was empty, and meandered in the general direction of one of the town spokes. The spoke jabbed into the heavens above all rooftops, a tessellation of wrought-iron girders barnacled here and there by shanty huts built by desperate homeless people. Some spokes had municipal elevators in them and were quite well-kept; this one was a rusty derelict unlit from any source.

"It's just lucky we have a man in Fanning's network." Miles had disappeared in the darkness ahead. Hayden followed his voice, idly wondering if he'd been lured in here to be mugged. "This time they weren't going to just hold your papers up to a light and check the birth registries. Friends, family, coworkers—I had to come up with them all at the last minute."

"But how did you know about it?"

"Ah, finally, a sensible question. Here, watch your step." They had reached the gnarled fist of beam and cable that was the spoke's base. Someone had built a crude set of stairs by simply jamming boards into the diamond-shaped gaps in the ironwork. Miles plodded up this, wood bending and twanging under his feet.

His voice drifted down from overhead. "I review intercepted dispatches about security checks. It's my job in the Resistance."

Hayden stopped climbing. "Resistance? You still believe in that?"

Miles spun around, glaring. "Hayden, how can you of all people say that? You were born into the Resistance—you were the first baby born of two members, didn't you know that?"

He shrugged uncomfortably. "That's not the point, is it? When they blew up the sun they beat us. It was our last hope."

"Is that what you thought?" Miles sounded outraged. "Son, we were just getting started! And after the attack we needed you more than ever. We searched for you for days after the attack . . ."

"I didn't know. I fell into winter." He looked down, noticing distractedly how the rooftops looked from just overhead, with their shingled peaks and streamlined eaves. From here the whole circular geometry of the town spread out below him, with its mazes of close-packed buildings, streetlights glowing overhead and on two sides, and the permanent winds of Slipstream whistling from the dark open circles of night to left and right. A gust shook him and he realized that he'd fall hard enough to be killed if he got blown off this precarious vantage point. Keep following Miles or go back? Hayden reluctantly groped for the next ladder-like step. "Where are we going, Miles?"

"There." The lean ex-soldier—who, when it came right down to it, Hayden didn't know that well—pointed straight up. The inside of the open-work spoke was blocked by a wood ceiling ten feet farther up. The surface was white with strange, broad black bands painted across it. With a start Hayden realized they were intended to look like shadows; this box was supposed to be invisible if looked at from some particular perspective—probably from the direction of the Office of Public Infrastructure.

Miles ascended the last distance by ladder and raising his fist, knocked it against wood. A square of light appeared above his head, and he clambered up. "Come on in, Hayden."

He cautiously raised his head above the lip of the trapdoor, and then, for the first time in many years, he entered a cell of the Resistance.

"No, it's not our headquarters," said Miles as Hayden looked around the little room. "Just a watching post. We're at a rare spot that lets us look down the window of the semaphore room in the Admiralty. But we also store sensitive materials here—like guns." He gestured to a stack of long boxes on the floor.

The place was little more than ten feet on a side, though a ladder led up to what was presumably a second level. Blackout curtains covered three walls. A little chair in the out-of-fashion Lace style perched in front of a desk where a man with thick glasses and a halo of white hair sat muttering over a pile of paper. In the opposite corner crouched a lanky man dressed entirely in black. He was walking his fingers over a map of Rush, evidently trying to gauge distances in one of the cylinders.

"Meet Hayden Griffin. He's the son of the original sunlighters."

The man in black just grunted; but the balding fellow at the table sat up straight and cranked his glasses down to get a look at Hayden. "Grace! So it is! You probably wouldn't remember me, Hayden, but I babysat for you when you were four."

"Martin Shambles," said Miles. "And this one, he's V.I.P. Billy. Our assassin."

Hayden nodded to them both, trying not to sneak another look at Billy. Shambles stood up and held out his hand. "Well met, Hayden! Looks like we saved your ass today."

"I wasn't aware it needed saving," said Hayden. But he shook the offered hand.

" 'Course, it would have been easier if we'd known you were still alive." Shambles sat back down, chuckling. "And working in the Fanning house, no less! That caused a stir. Some of our boys went so far as to claim you'd turned, gone over to their side—"

"But we know you wouldn't do that, would you?" asked V.I.P. Billy, who was now standing. Hayden suddenly realized that he was unfavorably placed with his back to a corner, with Miles and Billy on either side of him.

"Of course, there's the question of where you've actually been the past several years," continued Shambles, who was unconcernedly peering at his papers again. "We had a back story ready for somebody else, papers, friends—it's the sort of in-depth investigation Venera Fanning goes in for. She's much more thorough than the Admiralty that way. I mean, we traced you as far as we could, but that wasn't far. Not far at all, in fact."

Despite the cold air, Hayden was starting to sweat. "But—but I could ask you the same thing," he said. "Where were you? When the sun blew up and I fell into winter, where were you? It wasn't the Resistance who found me and nursed me back from frostbite. Hell, I fell *four hundred miles* before I finally hit a mushroom farm run by this weird old couple. . . . Nobody came after me. Did you even look?"

Miles nodded gravely. "We looked. Your falling into winter was one possibility. Being captured by one of Fanning's ships was another. It was fifty-fifty which had happened."

"These people . . ." Hayden had trouble thinking of what to say. He knew his life was on the line here. "They were exiles. A man and woman named Katcheran. Said Aerie had kicked them out twenty years ago. They had no gravity, they were as fragile as birds. They grew mushrooms on this little rock they'd found in the emptiness, and occasionally they'd jet over to the outskirts of Aerie to drop some off for supplies. But it took them ages to ferment enough alcohol for fuel . . . he tended to drink it away."

Miles looked skeptical, but Shambles perked up. "Did you say Katcheran?" Hayden nodded. Shambles pursed his lips. "Haven't heard that name in years." He tilted his head to one side and looked at Hayden shrewdly. "Go on."

Hayden did his best to describe his stay in the dark regions outside civilization. The volumes of air there were vast, and not all of it was cold, or dark. The little mushroom farm was just a cave to live in hollowed out of a clay ball no more than fifty feet in diameter. Katcheran and his wife bickered in a constant, monotonous murmur. Hayden had spent most of his time outside, watching the skies for any sign of a passing ship.

The distant beacons of Aerie teased him whenever he looked in its direction. But every now and then dawn would come as clouds parted around some distant sun. Then he could see just how far away from home he'd come. Hazy depths of emptiness opened out to all sides, not even a stray boulder or water ball visible for miles upon miles. He was stranded in a desert of air, and a few times he'd curled into a ball, hovering above the stinking fungus, and wept.

On two or three occasions, though, he saw more. The shells of cloud that enveloped the center of Virga sometimes parted, revealing the sun of suns, Candesce. Daylight would suddenly flash out to fill the entire volume of winter. Each time, Hayden had stood on the air, amazed at the brilliance of it—at the sheer size of an ancient, untended fusion engine that put all other suns in Virga to shame. Dozens of civilizations depended on that single central light, he'd heard. It was the greatest source of heat in the world; it drove the circulation cells in which Aerie and the other nations migrated slowly inward and outward.

The core components of his parents' sun had come from Candesce; the sun of suns was the wellspring for all of Virga's lesser lights.

"It was a year before Katcheran had enough fuel for us to fly back, and then he followed the beacons he knew, which brought us in a hundred miles away from Gavin Town. Of course, the town was a legend by then, but nobody knew much about it. Any pieces that were left after Slipstream attacked had been dismantled or drifted away. I didn't have anybody to go to . . . any way to get in touch with the Resistance, unless I came to Rush, and I didn't have any money to travel. I got a job in a kitchen in Port Freeley and saved until I could get passage here.

"But you know what I found out when I finally got back to Aerie? Nobody knew about our sun! Nobody knew. We'd built it in secret, and Slipstream attacked in secret, and nobody told the people what had happened. If they'd known . . . something might have been done." He shook his head. "Maybe the Resistance couldn't have kept Slipstream from finding the sun and destroying it. I don't know. But you could have told—you had the responsibility to tell the people of Aerie what had happened.

"How could I get involved with you again after that?"

Miles looked troubled, but Billy just raised an eyebrow. "So why are you working for the Fannings? It took you a lot of effort to do it—you even forged your Slipstream citizenship yourself, by the looks of it."

Hayden stared at him. "Well, why do you think I came here? I came to kill Admiral Fanning."

There was a brief silence while the other three looked at one another. Then Billy cracked a slight smile. "Why in Virga would you want to do that?"

"*Because he's the one.*" Hayden didn't care that the man in black was a killer. The indignity of having his motives suspected was just too much. "I saw the name on the side of the flagship that attacked us. The *Arrogance*. It was Fanning's ship when he was still commodore. He blew up our sun! He killed my mother! I care about that. Don't you care? What have you been doing here, all these years? What kind of a resistance is this? You're supposed to be an assassin, why haven't you killed him?" He stepped over to Shambles's table and tossed some of the papers in the air. "What, are you gonna *plan* them all to death? Is that the idea? Well, while you've been squatting on your asses in your little box, I've been doing something with my time. I was ten feet away from him today; tomorrow I'll be right there, and then he'll be dead."

He glared at them. "That's why I came here. That's what I'm doing. So what are you doing?"

Shambles adjusted his glasses and patted down the papers. "Well, Hayden my lad, we're trying to save our country. That would seem like a very different goal from yours, now wouldn't it?"

"Oh, please," said Hayden, crossing his arms. "What's to save? Slipstream annexed Aerie ages ago. I don't even *remember* how it was before that happened. It's ancient history."

"What you say is very true," said Shambles with a thoughtful nod. "However, it is also true that, since Slipstream is a migratory nation, it will someday migrate its way out of Aerie. Our concern is with what happens when that occurs."

Hayden looked at him blankly.

"Hmm." Shambles turned in his chair, crossing his legs. "It is a fact of youth that it has no concept of the future. Yet that is what we are here to discuss. The future of Aerie—and your future."

Hayden snorted.

"Tell me," said Shambles, "what is it, fundamentally, that keeps a nation together?"

Hayden decided to take the bait. "A sun."

Shambles shook his head. "No. It's *formation flying*. That is what keeps a nation together. If all your towns and farms and water balls are sailing off in different directions, it hardly matters if you've got a sun of your own, does it? What's essential is that you keep everybody flying on the same heading, maintaining the same altitude and position above the Sun of Suns. Aerie is still doing that—for now. The danger is that the presence of the Slipstream sun in our skies will cause parts of the nation to drift away, leave the formation, and join other countries. Hayden, that is a threat far greater than any police actions or propaganda by Slipstream could be."

"For ten years now we've been keeping Aerie in formation," said Miles. "That's what the Resistance does. What possible good would revenge do us? If you kill Fanning, he'll just be replaced."

"Yes," said Hayden, "but he'll also be dead."

Miles sighed. "I brought you here tonight because I hoped we could bring you back into the net. With your position in the Fanning household, you could be invaluable to us—especially now that Slipstream's finally moved close enough to our neighbors that it's been perceived as a threat. Mavery is moving against Slipstream. Slipstream will move into Mavery territory in a year or two and at that point they'll find themselves fighting a two-front war, against Mavery and us. Our job is to prepare for that, and to make sure that when the time comes, we either win or convince them to commit all their forces to Mavery, and leave us behind. If we had a spy in the very heart of the Admiralty . . ." His expression was greedy.

"Aerie is gone," Hayden said. "When Slipstream leaves they'll take their sun with them. Without a sun, Aerie will freeze in the dark. The people will leave. I've lived in winter. I know what it's like."

"We're working on that," said Shambles. "With the right components we could—"

Hayden shook his head. "I'm only here to do one thing. And after that . . . I don't care."

"But, Hayden my boy," purred Billy as he put an arm around Hayden's shoulder, "the problem is, we care. It's a worry, you know—the vision of you shooting Fanning and then being caught and tortured. You might talk about us, you see."

"Oh! No, I—"

"Now it would be supremely gauche of me to threaten your life at this point," Billy went on. "After all, as you say, you have your own path to take. That's fine. But if you're not going to join us, then we have one simple request."

"What's that?"

"If you're going to kill Fanning up close and personal like, say in the middle of the Admiralty itself . . . Just make sure you kill yourself too, hmm? As a favor to us, you see. So we don't have to."

Hayden bolted to the trapdoor and flung it up. "You know where to find us if you change your mind," Shambles called cheerfully.

"You won't hear from me," snapped Hayden as he lowered himself down to the invisible ladder. Slamming the trapdoor he began clumsily backing his way down to the city, fuming and muttering as he went.

He was just above the rooftops when a lurid orange flash lit up the sky. A distant grumble like thunder reached his ears. Hayden paused, clinging to the swaying planks, and listened.

The tearing sound of a jet could be heard fading in the distance. Then another one, growing closer. Funny; he knew all about bikes, but he couldn't identify the type from this one's sound.

Then something flashed by outside the iron stanchions. He poked his head out between the girders in time to see something bright shoot straight into the lit window of a mansion near the far end of the cylinder. To his amazement, the outer wall of the house seemed to dissolve in flame and the whole roof lifted off.

Another missile tore past, this one miraculously threading its way through spokes, guy wires, and ladder-ways to exit the other end of the cylinder. Seconds later he heard gunfire, and a distant bloom of light signaled the missile's destruction.

A head poked out next to his. The windburned homeless man spared Hayden a single glance before gaping at the next missile to appear out of the darkness. Belatedly, sirens were starting up throughout the city, animal voices Dopplered weirdly by distance and rotation.

The new missile hit one of the other spokes. The unfolding red flower lit the stubbled face next to Hayden's, tiny arcs of reflection glinting in the man's eyes.

Then he heard shouts from above. Miles and the others were coming down. Hayden pulled his head in and clambered the rest of the way down to the street, where people were now running back and forth shouting.

He felt a momentary surge of exultation. Slipstream was paying at last! He hid his grin; laughing out loud would probably be a bad idea right now.

Hayden walked through the chaos for a few minutes. No more missiles appeared but firefighting crews were battling their way through the mob and fights were breaking out. All lights were on and somewhere engines were throbbing. He felt a pull to the right and creaking, groaning sounds echoed through the street as his weight diminished. The hit on that spoke must have spooked the gravity department.

His feet had unconsciously led him toward the docks. When he realized where he was, he frowned. He should just go home—ride this out. But where would Fanning be just now? This attack meant that the fleet would be mobilized. For all he knew, the admiral might be aboard his flagship already, and then Hayden would never get a chance at him.

With a curse he ran for the docks, where he had parked his bike.

AT THE DOCKS the master was screaming, "No civilian craft, no civilian craft!" at a hundred panicked men crowding the doors. Hayden showed the security guard his pass to the Fanning estate and the grim-faced man reluctantly let him by. Once through the press of people he leaped on the back of his jet and kicked it into life. He dropped into turbulent air and the wail of attack sirens.

The sky was a storm of vehicles. Hayden had to twist and turn to avoid colliding with flocks of police bikes and ambulances. He kept his speed way down and held up his pass as he shot through narrow checkpoint gaps in ship-catcher nets that hadn't been there an hour before. In the distance other nets were slowly unfurling, distance making them appear like gray stains spreading in water.

Hayden never tired of flying between the cylinders of Rush at night. Even in this emergency, he found himself turning his head to watch the running lights of Quartet One, Cylinder Two as it showed him its black underside and, after he passed it, a crescent-shaped vision of glowing city windows and rooftops inside. The air was normally full of lanterns showing where invisible cables and stations waited in the dark; the lights were doubling, tripling now as he flew. To complicate matters, it looked as though a lightning storm was moving in: the sky below him was lit with intermittent flickers of white.

He was coming up underneath the Admiralty cylinder when

bright radiance slapped his shadow against the town's spinning metal hull. He nearly missed the entrance slot in surprise: they'd turned the sun on, seven hours early!

After he'd hooked his bike to its crane and climbed off, he saw that this wasn't a normal dawn cycle. The skies visible through the arched windows of the dock were still a deep indigo. There must be some sort of spotlight feature to the sun that he'd never heard of before; Rush was pinioned in a beam of daylight but the rest of the world was a cave of night.

Another pilot was standing by the windows. "Now I believe it happened," he muttered under his breath. Hayden frowned and hurried out of the dock and up the stairs.

He could hear the tumult in the Fanning household before he even opened the servants' door. Inside, the kitchen staff were running back and forth piling cutlery in boxes, searching for anything with the Fanning monogram on it.

"What's going on?" Hayden asked mildly, sitting down at the large table beside the stove.

"They're going to war," said a maid on her way past. At that moment the chief butler swept into the kitchen and immediately spotted Hayden. "Griffin! Get into uniform. We're going to need you."

"Yes, sir."

He felt a pulse of resentment, but as he turned to go to the cloakroom Lynelle, another of the maids, passed close by and whispered, "This throws all my well-laid plans to waste."

"Uh, what?" He turned to look at her as she leaned in the kitchen doorway. She was pretty, he hadn't failed to notice that. But maybe he'd failed to notice her noticing him.

"I was going to throw a little party at my place on our shift's off-day. And I was going to invite you when I saw you tonight." She shrugged sourly. "Can't do it now."

"I—, I guess not." He backed away.

She followed. "Was it really an attack by Mavery?" she asked.

"I don't know. Listen, I . . . I have to get ready for work."

"Oh. All right, see you." He knew she was watching him walk away; his ears burned.

Hayden had been careful to cultivate a respectful attitude since being hired. In truth, he hated it when the other servants were nice to him. How could good people, in all conscience, work for a monster? It seemed perverse and incomprehensible to him. He went to his locker in the men's cloak room and donned the livery of the Fanning household. Once he was dressed, he sat down on the dressing bench for a moment to gather his courage.

Obviously, he would never get a better chance than this—if Fanning was home. Chances were he was in the Admiralty office or the palace right now. But Hayden would have to assume otherwise, and do what so far he had not had a chance to do: venture unescorted into the Fanning's living quarters. He checked that the knife in the back of his belt was accessible, then stood up.

One little detail kept nagging at him. Hayden's search for his mother's killers had led him here. He had verified that the *Arrogance* was under Fanning's command at the time of the attack on Aerie's new sun. But there was a troubling photograph in one of the hallways of this mansion. It showed Chaison Fanning standing with an academy graduating class, his easy smile contrasting their own serious pride. He had given a speech and attended a dinner there, six hundred miles away from the edge of Aerie.

The picture was dated the very day of the attack.

His hands were trembling. With a curse he strode out of the cloakroom and made for the stairs. Somebody shouted after him, but he ignored them. Let them think he had business upstairs—well, it was true anyway.

He was feeling lightheaded. The lamps in their amber sconces throwing rings of light on the ceiling; the looming portraits of

ancestral Fannings glaring at him from all sides; the distant shouting
and clanging, all lent an unreal atmosphere to the night. Hayden
passed several people on the stairs, one of whom was an admiralty
attache; they all ignored him. As he reached the landing to the second floor he heard muttering sounds coming from the admiral's office. So Fanning was here after all.

But not alone. Hayden paused outside the door, which was ajar.
Fanning was talking to someone in low, clipped tones. It came to
Hayden that this was exactly where Miles and the other Resistance
members would have wanted him to be, had he agreed to join their
cause. For a moment the wild thought came to him that he might
be able to kill Fanning and escape, and that if so, he could pull a
double coup if he returned to Miles with strategic information. So
he listened.

". . . Won't accept any of it. He's getting way too trusting in his
old age." Hayden recognized Fanning's voice, which he had only
ever heard from behind closed doors. Was the admiral talking to
only one person, or was there a full-blown staff meeting going on
in there? Hayden couldn't find an angle where he could look
around the door without being seen.

"But our orders are clear," said another man. "We're to take the
Second Fleet into Mavery and deal with them now."

"We don't need the Second Fleet to eradicate Mavery," said Fanning contemptuously. "And the old man knows that. He's afraid
that the First Families are going to side with me and order the fleet
to investigate this buildup of ships in the sargasso. If he moves us
all into Mavery we can't do that."

"He doesn't believe the sargasso fleet's a threat?"

"He doesn't believe it's *real*." Hayden heard papers shuffling. "So.
Here are your orders."

There was a pause, then Hayden heard a sharp intake of breath
from the other man. "You can't mean this!"

"I can. We'll deal with Mavery, like the old man wants. But I'll be damned if I'm going to sit in the air occupying a second-rate province while somebody else moves in full force against Rush."

"But—but by the time we do this—"

"The sargasso fleet's not ready. That's clear from the photos. And we won't be able to put Mavery down right away; it'll take a minimum of two months before we're inextricably engaged with them, and who-ever's behind this knows to wait for that to happen. We have the time."

The other muttered under his breath, then seemed to catch him-self. "Sir. It's audacious, Admiral, but . . . I can see the logic of it."

"Good. Well, go to it, Captain. I'll join you when I've completed preparations here."

Hayden just had time to close the door of the linen closet as a captain of the navy in full dress attire strode out of Fanning's office and down the stairs.

As soon as he was gone, Hayden was out and sidling up to the door to the office. There was no one but Fanning in there now, he was sure of it. His mouth was dry, and his pulse pounding in his ears as he steeled himself for what he had to do. In all likelihood he wouldn't survive the night, but he had a debt to pay.

Taking a deep breath, he reached for the doorknob.

"There you are!"

He snatched his hand back as if it had been burned, and turned to find Venera Fanning standing at the head of the stairs. She had a hand on one cocked hip, and was glaring at him in her usual with-ering way. She was dressed in traveling attire, complete with trousers and a backpack thrown over her shoulder.

"I'm going to need a good driver," she said as she stalked up to him. "You're the only one I know who can handle himself outside of an air carriage."

"Uh—thank you, ma'am?"

"Wait here." She swept past him and into the office, leaving the door wide open. This gave Hayden his first glimpse of Fanning's office; it was not what he'd expected. The place was a mess. All four walls were crammed with bookshelves of differing pedigree. Books swelled out of the shelves and sheets of paper stuck out between the volumes like the white leaves of some literary ivy. More papers stood in precarious stacks on the floor, all leaning left to accommodate the Coriolis tilt of the town's artificial gravity. The admiral himself was leaning back in his chair, one foot propped up next to the table's only lamp. He scowled up at Venera as she walked in.

"This is low even for you," he said as he tossed a sheaf of papers onto the desk. He looked older in person than in the photos Hayden had seen, with crow's-feet around his eyes, and his hair was starting to recede. Whipcord thin, he nonetheless moved gracefully under gravity, unlike people who spent most of their time in freefall.

"Oh, come now," Venera was saying. "I'm just asserting my prerogative as a wife, to be with her husband."

"Wives don't travel on ships of the line, especially when they're going into battle!" As if to emphasize his words, a flash of lightning lit the sky outside the office's one narrow window.

"I admit I underestimated you, Venera," continued Fanning. "No—actually, I misunderstood you. This intelligence network you created, it's . . ." He shook his head. "Beyond the pale. Why? What's it for? And why are you so insistent on joining the expeditionary force that you're willing to blackmail your own husband to guarantee that I'll say yes?"

"I did it all for us," she said sweetly as she came around the desk to lean over him. Venera smoothed the hair away from Fanning's forehead. "For our advantage. It's the way we do things back home, that's all."

"But why come along? This will be dangerous, and you'll be leaving the capital just when it would be most advantageous for you to remain here as my eyes and ears. It's a contradiction, Venera."

"I know you hate mysteries," she said. "That's what makes you good at your job. But I'm afraid this particular mystery will have to remain unsolved for a while. You'll see—if all works out as I hope. For now, you'll just have to trust me."

He laughed. "That's the funniest thing you've said in a long time. Well, all right then, pack your things and get down to the docks. We'll be sailing tonight."

"Under cover of darkness?" She smiled. "You do some of your best work then, you know."

Fanning just sighed and shook his head.

Venera returned to the hallway, and taking Hayden's arm, drew him away from the office and toward the stairs. He let her do it. "I'm going to send a man around to your flat," she said to Hayden. "Tell him what to collect for you. You're not to leave the house to-day; wait for me by the main doors at six o'clock tonight, or your contract is terminated. Is that understood?"

"But what's—"

She waved a hand imperiously, indicating that he should retreat down the stairs.

She stood between him and the man he'd come to murder.

"Well?" she said. Venera seemed to see him for the first time; a muscle in her jaw flexed, causing the star-shaped scar there to squirm. "What are you waiting for?"

Hayden took a step down. He'd been planning this moment for years. In his mind it had always been clear: the traitor revealing his cowardice at the end, Hayden making some pronouncement— different every time—of just vengeance for his people's loss. An ex-ecution, clean and final.

But in order to get at the admiral now, he would have to leave Venera Fanning bleeding out her own life in the hallway.

He took another step down.

Something came over Venera's face. Softness? Some subtle giving-in to an interpretation of his actions that he didn't understand? "It will all be made clear tonight," she said in as soothing a tone as she was likely capable of.

He could have retreated around a corner, waited for her to leave. He might have staked out Fanning's office for the rest of the night. Instead he found his feet take another step and another, and then he was turning and clattering down the steps as though he actually had some other place to go. Somehow he ended up passing the photograph of Fanning posing with a graduating class. He stopped and stared at the date written on it until a hand descended on his shoulder and someone spoke his name.

He pushed past the other manservant as the world spun around him—and when he came to himself again he was kneeling in one of the servant's washrooms vomiting wretchedly into the privy.

5

ADMIRAL CHAISON FANNING pulled himself hand over hand up the docking rope and did a perfect free-fall flip to land on the quarterdeck of the *Rook*. He'd practiced that maneuver many times when he was younger, just as he'd practiced wearing the uniform of the Admiralty, keeping the cut of the jacket just so, the toeless boots polished to perfection and his toenails manicured and clean. The men watched for weakness using every possible standard—some couldn't follow a man with a thin voice, others couldn't respect an officer who didn't occasionally smile. Sometimes it seemed he'd spent the past two decades learning sixty varieties of playacting, with a special role for every rung on the ladder to his success.

There was a particular style to be cultivated when you were leaving port; he needed to project confidence and purpose to the airmen so that they didn't look back and obeyed his orders without question.

Rook was not the flagship of the fleet. A midsized cruiser, she was beginning to show her age, and several years ago had been refitted to buttress Slipstream's dwindling winter fleet. Still, she was a good ship: a hundred feet long, thirty in diameter, basically cylindrical but with curving ends that terminated in vicious spiked rams. Her thick wooden hull was festooned with hatches and ports through which could be thrust rifles, rocket racks, jet engines, braking sails, or mutineers as the situation warranted. Many of the hatches were open as she hung in the air next to the docking scaffolds, a mile from the Admiralty. The sun was glowering from behind the docks, whose caged catwalks cast long curving shadows across the amber hull of the ship, while tongues of light had found and lit random intricacies of its interior. Inside, the ship was a series of interlocking cells, most of them made of wooden lattices through which you could see men working or the tanned sides of tarpaulined and lashed crates. Some of the cells were big blocks of metal, such as the armory and the rocket magazine. And to the fore of the ship, just behind the bridge, an exercise centrifuge spun lazily. Its side walls made a turning mandala of Admiralty notices, wooden walls, and plumbing. The men were required to spend a few hours a day in the centrifuge, and he would too; nobody was going to lose their fighting trim on this voyage.

Captain John Sembry saluted the admiral. His staff were lined up in midair behind him, their toes pointed precisely in the same direction. "The ship is ready, sir," announced Sembry.

A quick glance told Chaison that everything was where it should be, and the men were all working hard—or at least giving the impression of working hard. That was all that mattered, if things were truly ready. "Very good, Captain. I'll be on the bridge. Carry on." He turned and did a hand-over-hand walk through a narrow passage under the centrifuge, heading for the prow.

On the way to the bridge he checked his cabin. Venera was not there. Neither was her luggage. Fuming, he continued on up to the cylindrical chamber just behind the fore rocket battery. The navigator and helm were waiting, looking expectant. They hadn't yet received their orders and were expecting to be told to set a course for Mavery. He was going to surprise them.

But not, apparently, yet. "Where is she?" he demanded of a petty officer. The man snapped to attention, slowly drifting upward and away from his post.

"Semaphore said, on her way, sir!"

"And when was that?"

"Half—half an hour ago, sir."

He turned away, composing himself before the man could see his mask of professionalism slip. He was looking for something to do—a tie-down to criticize, a chart crib to fold—when the navigator said, "She's here, sir," with some relief in his voice. He was floating next to a porthole; Chaison stepped over fifteen feet of empty air to join him there, and look where he pointed.

Hanging limbs akimbo in the cage of a docking arm twenty meters away was a long-haired woman with an imperious nose and heavily made-up eyes. She wore an outlandishly bright jumpsuit that was also too tight in all the right (or, on a ship like this, wrong) places. Her hands were twisting nervously, but her expression was intent and focused as she directed some navvies to push a small mountain of crates and trunks through the narrow exit of the docking arm.

Aubri Mahallan was not the "she" Chaison had been hoping to see. He'd assumed this particular passenger was already on board. Forgetting himself he frowned virulently at her, as if she could see him behind the sun-drenched hull.

"That . . . costume . . . will not do," he muttered under his breath.

"Two women on board, sir," said the navigator neutrally. "It's—"

"Far from unprecedented," Chaison finished smoothly. "There's a great tradition of female ship officers in Virga, Bargott—just not of late in the enlightened principality of our beloved pilot."

"No, sir, ah, yes, sir."

"Summon the armorer to the chart room when she boards. I'll meet her there." Chaison left without another glance at the bridge staff.

Located behind the bridge, the chart room was the traditional inner sanctum of the ship's commanding officer. Nobody was allowed in here except the bridge staff and Chaison himself—nobody except for the one person he did find when he entered the drum-shaped room. Gridde, Chaison's chart-master, was fabulously old and bent over—so much so that he retained the stoop even in freefall. As Chaison entered he was teasing a tiny ruby clip out of its nestle in the crook of two fine hairs inside the chamber's main chart box. "Ah, Admiral," he said without turning around, "it's an interesting challenge you've given me this time."

Chaison's irritability evaporated, as it always did around Gridde. "It would have been a shame for you to retire without helping us navigate winter."

"I've done it before," wheezed Gridde, smiling at Chaison's surprise. "Thirty-five years ago," continued the chart-master. He returned his attention to the large glass chart box. Inside the box was a three-dimensional lattice of fine, almost invisible blond strands—actual hairs, harvested from the rare young lady whose locks met Gridde's standard. Clipped to these strands were dozens of tiny jewel-clusters: a single sapphire stood for a small town, double-sapphires for larger towns, and so on. The box was a scintillating galaxy of light: sapphires, rubies, emeralds, topaz and jet, pale quartz and peridot. At the very center of the chart was a large diamond, which stood for the Slipstream sun. Gridde was adjusting the position of a ruby according to the latest semaphore information.

"Well, don't leave me drifting," said Chaison, crossing his arms and smiling. "What happened thirty-five years ago?"

Gridde snorted. "Why, the whole damn nation nearly drifted into winter! Don't they teach you any history at that academy? I remember a day when half the chart box was empty!" Despite the vehemence of his tone, his fingers were absolutely steady as they gripped the tiny ruby between a pair of wires and moved it infinitesimally to the left. "There. That ought to hold you for a day or two."

Chaison gripped the side of the chart table and pulled himself close to examine the three-dimensional representation of the one hundred miles of air surrounding Rush. "And our course?"

"Don't push me." Gridde slowly withdrew his wires and shut the case. "See, if this was one of those new gel charts, just drawing the wires out would move everything! You can't let them standard-ize on gel charts, sir. Would be a disaster."

"I know, Gridde, you've only told me a thousand times."

The chart-master sailed over to the wall and shut the metal bul-let shield over the porthole. Now the room was lit only by the gleam of a gas lantern. Chaison wound up the lantern's little fan, without which it would starve itself of oxygen in seconds, and handed it to Gridde. The chart-master closed the metal door of the lantern, and now light only shone out of a tiny pipette. He carefully arranged this miniature spotlight in a set of flexible arms attached to the chart table, and aimed it.

Only a narrow column of jewels was lit now; the big diamond gleamed at its end. "The way-point," said Gridde, "is Argenta Town, the double-ruby." The two little red gleams were the only town within the beam of light. The beam represented the course the ex-peditionary force would take; Chaison could see that they would pass unseen by the majority of the local population.

"Good—" Chaison turned his head at a rap on the door. "Enter!"

Sunlight washed away the illusion of hovering above a miniature world. Silhouetted in the doorway was the curving shape of Aubri Mahallan. "That will be all, thank you, Gridde," said Chaison. "Come in, Armorer."

AS VENERA FANNING'S small party wound their way through the labyrinth of docking arms, Hayden stared at their desti-nation with claustrophobic dread. Above him, below, and to all sides hung the bannered cruisers of Slipstream. These were the very ships that had invaded and conquered Aerie. He found himself searching the nearest ship for some sign of a scar—of burned hull, long since painted over—though the ship he had flown Can Two into six years ago had been incinerated before his eyes. He would not have been surprised had it turned up here, intact, a malignant ghost. Indeed, the cluster of bloated cylinders that shadowed the walkway seemed more nightmarish than real. This was the very last place in Virga he would have chosen to go.

"I'm definitely going to miss those Friday evening soirees," Venera was saying to some acquaintance of hers who had come to see her off. "Strange. The crowd has stopped cheering."

Only a low muttering came from the wall of people who pressed against the naval base's security netting. Hayden knew exactly why, but he was obligated to hold his tongue in the presence of his mistress. The crowd had come out to watch the fleet depart. They were eager for spectacle—for the proof that the Pilot was acting decisively after last night's outrageous attack on the city. People had been arriving all day, forming a curving half-shell made of human beings like tiles in a mosaic, that gradually came to obscure the backdrop of Rush's whirling towns. Charged up and indignant, they periodically broke into chants and songs, while continuously flinging sandwiches, drinks, and children up and down the surface of the wall. Bikes and folded wings, picnic baskets and man-sized wicker spheres containing food and souvenir vendors made a kind of base coat behind the human surface.

The fleet had been due to depart an hour ago. The sun was shutting down for the day, its light sputtering and reddening. The light made the docks seem like an alternation of photographs with different exposures and tints—now sepia, now plum-red, now black-and-white. As soon as the sun shut down, heat would flee the air. Few in the crowd had dressed for that. So now they were complaining.

Also muttering were the noncoms and military police who were hurrying Venera's party down the arm to the shadow-striped Rook.

As they approached, the ship's jets growled into life for a moment, and it began to rotate until it was vertical compared to the approaching party. The rest of the ships began executing the same turn as word of their initial course and heading was relayed from the Rook.

"Ooh, Venera," said the socialite clinging to Fanning's arm, "they're excited to see you!" She waved at the crowd, which had burst into song again at the sight.

The grumbling engines and motion of ships made Hayden's head spin—but he kept going. There was only one way for him to redeem himself for his earlier cowardice. Fanning was leaving Rush, and Hayden had to follow.

And if—an idea so heretical he refused to take it seriously—if he should be unable to kill Fanning (he would never *choose* not to!), then Hayden could still do some good by acting as a spy aboard the Rook. If what he'd heard outside Fanning's office was any indication, there was more to this expedition than met the eye.

They reached the end of the docking arm. Hayden hauled on the rope to halt the forward drift of Venera's trunks while she showed her papers to the waiting deck officer. He barely glanced at them, waving her on.

"Now don't forget my camera!" shouted the socialite from behind the shoulders and arms of the MPs. Venera's other friends waved and shouted similar platitudes, as though Lady Fanning were going on a Sunday cruise and not leaving the country under mysterious circumstances. Hayden gathered the two trunks, each by its leather handle, and stepped across the two-meter gap between the arm and the ship.

As the big doors swung shut behind him Hayden was met by a chaos of detail: beams and ropes in gaslight, the smell of jet fuel and soap, racks of rifles and swords, the flickering motion of a giant centrifuge wheel—and everywhere people, a mob of silent men all of whom seemed to be looking at him.

He spun around, because it was Venera Fanning they were staring at. She stared back for a second, a half-smile crinkling the scar on her chin. Then she turned and shot in the direction of a narrow corridor that passed under the centrifuge. Hayden was left holding her bags.

As he moved to follow her he realized that only one other person had accompanied them on board: a nondescript, passive-faced man of middle age. He looked like some minor bureaucrat. Now he smiled at Hayden.

"But the other servants—" They had come here in a large group. Surely Hayden wasn't the only one who was going?

"You're the driver?" asked the bland man; his voice was as colorless as his appearance.

"Uh . . . yes."

"Stow the bags in the captain's cabin and then go to the centrifuge. You bunk with the carpenters."

"Ah." He stuck out his hand tentatively. "I'm Hayden Griffin."

The man shook it distractedly. "Lyle Carrier. Get going, then."

Hayden grabbed the trunks in an awkward embrace and went to find Venera Fanning.

DARKNESS SHUTTERED THE sky well before the last ship had left the docks. Chaison Fanning sat in the command chair, chin on his fist. He had no duties at this moment: the ship was in the hands of Captain Sembry. Sembry's voice rang out confidently, sending commands down the speaking tubes to the engines and rudder gangs. All eyes were on him just now, and that was a relief.

Chaison rotated a little cup-shaped object in his fingers. It had been given to him by that problematic armorer, Mahallan, a few minutes ago. This device was intended to make real for him an idea he'd thought ridiculous when Venera had first brought it to him. He supposed he should try it.

It was hard to focus past his anger, however. He glanced around; nobody was looking at him. No, they wouldn't. But it would be all through the fleet in hours. This was a humiliation he wouldn't be able to escape.

Why had she done it? He wondered. More importantly: why had he let her? He could have set sail and forced her to catch up. Except that she had information that she could—and would—use against him, her own husband, if he didn't do exactly what she said. He had no doubt she would move against him, he had known Venera long enough not to doubt her ruthlessness.

He gripped the cup tightly and almost threw it at the wall. But that would just add to the talk later, he knew. With a sigh he held it up to his ear.

The sound was surprisingly loud—he pulled the cup away, then gingerly replaced it. What he heard was a roaring din—a steady hissing, weird warbling noises that came and went, and a sound like giant teeth grating. Overlaid on all this was a deep tearing sound, like some impossibly heavy fabric being ripped. It went on and on, hypnotic, an argument between demons.

He took the speaker away from his ear. This was supposed to explain everything, this incessant grumbling. He did admit it was a compelling demonstration, but in no way did it lend credence to any of the wild claims Venera had made.

Anyway, he didn't care. All Admiral Fanning could think of right now was the fact that his wife had, no doubt deliberately, made the national fleet of Slipstream . . . late.

6

A COLUMN OF ragged clouds twisted like smoke in the night. The shapes wheeled grandly like wary duelists, occasionally testing one another's defenses with half-hearted lightning bolts. Every now and then, a transient corridor of clear air would open to some distant sun through the shuffle of gray shapes that receded for thousands of miles in every direction. Then the flanks of one or another silent combatant would momentarily throw the rest into invisibility as it shone in shades of dusty rose and burgundy.

These were young clouds, the progeny of a mushroom-shaped column of warmer air that had penetrated into Slipstream territory earlier in the day. Being young, these banks and starbursts of mist had just begun to condense. The realm through which they drifted was filled with the remnants of an earlier mass of clouds: its droplets had come together and fused over the hours and days, each collision making fewer and larger drops. Now great spheres of water, some head-sized, some as large as houses, punched through the clouds like slow cannonballs, adding to the chaos of the mixing air.

Wakeful citizens on bikes hovered outside the two towns and a farm that were the only habitation for miles. The sentries kept a watch out for any large mass of water that might loom out of the dark on a collision course with the spinning wheels, or the dark nets of the farm. For one sentry, the only sound was the whirring of the little fan that kept his lantern alive as he waited in silence, cloak drawn around his shoulders to ward off the damp, feet ready on the pedals to kick his bike into motion.

Thus huddled, he at first didn't notice something nose out of a cloud shaped like a bird's head. When he finally spotted it he muttered a curse, because initially it looked like a town-wrecker of a water ball. He reached for his horn with numb fingers, but as he raised the brass horn to his lips he hesitated. The shape no longer appeared rounded, but rather like an extra beak to the diaphanous bird, this one hard and sharp. It was the prow of a ship.

Now that he could see what it was he realized he'd been hearing it for a minute or two already—a distant whine in several keys from its engines. He could also see two spotter bikes weaving in spirals ahead of it. You never knew what might lurk inside a cloud, so the spotters went ahead of the ship to ensure that there were no rocks, water balls, or habitations in the way. On dark nights like this, spotters sometimes found obstacles by running into them. So ships tended to move slowly at night.

They also used headlights to probe the blackness—that was simple prudence. This ship, however, was running dark. As it left the cloud in a whirl of eddied mist, another nose appeared behind it, and another.

The sentry raised the horn again, suddenly fearing an invasion; then he saw the lantern-lit sigil of Slipstream on the hull of the lead vessel. He slowly lowered the horn and clipped it to his saddle. He was a citizen of Aerie; he would not pick a fight with Slipstream tonight. In fact, he would be happy not to be noticed by them at all.

Seven big vessels passed by, all dark except for their running lights. As they disappeared into the black the sentry shivered and turned his attention back to his watch. This would be a story for the morning, perhaps, but he wasn't about to fly over to the other watchers to compare notes. Somehow he felt it better not to speak of these ships while darkness reigned.

HAYDEN HID IN his coffin-sized bunk for as long as possible. He'd spent an uneasy and unpleasant night, but staying here was preferable to climbing out and facing the reality of the situation. He had been shanghaied—pressed into service to the same enemy he was sworn to destroy. It was all some sort of absurd nightmare.

His bunk was at the bottom of a stack in the exercise centrifuge. He felt like a disused book shelved away in a particularly cramped library. He couldn't sit up because the bunk above his was only inches away from his nose. Each time he rolled over the world seemed to turn in the opposite direction—a familiar enough sensation from town living, but magnified by the small size of this wheel. The thing rotated five times a minute but only provided a tenth of a gravity for all that effort. Its axles had creaked monotonously, men on either side of him had snored in different rhythms, and someone had created prodigious amounts of bad smell that hovered in the air for what seemed hours.

Now his bedding was vibrating with footfalls as an endless parade of airmen ran laps around the wheel. The sleeping level had only one narrow aisle between the stacks of bunks, so the runners' feet slammed down inches from Hayden's head. Finally, when someone stumbled and kicked his shelf, he cursed and rolled out into the narrow space between the bunk stacks.

"Out of the way!" The shark-faced boatswain pushed Hayden as he made to step into the aisle. For the next few minutes he ducked from bunk stack to bunk stack as other airmen made a game of trying to hit him on the way by. Their crude laughter followed him as he scrambled up the ladder to the upper level of the wheel.

Last night the boatswain had made it very clear that on board this ship, Hayden was little more than dead weight. He had gone to bunk with the carpenters as ordered, but they didn't want him around either. He'd found an empty berth in the centrifuge, but clearly he would have to locate some less trafficked part of the ship or he was going to be covered in bruises before the end of the day.

The upper level of the wheel was simply a barrel fifteen feet in diameter. Half of it was taken up with crates, the other half was bare flooring where men with swords were circling one another under the watchful eye of a drill sergeant. Hayden eyed the crates, and finally climbed up on a stack, losing weight with every step. He settled in to watch the fencing technique of the men below.

"You!" He looked down. It was the boatswain again. He was a florid man with a crisp uniform and a shock of carrot-red hair. His eyes protruded when he glared, which was most of the time. Now his lips flapped as he said, "That's delicate equipment, get off it!"

Hayden sighed and hopped from the crates up to the centrifuge's entranceway, at its hub. Surely there must be a quiet spot somewhere.

All the ship's ports were open, it seemed, and a cold wind blew through the interlocking chambers of its interior. Everywhere he looked men were hauling ropes, shifting boxes, or hammering something. He decided that an open cargo door was his best bet and flew over to perch on its inside. A stiff wind flapped past just a foot away but he'd found a pocket of relatively still air. He curled up to look out.

The sun glowed far to aft. It was dim and red with distance; they must be near the border. The clouds they passed threw hazy shadows like fingers pointing the way ahead.

Dotting the sky around him were other ships. He counted six; there might be more on the other side of the vessel, but this was a far cry from the dozens that had left port. As the Rook slowly rotated around its axis he was able to verify that there were only seven ships in this group, counting his own. Where was the rest of the fleet?

They skirted the sides of a cloud-mountain and suddenly the air ahead opened up, clear of obstructions. Hayden blinked in surprise. He faced a deep blue abyss—a span of darkness that ran from infinity below to infinity above, and stretched endlessly to both sides. The *Rook* was driving straight into winter.

He couldn't understand how he'd come to be here. He'd had the chance to kill Fanning, and he hadn't done it. That made him a coward—but, undeniably, there was also something big going on, something beyond an imminent attack on Mavery. He might be the only spy Aerie had aboard these ships. As he'd tossed and turned last night, he'd kept coming back to the conclusion that it was his duty to find out what he could, and report it back.

"Hey you!" He turned to find himself facing a boy with a ratlike face who wore an airman's uniform several sizes too big for him. "You Griffin?" he asked belligerently. When Hayden nodded, he jabbed a thumb in the direction of the centrifuge. "Yer wanted in the lady's chamber." He smirked.

"Thanks. You can call me Hayden. What's your name?"

"Martor," said the boy suspiciously. "I'm the gopher."

"Good to meet you, Martor. By the way, where can a guy get a meal around here?"

Martor laughed. "You missed it. That was six o'clock. Not that you could have et with us men, anyway. Yer gonna hafta find yer own meals."

"How much to get that arranged for me?"

Martor's eyebrows lifted. He thought about it. "Six. No less."

"Done." Hayden went forward, a little less deferential to the other men now that he had a destination.

It wasn't Venera waiting for him outside the captain's quarters, but the bland Carrier. He stood on the air with his arms crossed, toes pointed daintily. He frowned at Hayden. "You have duties," he said without preamble.

"I, uh—yes?"

"Lady Fanning has secured a bike for our use. This is not a military machine but a fast racer with sidecars. You are to familiarize yourself with it. Three hours a day, no more no less."

"Yes, sir!" So they wanted him to fly? Well, it would be their funeral. "What model is it?"

Carrier waved a hand negligently. "Don't know. Anyway, the rest of your time will be spent assisting the new armorer. We were *told*," he said with a faintly unpleasant moue, "that you were mechanically minded."

"Well, I tinker with bikes—"

"Good. You are to report to the armorer immediately. That's aft," Carrier added helpfully.

"Okay, but what will I—" Carrier didn't even frown; he just turned his head away almost imperceptibly. Hayden got the message.

A little of the stifling gloom that had settled on him last night lifted as he headed aft, but he was still bewildered at how quickly and thoroughly he'd gotten himself into this situation. If he'd had any sort of courage he'd have killed Fanning yesterday. The fact that he hadn't, and was now effectively working for the enemy, made him feel deeply sick.

"Know where you're going, do you?" said somebody. Hayden looked down to find Martor squinting at him. "It's this way," he continued, pointing past the drooping bellies of a row of fuel tanks.

"Thanks. Hey—when I looked outside earlier, I saw we were headed into winter. What's all that about?"

Martor looked uncomfortable. "Don't know. Nobody's telling us anything, not yet anyway. You saw we split off from the main fleet? Rumor is we're going to come around behind the enemy. But that don't make no sense. Enemy's farther into the suns, not out here."

"You mean Mavery?"

"Who else would I mean?"

Martor was trailing Hayden now, shifting his weight and fiddling with his hands, much more like the boy he was than the tough man he tried to be. "Winter's nothing to worry about," said Hayden. "I've been there."

"You have? Is it true that there's capital bugs with suns in their bellies? And whole countries frozen solid, guys about to stick each other with swords when their suns went out and their whole armies covered in ice now?"

"Never saw anything like that . . ."

"But how would you know, since it goes on forever?"

"*Forever?*" Somebody laughed. "I don't think so."

An irregularly shaped box was stapled to the outer hull under a mad web of netting. The box had a perfectly ordinary door in one of its facets. The laughter had come from that direction. It sounded suspiciously like a woman's.

"You're gonna tell me that's the armorer," Hayden whispered to Martor. Martor nodded vigorously. "Thought so."

He stuck his head through the door. There was indeed a woman fitted into the intricate mess like a main cog in a watch. She was opening one of several dozen boxes crammed in around her, and was currently upside down compared to him so that all that registered at first was the halo of writhing brown hair that surrounded her face and the fact that she was dressed entirely in black save for a glimpse of scarlet silk that peeked out below her collar. He rotated politely to match her orientation and stuck out his hand. "I'm Hayden Griffin. I was told to assist you."

Her hand was warm, her grip strong. "Aubri Mahallan. Who told you to assist me?"

"Um, man named Carrier."

"Oh, *him.*" She dismissed the man's entire existence with those two words. Mahallan had a heavy accent, bearing hard on sounds like *er* and *oh*. Right side up, she looked as intriguing as she sounded, her skin pale and perfectly unblemished like the most pampered courtier, her eyes wide in a perpetually startled look and overemphasized with black makeup. Her mouth was broad and was always twisting into one or another expression so that a constant parade of impressions flickered across her face. Just now she was pursing her lips and squinting at Hayden. "I suppose I can use you for something. And you!" She aimed her expressive gaze past Hayden at the open door. "This is the fifth time you've blocked my light this morning. Guess I'm going to have to find something for you to do as well."

"Yes, ma'am," came Martor's voice faintly from somewhere outside.

"But I can't have ignorant savages working for me," continued Mahallan as she spun and opened a porthole to let a blast of fresh air into the junk-filled cell. "Winter does not go on forever—or rather, it does, but only in the sense that you could go around the outside of a dinner plate forever. Do you understand?"

"No, sir!" said Martor, still invisible.

"Come in here!" Martor peeked around the doorjamb. Somewhere outside, a gang of airmen was engaged in a swearing contest. "And close the door, will you?" added the armorer. Hayden shifted to let Martor do that, and found himself close enough to Mahallan that he could smell her perspiration.

Her attention was fixed on Martor. "Do you believe this world goes on forever in all directions?"

"Yes, ma'am," said Martor with no trace of irony. "Rush came out of Forever, two generations ago, and we attacked the countries here. After we've cut through them all, we're going back to Forever, out the other side of the countries."

"I see we have our work cut out for us," said the armorer with an amused glance at Hayden. "Young man, do you know what a balloon is?"

"A bag for storing gas," said Martor instantly.

"Good. Well, Virga, your world, is a balloon. It is an immensely big balloon, in fact, fully five thousand miles across and orbiting in the outer reaches of the Vega star system. Virga is artificial. Man-made."

"Ma'am, that's very funny," said Martor with a stilted grin.

"It's utterly true, young man. Is it not a fact that your suns are artificial? So, then, why not the rest of the world, too?" Martor looked a little less sure of himself now. "Now, the problem is that even a fusion sun capable of heating and lighting everything out to a distance of several hundred miles is just a tiny spark in a volume this size. Especially when clouds and other obstacles absorb the light so readily. Sixty, eighty, even a hundred suns aren't enough to illuminate the whole interior of Virga. So, we have large volumes of air that are unlit, unheated—volumes of winter."

"I'm with ya," said Martor.

"But these volumes don't go on forever. They end, one way or another, at the lighted precincts of some other nation, or at Candesce if you head straight toward the center of Virga. Or they end at the skin of the world, where icebergs crowd and grind like the gnashing teeth of a god. And your asteroid, Rush, orbits very slowly around the middle of this world, tugged by the almost imperceptible gravity the air creates."

"Now you're having me on," said Martor.

Mahallan sighed extravagantly, but couldn't hide a smile. "Go on. You're taking up my air. You," she said to Hayden, "stick around and help me unpack some of these boxes."

THE SEVEN SHIPS killed their engines a dozen miles into winter. They drifted for a few minutes, then with slow grumbles of their turning engines they slid into a star formation, each one pointing out from a central point. Lines were cast from nose to nose, and the captains of six ships hand-walked across to an open port in the side of the *Rook*. In all directions, darkness swallowed distance and detail.

When Admiral Fanning entered the *Rook's* chart room he was pulled up short by the vision of the captains clinging to floor, walls, and ceiling like wasps in a paper nest. They were all identical in their black uniforms, rustling and moving slightly. He could practically hear a subliminal buzz coming from them.

He shook off the impression and glided to his chair by the chart table. "You've all been very patient with our secrecy," he said as the last visiting captain ducked past him to loop a hand through a velvet wall-strap. Now that he thought about it, the idea of these men as wasps seemed more and more apt. They were dangerous, focused—and for the most part, dumb as planks. Perfect for the job he had in mind.

"I'm sure you've had your suspicions about where we're going. I'm equally sure," he said with a smile, "that your crews have been devising all kinds of extravagant ideas of their own." There was a polite smile from the swarm in return.

"Now that we're out of semaphore-range of any potential spies, we can make a general announcement."

"It's about time!" Captain Hieronymous Flosk, the oldest and least patient of the company, leaned into the light from the chart table. The glow made his face a mask of crevasses and pitted plains. "This secrecy is ridiculous," he grated. "We don't have to skulk around hiding from Mavery. Hit them direct, and hard. You'd think that would be obvious," he sniffed.

"Well, you'd be right," said Fanning, "if Mavery were our target."

Several of the captains had been muttering together, but these words shocked them silent. "What do you mean?" asked Flosk, his voice momentarily reduced to a whine. "After the damned sneak attack the other day—"

"Almost certainly not them," said Fanning drily. "Oh, their

munitions, right enough. But Mavery's border dispute with us has been trumped up by a third party—one with deep pockets and spies throughout Slipstream." He took one of the slides his wife had prepared for him and slipped it into the hooded lantern under the chart box. Opening a little door on the side of the lantern, he projected the image onto the wall behind him.

"This," he said, "is a secret shipyard of Falcon Formation. One of, uh, our spies took this photo less than a week ago." Several of the captains rotated in place to try to find a better view of the picture. Fanning glanced back to verify that he'd chosen the correct slide: it was Venera's picture of the giant warship.

"The dreadnought you see in the deep background is fifteen hundred feet long," he announced. Again, the captains went still. "Nothing like it has ever flown in Virga. It's big enough to be a carrier for midsized hunter sloops, as well as a substantial assault force. We believe she will be the flagship of a fleet aimed at Slipstream. We have learned that they are using the dispute with Mavery as a ruse to draw our forces away from Rush. Once our fleet is entangled in Mavery, they will move in and take the city." He didn't have to add that Rush *was* Slipstream. Take one and you had the other.

There was a long silence. Then Flosk said, "Who's this 'we' who believes all of this crap? You and the Pilot?"

"The Pilot, yes," Fanning lied. "He is well aware of our nation's failings in the espionage area. He's taken steps—hence the pictures." He changed the slide for another that showed the shipyard itself. "That's the strategic situation. I'm sure you can appreciate how important it's been to keep our knowledge of the situation secret."

"Wait," said someone. "You mean we're going to attack *Falcon*?"

"Suicide," someone else mumbled.

"Clearly we need any advantage we can get," said Fanning with a reluctant nod. "Your ships were either designed as winter ships or have been refitted as part of a winter fleet. These upgrades have been going on for some years, since my predecessor discerned a need for such a fleet."

"But these are hardly the best winter ships," objected Flosk. "The new ones are off with the force that's heading to Mavery."

"Naturally. Mavery and Falcon will notice if our finest winter ships don't show up for the border dispute. Your ships—and I hate to put this indelicately, gentlemen—are the inconspicuous ones. Not very powerful, not very important. Nonetheless, they are all rigged for operations in cold, darkness, and low-oxygen conditions. They will be sufficient."

He closed the cover on the projector and restored the light to the chart box. "This is the local constellation of nations," he said. "We are here. Falcon is there." The chart box contained dense clouds of colored sparks, each hue representing a different nation. The nations coiled around and pressed against one another in intricate contact, like the internal organs of some creature of light. "The chief nations of Meridian all follow the rise and fall of the Meridian Five Hadley cell that's powered by heat from the Sun of Suns, which is below the table in this view. Rush Asteroid is largely unaffected by the air currents and continues to follow its orbit around Candesce, at something less than walking speed. As you can see, Rush will soon leave Aerie and migrate into Mavery's territory. But after that . . ." He turned the box to show a mass of glittering green stars that took up much of one side of the box. "After that we will, by force of celestial mechanics, have to pass through Falcon."

Three suns—diamonds among emeralds—gleamed within the broad dazzle of green.

"Now, here is the location of the secret shipyard we discovered." He flipped a lever in the base of the map box. All the little pinpricks of light dimmed save for one amethyst that lit up deep inside Falcon territory.

The captains broke into a babble of complaint. Flosk burst out laughing. "How are we expected to get to that spot without fighting our way through the whole of Falcon?"

"Simple," said Fanning. "The location of the shipyard is secret because it's in an underpopulated area—a volume filled with sargassos. It's really at the terminus of a long tongue of winter that extends hundreds of miles into Falcon. The sargassos shade this volume and much of it is oxygen-poor. A wilderness. We're going to circle all the way around the Meridian constellation and sneak in through this alley of dead air."

". . . And raid the shipyard," said somebody. There were nods all around.

"Well, it's bold," said Flosk grudgingly. "Still suicidal. But then we're not too many ships. Slipstream can afford to lose us."

"I have no intention of sacrificing us," said Fanning.

"But how are we going to survive and get home again?"

"That's a part of the plan that has to remain secret for now," said the admiral. "But what it means in the short term is that, before we circle around through winter, we have to make a . . . a detour."

7

IT MIGHT HAVE been two thousand miles away; it could have been twice that. They were never able to tell her for sure. But some-where, and not too long ago, there had been a war.

Nobody knew whether the shot was fired by a lone sniper, or whether it was one of a salvo loosed in the midst of a confused melee involving thousands of men. But it was a military-grade weapon of some sort, that much was sure. The bullet had come out of its muzzle at a velocity of more than a mile per second. It outran its own sound.

She knew what had happened next. The bullet had gathered its experiences with it as it flew, remembering what it saw and where it went; and these memories came to Venera Fanning now and then, as dreams and nightmares. They must be from the bullet, there was no other possible source for them. She herself could never have imagined the vision of fantastically prowed vessels ram-ming one another and tumbling in burning embraces into blood-red clouds. Nor could she have thought up the rope-connected freefall city the bullet had sailed through shortly after being fired. The city owned no wheeling towns. Its towers and houses were nodes in a seemingly infinite lattice of rope, and its scuttling citi-zens were long as spiders, their bones fragile as glass. The bullet passed through the city going hundreds of miles per hour, so the faces and rippling banners of the place were blurred and unidentifiable.

The bullet shot past farms and forests that hung in the air like green galaxies. In places the entire sky was alive with spring colors as distant suns lit the delicate leaves of billions of independently floating plants, each one clinging by its roots to a grain of dirt or drop of water. The air here was heady with oxygen and, for the humans who tended the farms, redolent with the perfume of growing things.

In contrast, the vast expanses of winter that opened up ahead of the bullet were clear as crystal. Falling into them was like penetrating a sphere of purest rainwater, a deep fathomless blueness wherein the bullet cooled and shrank in on itself just a little. It threaded through schools of heavily feathered, blind fish and past the nearly identical birds that fed off them. It entered a realm of sky-spanning ice arches, a froth of frozen water whose curving bubbles were tens of miles on a side. Black gaps pierced their sides. Snow nestled in the elbows of icicles longer than Rush's shadow. Here the air was dense, exhausted of oxygen as well as heat. The bullet slowed and nearly came to a halt as it reached the farther edge of this shattered cathedral of ice.

But as it began a slow tumble and return to the blue intricacies behind it, an errant beam of light from Candesce welled up from below. The glow heated the air behind the bullet just enough to make a sigh that welled out and pushed it away. Again it tumbled into dark emptiness.

Winter did not rule all the empty spaces of Virga. There were columns of warm air hundreds of miles long that rose up from the Sun of Suns. Before they cooled enough for their water to condense as clouds, they were transparent, and Candesce's light followed them up, sometimes penetrating all the way to Virga's skin. The bullet strayed into one such column and changed course, rising now and slowly circumnavigating the world.

It was the passage of an iceberg that galvanized the bullet into motion again. An eddy of the passing monster put a sustained wind at its back and soon the bullet was cruising along at a respectable thirty miles an hour. On the crest of this wavefront it entered a dense forest that had supersaturated itself with oxygen. It narrowly missed a hundred or so of the long spiderweb filaments of trunk and branch whose weave made up the forest. But then it happened: the bullet rapped a solitary, tumbling stone a few miles in and some sparks swirled after it. One spark touched a dry leaf that had been circulating in the shadowed interior of the forest for ten years. The leaf turned into a small sphere of flame, then the other leaves floating nearby lit, and then a few nearby trees.

An expanding sphere of fire pushed the bullet faster and faster. Mile after mile the storm of flame pushed through the supercharged air, in seconds consuming threadlike trees bigger than towns. The forest transformed itself into a fireball bright as any sun in Virga. When it burned out its dense core of ashes and smoke would contain a sargasso—a volume of space sheltered from the wind by leagues of charred branch and root, where no light nor oxygen could be found.

The bullet was indifferent to this fate. It rode the explosion all the way out of the forest. When it left the roaring universe of flame it was once again speeding at nearly a mile a second. Several minutes later it entered the precincts of Aerie. It flashed past the towns and outrider stations of Slipstream. It narrowed its focus to a quartet of towns in the formation known as Rush. It lined up on a single window in the glittering wheel of the Admiralty.

It stopped dead in Venera Fanning's jaw. Some blood tried to continue on, but that only made it a few meters farther. And while the doctors did dig it out of Venera's throat, it had remained in the Admiralty ever since.

Until now. As Venera slept uneasily and dreamed her way back down the long trajectory of the projectile, it bumped slowly back and forth inside the lacquer box in her luggage where she kept it. Its journey was not over yet.

8

THE *ROOK'S* HANGAR was a deep pie-shaped chamber tak-ing up one-third of the length of the ship. Most of the space was bikes, all lashed to the walls like somnolent bees in a hive; but two big cutters made the stern area into a well of shadows, each boat a forty-footer armed to the teeth. Hayden eyed these as he slammed an access panel on the bike Venera Fanning had brought for him. The cutters were weapons, of course, and so distasteful to him; but they were also ships, and he couldn't help wondering how fast they were and how maneuverable they'd be to steer.

The bike was ready. He gave it one last appraising look. This wasn't his bike, but it was a racer, complete with two detachable sidecars and a long spool of grounding thread for those situations where you outran your own rate of static charge drain.

Hayden had been staying up late so as to be awake during nightwatch—there were fewer people around—so he was startled when Martor's thin face popped over the bike's small horizon like some parody of the sun. "Watcha doin?" said the gopher in his usual challenging way.

"Shouldn't you be asleep?" He unclipped the bike from its dry-dock clamps and hefted it, judging its mass. There were traces here and there of red paint, but sometime very recently it had been re-done a glossy black. He didn't mind that.

"Could say the same about you." Martor hand-walked around the clamps to look at what Hayden was doing. As he did the wind keened particularly loudly past the ship's outer hatches. Martor jerked his head in that direction.

"Still worried about winter? It's a bit late for that," Hayden pointed out. "We've been in it for days."

"You're not taking that out in it?" Martor watched in distress as Hayden dragged the racer in the direction of the forward bike hatch. "Ain't it'll freeze you like a block of ice?"

"It's not that cold." The bike started to drift as they passed the center of the chamber so Martor steadied it with his own mass. "Clouds insulate the air," said Hayden. "So it only gets so cold. Usually doesn't even get down to freezing, most places. Hey, why don't you come along for the ride? I'm just taking her out for a practice run."

Martor snatched his hands back from the bike. "You crazy? I'm not going out there."

"Why not? I am."

A couple of members of the hatch gang had heard this and laughed. They were lounging next to the big wooden doors, awaiting any order to open them. Hayden nodded and they reluctantly abandoned their cards to man the winch wheel.

"Hang on there!" Both Hayden and Martor turned. The eccentric armorer, Mahallan, was poised at an inside doorway. Her silhouette was very interesting, but she only perched there a moment before flying over to the hatch. "You boys going for a night flight?"

Hayden shrugged. "All flights are night flights right now."

"Hmm. Glad to see you've overcome your fear of winter," she said to Martor. The boy blushed and stammered something.

"Listen," continued Mahallan, "I'd like you to do something for me. While you're out there—I know it'll be dark so you probably won't see them—if you spot anything like this, could you bring it back?" She opened her fist to reveal a bent little glittering thing, like a chrome wasp.

Martor leaned close. "What's that?" Hayden plucked it from the air and turned it so its wings rainbowed in the gaslight. "I've seen these before," he mused. "But I don't know what they are. They're not alive."

"Not by ordinary standards, no," said Mahallan. She was perched on his bike, an angel in silhouette; rearing back she said with some obscure sense of satisfaction, "They're *tankers*."

Martor smiled weakly. "Ha?"

"Tankers. That little abdomen is an empty container. Usually when you catch one and open it, you'll find the tank full of ugly chemicals like lithium pentafluorophenyl borate etherate, methoxyphenyl-boronic acid or naphthylboronic acid. Very interesting. And where do you suppose they're taking it?"

"Couldn't tell ya," said Martor, whose eyes had gone very wide as the multisyllabic chemical names tripped off Mahallan's lips.

"They're going in," said the armorer. "Toward Candesce." She snatched the metal wasp out of the air. "Find me some more. If you can."

"Yes, ma'am." Martor saluted and turned to Hayden. "Let's get goin', then."

The hatch gang spun their wheel and the bike door opened into total darkness. As Mahallan kicked away to presumably return to her little workshop, Hayden leaned in to Martor and whispered, "You forgot the passenger saddle. It's over there." He pointed.

"Ah. Uh, thanks."

Mahallan left, and Hayden waited for Martor to back out of his impulse to come along. But he returned with the saddle and duti-fully waited while Hayden strapped it to the side of the bike. And he climbed aboard meekly and waited while Hayden guided the fan-jet to the open hatch and shoved it out into the light breeze, following himself a second later.

"IT'S NOT COLD at all!" Martor squinted over his shoulder as Hayden opened the throttle a bit. They shot away from the *Rook*. The bike was admirably quiet, so Hayden was able to lean back and say, "Like I said, the clouds trap the heat."

Now that they were in winter, the ships of the expeditionary force had all their lights on. Distant clouds made a tunnel that curled away ahead of them, but the air was clear for miles around. It was an opportunity to open up the ships' throttles that their pilots were stolidly ignoring. True, they were making twenty or thirty miles per hour, but each could do five times that without straining.

"Shall we see what she'll do?" Hayden asked. He didn't wait for Martor's answer, but gripped the throttle and twisted it. The fan-jet's grumble became a roar and they shot ahead and into the full blaze of the *Rook's* headlamp.

Martor pounded him on the back. "Quit showin' off!"

Hayden laughed. "No! Look back!"

Martor turned awkwardly and gasped. Hayden knew that their corkscrew contrail would be gleaming in the cone of the *Rook's* headlight like a thread of fire.

"Come on, Martor. Let's do some stitching!"

The bike was capable of nearly two hundred miles an hour, and he tested it to this limit over the next few minutes, running lines back and forth parallel to the *Rook's* course. Laying down parallel lines like this was called stitching. Following his own contrail was the safest way to test the bike's speed; if he entered cloud or deviated too far from air he knew was clear, he could kill himself and Martor if he ran into something unseen.

Hunkered down behind the windscreen, he could nonetheless feel the rip of the air inches away, and cautioned Martor not to stick his head—or hands or feet—out lest he get them ripped off. The bike performed well and he quickly got a feel for it.

"Right!" he said eventually. "Let's do a bit of exploring." He eased back on the throttle and nosed them in the direction of the encircling clouds. As they were about to enter a huge puffball he turned the bike and hit the throttle again; the ground wire trailing behind them whipped ahead into the cloud, and sparks flew.

"Is this a good idea?" Martor had been whooping with delight a minute before. He seemed afraid of anything new, Hayden mused.

"It's a great idea." Now that they'd shed their static potential, it was safe to push the bike into the cloud, a transition noticeable only in the drop in temperature and sudden appearance of the cone of radiance from the bike's headlight. Hayden glanced back; the *Rook* was invisible already.

Martor shook Hayden's shoulder. "H-how are we going to find the ship again?"

"Like this." He reached down and shut off the engine. As the whine faded, he heard a distant grumble—the other ships—but it seemed to be coming from all around them at once. "Wait for it."

The foghorn's note sounded low and sonorous through the darkness. "Where did that come from?" he asked Martor.

"That way?" The boy pointed.

"Right. Now, we're not going far. I just want to see if there's another side to these clouds." He spun up the bike again.

The mist seemed to go on forever, an empty silver void. After a few minutes, though, Hayden began to see pearl-like beads gleaming in the headlight. They shot by on either side, and at their lower speed Martor was able to reach out and grab one. It splashed into a million drops in his hand.

The water spheres grew more numerous and larger. "Could they stall the engine?" asked Martor nervously.

"A big one could," he replied. "Like that one." He dodged the bike around a quivering ball the size of his head.

Visibility was improving. They were now idling their way through a galaxy of turning, shivering drops, some of them tiny, some big as men. Reflections and refractions from the bike's headlamp lit the water cloud in millions of iridescent arcs and glints.

Martor was silent. Hayden looked back at him; the boy's jaw was slack as he gaped at the sight.

"Look." Hayden cut the engine and with the last of their momentum steered them over to a water-beaded stone that hung in solitary majesty amid the water. The rock was less than two feet in diameter.

"Well?" he said to Martor. "Aren't you going to claim this piece of land for Slipstream?"

The boy laughed and reached up to grab the stone. "Not like that!" Keeping one hand on the bike, Hayden flipped himself out of the saddle and wrapped his legs around the rock. "You've got to sit on a piece of land to claim it, you know.

"I decree this land the property," he said, "of . . ." *Aerie*.

"Of Hayden Griffin!" shouted Martor.

"Okay. Of the sovereign state of Hayden. Uck, it's wet." He kicked it away and settled into a perch on the windscreen of the bike.

"I didn't know it was like this out here," said Martor. "I grew up in Rush."

"What are you doing here, anyway? You're—" He was about to say "just a boy" but figured Martor would resent that. "—not a volunteer."

"Press-ganged," said Martor with a shrug. "I don't mind. It was that or the orphanage. I been in the fleet a year now, but this is the first time I've been out of dock."

"So you don't know much about the fleet—say, the admiral?"

"I do." Martor glared at him. "Admiral Fanning's the youngest one to take that job. Got it by doing some sort of secret mission for the Pilot, years back. 'Cept he really doesn't like to talk about that, I saw him get all red in the face one time when somebody just mentioned his promotion."

"Maybe it was his wife who got it for him," speculated Hayden. "She's at least as dangerous as he is."

"Ah," said the boy, "she's pretty, that's sure."

"Actually," said Hayden drily, "I meant put-a-bullet-in-you dangerous. But yes, she's pretty."

Hayden sighed and looked off into the dark. "Well, I hope you get a chance to see more of the world. It's not all like this out here." He smiled slyly. "There's . . . things in the dark, you know."

Martor looked alarmed. "I thought you said there wasn't!"

"Well, I've never seen anything. But you hear stories. Like the ones about the black suns. Ever heard of them?"

Martor's eyes had gone round.

"Pirate suns. They're small and weak, they only heat a few miles around them but it's enough for several towns to thrive. And they only shine through a few portholes, to spotlight the towns and nothing else. Black suns, they call them, each one surrounded by the ships the pirates have captured, in a cloud of wreckage that hides the glow of the towns. . . . They're migratory, like Rush, and they could be anywhere. . . ."

"You're making that up."

"Strangely enough, I'm not." The chill was starting to eat at him, so Hayden swung back into the saddle and pedaled the engine to life again. "We should get back."

They flew in the direction of the most recent foghorn, not talking for a while. As the water cloud tapered out, replaced by mist again, Martor said, "Do you think we'll be coming home? After whatever it is we're out here to do, I mean."

Hayden frowned. "I don't know. I . . . wasn't counting on it, personally." *What's there to come back to?* But he didn't say that.

"Do you suppose there's something in winter that's threatening Slipstream?"

"Seems unlikely."

"And what about the armorer?"

"Huh? What about her?"

"I overheard some of the officers talking. They said she's . . . not from here. Not from the world."

"What do you mean, not from the world?"

"Not from Virga. That doesn't make any sense, does it?"

Hayden thought about it. She did have a funny accent, but that didn't mean anything. He dimly remembered his parents talking about a wider universe beyond Virga; he tried to recall what his father had told him. "There's other places, Martor. Places that are all rock or all water, just like Virga's all air. It could be that she's from somewhere like that. After all, they say we all were, originally."

"Oh, now you're—" Martor swallowed whatever he was going to say, as a giant shape loomed up ahead of them. It was one of the ships, though not the *Rook*.

"Home again," said Hayden. "Let's find our own scow."

"Hey! Don't call the *Rook* a scow!" They accelerated past the ship and into its light. Hayden intended to make a spiral and locate the other ships by their lights, so he took them ahead of this ship's outrider bikes, into the night.

So it was that he had several seconds in which to be surprised as he saw a gleam of light shooting straight for him, a gleam that quickly resolved into the light of a bike—a light that quavered and shook—and time to shout a curse and turn the racer, nearly toppling Martor off his saddle. Time to hit the collision warning on his horn and narrowly miss plunging them into the solid wall of black water that blocked the sky in all directions.

Time enough to turn and watch as the ship they'd passed sounded its own alarm and began to deploy its emergency braking sails. Too late: it flew in stately majesty into the wall of water and disappeared in a cloud of foam and spray.

———

SPOTLIGHTS PINIONED THE crashed ship—although it wasn't so much crashed in the small sea as embedded. The surface of the sea curved into the mist in four directions, and clouds formed another wall directly behind the six free vessels whose headlamps were aimed at it. The cones reflected off its intact sides and into the water, making a diffuse blue aura there that was attracting fish.

The Tormentor was stuck three-quarters into the water, its forlorn tail orbited by a halo of water balls. As Hayden and Martor watched from the hangar hatchway of the Rook, gangs of engineers and carpenters were slinging lines to the other ships to pull her out. A breeze, chilly and damp through and through, teased and prodded at the warmer air inside the ship, and intermittently ruffled the surface of the sea.

"Who sounded the alarm?" somebody asked behind Hayden. Without thinking, he said, "I did."

"You're not one of their outriders." He turned and found himself facing Admiral Fanning, who floated in the hangar in a cloud of lesser officers.

"W-what?" Hayden felt like he'd been kicked in the stomach. He'd hated this man at a distance for so many years that the very idea of talking to him seemed impossible.

"He was doing a practice flight on my instructions." Venera's bloodless servant, Carrier, hung in the shadows to one side.

"Ah." Fanning rubbed his chin. "I can't decide whether the warning helped or did more damage. If they hadn't tried to extend the braking masts they wouldn't have snapped off when they hit the water. However, doubtless your heart was in the right place." He peered at Hayden, seeming to notice him for the first time. "You're one of the civilians."

"Yes, Admiral, sir." Hayden's face felt hot. He wanted to squirm away and hide somewhere.

The admiral looked disappointed. "Oh. Well, good work."

"Lights!" someone shouted from the absurd jut off the Tormentor's tail. "Lights!"

"What's he going on about?" Fanning leaned out, right next to Hayden, his face a picture of epicurean curiosity.

"Shut down! All! Lights!" It was one of the foremen, who while yelling this was pointing dramatically at the water.

They looked at one another. Then Fanning said, "Well, do as the man says." It took several minutes, but soon the spotlights and headlights were going out, one after another, leaning shadows back and forth through the indigo water.

"There!" The faint silhouette of the foreman was pointing again. Hayden craned his neck with the others. The man was indicating a patch of water near the Tormentor—a patch where suddenly, impossibly, a gleam of light wavered.

When Hayden had seen the size of this sea, he'd wondered. Now he was sure.

"It's just a glowfish!" somebody yelled derisively. But it wasn't. Somewhere in the depths of the miles-wide ball of water that the Tormentor had hit, lanterns gleamed.

"Do a circuit!" shouted Fanning to a waiting formation of bikes. Their commander saluted and they took off, contrails spreading to encircle the spherical sea like thin grasping fingers. Almost immediately one of the bikes doubled back. It shut down and did a high-speed drift past the Rook. "There's an entrance!" shouted its rider. "Half a mile around that way."

Hayden nodded to himself. You could dig a shaft into a water ball as easily as a dirt or stone pile. Farmers regularly used such shafts as cold-storage rooms. From the faintness of the shimmer here, though, the ones who'd dug this tunnel had taken it deep into the sea. And the extent of the lights suggested more than just a few rooms carved out of the cold water.

"*Warea*," he muttered. He turned to Martor. "This might be Warea."

"Huh?" Martor goggled at him. "What you talking about?"

"Warea. It's one of the towns I . . . heard about back when . . . when I lived with some folks who traded into winter. I heard that Warea was dug into a small sea, as a defense against pirates."

"You know this place?" Fanning had noticed him again. Hayden silently cursed himself for speaking up.

"It's a small independent station," he told the admiral. "Paranoid about pirates and military raids—they won't take kindly to seeing your ships out here, sir."

"Hmm. But they could have some of the supplies we need to fix the *Tormentor's* masts, eh?" Fanning squinted at the distant glow. "They've probably got divers in the water now, watching us dig her out. Can't hide that we're military . . ." He thought for a second, then nodded. "You, the boy, Carrier, and two carpenters. Go in, negotiate a purchase. Foreman'll give you a manifest. Tell them we've no interest in them beyond buying what we need."

"But why us?"

"You because you know the place. The boy because he looks harmless. Carrier because he also looks harmless, and because you and he are obviously civilians." He looked down his nose at Hayden's shabby shirt and trousers.

"Sir!" It was the armorer, Mahallan, coming up from below. "This settlement—they might have some of the things I need."

"Go on with you, then." Venera Fanning had also appeared. As she sailed in from the left the admiral glared at her and said, "Not a chance."

"He's my pilot." She indicated Hayden. "He takes orders from me."

"I'm the only one who gives orders on this ship." Fanning turned away from her. Venera's eyes narrowed, but then she smirked good-naturedly, and Fanning grinned back for a second. Hayden was surprised; he'd never seen Venera acquiesce like that, hadn't even known it was possible for her.

One of the carpenters thumped a hand onto his shoulder. "Stop gawking and get your coat, boy. We're going to town!"

9

"THERE'S NO SIGN," muttered Slew, the head carpenter. Hayden shot him an incredulous look. There certainly was no garish, brightly colored sign over the entrance to Warea. "You mean one that says 'Loot Me'?" he asked.

"How does it work?" Mahallan climbed down from one sidecar of the bike as Hayden reached out to clip a line to the nearest strut of the entrance framework. They floated just outside the dark shaft that led into Warea; nobody had come out to greet them. Mahallan's question was unnecessary, though. The scaffolding of the entrance shaft stuck ten feet out of the water, far enough to make it plain how it was constructed.

"Look, it's simple," he said, slapping the translucent wall of the shaft; it made a faint drumming sound. The builders of Warea had taken a simple wooden skeleton, the sort the Rush docking tubes were made of, and wrapped it in wax paper. Then they'd stuck the assembly into the side of the sea, like a needle into the skin of a giant. Up this close, he could see faint striations of tangleweed matted under the surface of the water. Warea probably cultivated the stuff—which was an animal, not a plant—to provide structural integrity to the vast ball of water in which they lived. Without it, a stiff breeze could tear the sea apart.

The shaft made an impenetrably dark hole in the water, unlit, possibly leading nowhere—except that a tickle of air teased Hayden's brow, and his bike was slowly being sucked inward.

"We're wasting time." Carrier kicked forward, his foot-fins driving him quickly into the dark. Hayden flipped off the bike and gestured for Martor to follow. Mahallan was already inside the tunnel, flanked by the carpenters.

Inside there was little to tell they were entering a world of water. The tunnel was a lattice of beams, like those of any freefall scaffold. The surface stretched between them could have been stone in the dimness of lamplight. Only the clammy chill suggested the nearby presence of the sea.

"I would have thought the walls would bulge inward or something," said Mahallan. "But of course they don't. No gravity, no pressure."

"I've heard that word before," said Martor in an overly casual way. "Gravity. Spin makes it, right?"

Mahallan had been doing a hand-over-hand walk along the struts. Now she stopped to look at Martor, and in the dim light he saw her eyes had gone wide. "Sometimes I forget," she murmured, "that the strangest of things here are the ones I talk to."

"Now what's that supposed to mean?" But she had turned away already. Ahead, Carrier shouted for them to be quiet.

He was silhouetted by flickering lamplight from a number of fan-driven lanterns. Beyond him the tunnel opened up into a broad space—a cubic chamber walled in wax paper and about forty feet on a side. This was a hangar, Hayden realized, for it was filled with bikes and other flying devices. The air here was cold and damp but the six men who were pointing their rifles at the newcomers didn't seem to feel it. They were uniformly dressed in dark leathers, and their narrow pale faces had the sameness of kin. It seemed like a small welcoming committee, but Hayden was sure that the faint motion of the paper walls next to him indicated more men hiding in the water outside.

"State your business," said their leader, who was clearly the oldest. The father of the others, perhaps?

"Trade," said Carrier. "Carpentry supplies. We can pay you whatever you think is appropriate."

"We're not trading," said the older man. "Be on your way."

There was a momentary silence; Carrier hung perfectly still. "What now?" Mahallan whispered to Hayden. "Does he threaten them?"

Hayden shook his head. "It's hardly worth our while to fight a pitched battle for some nails and wood, and they know it. I don't know what he'll—" He stopped, because Carrier was speaking again.

"As you can plainly see," he said, "our charting expedition is well-enough supplied that we don't *need* your help. But it'll shorten our stay if you do help us."

"Charting?" The older man looked alarmed. "Charting what?"

"Oh, just the various objects in this part of winter," said Carrier with a negligent wave of his hand. "Forests, rocks, lakes—anything that might drift into our space someday. Or that might be useful or militarily significant."

"We're of no use to nobody," said the leader. He was visibly tense now. "We want to be left alone."

"Well, then," purred Carrier, "I'm sure our captain could be persuaded to leave one or two objects off of the charts. If, that is, we received something in return."

"Wait here." The man turned and left through a prosaic-looking door that opened out of the hangar's far wall. A few minutes later he returned, looking unhappy. "Come ahead," he said. "You can trade."

So it was that they entered Warea and learned how the cast-out and the fugitive lived in the empty spaces between the nations. The walls of the short corridor between the hangar and the town complex glowed from distant lamplight; long shadows cast on the paper walls suggested some sort of layered barrier between the cold of the sea and the town. In fact as they passed through the next door the temperature rose and the dampness receded. The silhouetted bodies of the people in front of Hayden split off one by one, opening more and more of the space to his view until he was there himself, gaping about at the cave that was Warea.

Mostly it was just a cube like the hangar, but several hundred feet across. Floating in this space in a disorganized jumble were various multisided houses, each one tethered to its neighbors or the space's outer struts. Numerous openings led off from the main cube, some terminating almost immediately in walls of gelid water, others twisting away, their lamplit outlines faintly visible through the paper walls of the cave. The place reeked of burning kerosene and rot but it was reasonably warm, and the big industrial lanterns with their grumbling fans at least prevented an aura of total gloom from overtaking the citizens.

Some of these were staring in open hostility as Carrier led his group into their crowded airspace. The town elders who had decreed that they could enter had discretely retreated, or chose to remain anonymous within the mass of people. Carrier stopped to ask directions and while he did, Hayden examined the people. They had a familiar look: sallow, overstretched, and glum. For the most part they were exiles who remembered growing up within the light of a sun. Unhappy they might be, but few of them showed the signs of weight-deprivation.

In a few minutes he saw why. The far wall of the cube was moving—swinging up and to the left with a constant rumble that quivered the walls. The cube was only part of Warea. An entire town was embedded in the sea, and on part of its rotation the wheel passed through the cube like a giant saw cutting into a block of wood. Hayden watched houses, shops, and markets pop out of the cube's wall and swing up to vanish through the ceiling in steady and relentless motion.

"It's not a small place," muttered Carrier. "There's two markets. Dry goods on the wheel, Armorer. Building materials here."

"We'll split up, then," said Mahallan helpfully.

"I'll join you in a few minutes," said Carrier with a disapproving frown. "Watch yourselves."

Hayden, Martor, and the armorer watched the others vanish into a cloud of people in the building market. The place was crowded with huge baskets filled with white bricks and beams. "Looks like they'll find what they need right off," said Mahallan worriedly. "Let's hurry, we wouldn't want to keep them waiting."

Hayden shrugged and turned to coast in the direction of the wheel's axis. "I didn't see any wood back there," he commented.

"But what was all that white stuff?"

"Same as these houses are built with." He did a course correction by slapping one on the way by. Its white brick surface undulated slightly. "Paper. They fold origami bricks and beams in triangular sections and then fill them with water. You get beams and bricks that are stiff and incompressible."

"Really?" She seemed inclined to stop and admire the buildings. Hayden pressed on; now that he'd escaped Carrier's roving eye, he could run an errand of his own.

Mahallan and Martor caught up to him as he was entering the big barrel-shaped axis of the wheel. A sullen local flapped by on ragged foot-wings, and the armorer watched him go. "Who are these people?" she asked. "They don't seem happy to see us."

"Refugees, most of them," he said. "A lot of them will be from

Aerie, which was conquered by Slipstream about ten years ago. And some are pirates."

"This is a *pirate* town?" Mahallan laughed in apparent delight as they hand-walked down the top few yards of the yin-yang staircase that led to the rim of the wheel.

Where the curve of the staircase began to flatten out the rungs of the staircase were replaced with steps, at first improbably tall ones. As Hayden flipped over and began using his feet he said, "You asked who these people are. Can I ask who you are? You don't seem to know the first thing about how the world operates, and yet you're our armorer. That's more than a little . . ."

"Odd?" Mahallan shrugged. "It's a fair question. But I'm surprised nobody told you. I'm not from Virga."

"Told you," mouthed Martor behind her back.

"Then where . . . ?"

The nearly vertical staircase rapidly leveled out as they descended past the town's rooftops. Weight and the familiar, homey sensation of vertigo increased with each step. As she entered gravity, Mahallan seemed to shrink. Her normally cheerful face was clouded by unhappiness.

"Where is a difficult thing to answer," she said. "My world isn't like yours. Oh, I expect you'd think I mean that I come from a planet, with land and mountains and so on." Hayden had never heard either of these words before, but he kept his expression neutral as Mahallan went on. "But the rules . . . of reality . . . you might say . . . are different in my world. Identity and location are very fluid things. Too fluid. Too arbitrary; I prefer it here."

He shook his head. "I don't understand."

"Good," she said with a sad smile. "That means we can still be friends."

They had reached the street. Down had made itself forcefully known, and if it wasn't quite perpendicular to the decking but heavily skewed in the direction of the town's rotation, it was still comfortable to Hayden. "That looks like the market up there," he said, pointing.

"Excellent." Her smile was back. "Let's look for some chemicals I need. They'll likely be lurking in ordinary household materials—"

"Listen, I'll catch up to you," said Hayden. "I need to, uh, use the privy."

"Oh, well, whatever. We'll just be up here." She and Martor walked away, heads leaning together in intense dialogue. Hayden watched them go for a minute, then paced in the opposite direction.

He'd had time to scribble a few lines while fetching his coat. The folded scrap of paper in his pocket seemed to weigh a hundred pounds. Even now, as he hurried to find the local post office, he doubted the wisdom of his decision.

The paper read:

The Occupants
Strut Fourteen, Tromp L'oeil Elevated Platform
Quartet 1, Cylinder 2
Rush, Slipstream

6th Recession, Year 1580 A.V.

Seven Ships of the Slipstream Expeditionary Force split off from the main party near the diametric border of Aerie on 1st of Recession. The ships are the Severance, the Tormentor, the Unseen Hand, Rush's Arrow, the Clarity, the Arrest, and the Rook. *ADMIRAL FANNING IS COMMANDING THE ROOK.*

These ships continued on a diametric course outward from Aerie for four days before stopping at the winter town of Warea. Their destination after this is UNKNOWN, but they are all equipped for winter navigation and well supplied.

The expedition appears urgent. Also aboard are Lady Fanning and an armorer from outside Virga named Aubri Mahallan.

Regardless of the ultimate purpose of this force, its absence from the main body of the fleet may make for a strategic advantage.

Yours,

A reluctant recruit

Mail was an adventurer's game in winter. There were no regular lines, just bags exchanged by ships and the occasional courier who flew dedicated runs, dodging pirates, weather, and the beasts of the void. These men were used to hand-deliveries—and to not asking questions. Provided Hayden paid well enough, he was reasonably sure his little envelope would get through.

The town didn't have a post office as such, but after asking a couple of locals he was directed to the mendicant's lodge. The bartender there handled what little mail came out of the town.

He had just found the place and was tensely walking up to the doors when a hand fell on his arm.

"You're a bit late," someone snarled.

Hayden whirled to face the man. "Do I know . . ." But he did know him.

Bright gray eyes in a pasty-white face stared up at him. "You were due to meet us at the docks, what . . . a year ago, was it? Just come to trust you, and the first day we let you loose on your own, you fly."

"I got detained, Milson," said Hayden as he backed away.

"Detained, sure." Milson sneered. "Desertion's a crime, little rat." He loosened his sword in its scabbard. "You better come with me."

"Excuse me," said Carrier, who had appeared out of nowhere. He smiled vapidly at Milson then turned to Hayden. "Where are the others?"

"Er, just up the street. Listen, I—"

"Come, then." Carrier took Hayden's elbow and turned him about, smiling at Milson in a dismissive manner.

"Oh no you don't—" Hayden heard the scrape of a sword being drawn behind them; then suddenly Carrier wasn't at his side anymore. He heard a swishing sound and a faint "urk" but in the second it took for him to turn he missed all the action. Carrier and Milson were walking together toward an alley; Carrier had one arm around Milson's greasy shoulder and only an observant man would have noticed that Milson's feet weren't quite touching the ground.

The two men entered the alley. One, two, three, four . . . Carrier emerged, dusting his hands, every bit the mild bureaucrat again. He smiled at an old woman as he passed her and fell into an easy stride next to Hayden.

"What was that all about?" he asked. His voice was flat, completely belying his jovial expression.

"Uh . . . apparently they resent the presence of battleships outside their doors," Hayden improvised. "I think I was about to get mugged. Thanks."

"I'm not here to clean up your messes," hissed Carrier. "Understand this: if there's a next time, I'll laugh along with the crowd when they stick you." He smiled. "Now, let's make sure the other two aren't being similarly harrassed."

Hayden put a hand in his pocket. Before they'd gone twenty feet he'd balled the message into a tight wad; when Carrier turned his head away for a moment, he angrily flicked it onto a pile of trash.

So much for joining the Resistance.

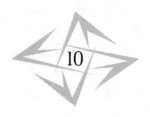

10

BY HAYDEN'S RECKONING, the ships were making barely fifteen miles per hour—nosing cautiously through the dark clouds, occasionally stalling while the commanders tried to figure out their current position by peering with narrowed eyes at the tracks their gyroscopes had made through tanks of glycerine. Twice great oceans of clear air opened up in front of them. The admiral took the opportunity and ordered full speed ahead. Hayden tracked down Martor on these occasions and took him for rides aboard his bike, opening it up to top speed and once tearing the poor boy loose entirely. Hayden circled back to find him arrowing on through the dark, sleeves rippling in the wind and utterly calm in his certainty that Hayden would return for him.

In the quietest hours of the nightwatch, he and Martor would meet Mahallan in her little box-shaped workshop. She had them building things—though what those things were, she wouldn't explain. "It's to do with electricity," was all she'd said. The devices (significantly, there were seven of them) were boxes full of metal wires that poked into and through various other, smaller boxes and tubes. Mahallan spent most of her time working on these little containers, filling them with carefully mixed pastes and powders that stank of oils and metal. Every now and then she would get Martor or Hayden to pedal a stationary bike that was attached to a big metal can connected by more wires to one of the boxes, and then she would poke about inside the new device using some metal prods. It was by turns fascinating and boring to watch. So, they whiled away the time by talking.

Hayden wanted to know about the strange outside world where Mahallan was from, but he could barely get a word in edgewise, what with Martor's constant babbling. The boy was thoroughly infatuated with the armorer.

When Hayden did get a chance to ask her about her past, Mahallan was evasive. But on the third night, as they hovered around one of her strange boxes watching an expanding sphere of smoke extrude out of its side, she sighed and said, "This is the most wonderful thing, for me."

"What's that, lady?" Martor had turned to fetch a leather curtain. She waited as he deftly scooped the smoke into it and glided over to the porthole to squirt it outside. When he returned, she pried open the lid of the box and said, "It's wonderful to me that we can sit here and build things whose behaviors we design ourselves. Like this ship." She patted the wall. "Things like this are made using *knowledge*." She savored the word.

"Don't you have knowledge where you come from?" Hayden asked the question facetiously, but to his surprise, she shook her head.

"No, we don't. Not about the physical world, anyway. The systems of Artificial Nature make it unnecessary for us to know anything." She saw his look of puzzlement and grimaced. "I know, it's hard to explain. That's why I haven't talked about where I come from. Listen, in the worlds beyond Virga, humans no longer have to make things for themselves. Artificial Nature makes them for us. And no two devices or machines are alike; each one evolves in its own pre-physical virtual world. Even two tools intended to do the same job, while they may look identical, might work in totally different ways. And because each device is evolved, not . . . *designed*, is the word you use here . . . no one can say how a given one works. You could spend years studying how one engine operates, but that wouldn't tell you how other engines necessarily function. So there's no incentive to try. It's been this way on most worlds for thousands of years.

"So Hayden, Martor, you can't begin to imagine the excitement I felt when I came here and first saw two of your ships sailing out of the clouds. They were *identical!* They worked the same way, used exact copies of the same machines. Here were people who could take their own mental models of objects, and make them physically real. Virga is a wonder to me, because here you have knowledge and you use it to make more than one of things. Every time I see a new one of something I've seen before—like these ships—I'm thrilled all over again." She beamed at them. "You live in a very special world."

As she had been speaking the box she'd been working on had been slowly, strangely, drifting toward one wall. She noticed it and seized it. "*That's* not a good sign," she muttered.

Martor rubbed at his chin, considering. "Is that why you seemed surprised that I'd heard of gravity, the other day?"

The armorer nodded. "Gravity, exactly. Uh . . . yes, most of the worlds I know are replacing concepts like gravity with new mythologies their artists are crafting." Hayden and Martor must have really looked lost at this point, because Mahallan laughed richly when she glanced over at them.

"I'd heard," ventured Hayden, "that the people from beyond Virga live forever, can travel anywhere in the universe, and can do anything."

Mahallan shrugged. "Oh sure. And that means we have no more need to *know* anything. That's a tragedy. I spent years learning what you call the *sciences* but it was difficult to find entities who knew how to teach them. Most such knowledge is implicit in the construction of things . . . not written down, as it were. In fact, that's why I came to Virga. It was the one place I knew where there was no Artificial Nature."

"Why is that?"

She leaned forward like a conspirator. "Candesce disrupts the systems of Artificial Nature. It was refitted to do that centuries ago, in order to keep my people's civilization out of Virga. There's side effects that aren't good for *your* civilization, though—and that's why we're building these." She waggled the burnt-out box.

"What do they do?" Hayden had asked this very question a dozen times now, and she'd sidestepped the issue every time. Maybe now that she wanted to talk, she'd give it away.

But Mahallan just smiled enigmatically and said, "They'll help us win."

At that moment there was a knock on the door. Before any of them could move, Venera Fanning poked her head into the tiny chamber. "Aha," she said. "The night owls are up, as promised."

"Venera," said Aubri neutrally. The admiral's wife swept into the room, frowning as she spotted Martor.

"So, the little spy-for-hire has wormed his way into your good graces. Get out, or I'll have the boatswain chop off your fingers."

Martor scrambled past her and out the door. With a faint smile of satisfaction, Venera closed it behind him. Turning to the other two, she clasped her hands before her and said, brightly, "How is it coming along?"

"It was coming along just fine, until you ejected my assistant," said Aubri.

"Bah!" Venera waved away the problem. "You still have this one. Though not for long, I need him to pilot me tomorrow. We're going on a little trip. You're coming too."

Aubri carefully placed the device she'd been working on in a dark wooden case and shut it. "Where is it that we're going?"

"Our first stop. First official stop, I mean. I want you to come with us because you've been here before."

"Really?" Aubri shifted uncomfortably. Hayden thought she looked very unhappy all of a sudden. "Have we circled back to Slipstream, then?"

Venera barked a laugh. "You know that's not where I mean. We're coming up on the tourist station! That was your first home when you came to Virga, wasn't it? You should know your way around it pretty well."

"As a matter of fact, I don't. And I don't appreciate being taken back to it without consultation. Unless—" She paled suddenly. "You're not sending me back . . ."

"Of course not, silly woman. I need you to find someone for me—talk to them, make a deal. That's what this is all about, isn't it? Our deal?"

"Yes," murmured Aubri. To Hayden's astonishment he saw that she wouldn't look Venera in the eye. Venera either didn't notice this, or accepted it as normal. She turned to Hayden, smiling her predatory smile.

"Be ready to fly at eight o'clock sharp. We'll be taking the bike and sidecars, so they'd better be put together."

"Yes, ma'am."

"Good." Without another word, Venera left. As soon as the door closed Aubri spun and went to the porthole. She yanked it open and stuck her head outside. Hayden heard muffled cursing coming from beyond the hull. "What's going on?"

She pulled her head back in and grimaced at him, gesturing at the open porthole. He slipped by her and put his own head out into the cold whispering wind.

For a moment he saw nothing but the usual darkness and clouds. Then with a start he realized that what he had taken to be a giant puffball of vapor was made of facets and sweeping curves of glittering ice. They were sailing past a frozen lake: an iceberg as big as any of the cylinders of Rush.

He brought his head back in. "There's an iceberg outside."

Aubri shook her head dejectedly. "Look again." Puzzled, Hayden looked out again. Well, there was the iceberg, and actually there was another one on the other side of it. And another—they were attached tip-to-top, making a kind of chain.

A wreath of cloud slipped over and past the ship, and in the opening that followed he saw what Aubri wanted him to see—and gasped.

The Rook's running lights reflected faintly from shimmering planes of ice, a thousand angles of it receding into blackness. The ship's cyclopean headlight cast a cone of radiance into the dark and where it lit, Hayden beheld a forest of icebergs. They clung to one another by merest filaments and blades; a dense fog insinuated itself into every hollow and space between them. The Rook wove slowly around the giant spires of ice, each giant receding into the haze as others emerged ahead.

Hayden's eye followed a line of bergs as they passed it, and he realized that they thickened and converged miles away until they were jammed together cheek by jowl. Dark crevasses gaped between them. He was reminded of the forest that carpeted Slipstream's asteroid, only instead of the crowns and cones of trees rising up from darkness, here was endless ice.

"It's like a wall," he said. Just then his chin bumped the edge of the porthole. For some reason he'd started to drift into the ship—probably the air pressure.

"It's not a wall," said Aubri sourly. "It's a ceiling. The ceiling, to be precise."

"The . . ." He got it then. "This is the world's skin?"

"The skin of the balloon, yes. Everything else in Virga is below us here. That's why we're feeling gravity. I should have realized it from the way the engines were straining."

In the distance a thunderous *crack!* echoed through the berg forest. Hayden looked out again, and beheld a mountain of ice majestically disengage itself from its neighbors. He watched it as it faded into the ice fog behind them; he was almost sure he could see it moving away from its brothers.

"Candesce drives convection currents in Virga," said Aubri, startling Hayden because she was right next to him, just below the porthole. "Rising water vapor condenses into lakes, and if it makes it all the way up here, it freezes. The skin of Virga is very, very cold. But the skin is also the top of Virga's gravity well, slight though that may be. As these bergs grow they become heavy. Eventually they dislodge and fall, melting as they go. The biggest of them make it almost to Candesce before they evaporate."

Hayden contemplated the gargantuan icicles—for that was what they were—for a long time. Then he drew his head into the ship and said, "Why are we here?"

Aubri's face was only inches from his own. He had never been this close to her, and it gave him an uncomfortable pleasure—but she was looking miserable. "What's wrong?"

She pulled herself back to her workstation and fiddled with the lamp for a moment. "If I'd known we were coming here, I wouldn't have joined this expedition."

Hayden crossed his arms and waited. After a few seconds Aubri sighed heavily and said, "Look, I came to Virga to get away from *that* world." She jabbed a thumb hullward, aiming, he supposed, past the skin at the universe beyond. "I'm a refugee here, and I don't like to be reminded of what I left. Even less do I want to revisit that insipid tourist station."

He descended to sit on the air next to her. After musing for a few moments, he said, "I think I understand. I was born and raised in Aerie. Slipstream conquered it when I was still a boy. But I remember it—and there's reminders of it everywhere you look, from the crafts they sell in the market to the accents of people in the streets. They're . . . painful. You start avoiding them. And then you feel guilty about it."

She shook her head. "It's not like that. Not quite like that, but yeah, I don't like to be reminded." She smiled suddenly. "I didn't know you were from Aerie."

"Well, neither did anybody else before tonight," he said, clasping his hands in front of him. "Are they going to know by morning?"

Aubri raised an eyebrow. "No—no reason why they should."

They sat in companionable silence for a while. Then a faint shudder went through the ship, and simultaneously the whine of the engines changed tone.

Aubri groaned. "Are we there already?"

The howl of the alarm Klaxons drowned out any reply Hayden might have had, or any thought. He bounded to the window and looked out, in time to see bright streaks converge on one of the other ships from inside a vast cloudbank. Bright flashes lit the side of the ship. He was able to close and dog the porthole before the staccato noise of explosions reached the *Rook*.

"We're under attack," he said unnecessarily, but there was no reply as Aubri Mahallan had already left the room.

CHAISON FANNING THREW on a jacket while an aide with a hand on his back steered him through the connecting passage to the bridge. Behind him the whole ship was awake and churning with activity. "How many are there?" he shouted ahead at the suddenly alert nightwatch. "What weapons?"

"Admiral, it looks like winter pirates," said the frightened-looking Helm. He was a junior officer on one of his first watches. Probably more afraid of messing up than of the enemy.

Chaison glided to the main periscope and took hold of its handles, slipping his feet into the stirrups below without having to look for them. For a few seconds he blinked, trying to figure out what he was looking at. Then practiced reflexes took over and he began counting and evaluating.

"I see ten enemy craft. It's a whole fucking fleet. I bet there's more maneuvering inside that cloud bank."

"Somebody at Warea must have told them about us," said Captain Sembry from behind him. "We're probably the biggest prize that's ever wandered into their territory."

"It's pure foolishness—they're not a navy, just a ragged flock of crows. What makes them think they can outmaneuver us? . . . Ah." He laughed humorlessly as he made out more details of the distant ships. "Some of them look like Aerie frigates. I take it back, they're not after booty. At least some of these people are carrying a grudge."

He spun and offered the periscope to Sembry. "Captain, it's a classic night engagement. They've got us trapped in the center of a cylinder of cloud. Their ships have plumbed those clouds, and I don't doubt at all that there's some big icebergs lurking in there if we were foolish enough to follow them. They're going to hit and run out of the fogbanks because they know what's inside them. We have to take away that advantage."

He turned to the disheveled but alert semaphore team. "All ships: launch bikes. Bikes to reconnoiter clouds, not to engage enemy unless attacked. All ships: rolling torus formation. All ships: ready rocket barrages.

"Fire at will."

"CIVILIANS TO QUARTERS!" The boatswain waved his sword at Hayden for emphasis. "That means you, errand boy. And strap yourself in—we're going to be pulling heavy maneuvers."

After a few moments of hesitation, Hayden retreated back to

Mahallan's workshop. This was probably the only place in the ship where he'd be left alone. He nearly missed his grab for the door as the entire vessel shuddered. The sound of the engines was momentarily deafening, and a squeal of seldom-used brakes echoed from the fore. They were stopping the centrifuge so the Rook could maneuver without having to take gyroscopic effects into account. Somewhere in the distance he heard crashing sounds as the personal effects of dozens of airmen slid and tumbled inside the wheel.

He stuck his head out the porthole, wary of getting it shot off. What he saw was a jumble of ships, lit intermittently by rocket fire, moving at all angles to one another with no way at first to tell friend from foe. Some of those silhouettes were familiar, however. Hayden knew the sleek forms of the winter pirate vessels all too well, having spent some time on one of them during the years of his exile. He'd lied when he told Miles and the other Resistance fighters that he'd spent all his time sitting on a mushroom farm in the middle of nowhere. The truth was more dangerous to admit.

More details resolved as his eyes adjusted to the darkness. Clouds of bikes were tumbling out of the ships now, their tearing buzz filling the air as they swarmed around one another. The whole tableau was framed by black cloudbanks that pressed in on all sides. And now a huge frigate emerged as if by magic from one of those clouds, tongues of red fire erupting from its side as it fired a salvo of rockets point-blank into the stern of a Slipstream vessel. A good half of the rockets bounced off the cone-shaped end of the ship, drawing scarves of light on the darkness, but the remainder exploded. Beams and planking flew everywhere. The pirate rolled, jets screaming, and lined up its dorsal rocket battery. This time the bulk of the volley shot straight down the length of the Slipstream ship's exposed interior. A chain-reaction of explosions convulsed the victim and then the clouds flashed into flame-lit visibility as the ship burst like an overripe fruit. Men and materiel tumbled into the cold air while thunder banged and rolled around them.

Hayden smiled in grim satisfaction. That was one less Slipstream ship. On the other hand . . . he suddenly realized that the expeditionary force might lose this battle. If they were overwhelmed, there would be no prisoners taken. Everyone would be killed, from Admiral and Lady Fanning to Martor and Aubri Mahallan.

He would cheer the deaths of the Fannings—or at least of the admiral. Venera . . . he didn't know what to think of her. But her fate was out of his hands, he realized with a pang. She would never agree to escape with him. But maybe he could convince Martor and Aubri Mahallan to climb into the sidecars of his bike. They could arrow out of here, make for the tourist station, which he could now see through a gap in the clouds. It was miles away yet, an inverted, glittering landscape of towers; a city not rolled into cylinders but flattened out across the black ceiling of Virga.

They could make for that swirl of light. They could survive.

He turned and bolted for the workshop's door.

"WHO KNEW THERE were this many pirate ships in all of Virga?" muttered a crewman. Chaison Fanning didn't acknowledge the comment, but he'd been wondering the same thing. Had they gathered this fleet from all over the world, just to attack his little expeditionary force? Right now it seemed that winter really was the vast dark empire of freebooters and privateers that some popular stories and songs made it out to be.

Unbelievably, they'd already lost *Rush's Arrow*. The effect of the ship's explosion on the men had been immediate and dire. Chaison was now on his way through the ship, hurling orders and optimistic quips to the men as he went. He needed them to know that he trusted Sembry to command the *Rook*, and that his primary concern was them. But he was followed by a stream of staffers and he paused at every porthole to stare out at the battle, and occasionally issue a terse order for the semaphore team.

He stuck his head into the bike hangar. The place had been emptied out, all bikes in the air except for Venera's absurd racer with its sidecar, which her driver was laboring over. The hangar doors were wide open and men with rifles perched on them at various angles, haphazard gargoyles ready to fend off any comers. On his orders the ships had tossed out flares and so the clouds outside were lit a lurid green.

Actually, the view from here was excellent, better than the bridge, even. Chaison leaped over to one of the doors and anchored himself next to a surprised airman. "Do you have any more of those?" he said, pointing to the man's rifle. "I'm aiming to take some personal vengeance for the *Arrow.*"

The airman grinned and shouted back, "A rifle for the admiral, boys!" One was passed up, the last several hands being those of his staffers, who looked uneasy and disapproving.

He motioned for them to join him. "Run a speaking tube from here to the bridge," he said. Just then the *Rook's* rotation brought the black-sided hull of a pirate corsair into view. The ship was less than three hundred feet away; he could see lights through its open rocket ports.

"Hit that ship!" he yelled, and opened fire with his rifle. The men cheered and a satisfying volley erupted around him. Moments later the bright darts of rockets followed from the *Rook* and from somewhere behind it. That would be the *Severance,* he guessed, which should be in triad formation with the *Rook* and the *Unseen Hand.*

"Concentrate your fire on the engines!" He squeezed off several shots to demonstrate. In a battle like this you kept moving, but you were also rolling the ship constantly to bring the rocket batteries to bear on the enemy. In order to do this the ship had to stick its engine nacelles out and turn them ninety degrees; this made them vulnerable to rocket and small-arms fire.

The *Rook* was rolling now and it made for a bit of gravity; Chaison had to turn himself around and cling to the hatch because *out* was now *down* and he was firing past his own feet. This was why you lashed yourself to any handy ring during a battle. You could easily fall out of the ship.

As the hangar rotated out of sight of the corsair Chaison caught a glimpse of one of his bikers plunging in from behind it. The man held a grenade over his head and as he passed the corsair at over a hundred miles an hour, he threw it. The green-lit ball disappeared into one of the corsair's engines and it blew up, just as the outthrust hangar doors cut off Chaison's view.

But now the rest of the battle swung into sight again. *Tormentor, Clarity,* and *Arrest* had good crews and had maintained their triad even though they were surrounded now by six ships. One of those ships was on fire and as Chaison watched it veered away into the safety of the clouds. A coordinated volley of rockets from the triad enveloped another pirate and its sides buckled under the explosions. Silent and dark, it began to drift.

The ships and cloudbanks were lit flare-green but now yellow and red lights also glowed inside the clouds. Those were locator flares his bikes had dropped where they'd found ice or other hazards inside the mist. The bikes should be returning now. He turned to his staffers. "All bikes: attack enemy at will."

Seconds later he heard the buzzing snarl of jets as bike formations began to appear, swirling into the disorganized knots of the pirates' own riders.

The roar of a bike sounded, very close. It might be one of the Rook's boys coming back, maybe wounded, or . . . He swung down and looked around the edge of the hangar door. Not thirty feet away, a black can trailed flame as it tried to match the rotation of the Rook. Its rider wore a lime-green jacket and burgundy trousers. He was straining to snag a passing porthole with a hook lashed to a grenade.

Chaison leaned way out, standing now on the very bottom of the open door with only a rope around his waist tying him to the Rook. He aimed and fired in one motion, and saw the rider convulse and the bike veer away. Before he swung back up he verified that the grenade had followed them into the dark.

Dangling there, vaguely aware of cheering coming from up above, he watched the battle progress. His forces had a clear advantage in weaponry, armor, and discipline, but they were outnumbered. The pirates—or expatriate Aerie airmen—kept swinging in and out of the cover of the cloudbanks. They had men on bikes tracking down the flares Slipstream's own bikes had laid down; as Chaison watched, the glows that marked the location of obstacles in those clouds were snuffed one by one. Having previously set the positions of those ice and rock chunks in their inertial navigation systems, the pirates themselves had no need of lamps to know where they were.

Another swing around and *Severance* and the *Unseen Hand* appeared, locked into a fierce rocket battle with three black cylinders. Their formation was broken and the two ships were drifting away at a quickening pace. As Chaison was about to ask why Sembry wasn't pursuing them, the Rook's rotation took them out of sight, and something huge cut off any further view of the sky.

It was the black hull of a pirate, and it was barely yards away. The bastard had somehow snuck up on Sembry. Looking to the side,

Chaison realized that the pirate had already looped rope around the spinning *Rook*. If friction or snags didn't break them, the pirates could drag the *Rook's* hull into contact with the jagged rams that were even now being thrust out of its rocket ports.

"Sembry!" roared Chaison. He'd have the man towed for a day behind his own ship for this. The riflemen around him were gaping, so he yelled, "Fire on those ports!" and did so himself as an example.

Then he turned to his staffers. "Ready the ship for boarders. And find out why Sembry's not moving us!"

"It's mines," somebody said. "They've mined the air between us and the others."

Sure enough, as the ship spun around again he caught glimpses of green-lit star shapes tumbling in the space between the *Rook* and the receding *Severance*. "I need those cleared!" Even as he said this he realized that none of Slipstream's bikes were nearby. The bulk of them were caught up in a gigantic dogfight at the opposite end of the battle. Some drifted, dead or burning. The rest were missing.

He whirled and pointed at Venera's driver. "You! Get out there and clear those mines."

"W-what?" The young man blinked at him dumbly. Of course, he was just a civilian.

Chaison appealed to the riflemen. "Can anyone else here fly a bike?"

"No, wait, I'll do it." The driver was glaring at Chaison as though he'd received a mortal insult. "But . . ." The black-haired young man glanced to one side slyly. "I'll need help." He indicated the bike's two sidecars.

"Whatever," said Chaison with a negligent wave of the hand. "Take whoever you need.

"Bring me a saber and a pistol," he said. As he waited he watched the driver manhandle his bike toward the open hangar doors. *Venera's not going to be happy if I wreck her nice little taxi,* he thought. The idea made him smile.

"MARTOR!" HAYDEN WAVED frantically as he saw the boy pass the inside door to the hangar. "Get in here!"

"But I gotta go to—she's got nobody to—"

Hayden grabbed him by the arm and aimed him at the bike. "Are you talking about Aubri Mahallan?" he asked. Martor nodded quickly. "Well then go get her and bring her here. Fast!"

He did his best to be slow about winching the bike over the open doors. Every few seconds the scarred hull of the pirate would flash into view and the ships would exchange rifle fire. Bullets hummed past on all sides when that happened and Hayden hid behind the substantial metal of the bike.

When he poked his head out the third time he saw Martor literally dragging Aubri Mahallan into the hangar. "What's this all about?" she asked impatiently as the two came to land on the sidecars.

Hayden turned to Martor. "Martor, can you fetch us an extra set of stirrups?"

The boy looked suspicious. "But why—" Hayden turned away from him, to face Mahallan. In a low voice he said, "We're going to lose this battle. Come with me if you want to live."

Her eyes widened. She glanced at the opened doors below them just as black hull appeared there. "Down!" Hayden grabbed her shoulders and pushed her into the open mouth of the bike's jet as gunfire sounded all around them. Abstractly he noticed how fine-boned her shoulders were. Behind them, two of the *Rook's* riflemen convulsed and tumbled forward to hang at the end of their lines.

Aubri cried out and covered her eyes.

"We have to go," Hayden said to her, "and we have to go now! The *Rook's* about to be boarded. You have no idea what they're going to do with a woman if they catch you."

The gunfire subsided as the pirate swung out of sight again. Aubri Mahallan looked out at the bullet-scarred space, its air blue with gunsmoke, and bit her lip in obvious indecision. Then she pushed Hayden aside angrily. "Get out of my way," she hissed. "I'm needed here."

"What are you talking about? You'll be killed if you stay!"

"I can't go," she said, looking frantic. "Too much has happened— is at stake now. It would be—"

"You have to choose your battles, Aubri."

She shook her head angrily. "Fine. I choose this one. You run away, if that's what you want."

Hayden was too astonished to stop her as she jumped back up to the inner door. Martor was coming back with the spare stirrups and gaped at her as she went by. "What did you say to her?" he yelled at Hayden. At the same time, another heavy body landed on the bike next to him, making it rock.

"Hey!" shouted the red-haired boatswain, who held a bundle of rope and rockets under his arm. "Cut us loose, errand boy!"

Hayden cursed and mounted the bike. "Come on, Martor! We need you!" He and the boatswain dragged the protesting boy onto the bike. Hayden glanced down to make sure the pirate wasn't below them, and then pulled the pin on the winch. The bike did its curving fall into the dark air, and he spun up the fan and lit the burner without thinking.

His two passengers were having a shouted conversation past his back. ". . . Tied to the nets," said the boatswain as the jet lit and they surged forward just in time to avoid the approaching hull of the pirate. "Snag a mine with the net and light the rocket. Make sure you aim the rocket away from the *Rook* first. If you can aim it at a pirate, great!"

The boatswain spun in his seat and hit Hayden in the midriff. "Get us out there! The *Rook's* about to be boarded!"

Hayden complied silently. This bike was dangerously fast, even with sidecars on it, so he was compelled to approach the mined air in a series of short bursts. This drew more insults from the boatswain. Meanwhile the battle continued to rage around them, at near points such as the *Rook*, and far away in flashes like lightning on distant clouds. Grumbling and roaring noises echoed strangely off the ice field that made a half-visible wall beyond the mists.

In the light of flares that Martor held over his head, the first mine hove into sight just yards ahead. Hayden puffed the engine a couple of times and the boatswain leaned out with his net to encircle the studded metal sphere. The net was tied to a rocket the length of his forearm; the boatswain lit it and the bike was showered with sparks. Hayden shielded his eyes for a second then watched as the rocket surged away, towing the mine into winter.

"Next!" roared the boatswain. Hayden turned the bike, glancing back at the *Rook* as he did. It and the smaller pirate seemed locked together now and men were spilling into the air between them.

He looked in the opposite direction. Far out there, the glittering lights of the tourist station beckoned. There was life for Martor and Aubri, if only he could figure out a way to get her off the *Rook*.

It was too late for her, he realized with a pang. But not for Martor.

The boatswain fired off another rocket. "Next! We've got to clear a tunnel for the *Rook* to fly through!"

"All right, all right!"

Hayden's heart was pounding. It was happening again: start to know someone, and all you got was the chance to lose them. True, he barely knew Aubri Mahallan. And true, a month ago he'd been willing to sacrifice his own life just to strike a blow against Slipstream. His most hated enemy was fighting for his life in the *Rook*, and Hayden should fervently wish nothing but disaster for that ship and all aboard it.

But he'd flown out from Gavin Town with a rifle in his hand and attacked Slipstream's cruisers while his mother decided her own fate in Aerie's unlit sun. And as Hayden had tumbled helplessly away into winter she had died. Was he really going to let Aubri go in the same way?

He swore, twisting his grip on the bike's handlebars. "Next!" yelled the boatswain and he turned the bike to find another glint of green in the light of Martor's flares.

Momentarily, he had an audience's grand view of the battle. Slipstream's ships were giving better than they took and several pirates were now drifting hulks surrounded by clouds of debris and dead men. The superiority of Fanning's disciplined crews was beginning to tell. The problem was that the pirates were able to use the cover of the clouds; they emerged just far enough to fire off a salvo, then retreated into invisibility.

Now that he could see the whole vista, though, Hayden realized that the pirates were only hiding in the clouds on one side—the side where the icebergs lay hidden in mist. They could use those bergs safely because the things didn't move, they were really giant icicles hanging from the outer skin of Virga. He had seen one of them begin a slow majestic fall just before the battle.

That gave him an idea.

"Next!" He looked around. There were dozens of mines, and there was no way they were going to clear a path for them before the boarding action on the *Rook* was decided one way or another. He turned toward a nearby mine, but made sure that he brought it up to the bike on Martor's side. "You take it, rat," said the boatswain as he handed Martor a rope and rocket. The boy grinned fiercely and leaned out to lasso the mine.

Hayden pulled out his knife and cut the strap tying the boatswain to his seat. The man was watching Martor and didn't notice. Then Hayden took a net and threw it over the boatswain's head.

"Hey! You bastard, watch what you're—"

Hayden lit the rocket tied to the net just as Martor was lighting his own. Sparks showered everywhere and they both ducked down covering their eyes. When Hayden looked up again, both the mine and the boatswain were gone.

Martor stared at the empty seat. "Where'd he go?"

"I don't know." Hayden spread his hands, looking surprised. "One second he was here, then he was gone. Must have caught a stray bullet."

Far out there, if you knew where to look, the fading ember of a rocket poked into a cloudbank and disappeared. Hayden watched it go then turned to Martor. "Listen," he said, "this isn't going to save the *Rook*. I've got a better idea."

He took them over to the next mine and Martor netted it. "Don't light the rocket," Hayden told him. "Just string it out behind us." They did the same with the next mine, and the next. Soon they had five of them dangling in their way.

"Now we get out of here," said Hayden.

"But the admiral told us to—" Martor hastily grabbed the sides of his car as Hayden put on the power. They shot up and away from the mined air—and the battle—heading straight for the mists that hid the bergs.

"Light more flares. We'll need to see where we're going." He slid them into the clouds at an incautious speed, trusting to his own skill to avoid hitting anything. The flares made a sphere of leaf-green

light around them, and only the occasional wisp of moisture fluttering past showed that they were moving at all.

It was freezing in here, and Hayden took inspiration from that:
follow the chill. He slowed the bike and let it drift in the air currents until he felt it enter a river of cold. Then he cautiously nudged
them forward.

Out of the darkness, a vast turquoise shape emerged—a long
sleek fish-shaped mountain of ice covered with knobby protuber-
ances. Hayden could make out its tip off to the right, a dangerous
white spike intermittently lit by distant explosions. To the left, the
shape wove off into blackness.

He wrestled the bike in that direction. Martor was silent now,
puzzled but obviously intrigued. As Hayden circled the berg he saw
what he was looking for: there was a spot where the giant icicle
narrowed to a thickness of only a few yards. In the minuscule gravity created by Virga's collective air and water, this neck was enough
to hold up the rest of the bulk.

"Martor, I want you to fire a mine at that crimp there." He
pointed. Now the boy's eyes widened with understanding and he
hurried to obey.

Hayden ducked away from a cascade of sparks, then looked up to
see that Martor's aim was good. The mine sailed silently at the ice,
contacted it and—

A flash of orange lit the night and moments later the thunderous
bang of the explosion made Hayden flinch. As the smoke cleared he
saw that the neck of ice had been severed. A white splinter shot past
his head, barely a foot away, but he hardly noticed. He was watching the gap that now existed between the ice attached to Virga's
skin, and the long berg that had hung down from it.

"It's widening," he said after a few seconds. "Martor, do you see
it? It's starting to fall."

The boy grinned. "Let's do another one."

THE SHIP WAS a madhouse full of screaming, gunshots, and the clash of swords. Chaison Fanning had his sword out, but his staffers were in the way. One of them interposed himself between Chaison and the silhouetted form of a pirate whom he was about to attack.

Chaison had a savage moment in which he considered stabbing the man to get at the pirate. What he needed above all else was to take the heads off a few of those swine who were threatening his ship, his men, and his mission.

Chaison slipped past the well-meaning fool and his sword fight, and dove for the hangar. A knot of men was struggling unsuccessfully to prevent the pirates from gaining access to the ship proper. Chaison flew over to join them, being careful to look past the heads and struggling arms in his way and assess the enemy. The hangar was mostly full of low-lifes and bullies who were unused to an even fight, but they seemed to be led by a tight vanguard of ex-Aerie naval officers who had thrown themselves across the space between the ships with no regard for bullets or blades.

"Shoot the leaders!" He grabbed a rifle and aimed past a pair of men who were fighting a freefall sword fight, blade in one hand, long curving belaying hook in the other.

"But sir!" The damned fly who'd buzzed around him earlier was back, panting but unscathed. "What about the fleet? Your orders?"

He whirled, murderous rage causing him to level the rifle at the man. To his credit, the officer paled but stood his ground. "They need an order," he said.

Chaison cursed and grabbed him by the throat. "Don't ever," he hissed, "make the mistake of thinking I can't fight and plan at the same time." Then Chaison dove past him, making for the bridge.

The way was blocked. He blinked in surprise at the staved-in beams and boards that filled the narrow passage beneath the centrifuge. That didn't look like rocket damage. A prow? Had they been rammed while he was looking the other way?

It hardly mattered. He pried some planks out of the way and stared out at the dark. The battle was going much as he'd expected; the pirates had the advantage of available cover and were using it shamelessly. But the five ships on the other side of the mined zone were making mincemeat out of them anyway. *They don't need my help,* he decided. Taking a moment to run down his list of priorities, he turned to the staffers and said, "Where's my wife?"

"Uh, the bridge, sir."

"All right. We're going to have to get there, that's where the scuttling triggers are located. Time to do a little outside climbing, boys."

He kicked at the broken planking and soon had made an opening big enough to worm through. The staffer who'd confronted him earlier put a hand on his arm as he made to go through it. "Let me go first, sir. We don't know what's out there."

Chaison looked at him in surprise. "What's your name?"

"Travis, sir." He looked more like an actor playing some idealized naval officer than a real man. Why, they were in the middle of a battle and his uniform wasn't even scuffed! But he looked calm and composed, unlike the rest of his team.

Chaison grinned at him. "You've got a fine sense of propriety, Travis, but you're a bit impertinent." Travis looked crestfallen and Chaison laughed. "Get going! We'll talk later."

Travis made it outside and apparently didn't die; his hand reached back through the gap to help Chaison and the other staffers clamber out. They found themselves at the bottom of a huge dent in the Rook's hull. Nothing that the carpenters couldn't take care of. Chaison looked out and saw that both the Rook and the pirate had stopped spinning. They were lashed together now by dozens of ropes. The nearest hatches on the pirate were twenty feet away, and while men were popping out of those every few seconds, none looked forward and spotted Chaison's small group. It was tempting to start picking them off, but that would be a fool's game; they wouldn't last a minute before somebody sniped them from behind a porthole.

"There's a fine irony," commented Chaison as he groped for purchase on the streamlined hull. All around was nothing but air, the endless abyss of Virga; a misgrab here would send you on a slow trip around the world, with the birds, bugs, and fish making a moving feast of you along the way.

"What's that, sir?" Travis appeared next to him. Both of them clung by their fingernails to the gaps between hull planks, moving themselves forward with slow swings so as not to lose that purchase.

Chaison shrugged and said, "We came out here to find a pirate's treasure, but it looks like we're going to become such a treasure instead."

Travis nearly lost his grip. "Pirate's . . . *treasure?* Admiral, sir, what are you talking about?"

Chaison gazed past him. Another of his ships was disappearing behind a pall of smoke. He doubted that it was a deliberate ploy, it wasn't evenly enough distributed. That did not look good.

They were approaching the portholes to the bridge. There was an impenetrable hatch there; they would have to talk their way in. *Shouldn't be hard,* Chaison thought absently. *Venera's not mad at me for anything at the moment.*

He risked another glance at the battle. Yes, that was definitely the *Clarity* on fire out there. Three pirates had it under sustained attack. They were using a wheel formation, he saw—that was far too sophisticated a maneuver to be undertaken by untrained privateers. The three ships had let out ropes and tied them together at a central point. With their engines on full they'd begun to spin around that central pivot point. Spinning up like that was easy; it was a standard way for groups of ships that lacked centrifuges to create gravity while on long voyages. What was hard was spinning and twist-ing while you spun to present a difficult target to attackers. These ships were doing that.

Two-thirds of the wheeling formation were inside the cloud-bank. The net effect was that a pirate would swing out of the white wall at a fierce clip, fire a volley of rockets, and then dive back into the mist in a much steeper turn than would normally be possible. The Clarity was firing rockets at the center of the formation, hoping to cut the ropes that held the three ships together. That was a long shot, however.

Travis had given up asking about the treasure and was pounding on the armored hatch. Chaison hardly noticed, mesmerized as he was by the drama unfolding in that distant patch of sky. *Get out of there,* he willed the Clarity, but its engines must be damaged. It was a hanging target, like a driver fallen off his bike and vulnerable in clear air. In seconds it could all be over.

The cloudbank pulsed orange once, twice, then dozens of times in rapid succession. Chaison had seen fireworks reflecting off clouds; that was what this looked like. He'd been mentally timing the ap-pearance of each ship from within the clouds, and the next one was late. No, not late—it wasn't coming out. Seconds passed, and the second of the three should have appeared, but it didn't.

Finally one appeared. The pirate left the cloudbank in an uncon-trolled tumble. Flashes of rocket fire showed long streamers of rope trailing behind it.

"They hit something," he said. Travis looked up, puzzled. Chai-son pointed, and as he did so another flash lit the clouds, this one miles away.

"Somebody moved the icebergs," he whispered. Then he started to laugh. Two spokes of the wheel had been lost within seconds—two pirate ships flown at full speed into an unexpected obstacle. The fools were too confident in their charts, and now they were blindly running into the mountains of ice they had been using to hide their maneuvering. It served them right.

"I don't see what it is you find so amusing about the situation," said a cold voice behind Chaison.

"Travis, cease your work," he said quietly. Turning, he raised his hands. "We have visitors."

VENERA FANNING CROUCHED on the inside of the bridge's hatch. She could hear voices outside; one had sounded like her husband's. Captain Sembry refused to undog the hatch, however, and she didn't have the strength. The damn thing was designed to resist an invading force. Opening was about the last thing it was capable of doing.

Rhythmic pounding came from the inner doors as well. A minute ago an explosive charge had gone off behind one of those doors, but it hadn't been enough to break the hinges. It was only a matter of time, though.

Well, she thought, this will be an interesting new chapter in my life. Captured by pirates! The prospects of various fates worse than death outraged and angered her, but Venera wasn't afraid. She was already wondering what leverage she could use to make the best of the situation.

"The gas?"

Venera came alert at those words. She looked over at the bridge crew, who were clustered around a set of valves and pipes at the back of the can-shaped chamber. Captain Sembry was shaking his head at whoever had spoken.

"Too late for that," he said. "We'd kill the boarders, but the rest of the pirates would just blow the stuff out and come in again."

"The charges, then."

Sembry nodded, reaching into his jacket for something.

"Captain?" Venera put on her best maiden-in-distress act. "What's happening?"

Sembry turned, looking patriarchal and sad. "I'm sorry, dear," he said, "but we can't allow a Slipstream ship to fall into enemy hands. I'm going to have to scuttle the *Rook*."

She widened her eyes. "But we'll all be killed, won't we?"

He sighed. "That is the nature of military service, I'm afraid."

"How do you scuttle a big ship like this?" she asked.

Sembry showed her the key in his hand. He nodded to a set of metal boxes on the wall behind him. "These charges can only be set off by electrical current," he explained. "This key—"

He blinked in surprise at the pistol Venera had produced from inside her silk pantaloons. Sembry opened his mouth to speak but Venera never learned what he might have said because at that moment she shot him in the forehead.

The rest of the bridge crew was nicely packed together, and consequently picking them off was just as easy.

Twitching bodies and drops of blood caromed around the bridge. Venera ducked through it all and grabbed Sembry, who still had a surprised look on his face.

First order of business, she thought: *dispose of this key.*

Second: open the doors and let in the pirates.

HAYDEN'S PLAN HAD worked. He and Martor hovered high above the action, at the only spot he'd found where they could see past cloud, contrail, smoke, and darkness. Four icebergs were nosing out of the mist now, trailing fog as they slowly gathered momentum in their long fall toward the Sun of Suns. The pirates had lost their advantage and were in disarray. The battle might have turned.

Something he hadn't anticipated was happening, though: as the icebergs fell, they brought their weather with them. The battle scene was fast disappearing in a vast billow of cloud. Already foghorns were sounding through the dimness as the ships struggled to avoid one another.

Martor was squirming with impatience. "Now back to the Rook!"

Hayden nodded and spun up the engine; but he was uneasy. With the ships separated by mist and mines it could be a long time before the Rook was relieved. He nudged them cautiously through the layers of mist, listening for the sound of gunfire or rockets. Ominously, he heard nothing.

A black hull loomed up suddenly and he had to spin the bike and hit the gas to stop in time. "It's the pirate!" said Martor as he groped for the sword he'd stowed in the sidecar. "Sounds like we've won!"

Hayden eased them around the hull, as quietly as he could. The pirate and the Rook were still bound together with rope, and lights burned in the portholes of both. He could see the gray shapes of men working on the Rook's engines, so the fight must indeed be over.

Martor was nearly bursting. "Come on, what are you waiting for?"

"Shh!" Cutting the engine entirely, Hayden let them drift toward the aft of the ships. The working figures resolved slowly, like images he'd once seen on a photographic emulsion.

"Hey, those aren't—" Quickly Hayden grabbed Martor's arm, putting a finger to his own lips. The boy pulled away.

"But that can't be! We have to do something."

"Martor, they've taken the Rook," Hayden whispered. "We can't go back now."

"But somebody has to protect Aubri! Listen," pleaded Martor, "we can catch a ride on the hull, like tired crows, and when they least expect it—" Hayden shook his head.

Martor tried again. "Then let's hang back in the clouds and follow them . . . What?"

"We have another ten minutes' worth of gas, tops. If they aren't out there already, the pirates are going to send out bikes any minute now to look for any followers. And you know perfectly well they'll check every inch of the hull, inside and out, for stowaways."

"You want to run back to one of the other ships? No! I'm staying to fight."

"Martor, that's ridiculous. You wouldn't last ten seconds." Let the boy think they were returning to the other ship. By the time he realized that their true destination was the tourist city, it would be too late.

Hayden felt sick at the thought of leaving. Consigning Aubri Mahallan to these monsters was another defeat in a lifetime of defeats. And for some reason, the thought that Admiral Fanning was dead or soon would be, was no consolation. *Who cares about him?* some unexpected part of him said. *Only you, and what do you matter?*

"I hate to do it," he said sincerely. "But we've got to—"

He glanced up just in time to see the black cylinder of a rocket, held in Martor's hands, swing toward his face. Then everything burst and went dark.

WHEN VENERA FANNING was a girl she lived in a room with canary-yellow walls. Little trees and airships were painted on them, and her bed had a canopy of dusty velvet and sat against one wall.

At night, if she pressed her ear to the uneven plaster, she could hear the screams of men and women being tortured in her father's dungeon.

She'd been reminded of home many times over the past day. Now, though, the sounds of screaming echoing through the Rook had died out. In the relative silence that followed she could hear someone big approaching through the lamplit dimness—whoever it was was banging back and forth off the walls in a freefall tantrum. As the figure passed the doors to the hangar where Venera was tied up, she saw that it was the pirate captain, Dentius was his name. It was apparent that he wasn't pleased with the results of the torture session.

Venera took the opportunity. "By now," she said loudly, "you'll have noticed that the crew have absolutely no idea where we were going."

Dentius whirled. His already small eyes narrowed further and his lips pulled back from his teeth. Swinging into the hangar he stopped himself by wrapping his legs around Venera's hips. He grabbed her by the throat.

"What do you know?" he shouted. "Tell me or you're next."

"Now, Captain," she croaked, rearing back, "there are easier ways. I'm quite willing to tell you . . . for a little consideration."

He sneered. Dentius wore the faded and patched uniform of an Aerie ship captain. His face, however, bore no traces of ever having been exposed to sunlight. Like most of his crewmen, his skin was as white as the inside of a potato, except where it was crisscrossed with pink scars. To Venera he looked like some giant, writhing grub stuffed into an officer's jacket.

She knew he was already inclined to treat her differently than the crew, who were mostly crammed into empty rocket racks or water lockers, out of sight and momentarily out of mind. Whether Chaison was with them, or whether he even lived, she had no idea.

Venera and Aubri Mahallan were tied up and on display in the hangar, "as an inspiration to the lads," Dentius had said—though both were still clothed because, he'd said, "there's a fine line between inspired and obsessed." Still, Mahallan was lashed spread-eagled in the center of the space and seemed dazed and despairing. Venera merely had her wrists fastened to a stanchion near the door.

It was clear what the captain had in mind for Mahallan. If he had no clear idea of what to do with Venera, she wanted to provide him with some alternatives before he thought about it too much.

He peered at her for a moment, then sucker-punched her in the kidneys. The pain was astonishing—but through Venera's mind flashed a memory of herself lying on marble tiles, moaning through a ruined mouth and staring at the blood-shrouded shape of a rifle bullet that lay next to her. While nobody came and her fury grew and grew . . .

Dentius grabbed her hair and pulled her head back. "Tell me!" he roared at her. "Or I'll kill you right now!"

"Th-that's the problem, isn't it?" She managed to smile, though her neck and jaw pulsed with pain and she could feel the hairs in her scalp starting to pull out. "You're going to kill me anyway. So why should I cooperate?"

Dentius grunted and drew back. He had the mentality of a shark, she'd decided: all straight-ahead brute force, but stupid and immobile when stopped. Her bravado seemed to have stymied him—or at least, it had reminded him of what she'd already done.

"Why'd you shoot the captain?" he asked suddenly.

Venera smiled. "Why? Because he was the one other person on board who knew our destination."

Dentius let go of her hair. At that moment one of his obsequious mates appeared in the doorway. "Inventory's done, Captain," he said in a familiar accent she couldn't quite place. "Strictly military, except for some paintings. Probably going to trade those at the voyeur's palace."

Dentius nodded, eyeing Venera speculatively. Then he drew a knife out of his boot. She drew back, but he merely reached up to cut the length of rope holding her to the beam. "We'd best talk further," he said, as he towed her out of the hangar and into the remains of battle: drifting droplets of blood and hanging balls of smoke, wood splinters, and tumbling scarves of bandage.

As he dragged her with bumps and jerks through the wooden ribs of the ship, Venera tried to keep her wits. She needed a sense of who was still alive, and where they were. The rocket racks were essentially iron cages, so it was easy to see their inhabitants. None of the senior officers was visible, only able airmen who stared at her listlessly or with fear. Was Chaison dead, then?

Dentius hauled her into the axle of the centrifuge, which had been spun up. Exhausted or wounded pirates lolled in hammocks at the rim of the wheel; she heard both moaning and laughter. "My cabin," she said to Dentius, pointing with her tied hands.

"Captain's cabin," he said. "You his woman?"

She shook her head. Chaison Fanning had appropriated Sembry's cabin, causing the *Rook*'s captain to have to bunk elsewhere. "I was the admiral's wife," she admitted. "But he's dead and lost in the clouds now."

Venera had no doubt that Dentius would have asked the tortured men about her. There was no point in trying to deny her status.

Without comment Dentius shoved her into the cabin, which was a shambles of overturned chests and jumbled clothing. Most of the contents had been Sembry's of course; Chaison traveled light.

Her jewel box lay on the floor, its lid up, the fated bullet that had struck her jaw still on its velvet bed inside. The centrifuge's spin was making her nauseated so Venera went to sit on the edge of the bed, making a show of straightening her clothes.

"So . . ." Dentius gnawed at one calloused knuckle. "Why'd you kill the rest of the bridgers?"

She shrugged. "They . . . objected to my tactics."

Dentius laughed. "Venera Fanning, that's your name, isn't it?"

"Aye," she said, lifting her chin. Her heart was hammering in her chest; raised though she was in the arts of deceit, Venera doubted she could keep her calm demeanor for long.

Dragging over a chair, Dentius sat down and clasped his hands in his lap. "So," he said in a horrible parody of politeness, "what brings you to our winter, Venera Fanning?"

"Treasure," she said promptly. "Somewhat ironically . . . pirate treasure, to be exact."

Dentius shook his head. "If there were anything worth having out here, I'd have taken it and built a fleet to reconquer Aerie, years ago. Nobody brings treasure into winter. Anybody here who's got it, takes it somewhere sunny."

"I know," she said. "But that wasn't always the case. There've been times when convoys ran through winter regularly, shipping goods between the principalities of Candesce and the outer nations. And during those periods, there was treasure to be had."

Dentius thought for a while. His face, which had appeared that of a brutal simpleton just minutes ago, relaxed by degrees into that of a weary, disappointed man. After a while he said, "I've heard the fairy tales. We all have. There was even a time when I believed in such things." With a faint smile he added, "It's Anetene, isn't it? You're talking about the—how would you put it, 'the fabled treasure of Anetene.'"

Venera frowned past his tired skepticism. "I was," she said. "We were on our way to the tourist station, because that's where the map is."

Dentius laughed. "You've got to be out of your mind," he said. "Anetene's a legend. Sure, he lived and he was a great pirate. The less intellectually endowed members of my crew swear by him. But the treasure's pure myth."

"Maybe," she said with a shrug. "But the map to it is real."

His lips curled in sly indulgence. "And what would an admiral of Slipstream be doing hunting pirate treasure in winter?"

"As to that . . ." She looked away, making a faint moue. "Slipstream's finances are not in the greatest of shapes at the moment, if you get my meaning. The pilot is not the cleverest of men when it comes to state funds."

"You've a deficit to pay off?" Dentius grinned.

"It's more like, the pilot has a deficit he's told the people about . . . and then there's the real deficit."

"You're wanting to forestall a political scandal, I get that." Dentius shook his head. "The whole story is preposterous on the face of it, and you know it. So why are you trying to put this one over on me?"

"Because the treasure is real," she said. "But I realize that I can't convince you of that." Now she hesitated: how far could she push this man? If she played the next hand, he might kill her. But if she gave in to fear he would have won; the bullet would have won. "There's another consideration," she said slowly. "I saw how you and your men fared during the battle. You have your own deficit now, Captain Dentius: you've just paid far more in men and ships than you've gotten back. Am I wrong in thinking that this is going to cause you some . . . political problems . . . of your own?"

Dentius's face flushed with anger. He stood up, knocking over the chair. "We're going to kill all of you for starters," he said. "Very bloody, very visible. My men will have their revenge."

"Yes but will that be enough?" Venera allowed herself a small, ironic smile. "You know that the other captains won't be impressed. You lost ships, Dentius."

He didn't answer. "Killing us will be a good diversion," Venera continued. "But you need a better diversion. One that will last longer, until the memories of this debacle have faded. You've got to give your men *hope*, Captain Dentius, or else you may be out of a job."

"In other words," he said, "it hardly matters at this point whether the treasure of Anetene really exists . . ."

"As long as there's a map. Something to give the other captains." She nodded. "And there *is* a map."

Dentius leaned against the wall for a while; he was obviously not comfortable in gravity. Finally he nodded once, sharply. "Done. You show us to the map, you get to keep your life."

"And my virtue."

"Can't guarantee that. But let's say it's on the table." He grinned and turned to leave. "Cabin's yours. Anything else your grace requires?"

Life, not death, lay ahead—at least for now—so Venera decided to ask about the one thing that Dentius might be willing to indulge. "There is something . . ."

Dentius turned, surprised. Venera knelt down and retrieved her jewel box. She plucked out the bullet and held it up, next to her jaw.

"We have a history, this bullet and I," she said. "If I live, and if someday I gain my freedom again, I want to know where it came from."

He was obviously impressed. "Why?"

There was no pretense behind her smile now. "So that I can go there," she said, "and kill everyone connected to it."

A BLACK WING lifted. Hayden blinked at a blurred jumble of shadows and silhouettes. Mumbles and tearing sounds came to his ears; someone was tugging at his shirt. He couldn't feel any surface under him so he must be weightless. He was also very cold. And in the distance, the faintly annoying two-tone sound of the *Rook's* engines rumbled.

That meant something bad. "Hey!" he tried to shout. The word came out slurred and weak.

"He's awake." He recognized the voice behind the tense whisper. "Pardon us, Griffin, we're sacrificing the hem of your shirt to a better cause."

"Wha—" Admiral Fanning's voice had been dry, almost raspy. But why was he of all people here? Hayden shook his head, which filled him with an awful vertigo and a pounding pain that radiated forward from behind his left ear. *Don't throw up,* he beseeched himself. *Don't throw up. There's no gravity today.*

The gray blurs became a bit clearer. He was curled in the fetal position in some cramped space defined by metal bars. There was no light source nearby, everything was shades of speckled gray with no color. Crammed into this unlikely place with him were three men and a boy. One of the men was Fanning. Another—he wasn't sure—might be Venera's manservant, Carrier.

Hayden's stomach did another flip, but not because of his own pain. The third man held Martor by a hand and a foot, stretching him out like a sheet about to be folded while Fanning tried to staunch a dark liquid welling from his flank. Martor's foot stuck out one side of the cage, his hand out the other.

"He's . . . stabbed?"

"Shot," muttered Fanning. "The bullet's still inside."

The sight had brought Hayden alert like a dash of cold water. "We need to dig it out," he said, focusing on making his uncooperative lips form the syllables.

"Really?" Yes, that was Carrier all right, his tone dripping sarcasm. "Keep your voice down," he added in a hiss.

Hayden wanted to ask why they were in this cage, but didn't want to hear any of the possible answers. The strange electric silence of the ship, the way these men flinched any time there was a noise in the distance . . . But overriding that curiosity was the need to know that Martor would be all right.

"Cut the man some slack," Fanning said quietly to Carrier. "He's concussed." He turned to Hayden. "The problem is that I can't reach the bullet with my fingers. And the only other thing we have is a couple of splinters of wood I pried off the hull." He held up two sharp spikes of wood. "If I go noodling around in your friend's abdomen with these, I'm going to puncture something for sure, and probably leave some splinters behind. That's bound to fester."

"Maybe you can help," said the man who was holding Martor like a sheet. Hayden recognized him as one of Fanning's staff. "We could heat the wood to sterilize it—without setting it on fire, of course. If we could reach that." He pointed.

Now Hayden realized where they were: crammed into the framework of a rocket rack, somewhere near the stern of the ship. The rack was mounted to the hull and surrounded by boxes that blocked the light. But where the staffer pointed, the corner of one crate was brightly silhouetted. Just around that corner was a lantern. Hayden held out his hand and felt the faint movement of air coming from its wind-up fan.

A cough sounded nearby and gruff voices spoke. The men in the cage froze, only their eyes darting in the direction of the sound. Seconds ticked by, and eventually they all sighed as one and relaxed from their positions.

"None of us can reach that lantern," said Fanning, as if nothing had happened. "But you're young and lanky. Care to try? We need these splinters heated but not burned."

"Ah." He took them in one shaking hand. "Okay." Drops of Martor's blood were drifting past his nose, scented of iron. Hayden carefully ducked around them and pressed his shoulder to the bars of the cage. Once again in middistance he heard grating, accented voices: that was not the crew of the *Rook*. The pirates might see his hand groping around the corner of the crate—it was going to be brightly lit, after all—but he'd be damned if he was going to seize up like a busted engine every time one of them sneezed. He had to try his part to save Martor.

By straining until spots appeared in his eyes, he was able to get his hand around the corner of the crate. He knew the shape of the little lanterns intimately: they were like tiny bikes, open-ended cylinders with a wind-up fan at one end to move air past the lamp's wick. He pictured the device in his mind, and moved one of the splinters until he figured it was near the flame. He waited a moment, then brought it back.

The splinter was still cool. He tried again, shifting position slightly. Five tries and he put it right into the flame, making it catch light so that he had to quickly blow on it while Carrier cursed him for a fool. But he was getting the hang of it now.

A few minutes later he gingerly handed two hot lengths of wood to Fanning, who grunted in approval. Hayden felt proud of himself, happy for the implied praise, and then angry at himself for valuing Fanning's opinion.

Now that Fanning was at work, Hayden felt he could finally ask the questions that were burning in him. "Who shot him?" he asked Fanning's staff member. The man looked over Martor's arm at him with a bemused look on his face.

"We were going to ask you the same question," he said. "They threw you both in with us an hour after we lost the fight. I'd heard a shot. . . . Were you outside the ship?"

Hayden nodded. "Clearing mines. . . . Now I remember. He hit me on the head because I refused to return to fight. You'd . . . already lost."

"Wisdom is often rewarded with a blow to the head," said the other. "My name is Travis. This is Carrier. You probably know the— uh, Ensign Fanning, here." Travis smiled ruefully. "You have the privilege of being stuck in the cage reserved for troublemakers. Fanning and I were caught sneaking outside the ship. Carrier made it all the way into the bridge of the enemy ship and killed six people before they subdued him. And apparently, you two attacked a fully armed pirate ship with one bike and two pistols. We're a pretty worrisome lot, I guess."

"But we're alive," said Carrier in a flat voice. "Stupid of them."

"They don't know—" Fanning's voice was distracted "—which of us might be valuable."

"They don't know who he is," Travis whispered, jabbing a thumb at the admiral. "But they know there was an admiral on board. His ransom might be the only profit they see off this escapade."

"Thought I was him," said Carrier with the first trace of amusement he'd shown. "Why they didn't shoot me on the spot."

"Ah!" Fanning hunched over, gritting his teeth as he slowly inched his hands back. At last he drew a gleaming metal slug into the dim light. "That's it. Let's patch him up."

They'd each torn strips off their shirts. Hayden reached to hand some to Fanning, and his hand faltered. "Just a sec—" he said.

Then the black wing descended again over everything.

"I'M NOT SURE that's such a good idea," said somebody. Hayden felt his body twitch once, then he was blinking around at a half-familiar vision of dimly lit bars and crowded bodies.

"Travis, I let you talk me out of surrendering myself when these criminals started torturing our men and now I feel ashamed of myself." Admiral Fanning sat on the air, knees up and his hands tightly gripping them. His breath misted in the cold air as he spoke.

Martor drifted, face pale and limbs akimbo, in the center of the cage.

"But it was to protect the details of the mission—"

"Hang the mission! These men are my responsibility. If I can spare just one of them the agonies we heard earlier, then I have to."

"Not if that ultimately kills them," murmured Carrier. "Quiet, someone's coming."

Hayden had been about to ask how Martor was. The sound of someone hand-skipping off the beams of the ship silenced him.

After a moment a lean, pale face appeared outside the cage. The pirate was young, almost grotesquely spindly, and dressed in layers of patched jackets, vests, and pantaloons. Keeping a safe distance, he shoved a couple of flasks in the general direction of the cage. "One's fer pissing, one's fer drinking," he said as they sailed over. "Don't get 'em mixed up."

Admiral Fanning cleared his throat. "Where are we going?" he asked in a calm tone.

"Voyeur's palace," said the pirate. "After we catch up to the rest of our fleet." He pushed off from the cage and began climbing away like a four-limbed spider.

"What's the voyeur's palace?" whispered Travis.

"I think he meant the tourist station," said Fanning. "That's bad news. It means they found out what we're up to."

Travis sighed. "Great. So you're telling me the pirates know the purpose of our mission in winter, while your senior staff still do not?"

Martor was breathing regularly, Hayden saw. He turned his attention to Fanning, who was looking chagrined.

"The revelation that we were looking for a famous treasure was to be kept from the men until we were actually there," said Fanning. "We felt it might . . . affect discipline . . . among the press-ganged members of the crew."

Carrier guffawed. "They might mutiny so they could set themselves up like kings, you mean."

"Yes, Mr. Carrier. That is what I mean."

Hayden stared from one man to the other. What was this about a treasure?

"But why undertake such an expedition now?" Travis shook his head. "We're at war with Mavery. There's indications that Falcon Formation is going to take advantage of the fact and stage an invasion. Why go running halfway around the world for gold? Unless . . ."

"Belay that thought, Travis," said Fanning. "We're doing this for the survival of Slipstream, and our present client nation." Hayden started at this mention of Aerie. "The fact is," Fanning continued, "our navy is no match for Falcon's. We need an edge, and since our Pilot has successfully alienated all our current neighbors, that edge can't be diplomatic. It has to be military."

"But a pirate's *treasure?*"

"Oh, forget the treasure, man. We'll divide that up between the men, I don't care about that. It's what's said to be kept with the treasure that interests me. Something that would be valueless to any of these men—or to pirates, for that matter."

"And that is . . . ?"

Fanning smiled enigmatically. "We sometimes forget, Travis, that we live in an artificial world—a world sustained by mechanisms so vast that we seldom realize that's what they are. And mechanisms built by man have doors, and locks. . . . I've said too much. Suffice it to say, if we find what we're looking for, Falcon Formation should be easy to handle."

Travis—and Hayden—waited. When nothing more was forthcoming, Travis said in annoyance, "Didn't you say 'hang the mission' a few minutes ago? Now you're being protective of it again."

"That's because our benefactor there," Fanning nodded in the direction the pirate had gone, "gave me an idea."

Hayden decided to reveal the fact that he was awake. "How's the kid?" he asked—though he also wanted to hear more about this treasure. His voice came out as a croak; he realized as he spoke how terribly thirsty and hungry he felt.

"The boy will recover," said Carrier. "What are you thinking, Admiral?"

Fanning reached up to pull on the bars of the rocket rack where they were riveted to the hull. "This ship wasn't originally designed for winter," he said. "It's a retrofit. Now, I once saw a rack like this pull free of the wall during a maneuver in winter. It was due to frost-heaving in the planks."

"Oh?"

"If we inject water in between the boards, here and here . . ." The admiral pointed. "It may push the wood apart when it freezes."

Carrier looked disdainful of the idea, but Travis appeared to be giving it some thought. "Since the ship's been winterized, the chinks have been sealed with tar against bad air coming in," he pointed out. "The water will have nowhere to go."

"Exactly," said the admiral. "Now, I don't propose that we use our drinking water, here." He held up the other flask. "Everybody piss. We'll use that."

Hayden shook his head as Fanning unlaced his own codpiece and proceeded to demonstrate. Maybe he was hallucinating. That would explain why he seemed to have heard Admiral Fanning talking about a treasure hunt, and why that same admiral was now proposing that they piss in the walls.

"What are you suggesting?" he asked sarcastically. "Are we four going to take the ship back with the strength of our own arms?"

Fanning shook his head. "Of course not. We will scuttle the Rook. Can't allow Slipstream military hardware in the hands of the enemy."

"Ah . . . And how do we do that?"

"Got to get to the bridge. I suggest we find a porthole and crawl outside to the—" Fanning noticed Hayden vigorously shaking his head. "Why not?"

"Because when winter pirates have a lot of prisoners they hang the excess off the hull. So they'll have a man or two out there to keep watch."

All three men turned to look at him. "And how do you know that?" asked Carrier.

Hayden hesitated, but his last reserve of cunning was exhausted. "Because," he admitted, "I was press-ganged by pirates five years ago."

Now they just frankly stared. Finally Carrier shrugged and looked away. "Things begin to become clear. Knew you weren't what you seemed. Pirates planted you in Fanning household?"

"No! Nothing like that." He'd done it now. Even if the pirates didn't kill him, Fanning would have him towed until he froze, or shot in front of the crew. There was just the faintest chance, if he told most of the truth—but not all of it—that he could avoid such a fate. "I . . . I eventually escaped and made my way back to Rush. And yes, I made up a cover story, that's true, I'd learned how to do that from a station infiltrator I worked for. But I wasn't spying for anybody. I really did need a job."

Carrier raised one eyebrow. "Interesting," he said. "You actually expect us to believe that?"

"We'll deal with that question later," said Fanning. "Right now I want to know why you're familiar with how winter pirates deal with their prisoners."

"Uh . . ." Hayden blinked. Fanning didn't care that he'd wormed his way into the service of his wife under false pretenses? Or was he really as focused on the here and now as he appeared? "Well, sir," he said, "I was brought on board the pirate ship *Wilson's Revenge*, somewhere in between being a slave and an apprentice. I couldn't leave; but I had the run of the ship."

Fanning waved a hand indifferently. "Press-ganged," he said. "Get to the bit about the prisoners."

Hayden took his turn at the flask and tried to organize his thoughts. "Ah. Um, being a pirate turned out to be the most unglamourous job you could imagine. It consisted of bullying fishing boats and birdcatchers and selling their tackle and nets at places like Warea. You could barely buy food, you had to hoard your ammunition, and beer was out of the question unless you brewed it yourself. Mostly it was just dark, dismal, and hopeless."

Fanning dug at the caulking between the planks, at the spot where the frame of the rocket rack was mounted to the hull with bolts. Once he had a finger-sized hole, he jammed the neck of the now-full flask into it and squeezed. "Go on," he said.

"Once in all that time I spent with these men, we heard about a yacht that was trying to sneak through the cloudbanks of the nations near Candesce. It was some young noble kid trying to reach his lover, who lived in a nearby nation the kid's nation was at war with. . . . You get the picture. My infiltrator boss had the word from one of his spies. So we went on the hunt and we found the yacht right where it was supposed to be. We . . . took it."

He didn't like being reminded of that incident, but now that he'd started talking about it, it seemed he couldn't stop. "Our ship was a modified birdcatcher, the same dimensions as the *Rook* but mostly hold—empty space. Thirty crew, tops. The yacht had that many plus a ridiculous number of manservants and cooks and such for the noble kid. The hold was full of bikes, so my captain made most of the survivors ride outside."

Without realizing it, Hayden had hunched around himself and drifted into one corner of the cage. "Most of them froze to death in the first day," he murmured. "I know; I had to stand one watch."

To his suprise, Fanning asked no more questions about his past. Instead, the admiral called a huddle to discuss tactics. Hayden supplied his best guesses about where the guards would be stationed, and Travis provided a detailed description of the inside of the ship, including sight lines. Reaching the bridge undetected from the inside would be difficult, but it could be done.

While they talked, Hayden periodically checked on Martor. The boy was breathing more easily now, and though he remained pale and cold, he was at least alive. Hayden wrapped his own jacket around Martor's feet to help keep him warm; out of the corner of his eye he saw Fanning nod approvingly as he did so.

That fanned the smouldering spark of his anger. Who was this murderer to deign to approve of his decency?

Something had been festering in the back of Hayden's mind ever since the attack. Now he turned to Admiral Fanning. "Sir, how did the pirates know we were here? They must have amassed that fleet with some foreknowledge of its target."

Fanning mused. "Don't think I haven't been wracking my brains over that. As best as I can figure, somebody in Warea sent the word that we were there. They might have dispatched a bike in secret before we'd even reconnoitered the lake."

Just then a sharp crack sounded from the hull. The rocket rack quivered and all four men turned to stare at the planking. A long splinter had popped up and the crack ran right under the bolted frame. "I don't believe it," whispered Fanning. "The damned thing worked."

"I'll never doubt you again," said Carrier. He almost smiled—but Fanning turned and looked down his nose at the man.

"Your confidence is not required, Mister Carrier," he said. "Now help me lever this thing aside. We need the youngest and nimblest of our party to slide under here."

They braced their feet against the hull and hauled on the bars of the rack. The bolt pulled free with a groan and a space opened between the bars and the hull. Hayden didn't feel particularly nimble at the moment, with his head pounding like a malfunctioning sun, but he eagerly wriggled his way into the opening.

He was through up to his hips and already thinking about how to deal with the guards he knew were lurking around these crates, when the sound of the ship changed. The engines changed pitch, and the sound of a ringing bell echoed through the space. Moments later the engines cut out entirely.

"Back, get back in!" Three sets of hands dragged him back under the pressing rust of the rack. Scratched and breathless, Hayden pressed himself against the hull as three pirates with pistols in their hands rounded the crates.

"Here's the catch of the day," said one with a laugh. "You gentlemen have the privilege of witnessing a grand display of fireworks to celebrate our reunion with the rest of our fleet.

"Well, okay," he admitted with an ironic wink at his companions. "You won't really be witnessing the fireworks. You're gonna *be* the fireworks."

They all laughed, and he came to unwind the chains holding the rack closed. "Get out!" he commanded.

"It's execution time."

13

"IT'S A TRADITION of mass executions to sail into port leaving a trail of blood in the sky," said Captain Dentius to his audience. "But that only works when you're near a sun. It's the visibility that's important, you see—justice must be seen to be done, eh?" He looked down at Venera and grinned. The grin had the intense focus of a man who's on stage and acting a part.

"So," he declaimed, "we pirates of winter have invented an alternative method. Rather than tying you all to the outside of your ship and riddling you with bullets, or slicing your arteries with knives and then flying into port trailing a grand banner of blood . . . rather than that, we choose to announce our executions with fire.

"This will be a truly grand spectacle!" he shouted. Dentius had his feet hooked into two leather straps on a T-bar that surmounted a long pole. The pole had been thrust out the side of the *Rook* so that he stood outside it, in commanding view of both his own ship and the *Rook*. Two of his lieutenants were similarly perched, and tied to the crosspiece by their wrists were Venera Fanning and Aubri Mahallan.

"Dentius, please," murmured Aubri. "You won't lose face if you spare these men. It—"

"Silence," he hissed at her. "I've already lost face." He turned back to the vista of the rope-twined ships. The portholes and hangar doors of the pirate were wide open, and everywhere lanterns were aimed at the *Rook*. The bright light obscured whatever waited in the darkness; it was as if only these two ships existed in the entire universe. *As far as we're concerned*, Venera thought, *that might as well be true.*

The crew of the *Rook* were tied in nets that trailed behind the ship on long ropes. Three pirates carrying a bag of kerosene and a mop were moving systematically around the nets, slopping fuel over the men of Slipstream.

Venera had also asked Dentius to spare the men. Not that she'd begged; he might have felt he had leverage on her if he thought she cared overmuch for them. And she didn't, of course; but one pair of eyes glaring up at her from the bullet-scarred hull of the *Rook* belonged to Chaison. He had survived and his men had not given him away. Both facts impressed Venera.

"Have you considered that some of these airmen might make good converts?" she asked now.

"They're Slipstreamers," Dentius said. "The original pirates. You execute pirates when you catch them, you know."

It was humiliating to be tied at the feet of these odorous maggot-colored men. She'd see them dead as soon as humanly possible. The thought cheered her somewhat, until she glanced back at the tangles of bodies hanging from the *Rook*.

Would her plan work with the degree of uncontrolled fire that was likely to be trailing the *Rook* in the next hour or so? She somehow doubted it; after all, if she played her hand now Dentius could always belay the fire and have the Slipstreamers shot instead.

She almost opened her mouth anyway to give Dentius her ultimatum—but he was addressing the crowd. "We will be rendezvousing with the rest of our ships within the hour," he shouted. "We've seen their semaphores blinking in the night air. The little Slipstream fleet has been utterly destroyed. To celebrate, as we sail into formation with our brothers, you will light our way. And your smoke will trail behind us for a hundred miles—two hundred miles!" His men cheered and Dentius raised a fist.

Dentius had come to her last night, and she'd submitted to his dark attentions. Venera's revulsion for the man had reached an almost religious pitch; she hadn't felt such intensity of emotion since the bandages were removed and she first saw her scar in the mirror. Yet she'd known he was waiting for her to try something. He would have happily taken the pretext to kill her, she knew. So instead of reaching for a hatpin or the comfortable heaviness of her jewel box, she had lain there and listened to him talk. He was a man crushed beneath the weight of his own history.

Dentius had once been a captain in the Aerie navy. Upon the fall of his nation he had escaped into winter along with some of his compatriots. But he still dreamt of a triumphant return, someday. Despite his own better judgement, the notion that the treasure of Anetene might be real had seized his imagination. He couldn't help talking about what he might do with a king's ransom in money: build a fleet and free his homeland. In his own mind, Dentius was still an embattled airman, biding his time. He was not really a pirate, though he acknowledged that he must play the role.

Venera had lain there with an arm across her eyes, willing him to shut up and die while he tried to justify and magnify his own existence.

Now he was clinging to the attention his men were giving him. "Are you ready?" he bellowed. The torch men raised their fists over their heads. "All right then. Light 'em up!"

Venera had to speak now or it would be too late. But it would do no good. As the first screams rose from the nets, Venera could only look away. Beside her, Aubri Mahallan was sobbing.

"All engines ahead slow," directed Dentius. "We want just a whiff of a breeze to stroke that fire back over the rest of them." The crew of the pirate were whistling and hooting now, a din to match that of the screaming coming from the Rook. Dentius looked down over it all like some pale bird on his perch, and laughed.

Venera became aware of the cracking sound only after something flickered in her peripheral vision. She turned to look but it was gone. Then, turning back, she blinked at the sight of twenty bikes swooping out of the darkness. Flashes from rifle fire lit them and suddenly Dentius's pirates were tumbling from the nets. Red dots of blood gleamed in the firelight.

"Get them!" Dentius began hastily clambering down the long pole, his lieutenants behind him. That left Venera and Aubri Mahallan pinned like targets between the ships.

The deep thrum of engines signaled the appearance of five cylindrical shadows. The *Severance*, the *Tormentor*, the *Unseen Hand*, the *Clarity*, and the *Arrest* fell into a star formation around the *Rook* and its captor. Droning bikes and gunfire filled the air.

The fires on the nets were going out. At the same time, the ropes connecting them tautened and the helpless men were drawn in until they were pressed against the hull of the *Rook*.

Now the pole holding Venera and Mahallan wobbled and began to move. They were being drawn into the *Rook*, she thought in relief. It was better armored than Dentius's own ship. Moments later she found herself on the bridge with Mahallan, Dentius, and his lieutenants. One of them slammed the metal hatch and the horrible sounds coming from outside dampened somewhat.

"Wait for it," said Dentius with a nervous chuckle. He pretended to count off seconds on his fingers. Before he reached ten, the sound of gunfire ceased.

He blew out a sigh of relief. "We've lashed their men to our hull," he said with satisfaction. "The bastards know they can't fire on this ship or they'll hit their own crew. We've got 'em by the balls." He turned to the pilot. "Let's get the hell out of here."

"If you try to leave they're likely to fire anyway," Venera pointed out. "They'll target the engines."

Dentius shrugged angrily. "Who cares?" He turned to the boy

who'd taken over the semaphore chair. "Send 'em a message. Tell 'em if they fire we'll start shooting the prisoners. The ones we lit up have gone out, right? Maybe they'll take that as a good sign." He rubbed his chin. "All we have to do is make the rendezvous and we're home free."

Venera felt a languorous wave of spiteful pleasure wash over her. "No, Dentius, you're trapped," she said with a smile. "Just one rocket in the wrong place and this ship is going to explode."

He had looked away from her and was about to say something to his men. Now Dentius turned, a quizzical look on his face. "What did you say?"

"You really think I shot the bridge staff because they knew our destination?" She laughed. "They were going to scuttle the ship, Dentius. I stopped them. But after I did that, I armed all the charges myself—and broke off the key in the control box's lock." She pointed.

Everybody turned to look at the inconspicuous metal panel on the bridge's inside wall. "Once the charges are armed, any kind of disturbance could set them off," she said. "They're supposed to be on a hair trigger."

A new salvo of gunfire sounded outside. "That would be your men, shooting at the bikes," said Venera. "You know there's going to be return fire."

One of the pirates was crouched over the control box. "It does appear to be a scuttling panel, Captain," he said. "And there's a key broken off in the lock."

Dentius swore softly.

"Close your mouth, you look like a fool," said Venera.

"Belay that message!" Dentius dove for the semaphore chair. "Tell them we request a ceasefire!"

"But . . . but . . ." Dentius's lieutenants looked at one another; at him; at Venera.

"Those five ships have no idea how fragile the *Rook* is right now," Venera pointed out. "And they've just watched their own men be set on fire. Do you really think they're going to be polite?" She shook her head. "It's time to come to terms, gentlemen. You can always threaten to blow us all to smithereens, so your situation's not hopeless. In fact, I'm betting you can escape with your skins and maybe even your own ship. But you'd better start talking fast."

Dentius's eyes were bulging and his face was bright red. He drew his sword and launched himself toward her.

She ducked behind the navigator. "You'd better negotiate with my husband, the *admiral*," she said quickly. "He's, ah, waiting outside. And Dentius, he'll be more inclined to accept your proposal if he knows I'm alive."

Dentius snarled. Then he turned to the semaphore man. "Send this: 'Request immediate ceasefire. Admiral to negotiate disengagement.' And somebody tell our men to stop firing!"

He glared down the length of his sword at Venera. "Be as smug as you want right now, lady. But I'm putting a price on your head that'll have every thug and cutthroat in Slipstream after you. I'll see you dead in a year, one way or another."

She shrugged out of the navigator's grip. "It'll be just like life back home, then," she said insouciantly. "But I wouldn't count on you living to put out that contract. Not once your own men are done with you."

There was silence after that, and then the outside hatch was opened and one of the lieutenants went out to fetch Admiral Chaison Fanning.

SLEW, THE HEAD carpenter, nodded in greeting as Hayden eased the bike into the hangar. The man was standing with the hatch gang, who all waved. One of them even grinned at Hayden.

Come to think of it, there hadn't been the usual delay in getting the hatch opened when he returned from his search run.

What was all that about?

Hayden was bone weary, having logged ten hours in the air at his own insistence. All the *Rook*'s bikes were out looking for the pirates; so far there had been no sign of them. Dentius and his mates had made a clean getaway, having negotiated a small head start as part of their terms of disengagement. None of the other ships had been seen either; Travis's theory was that they had a hideout somewhere among the icebergs.

Venera's racing bike was riddled with bullet holes and made an odd whistling noise now when it ran. It hadn't lost any performance, though. The thing was developing enough character that Hayden was beginning to think he should give it a name.

"Here, let me." One of the hatch gang whose name he didn't know reached out to help him hook the bike to its winch-arm. Hayden blinked at him in surprise.

"Thanks." He didn't know what else to say, so he ducked his head at the gang and left the hangar. Sick bay was at the back of the ship; he went that way.

A small mob of airmen, silhouettes in the lantern light, crowded around the angular box that was the sick bay. Somebody must have died, Hayden thought—and in a sudden rush of anxiety he elbowed his way through the crowd.

But no, he heard Martor's voice well before he got to the door. The boy was awake and talking. Not just talking: his voice wove up and down in pitch and volume, like a master storyteller's.

". . . So we's got this bag of mines, now, see. And Hayden sez, 'Let's take 'em and blow those icebergs!' So there we are weaving our way in and out of the rest of the mines, voom voom, and we're in the clouds. And sure as itches, there's this great awful wall of ice comes at us out of the mist. Got this little tiny neck holding it to the wall of the world and Hayden sez, 'Let her rip!' so I do. Boom!—ow! Oh, that smarts."

"In my report," came the surgeon's dry voice, "I shall state that Master Martor died of an excess of *hand gestures*."

"Yeah," somebody shouted over the laughter, "tone down the jumping about, boy. I want to hear how this ends."

Hayden paused at the doorway, uncertain of whether to go in. He didn't like that Martor had been talking about him, although that might explain why the hatch gang had been so polite just now.

Suddenly worried about what the boy had been saying, he tapped the man in the doorway on the shoulder. "Well, here he is, the man hisself," said the airman as he shifted to let Hayden past. He glided into the sick bay and grabbed the back of a cot to stop himself.

Wounded men tiled the floor, walls, and ceiling of the place. Nearly all of them were awake and apparently listening to Martor, who had pride of place, propped like some parody of a doorman by the entrance to the surgery.

"Hayden, I was just telling the guys how we blew the icebergs and saved the fleet!" Martor's ferretlike face was twisted into a quite uncharacteristic smile. "The pirates flew right into 'em, blam blam blam!" He laughed and immediately winced. "And then," he said to the general crowd, "he sez, 'Now let's go back and save the *Rook*!' Just the two of us, can you imagine? But he—"

"I did no such thing," Hayden said sternly. "I wanted to get the hell out of there."

"But *Hayden*," stage-whispered Martor. His eyes darted at the listening men. "Tell 'em how we attacked the pirates, huh?"

Hayden crossed his arms and gave his best adult's frown at Martor. "I don't remember us attacking the pirates, because after we saw that the *Rook* had been taken, this little snake rapped me over the head with a rocket when I tried to fly him away to safety."

He couldn't have said what he expected, but Hayden was vastly surprised as the assembled men broke into peals of laughter.

Someone clapped him on the shoulder. "Ah, Martor, I wondered just how far your lying instinct would take you this time," said one of the officers. "Too bad you had a witness this time."

"But it's true about the icebergs," Hayden said quietly. "At least— we did blow them. I can't vouch for whatever else he might have worked into the tale."

"Like the emergency stop at the whorehouse?" someone asked.

"Or the sword fight with the hundred pirates on bikes?"

"Or the—"

"I never said that stuff!" Martor tried to get out of his bed, grimaced, and let the elastic sheet flatten him back against the wall.

"This has gone too far!" shouted the surgeon. "The lad really is going to bust a kidney if you all keep this up. Out! Out! That goes for you too," he said, waggling a finger at Hayden.

Hayden couldn't suppress his grin. "Since I know you're not dead, I'll be on my way," he said to Martor. "But no more lies about me, you hear?"

"Yes, sir," said the boy sullenly.

Hayden headed for Aubri Mahallan's little workshop. All around him the ship was abuzz with talk. He knew this, he'd seen it before after the few one-sided fights he'd been in when he was a pirate himself. The trauma of the battle and captivity had to be exorcized somehow; there were some fights, the settling of scores, but mostly, the airmen were exchanging their stories. In the process they were building a whole mythology around the battle.

It seemed that Hayden had unwittingly placed himself at the heart of the myth.

He nodded at another airman who had casually saluted him on the way past, and knocked on the door to Mahallan's wooden cube. There was no answer.

Was she hiding? Hayden hadn't talked to her since the battle. He had only seen her, looking starkly grim and pale, her hair a rat's-nest and her fingernails chewed to the quick. She had avoided his eyes. He was worried about what might have been done to her by the pirates, but so far that part of the incident had not been worked into any shipboard stories.

"She ain't there," said the airman who had saluted him. Hayden turned, eyebrow raised.

"Up at the bow, talking to the lady," said the airman. Venera Fanning was another hero of the day; her quick thinking in palming Captain Sembry's key when the pirates burst into the bridge and killed everyone had ultimately saved the Rook. A craftsman was apparently on the bridge right now, delicately teasing the broken key out of the lock to the scuttling panel.

"Lucky thing the admiral gave a good account of himself in the fight," someone had said earlier, "else we'd all be saluting his wife instead of him."

"Well go on," said the airman now. "They'll be wanting you anyway. We're arriving at that weird tourist city, and Mrs. Fanning wants to visit it."

ADMIRAL CHAISON FANNING felt very small in this place. He didn't like the sensation at all.

The tourist "station" was really a city that dwarfed any place he'd seen—or even heard of—in Virga. It spread for miles across the ceiling of Virga, a glittering chandelier of towers like fiery icicles, globular dwellings hanging from long tethers, and vast spinning cylinders, each one three or four times the size of the towns of Rush. It was to the axis of one of these cylinders that the Rook had gone, under Aubri Mahallan's instruction. Now Chaison walked the streets of a city that seemed more delirium dream than reality.

Some cunning of artifice had hidden the shape of the town; it didn't appear to be rolled up and spun, as it really was. Above Chaison was an endless sky of blue, and the city's confectionary towers were laid out on a seemingly flat surface. The streets converged in perspective until they blurred into the hectic detail of buildings, people, and floating unrecognizable glowing things. Signs, some of those—but more were mobile, and some, he'd noticed, could speak.

The people were just as bizarre. They were dressed—when dressed at all—in sloppy imitations of Virga's fashions. They came in all sizes and skin tones, including unlikely shades like blue and vermillion. They crowded the streets in their millions, gabbling and waving their hands at faint squares of flickering light that buzzed around their heads like bees. Images flashed across these squares like heat lightning and everywhere there was a chaos of noise.

He and Venera had to hurry to keep up with Aubri Mahallan, who stalked through the crowd with her head down and her shoulders hunched. The strange gatekeeper who had met the Rook at the docks had insisted that no more than two natives accompany her. "Take no pictures," he had said in a sibilant accent while smaller versions of himself—identical right down to the clothes—perched on his shoulder or ran laughing down the hall behind him. "Take no items, leave anything you want."

"We've come to recover a work of art loaned to one of your museums two hundred years ago," Venera had said. "It's ours, not yours."

He'd raised an eyebrow while one of his smaller selves stuck out its tongue. "Take it up with the museum," he'd said. "Not my area of concern."

Chaison quickened his pace until he was walking abreast of Mahallan. She still looked drawn and grim. He cast about for something to say, finally deciding to directly confront her most likely complaint. "I had to let the pirates go," he said. "We might have reneged on our bargain and blown them up as they left, but then they might have gotten a rocket or two into the Rook at the same time."

After a few moments she looked over at him, an expression of distaste on her face.

"Is that why?" she asked. "Because you were afraid they'd blow up the Rook?"

"It's a sufficient reason," he said. "But no, that's not all. We did make an agreement. And while my entire crew and all of my officers howled for revenge, I am bound as a gentleman to keep my word. Even more importantly than that, I just had no desire to cause any more deaths this week."

Mahallan mulled this over, but the dark expression on her face had not lifted. "Are you happy to be back among your own people?" he asked her.

"No."

The silence drew out. Clearly companionable solicitations were not going to work. "Well, you've seen the ships of the fleet in a real engagement," he said after a while. "If your opinion about the usefulness of your devices has changed at all, I hope you'll tell me."

Mahallan glared at him. "Is that all it was to you? An 'engagement'? Something to be picked apart afterward, analyzed and stuffed for future consideration?"

Her anger didn't impress Chaison. "As a matter of fact, it's a requirement of my position that I view it that way. Why? Because understanding everything that happened is the only way that I can hope to save more lives next time we're forced to fight. And saving lives is my job, Lady Mahallan. I bend every effort to achieve military objectives with the least possible loss of life. That is why we are in this city, walking these streets, isn't it?"

She stopped and pointed down a shadowed and empty side street. "There. The entrance to the Museum of Virgan Culture's storage depot." Then she took off down the narrow way at a renewed pace.

"I—I'm sorry you had to be part of that, Ms. Mahallan," he said before she could get out of earshot. "The incident has been hard on us all."

"Don't bother," said Venera cheerfully as she took him by the arm and sauntered after Mahallan. "She's bitter. People enjoy being bitter. It gives them license to act childishly."

"Aren't you the philosopher," he said with a laugh. "Are you unscathed by, ah, recent events?"

"I wouldn't say that," she said, glancing down.

"Dentius didn't touch you, did he? I know you told me not when we were negotiating with him, but you knew I'd have run him through if I thought he had."

She looked him in the eye. "He didn't lay a finger on me."

"I didn't want you to come," he said. "Things like this happen. This is no society outing, Venera."

"I coped."

At the end of the street was a reassuringly real-looking door. Mahallan was waiting impatiently for them in the shadows.

"Admiral and Lady Fanning, this is Maximilian Thrace, the curator of the museum," she said in a voice that had suddenly gone sweet.

Beside her hovered a ghost. That, at least, was Chaison's impression of the apparition; he could see right through it. Thrace bore many resemblances to a human being, but there was no color to him, only stark white and shades of gray. His head was disproportionately large and he had huge eyes. "Max is a Chinese Room persona from a very old and respected game-church," Mahallan whispered. Chaison nodded politely.

He bowed to the vision. As he was straightening, Venera said, "We've come to recover an artifact you've had on display here for a long time. It's called the . . ." She turned to Chaison, one eyebrow eloquently raised.

"*The Winding Tree of Fate,*" he said with a smile. "It's important to a small but influential group of artists in Slipstream, our home. Our documents show that it was placed on loan here, two centuries ago."

Thrace's frown was magnificently overdone, a great downturning of the mouth that distorted his whole jaw. "You wish us to return all representations, versions, models, simulations, and copies of the piece? That could be difficult, it will require viral legislation that could take months—" Mahallan was shaking her head.

"We just want the original."

Thrace's eyes narrowed ever so slightly. "The what?"

"The artwork itself," said Venera. "The item that your, ah, copies are based on."

"That's why we asked to meet you here," added Mahallan, "at the storage depot."

"You just want the original? Nothing more?" Thrace looked tremendously amused. "You could have just sent us a . . . what do you call them? A letter. We'd have mailed it back to you!" He turned and gestured, and the door in the wall opened by itself. Chaison jumped at this, but nobody seemed to notice.

As Maximilian Thrace drifted into the dark hallway revealed by the open door, he said, "Space is expensive here. It would have cost us less to send it back to you than to continue to store it. We could even have hired escorts if you wanted."

Chaison stopped walking. Thrace's ghost continued on; Venera had given him her arm, so apparently he had some solidity although his tiny feet waved impotently some inches above the floor. Chaison shook his head and looked away. There was nothing else in this long narrow corridor to look at, except Aubri Mahallan, who had paused to look back at him.

"Did you know this?" he asked her. She looked apologetic.

"I doubt he's telling the truth about the escort," she said, falling back to walk beside him. "I knew they would ship it to us if we asked. But we'd have had to send a courier ship here to do that, and then wait . . . time was tight. It didn't seem practical."

"In the future," he said tightly, "please allow me to make such judgements."

"Sorry."

Civilians! He hated them as a species. Chaison trudged along, thinking about the lives lost in getting here. They were all ultimately his responsibility. But it was an awful thing to make choices in ignorance of potential alternatives.

Mahallan seemed to just be realizing her mistake. "Listen, if I had known—"

"What is he?" Chaison gestured at the wraith who was walking and laughing with his wife. "Is he a real person?"

"Ah." Mahallan shrugged awkwardly. "Define 'real.' Max is a Chinese Room persona, which makes him as real as you or I." She saw his uncomprehending stare, and said, "There are many game-churches where the members of the congregation each take on the role of one component of a theoretical person's nervous system—I might be the vagus nerve, or some tiny neuron buried in the amygdala. My responsibility during my shift is to tap out my assigned rhythm on a networked finger-drum, depending on what rhythms and sounds are transmitted to me by my neural neighbors, who could be on the other side of the planet for all I—" She saw that his expression hadn't changed. "Anyway, all of the actions of all the congregation make a one-to-one model of a complete nervous system . . . a human brain, usually, though there are dog and cat churches, and even attempts at constructing trans-human godly beings. The signals all converge and are integrated in an artificial body. Max's body looks odd to you because his church is a manga church, not a human one, but there's people walking around on the street you'd never know were church-made."

Chaison shook his head. "So this Thrace is . . . a fake person?"

Aubri looked horrified. "Listen, Admiral, you must never say such a thing! He's real. Of course he's real. And you have to understand, the game-churches are an incredibly important part of our culture. They're an attempt to answer the ultimate questions: what is a person? Where does the soul lie? What is our responsibility to other people? You're not just tapping on a drum, you're helping to give rise to the moment-by-moment consciousness of a real person. . . . To let down that responsibility could literally be murder."

He looked at her sidelong. "You seem awfully passionate about this for a voluntary exile. Did you belong to one of these churches before you came here?"

"Oh!" She looked like someone who had just realized that she'd said too much. "No, it's just that—"

"They told me you were here!" said a voice behind them.

Chaison turned quickly, hand going to his waist where his sword should be—but wasn't. An ordinary-looking man of medium height and age had come up behind them as they talked. His accent had not been like Aubri's, Chaison realized. He had sounded like he was from Virga.

"Aubri Mahallan," he said now, arching one eyebrow. "What could you possibly be doing back at the station?" She shrank back.

Stepping between them, Chaison said, "And you are . . . ?"

"Aston Shen," he said, holding out his hand for Chaison to shake. "Virgan home guard."

"Home guard?"

"You've never heard of us? Good! Then we're doing our job." Shen smiled at Chaison's expression. "There are always some people of every generation who become curious about the outside world, you know. A few hundred find their way here every year. Some emigrate and never return. But some of us . . . find a higher calling. The home guard exists to protect Virga from outside influences. We try to ensure that no bad elements enter our world." Deliberately, he looked past Chaison at Mahallan. "And when they do . . ." He eased past Chaison. "So, Aubri, what have you been up to?" he asked. She shrugged.

"Just living my life, Aston. As best I can, now that I'm here."

"So? And the purpose of your business in the station?"

Chaison interposed himself again. "She is here on my business. We needed a native guide. I'd kindly ask you not to interfere."

Shen held his hands up solicitously. "Wouldn't think of it, old man. As long as you know to be careful with this one. She's not to be trusted."

"Oh really? I—" They were interrupted again as Venera returned carrying something. She held it up triumphantly and beamed at Chaison.

"We got it!" The thing appeared to be an intricate branch with extremely tiny leaves, if those finest bifurcations were leaves at all. Jewels glinted here and there inside its tangles.

"I'll expect delivery of the paintings tonight, then?" Thrace was saying to her. Venera nodded vigorously. "Come dear, we should get back." She noticed Shen. "Well, hello."

"Ma'am." Shen turned back to Mahallan. "We'll do a full-pass sweep of you and your companions before you're allowed to leave. I thought it polite to let you know." Seeing Chaison's expression, he smiled and bowed. "You won't even know it's happening. Just re-member," he said to Mahallan, "we're watching you." He walked away.

Venera watched him go. "What an unpleasant person," she said. She had that appraising look that Chaison had learned meant that her instincts for paranoid intrigue had been triggered. "Let's get out of this place," she said to him as she smiled again at Thrace.

As they walked back to the ship Chaison tried to sort out every-thing he'd just seen and experienced. But he was tired, and Venera's excitement just too infectious. By the time they reached the *Rook*, he had forgotten Mahallan's explanation of her people's churches, and couldn't bring himself to speculate about the Virga home guard or Shen's cryptic warnings.

None of it mattered anyway. They had the map they had come to find.

14

THE SCENE WAS an eery repeat of Dentius's call to execution, only now it was Chaison Fanning who perched atop the T-bar and addressed all six of the ships. The vessels were temporarily lashed together into a loose star formation. Their crews sat or stood on their hulls, dark silhouettes casting long shadows from the spot-lights that lit Fanning.

The admiral gestured with his bullhorn. "We are a long way from home. We have gone through the trials and tribulations of a minor war, and yet I have not told you why.

"Now, I will tell you why."

A murmur went through the assembly. Hayden Griffin, who sat astride his bike comfortably invisible in the dark air, strained to hear what the crewmen were saying. Resentment battled respect among them, he knew. Fanning was known to have fought gallantly against the pirates, but then he had also let Dentius and his men escape. There were airmen listening now who would always bear the scars of Dentius's torturer.

This had better be good, Hayden thought, knowing that the same thought must be going through everybody else's minds as well.

"Before I explain our mission in full," said the admiral, "I'm going to tell you a story." He held up a hand, face slightly turned away. "This is no cocktail-party anecdote, designed to soften up an audience.

I know you're exhausted. This story is vital to your understanding our purpose. It's a story that concerns pirates, in fact.

"Two hundred years ago, winter was not the quiet place that it is today." If he expected a laugh at this point, Fanning didn't get it. "We've tangled with a modern pirate armada. But Dentius's force is nothing compared to the old ones. Once, pirate navies fought their way into the heart of civilized nations. They plundered suns. Their blades reached all the way to the precincts of Candesce itself. And the greatest of the pirates of that age was Emile Anetene.

"Anetene was a fop. He was an educated man, with refined tastes. Such men become the most savage of killers, and Anetene was the finest at it. He plundered the principalities of Candesce; he terrorized Slipstream's borders; and eventually, he inspired the wrath of the whole world, so that a vast navy was assembled, comprising ships from most of the worlds of Virga. And they hunted him down.

"Now, you might think that it was Anetene's depredations that caused the nations to finally react so. Most people think so; we in the government have always encouraged the impression that it was out of compassion for our set-upon citizens that we hunted Anetene down. But that's not true.

"Anetene stole one particular thing—a small, seemingly insignificant object. When the heads of Virga's states found out—particularly the principalities of Candesce—they acted instantly. No amount of rapine and slaughter could have galvanized them to do so. One theft did."

Fanning paused. The men were silent now, confused but also curious. The admiral looked away into the darkness, appearing to gather his thoughts. His expression was serious.

"This expedition was undertaken after certain facts came to the admiralty's attention," he said. "We knew all about the threat from Mavery, and you and I know that this threat was never great. We were always able to defend ourselves against the likes of them. But let me ask you something. Their rocket attack on Rush—the one that so surprised us all, and that precipitated the Pilot's order to send out the fleet . . . many of you were there. You are military men. Did that attack *make any sense to you?*"

Fanning nodded, as though to himself, and said, "That attack was a deliberate provocation. It was designed to draw us out. But why would Mavery do that? —When we were sure to make mince-meat of their navy in the ensuing battle?"

Now the murmurs started again. "Somebody's with 'em!" someone shouted.

"Exactly. They've got allies. To be precise, they have *one* ally that intends to join them to crush Sliptream. That ally is Falcon Formation."

Shouts of anger and dismay met this news. Hayden nodded to himself. He remembered now the photographs he had seen in Venera Fanning's hand. A fleet being commissioned.

"Sliptream's very existence is threatened!" shouted Fanning. Hayden leaned forward, his mouth dry. For years he had dreamed of hearing such news—but that it should be the Formation . . .

"Falcon Formation is our most powerful neighbor," said the admiral. "We've had little to do with them because our long journey of exile has taken us on a tangent course. It's a good thing we never attracted their attention before, even when we were conquering their neighbor Aerie. The Formation is a dark bureaucracy, a super-Confucianist state ruled by a hereditary caste of bloodless clerks. They are fanatics who are determined to one day rule over all of Virga. And they have decided that Sliptream is a prize worthy of their ambitions.

"We might be able to hold off an invasion by the existing Formation fleet. I beseeched the Pilot not to fall for Mavery's diversion. We would need all our ships to thwart an attack by the Formation. But a month ago we learned that Falcon Formation is building a new weapon that they are going to use to crush us."

As Fanning told the men about the Formation's secret shipyard and the dreadnought being built there, Hayden found himself wracked with conflicting emotions. The prospect of Slipstream being conquered was exhilarating. On the other hand, if Falcon Formation moved in on the conquered territories of Aerie, they would never give them up. Aerie's people would be assimilated into the cold dictatorship of that notorious bureaucracy, and Aerie itself would be erased from the history of Virga.

". . . No allies will come to our aid," Fanning was saying. "Therefore, we need a miracle. You, men, are here in winter to provide that miracle.

"The stories they'll tell about you! Each and every one of you will be entered into the roster of Slipstream heroes when our journey is done. For we are on our way to destroy the navy of Falcon Formation!"

A stunned silence greeted these words. Fanning looked around slyly. "Is he mad? That's what you're wondering. How are six ships—and the ghost of a seventh whom we will never forget—how will such a tiny force prevail against the hundred cruisers and carriers of Falcon?

"I will tell you how.

"There exists a weapon that will give us an unassailable tactical advantage over Falcon's ships. It will allow us to maneuver in darkness and fog as though we were in clear and empty air. It will let us fly and bank and turn in utter darkness at two hundred miles an hour, all the while keeping Falcon Formation's ships centered in our crosshairs. We have come to winter to acquire that weapon!"

A babble of protests, shouts of delight, and heated arguments wafted through the dark. Fanning gestured for silence. "Please! I've heard all the objections before. If such a weapon existed, why isn't it being used? Why doesn't Falcon Formation have it?

"The reason," he said more quietly, "has to do with Candesce.

The Sun of Suns emits radiation that interferes with certain types of machine. Radar is one of the devices that won't work within Virga—though it works everywhere else in the universe. Anybody can build a radar set, it's just an electrical device. You've all seen electricity, we use it for lighting and electrolysis. But getting anything but noise' out of a radar set, that's another matter, here in Virga.

"But there is a way to make electrical devices work cleanly. The secret was lost two hundred years ago—stolen from the flagship of one of the principalities of Candesce by one of the most legendary figures in history."

Fanning laughed. "Yes. We come back to Emile Anetene. His story is almost mythological—indeed, it wasn't until we visited the tourist city and I saw the map with my own eyes, that I allowed myself to really believe that the legend of the treasure of Anetene is true."

Hayden had to smile at the muted reaction to this. The men had heard too much that was unbelievable already. One more preposterous notion piled on top of the rest made little difference.

That is, it didn't at first. Fanning explained how Emile Anetene had stolen something—a key, though to what he didn't say—and hidden it with the rest of his hoard. He then died in a hail of rockets, cornered by the allied navies of Candesce. Almost from the first there were rumors about the hoard. No one had plundered it, the legend went, because Anetene had left the only map with one of his women—and she had hidden it somewhere no one would ever find it.

"We found the map," said Fanning. "We have it. Within the week, you will be plundering Anetene's hoard." He laughed again briefly. "At this point, you needn't believe my story. Just lend me seven days of service, and we'll all know for sure if the legend is true. And if it is . . . then the treasure is yours."

"Now that's more like it!" yelled an airman with a broken arm. The others laughed.

"We will return with the treasure and working radar. We will demolish Falcon Formation's secret shipyard and anybody else who gets in our way. We will save Slipstream and you will return to your homes rich as Pilots.

"Anybody object to that?"

HAYDEN SPUN UP the bike and drifted it to the Rook's open hangar doors. Fanning continued to field questions, though he wouldn't answer any more about how this radar thing was going to work. Many of the men considered his story a ridiculous fabrication, but they agreed that giving him a week to prove it was fair.

Having worked with Aubri Mahallan to build the radar units, Hayden already believed.

After securing his bike he sought her out. The two of them still hadn't spoken properly, and he intended to find out why. Her workshop's door was tightly closed, so he rapped on it smartly. He waited, and when she didn't answer, he rapped again.

"I can keep doing this," he said loudly.

There was a long pause, then the door flew back. Aubri was braced just inside. Her eyes were red. "What?" she snapped.

"Can I come in?"

Silently, and with obvious reluctance, she drew back to allow him to enter. Her workshop was a shambles. The pirates had evidently ransacked it, but surprisingly little was actually broken—or not so surprisingly, he remembered now. Pirates had so little of their own that they prized, rather than destroyed, whatever they could steal of others'.

"I just wanted to see whether you were all right," he said after a long and awkward silence. Aubri shrugged, and finally nodded.

"Why did you come back after the battle?" she said in a subdued voice. "To make sure you were right? —About the Rook being taken?"

"I was hoping it wasn't."

"Or maybe you didn't come back at all," she continued. She wasn't watching him, but was nervously organizing the debris in the room. "Maybe you were on your way to the station when Martor figured out you'd abandoned us all. And that's why he knocked you out."

Anxious, but unwilling to back out now, Hayden shrugged. "Think what you will. I wasn't wrong, was I? The *Rook* lost the battle. The ship was boarded. If it hadn't been for Venera's quick thinking . . ."

"She's as savage as the pirates," said Aubri with a rueful smile. "I've never seen such ugliness as I saw here. Brutality . . . You people are animals."

"I couldn't agree more." She looked at him in surprise. "If the world needed saving it wouldn't be worth doing it," said Hayden. "Everything worthwhile ends up getting stolen by someone evil. You hate the pirates who tried to take the *Rook* and its people? Well, some pirates are so powerful they get to call themselves by other names. Names like 'Pilot of Slipstream.' What's Slipstream if not the biggest pirate armada in the world? So big that they don't capture and plunder ships, but whole nations."

"What are you talking about?"

He sighed. "Do you know anything about the people you're working for?"

Aubri narrowed her eyes, searching his face. "This is some sort of justification for why you wanted to abandon your friends, isn't it? They're bad people, so you're justified in only being in it for yourself, is that it?"

Angry now, he said, "I tried to save you. There's nothing for me out there. I haven't got a future. I just thought it might be worth saving the life of somebody who did have one."

"Then you picked the wrong person to save."

It took a few seconds for her words to register with Hayden. "W-what did you say?"

Aubri sighed heavily. "Listen, I don't need this right now. And I don't need your help at the moment, *assistant*. You know our machines are ready." She put her hand in the center of his chest and pushed. Confused and angry, Hayden let himself sail out the door.

Slew the carpenter had watched his exit and now smiled. "They're all trouble, kid. Take my word for it, that's as good as you're gonna get from her."

"Shut up." But Slew just laughed at him, and Hayden, ears burning, retreated to the hangar again.

FINDING ITSELF IN a stray beam of sunlight from distant Candesce, the capital bug shrugged awake. It unfolded its six legs and stretched them ineffectually into the cold air. There was nothing to grab on to for a hundred miles in any direction, but it didn't care much; it lived on stray flotsam and jetsam and could hibernate for months at a time. The heat of a sun could waken it, though, and as it felt the distant rays of Candesce it spread its diaphanous wings, and began to hum.

"Batten the hatches!" The *Rook's* new boatswain leaped from one side of the vessel to the other, following his own order. The lads in the hangar were hastily dogging the doors as well; but it did little good. The world-shattering drone of the capital bug wormed its way into every nook and cranny of the ship. The crewmen cursed and clapped their hands over their ears, but the buzz seemed to resonate all the more inside their skulls. One by one, across the ship, the windup lantern flames flickered in the choppy air and went out.

Hayden had been asleep on his bedroll in the ship's centrifuge. He was used to all its noises now, and even the thunder from test firings and target practice couldn't wake him. But the sound of the capital bug had him instantly alert.

As he exited the now-shaking wheel he saw Travis's face floating in the solitary illumination of the last opened porthole. "Will you look at that!" said the officer—or at least, those were the words his mouth shaped. Hayden couldn't have heard him from six inches away.

Over the past few days Hayden had discovered that Travis liked or at least respected him. The feeling was mutual; the man didn't treat the presence of civilians on his ship as a threat to his authority. So Hayden didn't worry that he was tempting fate by putting his head next to Travis's and looking out the porthole.

Dots of cloud patterned the air around the capital bug, throwing small lozenges of shadow on the vast, distance-blue curve of its abdomen. That flank was all Hayden could really see at the moment; any details about the rest of the beast faded into darkness or blue to either side. Cruising up and down the vast wall of flesh were flocks of birds or fish, apparently immune to the drone that could kill any man who came too close. Closer to the Rook—only a few miles away—a number of large black spheres turned lazily in the sudden sunlight. These were surrounded by wreaths of yellowish mist and swarming dots.

The buzzing stopped, leaving a ringing silence that was, in its own way, just as painful as the noise.

Travis grinned. "That's a real capital bug, isn't it?" It sounded like he was on the other end of one of the ship's speaking tubes.

Hayden nodded, digging in his ears and then checking his fingertips for blood. "Good thing we weren't any closer," he shouted.

"What're those things?" Travis pointed at the town-sized spheres of black in the middle distance.

"Bug shit," said Hayden. "You don't want to go near it. Great for growing mushrooms, though."

"I can't believe anything that huge could be alive."

"They're mostly empty space. A big balloon, like the world itself I guess. The bugs even have their own forests and lakes and stuff inside them, or so they say."

Travis gave one last wistful look out the porthole, then turned away to attend to his duties. Hayden stayed where he was as up and down the Rook men threw open the rest of the portholes. The heat of Candesce was very faint, but it was sunlight on his face, and its very presence was vastly soothing.

"Don't get too comfortable," said a voice next to him. Hayden turned, blinking, to find Lyle Carrier hovering in the shadows.

"What?"

"I know you think you've made friends in high places," said Carrier, nodding at Travis's retreating feet. "But it's not really that they trust you, you know. They're happy to smile and chat with you because they know I'm watching you."

Hayden scowled at him. "What's that supposed to mean?"

"There's a lot of unanswered questions about you, boy," Carrier said, his mouth pursed in a by now familiar moue of distaste. "And what answers you have given just don't add up. You see," he leaned in close, "I know you're up to something, and Venera knows I know. She has every confidence that I'll find out what it is. So she and your other betters are happy to indulge you for the moment. They know you're well taken care of."

Hayden stared back at him. It had taken him a long time to get Carrier's proper measure. He regretted not sizing the man up properly right at the beginning. Carrier was a killer; but Hayden wasn't afraid of him.

He cocked his head to one side. "You mean you've spent all this time skulking around watching me and formulating hypotheses on your own? And you never once thought to just ask?"

The slightest tremor passed over Carrier's left eyelid. It was enough discomposure to make Hayden smile.

"What are you up to, then?" said Carrier.

"None of your business," snapped Hayden. He turned back to the view.

"So that's the way you want to do it," murmured Carrier. "All right. Later, Griffin."

Hayden didn't hear him leave, but he refused to turn his head to check. For one thing, the sight outside was beautiful: the light from Candesce wasn't fading, if anything it was brightening, and no wonder for that was where the *Rook* and its sister ships were going.

But also, he didn't want Carrier to see his face right now. Carrier would have seen that Hayden knew he was now marked for death. You didn't insult a man like Lyle Carrier and get away with it.

So be it. Right now he needed an enemy he could hate unreservedly. His feelings about Admiral Fanning were too mixed to be satisfying. Carrier . . . that was another matter.

Hayden watched the *Rook*'s sister ships skirting the precincts of the gargantuan capital bug. They set their prows in the direction of the Sun of Suns, and as the air continued to be clear and fortunately lighted, they all opened up their throttles and arrowed toward Candesce.

TWO DAYS LATER, and the way ahead was bathed in perpetual light. First one, then two, then four suns peeked out from behind the perpetual cloudbanks of winter. At first each was little more than an orange smear on the sky, its light diffused and filtered by hundreds of miles of air, water, and dust. Over the hours they sharpened, becoming in time tiny pinpricks of actinic light embedded in discs and arcs of silver and green which were the collective reflection of thousands upon thousands of individual houses, towns, forests, lakes, and farms.

Gridde, the ancient chart-master, emerged from his velvet-lined chamber to hold up prisms to the light of these suns. He examined the miniature rainbows so created and consulted tables in a huge book that he had carried strapped to his back for so long that it had permanently dented the shoulder of his jacket. Then he pointed at each of the suns in turn and said, "The Nation of Tracoune, the Principality of Kester, the March Collective of the Hero Reeve and, er, what was the other damn one . . . that one's the Upstart Break-away Republic of Canso."

The crewmen who had gathered to watch this procedure nod-ded and muttered sagely to one another. Few had heard of any of these nations, and none had heard of all of them. They were halfway around the world from Slipstream and its neighbors. More importantly, these were countries that steered their way through the intermediate airs of Virga, hundreds of miles above the princi-palities of Candesce but hundreds more below the layers flown by Aerie and other familiar places. Between were layers of winter—dark, cold, and choppy air that had proven over the centuries to be unlucky for the founding of nations.

"Gridde told me it's because there's cyclones, jet streams," Martor said later. "Things drift apart too easy. I guess if they didn't there'd be no winter, just suns and countries packed from one end of the world to the other." He smiled wistfully. "Imagine that."

"Hmmpf." For lack of anything better to do, Hayden was polish-ing the racing bike for the tenth time. Now he looked at Martor with a sour expression. "There's too much junk floating around in civilized spaces. You can't take a bike above sixty miles an hour with-out getting somebody's discarded chamber pot in the forehead—or worse, the loose contents of one. Plus there's police every five miles waiting to ticket anybody who opens up their throttle. Far be it that you should rattle the windows of some rich man's house."

"I hadn't thought about it that way," said Martor.

"That's 'cause you haven't got enough bike time in yet. When you own your own someday you'll curse the density of civilized spaces."

Over the next few days Hayden's dim assessment of civilization was confirmed: the expeditionary force made little headway through increasingly populated air. Habitation began on the lowest level with basement spiders who wove long scarves of web that attracted flecks of soil and trash, gradually growing into rafts the size of dinner tables on which myriad other creatures thrived. The webs tangled in the Rook's vanes and had to be swept off with brooms. Birds, fish, and insects, most thumbnail-sized but some big as boats wove and ducked around the mats. As the light of the suns brightened the mats were seen to be festooned with grass and wildflowers. In the distance the watchmen began to spot trees and farms. And everywhere, now, there was ship traffic.

Most of the local suns followed the diurnal rhythm of Candesce, otherwise there would be no darkness here at all. Some renegades did use their own time scales, for historical or political reasons. The result was that the nights here were more glorious than any Hayden had known. The air and clouds deepened to azure tinged with shades of turquoise, mauve, and peach, and in this twilight a thousand town and house beacons glimmered. Hayden overheard Aubri say something about "the stars" as she gazed at the view from the Rook's hangar. He didn't approach her to find out what she meant.

Nor were there any fights or loud arguments among the men. A spell of grace had settled over the ships, all the more precious because they knew it wouldn't last. For a few days they were just airmen, entering strange and wonderful skies.

They didn't approach any of these suns; their destination lay farther in. The six cruisers threaded their way between border beacons, staying in international air as they approached the shell of civilization enshrouding the Sun of Suns. The principalities of

Candesce became visible as a vast haze that curved away to all sides—the misty outline of a bubble hundreds of miles in radius with Candesce at its center.

The man-tended suns of the outlying nations fell behind as Candesce's radiance grew. Here were dense forests like gargantuan heads of broccoli, each dozens of miles in extent. There were equally big lakes, some shaped by scaffolding into lens shapes that focused the light of Candesce into town-sized zones of incandescence for industry or waste control. The air began to smell hot and rich with life.

This was the most ancient part of inhabited Virga. Candesce had been here since the founding of the world, and some of the nations now visible had existed almost as long. The crew traded stories of fabled places and legends, of town wheels made of solid gold and forests as big as nations. The air was speckled with ships in all directions, and now they even spotted flying humans, intrepid individuals using leg-powered wings mounted on their backs, like angels, to travel between towns and houses. Ship traffic became constrained by beacon lanes and the six Slipstream ships dutifully kept within their boundaries.

Finally Gridde emerged from his cell again and went to perch like some ragged black bird on a hangar door. He measured the angles between Candesce and the suns they had passed, and eventually nodded. "Gehellen," he announced, "lies two days' journey that way." He pointed toward a part of the crescent of haze surrounding Candesce that looked to Hayden like any other part. As he folded himself back into the ship Hayden overheard him mutter to Admiral Fanning, "It's there that you'll find Leaf's Choir."

Two days later, the Rook and its sister ships stopped at a border beacon. The beacon itself was a wrought-iron and glass ball forty feet in diameter. Since it was day, its fires were banked, but the air smelled of kerosene for miles around. The lane markers had funneled all ship traffic into a choke-point here; all travelers had to pass near the rocket racks of an ancient, moss-encrusted fortress built of stone in a crude cube shape. Tethered to this were four baroque, heavily carven cruisers flying banners Hayden had never seen before.

As the Slipstream vessels arrived, a squadron of bikes exited the fortress and moved to surround them. The cruisers's engines coughed into life and they began to edge forward, blocking the way. And deep within the shadowed stones of the fortress itself, the noses of rockets slid into view.

"So," said Slew the carpenter, who was sitting with Hayden in the hangar, "welcome to Gehellen."

" . . . LADY AND BARON Castermond." Heads turned to acknowledge the new arrivals. Chaison Fanning bowed, but by now Venera couldn't be bothered. She looked beautiful today, so she could get away with bad behavior. She intended to.

This ballroom was a chamber to equal anything in Rush, constructed of stone and glass, with all the extra spin-up cost that implied; of course, grand reception halls were intended to intimidate. Anybody who thought their purpose more innocent was an idiot.

"You see? I told you all the best people would be here," said Ambassador Richard Reiss. Slipstream's representative in Gehellen was a portly man with a wine-stain birthmark on his cheek. He wore local apparel, with flounces at the wrists and ruffles at the throat. For once Venera Fanning was grateful for the austerity of Slipstream military uniform; her husband looked positively rakish next to the ambassador.

"It's just a shame that your exotic passenger wasn't able to attend," continued Reiss. "What was her name again?"

"Mahallan," said Chaison absently. He tilted his glass to greet someone he didn't know.

"She had . . . research to attend to," said Venera. "This isn't a holiday for us, Ambassador."

"Of course, of course. Nonetheless I'm glad we were able to throw this little soiree at such short notice." Reiss gently cupped

Venera's elbow and led her toward a drinks table. "This evening's festivities could be essential to greasing the wheels of progress. You know, your ships . . ."

He hardly had to remind her. The *Rook* and its sisters were sitting idle at the military shipyard on the other side of Gehellen's capital city of Vogelsburg. They had been there for three days now, ever since the Gehellen navy had escorted them in under watchful guns. Venera couldn't really blame them for being cautious; you didn't just let foreign warships traipse through your territory. Not without giving them every inspection and putting the question to their crews. Chaison should have thought of that before they got here.

Still . . . the delay did have its advantages. Venera's first sight of Vogelsburg had electrified her. She had dreamed of this place.

This was the weightless city she had visited in her sleep so many times—she was sure of it. Vogelsburg's buildings came in all shapes and sizes, but very few spun to provide local gravity. They had confectionary shapes, with many honeycombed sides, frescoes, statues, and minarets that stuck out all over. They looked like the diatoms her oldest brother had once shown her in a microscope. Joined together by ropes and kept apart by their minarets, they jostled in slow motion in the perpetually golden light of distant Candesce, just like in the dream. Vogelsburg's people flitted like birds in their thousands between the shifting structures.

The people themselves made Venera uncomfortable. Only the rich and powerful had regular access to gravity in Gehellen. Even they were much taller than she was used to—spindly and bandy, for the most part, though some of the women achieved a state of ethereal grace whose effect on her husband she didn't fail to notice. The lower classes were instantly recognizable: the servants in this ballroom could barely lift their heads, much less the drinks and canapes they served. They loomed like giant spiders over their betters, appearing uncomfortable and worried.

Venera could understand this dichotomy as the result of a deliberate policy to keep the poor weak. History was rife with examples of aristocracy reserving physical health and power for themselves, after all. What disturbed her was the possibility that this state of inequality might have come about through simple neglect. That would imply a shameful decadence on the part of the principalities of Candesce.

As Reiss grazed over the drinks table, Venera took her husband's arm and leaned in close. "This is a very strange assemblage," she said.

"You've never been here before," muttered Chaison. "So how do you know?"

"It's the mix of people, dear. My father threw a little banquet like this once, for some of the outlying provinces' tax collectors. He brought them all together in one place, sealed the doors, and had them shot from the gallery."

Chaison gazed off into space. "Sounds like your father."

"Anyway, I don't like it. Look around yourself. We're cut off from the ships. All the officers are here. There's guards on the entrances."

He looked askance at her. "But they left us our sabers."

"As if that will help. Oh, mark my words, Chaison, I'm sure there's not going to be some sort of massacre. These people value their architecture far too much to risk chipping it with bullets. But something's not right, I'm sure of it."

"Well," said Chaison. "You keep an eye on things, then. Worry all you like. Meanwhile, I'm going to enjoy the afternoon. These people have done nothing to threaten us."

"That's only because we have six fully armed warships sitting in their port," she whispered. At that point Reiss returned, a tall glass in his hand.

"Look who I just spotted." He nodded in the direction of a stiff-looking older gentleman who stood alone under one of the vast rose windows that dominated the ballroom's end walls. Colored lozenges of light from the stained glass dappled this man's dress uniform, and just now half his face was lit green. "General Harmond is here. I'll have to tell your husband—"

"Oh, I'll tell him myself," said Venera as she headed straight for the military man. Reiss made a surprised "Oh" sound as Venera outpaced him. Stopping in front of the general, she bowed. He instantly snapped to attention.

"General Harmond, isn't it?" she said, eyes wide. "I've heard so much about you."

"Oh?" He looked surprised and wiped his palms on his hips before extending a hand for her to shake. "You're with the Slipstream party. Sorry about locking down your ships like that, it's uh, protocol."

"Oh I'm sure it's necessary," she said, waving a hand to dismiss the whole affair. "Protocol isn't one of my strong points. But I do have my hobbies, General, and I was hoping to meet someone authoritative enough to be able to indulge one of them."

"Oh, indeed? And what hobby might you be talking about?" The poor man looked like he wanted to flirt, but had no idea how.

"Small arms," said Venera brightly. "I have a fascination with rifles, pistols—small bore weapons."

"Really?" He goggled at her.

"I'm also a bit of a history buff," she said. "Wars interest me, and I'm afraid I've not kept up with recent events in this part of the world. I was hoping that you might be able to enlighten me—and fill in some sad gaps in my knowledge of Candesce armaments."

The general preened. "I'd be delighted. Just as long as you don't ask me about any military secrets, you know."

"Oh, I wouldn't know it if I was," she said demurely. "I'll have to trust you to correct me if that happens."

"Hmmf. Well, then. Rifles, you say? Our armorers are unmatched in all of Candesce, if I do say so myself. Take the Matchley forty-five, for instance . . ."

Venera listened intently, while Chaison Fanning wove his way through a maze of courtiers and ingenues, now faintly worried.

THE ROUND WINDOW of the palace's reception hall flashed crescent rainbows for a moment as it rotated up and away. Hayden turned resolutely away from the government town; the Fannings were behind that intricate glass and for once, were not his problem. Now that the bike had been ejected from the wheel's small hangar it drifted under him as he took his bearings.

"The library's over there," said Aubri Mahallan, pointing.

"Yeah yeah."

She held up her hands, palms out. "Just trying to help," she said.

Aubri wore flame-red today, an outfit of silk with harem pants whose long slit sides showed off her legs. Fanning wouldn't allow her to wear anything like this on the *Rook*. Hayden was determined not to let her know he'd noticed.

She was his passenger reluctantly; the Gehellens refused to let any of the *Rook's* military bikes fly through Vogelsburg. In fact, they wouldn't let any of the crew off their ships. Once again, Hayden was benefitting from his ambiguous relationship to the expedition.

He had seen and learned a lot since he joined the *Rook*. It was time to send a report about his experiences back to the Resistance. Once he dropped off Mahallan he planned to find a local post office and draft some sort of letter. The problem lay in deciding what to write.

The bike's fan was whirring, so he leaned back and pumped on the ignition to send a spark into the bike's alcohol burner. It lit with a *whoosh* and the bike reared forward.

"Slow down!" Mahallan snatched at her handlebars.

"It always kicks like that when it starts. Don't worry, I'm not going to drop you."

"I'm more worried that you'll run into something. This place is *dense.*"

"No denser than where I grew up."

There was a momentary silence as they wove their way into the slower traffic of foot-powered wings and propellers that streamed into the disordered jumble of the city. Then Aubri said, "You grew up in Aerie, didn't you?"

"Yes. And Aerie has its cities too. Or, it did—before Admiral Chaison Fanning and his fleet dispersed them and killed or drove out everyone I ever knew."

"He wasn't admiral when Slipstream invaded Aerie," said Mahallan. "I *do* know my history. He was promoted after the conflict ended."

"You've been reading," he sneered.

She held his gaze defiantly, then said, "Talking to the crew. Because you were right to criticize me for not knowing enough about the people I'm working for."

This simple statement knocked most of the wind out of Hayden's sails, but by now he wouldn't back down. "They only told you their side, though," he said, "and haven't told you some things at all. Things like the reason Fanning was promoted. It seems he found a secret Aerie sun we were building and destroyed it, killing all the workers in the process. Some hero!"

"You know about that?" She shook her head. "But you've got the facts wrong. After a few drinks one night the admiral told his officers—I was there—how his promotion came about. He's quite bitter about it. Fanning was against the attack on the Aerie sun—it was the pilot's idea. In fact the pilot insisted on leading the expedition himself and even took potshots with a rifle from the flagship! He treated the whole thing like a sporting event but afterward he

realized his misstep; everyone involved was horrified at the outcome. So since Fanning had gotten in his face about it, he proclaimed
to the upper house that the whole thing had been Fanning's idea.
They promoted Fanning but the promotion came with a reputation
as a butcher. It's hung like a weight around his neck ever since. He
despises the pilot."

Hayden nearly ran them into a forty-foot-wide food net that was
being towed across his path by a flock of tame, feathered barracuda.
As he fumbled with the controls he stammered incoherent curses.
"My mother," he heard himself saying. "He killed my mother. The
pilot ordered my father executed, never saw him again. Killed them."

"*What?*" Mahallan leaned around the curve of the bike, unbalanc-
ing it so that Hayden nearly crashed them again. "Who killed your
mother?"

He shut down the bike, turned, and glared at her. "Fanning. Fanning killed her. I was there, at the new sun, when he came out of the
sky and killed everyone I knew."

She drew back. Angrily he spun up the engine again and opened
up the throttle all the way, dodging them around startled people
and cargo nets. "Don't tell me what happened because I know what
happened," he said even though she wouldn't hear him over the rip
of the wind. "I was there!"

The library, her destination, came up all too quickly. It would be
petty of him to overshoot it, or circle it; reluctantly, Hayden cut the
engine and deployed the bike's parachute.

"Hayden . . . of course I didn't know," she said. "This is the burden you carry everywhere, isn't it? If you'd only told me sooner—"

"It was years ago," he said, trying to pull back from the emotions she had stirred up. "There's nothing to be done—or said, really. Here's your stop."

For a few seconds he was absorbed with judging the final yards
of their approach to the library. This was not so much a building as

a concretion: perhaps it had originally been a box, or pyramid or sphere of wood with ordered rooms inside it. If that were true, there was no way to tell. Over the centuries, individual rooms had been screwed or nailed onto the original structure, jutting out like barnacles. Whole floors were canted onto it and makeshift galleries built to connect them to the whole. Shafts had been dug through existing levels while other municipal buildings that possessed their own logic of construction had been towed over and added to the assembly. The whole bizarre pile rotated by slow increments causing the light from Gehellen's sun to tangle in confusing ways in its interior. People drifted like flies in and out of this migraine-inducing architectural disaster, and smaller flecks drifted too in their thousands: loose books not yet snagged by the haggard and overwhelmed library staff who chased them down in ones and twos using nets on poles.

"So," he said awkwardly, "what do you hope to find here?"

She gazed at him sadly as he grabbed a strand of the big rope cone that framed the library's entrance. "The admiral wants me to research the destination our map points to," she said quietly as she unwound herself from the embrace of the bike. "But all I was really after was distraction."

"Well." He made to turn the bike around. "When would you like me to pick you up?"

"Wait!" Aubri stretched out to put a hand on his arm. "Stay, please. I'd appreciate the company—and the help."

On the way here Hayden had been telling himself that he would leave her here for a few hours while he tried again to contact the Aerie Resistance. He would report the important information that Slipstream was threatened by Falcon Formation. What, though, was the Resistance going to do with that information? Hayden had run through various scenarios in his head as he lay on his bunk listening to the snores of Slew the carpenter. His thoughts had not been reassuring. The Resistance was likely to take the information and try to cut a deal with Falcon; they wouldn't have any faith in this mad venture of the Fannings. Maybe, if Hayden were some sort of hero, he could steal whatever it was that Fanning was after, and bring a radar set or two home with him. Then what? Give them to Falcon? He couldn't see any deal with the Formation that wouldn't seal the fate of Aerie once and for all.

Aubri had seen Hayden's hesitation, and frowning she turned away. "Wait!" He hand-walked up the netting of the entrance funnel to join her.

They drifted into a long cylindrical space with branching entrances leading off to all sides. The entrances were marked by subject matter. Ropes with handhold loops crisscrossed the space and bright lanterns lit the walls, their windup fans gently whirring. Whatever the chaos of its facade, inside at least the library seemed remarkably well organized.

Aubri was watching him sidelong. "Slipstreamers are your mortal enemies, aren't they?" He nodded.

"And all this time you believed it was Admiral Fanning who led the attack on your sun? I can't imagine what it must have been like to be trapped on the Rook with him."

"It was intolerable," he admitted. At that moment Hayden was near having some internal dam burst and he knew it; one more sympathetic word from her and he would blurt out his whole life story like some maudlin teenager. He cast about for a way to change the subject. "Things haven't exactly been easy for you either."

She half-smiled. "Are you referring to the pirates? It was . . . bad, I admit. But that whole incident's over with, isn't it?" Her smile held sadness. "You should be grateful for traumas that have a definite ending to them. Some don't, you know."

"Believe me," he said, "I know." Then he narrowed his eyes. "You did this to me before."

"What?"

"Danced around the subject of why you're unhappy."

"Ah."

He grabbed a rope, and her hand, and stopped them above a square shaft that had the words MUNICIPAL ENGINEERING carved around it. For a long moment he felt her warm fingers wrapped around his; their eyes met. Then she drew her hand away.

He had to say something; what came out was, "I came aboard the Rook planning to kill Admiral Fanning, but you see I never expected to survive doing it. That's what I meant before, when I said I had no future. But when I said that, you suggested you didn't have one either. What did you mean?"

Aubri's expressive face twisted in eloquent distress. "I can't explain. Not in a way that you'd understand."

He crossed his arms and let himself hang in the air before her. "Is it because I'm an 'ignorant savage'? I believe you used that phrase to describe Martor a few days back."

She bit her lip. "It's not that. . . . I don't know how to explain it to you." She looked around, spotted something, and said, "I think we need to go that way."

Hayden thought she was changing the subject again, but as they flew down the hexagonal wood-paneled corridor to the library's history department, Aubri said, "I didn't come to Virga willingly. Not entirely willingly; I wasn't lying when I told you I had studied science and admired your people for their knowledge."

They entered a vast circular room that would not have seemed out of place under gravity—if one ignored the usual crisscross of ropes that various readers were using as perches. Light was provided by bright lanterns which lit the endless ranks of books lining the walls.

"It was my love of ancient arts like manufacturing that got me into trouble," continued Aubri. In this light she looked very beautiful to Hayden, a troubled doll drifting in lamplight. "Along with some others, I tried to overthrow Artificial Nature—locally, at least. We wanted to go back to noble pursuits like industry and construction! Work with our minds and hands again. I confess that . . . entities died. Not humans, you wouldn't understand them, they were surfers, standing waves in the stuff of A.N. Taking down A.N. killed them. As punishment, I was exiled here."

"I understand something about being an exile," said Hayden. Aubri smiled.

"Before I can return I have to fulfil a mission for Artificial Nature," she added with a sudden frown. "It hangs over my head like a sword. If I don't do it . . . I'll die."

"What? They'll send an assassin or something?"

She shook her head. "The assassin is already here, inside my body. It waits and watches. If I don't play my role to its end, it will strike me down."

This revelation was the last thing Hayden had expected from Aubri. He tried to imagine some alien machine coiled in her throat, watching him through the veil of her skin. The thought made his scalp prickle. "So what's this mission?" he asked after a long silence.

"I can't tell you," she said simply. "It might activate."

Confused and upset, he followed her to a cage mounted on one wall. There perched a bored-looking woman with arms like birds' legs, her prehensile foot crooked around a strap while she filed books in various slots in the cage. "Can I help you?" she asked, looking down her nose at Aubri.

"Hello, I'm not from around here. I'm looking for information about Leaf's Choir."

The woman's face brightened. "My, what an interesting accent! Well, welcome to Gehellen. And welcome to the library. Did you know we've been continuously open now for two hundred forty-seven years?"

"That doesn't surprise me at all," said Hayden.

"What about Leaf's Choir?" Aubri asked.

The librarian yawned. "The novels start over there, and wrap halfway around. Children's stories over there. Opera and plays, there."

"What about aereography?"

"Maps? That would be that section there." She pointed to the opposite side of the room. "But you won't find much, comparatively speaking. Leaf's Choir is much more interesting as a story than as a place."

"Why's that?"

"It's just a burnt-out shell now. Nobody can go in very far because of lack of oxygen, and occasional flare-ups. And whatever was in the outer layers was stripped decades ago. Leaf's Choir is a sargasso."

Suddenly Hayden understood. The extra fittings on the *Rook* weren't just for winter travel; they included air tanks and sealant for the portholes. The ship had a furnace but it also had a rock-salt battery for storing heat.

We're going in there, he thought, in sudden wonder.

"It must have quite a history to be the subject of all those novels," said Aubri as she gazed at the stacks. The librarian nodded.

"The original story's as fabulous as the novels," she said. "Once upon a time, two suns burned in the heart of Leaf's Choir. The suns were invisible from outside the nation because they were surrounded by a single, vast forest: millions of weightless trees connecting and reconnecting like the threads of a spiderweb through an intricate network of lakes and rock bits. The forest made a sphere over fifty miles across and within it were dozens of towns and hundreds of villages built out of the living branches of the trees." The librarian shaped the forms with her hands, long shadows cast by the lamps interpreting her gestures on the bookshelves behind her. "The impenetrable barrier of foliage provided protection as well as wealth to the citizens of Leaf's Choir, and they prospered.

"After centuries of peace, rumor began to circulate of the beauty of an heiress from Leaf's Choir, and that rumor attracted the attention of a warlord who determined to have her for himself. He laid siege to Leaf's Choir and was finally able to seize the giant air-pumping stations that kept the forest from supersaturating itself with oxygen. He threatened to blow up the stations unless the young lady was turned over to him. The government refused but the heiress secretly fled the capital and made her way to the warlord's encampment, and there gave herself up.

"To punish the nation, the warlord ordered the pumping stations blown up. Then he left—and behind him, the millions of trees of the forest continued to bask and produce oxygen. Leaf's Choir had cultivated them for centuries, to the point where it needed the artificial circulatory system of the pumps to ensure that oxygen did not build up to dangerous levels within the nation. Without the pumps, the least spark might set off an impossible conflagration—and so it happened, weeks after the warlord left. The fire raged out from the heart of Leaf's Choir and consumed everything, town, tree, and sun. All that was left when it was over was a sphere of charred wood and ash thirty miles across. That sphere is now tethered at the edge of Gehellen's territory; we've been mining it for its charcoal for centuries. It's very slow work because the heat of combustion is still trapped in airless pockets deep inside the sargasso. If oxygen reaches them, they break into flame again; so Leaf's Choir remains choked with stagnant, dead air. We have special ships that can go in, but navigation is a nightmare; it's all just black twisted wreckage that goes on forever. Leaf's Choir is ugly now—like a scar on the sky. Nobody goes there, unless it's for mining."

"That's very sad," said Aubri.

Yet somewhere deep inside it, Hayden mused, was the hidden treasure of the pirate king.

They spent several hours poring over maps of the place. The librarian was very helpful—Hayden and Aubri were a blessed break in her routine, it seemed. They both began to relax in each other's presence again. Hayden couldn't help but be distracted by occasional flashes of thigh or calf when Aubri reached for something; she pretended not to notice him noticing. The time went quickly.

Still, Hayden couldn't stop thinking about the assassin thing she had described. He wondered whether there were some way to pull the monster out of her, or poison or blind it. Aubri spoke no more of it, and he said nothing further about his own troubles. Perhaps out of a mutual need to turn their thoughts away, they focused with great intensity on comparing photos of Venera's map to the various charts. The charts were all centuries out of date. As the librarian had pointed out, the outer shells of the sargasso had been stripped away long ago, and the inner ways were char. It would take a miracle of navigation to find the treasure.

"I wish Gridde were here," Hayden said eventually. "He'd be able to sort all this out." As he said this he realized he'd felt a pang of affection for the crabby old man. Well, why not? Gridde was no soldier, he was just in love with his work. He was an innocent.

Finally they had compiled enough information to satisfy Aubri. "I think we've earned a break," she said. "There should be a restaurant near here, don't you think?"

They followed the librarian's instructions and soon found themselves back in the crowded sky of Vogelsburg. Distant Candesce was cycling into its evening phase, its light reddening slowly. Where the librarian had directed them, the air was so crowded with structures as to be nearly impassable. Blocks and spheres, triangles and loose basket-farms were jammed in together, all jostling for sunlight and air. People sailed every which way, and as they nearly collided they would reach out to push off from one another without rancor or pause. The air was full of the scent of cooking and of waste, as well as shouts and laughs overlaid with the distant, ever-present rumble of buildings grinding together.

Hayden had just spotted the wicker restaurant the librarian had recommended when suddenly Aubri clutched his arm. "Someone's following us," she murmured.

He restrained the urge to turn and look. "Are you sure? How can you tell in this crowd?"

"Because he followed us into the library. I spotted him dawdling in the history room when we were working. He was trying to see the maps, I'm sure of it. Now he's behind us again."

"Well . . ."

"He looks like one of them." He looked at her blankly. "One of the pirates!" she whispered.

Now he did contrive to glance casually behind him. Hayden spotted a shock of yellow hair moving through a swatch of sunlight and felt his scalp prickle with recognition.

"Come on." Hayden led them in a complicated path between buildings, just to see if their tail would keep up. He did, a constant in the churning flow of faces and clothing.

"Okay, forget about lunch. We'd better get back to the bike and tell the others about this." He grabbed a municipal rope to change his course; less gracefully, Aubri followed.

She touched his ankle. "Look, there's a police station. Should we . . . ?" Hayden wasn't inclined to trust the constabulary, but today might be a good time to make an exception. He grunted and they jumped in that direction.

"He's gaining on us."

"Wants to keep us from getting to the station, maybe?" Hayden didn't look around, but redoubled his efforts to get to the building, which was a cube built of stone and rust-streaked iron.

"He's right behind us!"

Hayden looked back, and hissed with shock: he recognized this man. He had been one of the two who had doused the *Rook's* crewmen with kerosene. Now he was only yards back, moving with great easy bounds between the buildings and carefully not looking at Hayden or Aubri.

The police station was just on the other side of a great crumbling apartment held together by rope and stretched burlap—but they weren't going to make it. "Fuck it," said Hayden; he grabbed the corner of the building and stopped himself. Then he reached for his sword.

The pirate dove toward him, but passed a good ten feet away, still looking the other way. "What the—" Hayden and Aubri watched in disbelief as their follower sailed on through empty air; with no ropes to catch and change course, he had only one possible destination.

"I don't believe it," said Aubri as the pirate disappeared into the funnel-shaped entrance of the police station. "What do you suppose that means?"

"I think I know exactly what it means," said Hayden as the entrance suddenly boiled with uniformed officers wearing powerful foot-fins. Somewhere behind the building he heard jets whining into life.

"We've got to get back to the bike!"

Aubri sat perched on the side of the apartment, staring at the cloud of oncoming policemen. "But what's—"

"He's working with them! Aubri, come on!"

"Oh, I think you'll find it's too late for that," said a familiar voice behind them.

Hayden spun around.

Captain Dentius stood on the building, not fifteen feet away. He was flanked by two policemen, and he looked very pleased with himself. "Hello again," he said in his grating voice. "It's always a pleasure to run into former clients . . . especially when you've got unfinished business with them."

"Bastard!" Hayden's anger finally had a focus. It was with something like joy that he drew his sword and leaped at the man, ignoring the policemen.

He spun until he was going feetfirst and nearly managed to put his blade through the captain's throat, but Dentius ducked out of the way at the last moment. The policemen couldn't react before Hayden planted both boots on Dentius's chest and kicked hard. He sailed back to Aubri with extra momentum on his side. "Come on!"

She took his hand and they careened around the corner. Angry shouts followed.

"I can't believe you just did that!" she shouted. A gunshot sounded very close by, and here came the police bikes, a black swarm emerging from behind the police station.

"Take the initiative and you turn bad odds around," laughed Hayden. "First thing they teach you in pirate school!"

"Apparently Dentius skipped that class. Now what do we do?" They were trapped on the plain of the apartment block, with men closing in on all sides. There was just one obvious direction to go; Hayden smashed the wooden filigree of a window with his sword, and Aubri climbed in ahead of him as the police yelled at them to stop.

They found themselves in a strange apartment shaped like the cells of a wasp's nest. Shouts erupted from the half-dressed couple in the nearby bed-nest. Their limbs grotesquely long and curving, they looked like spiders as they reached out for any handy objects to throw at the intruders.

"Sorry!" Hayden and Aubri ducked past as policemen and pirates crammed into the window behind them.

Out in the tubelike hall, Hayden saw doors opening in both

directions. The shouting and shots had alerted the whole building. He and Aubri went as quickly as they could from rope-hold to rope-hold but in seconds all the doors were open, and the citizens of Gehellen poured into the air around them.

16

"THAT'S A PRINT from the second dynastic era of Keppery," said the courtier helpfully, indicating the garish splash of lime-green and beige plastered like an insult on the banquet hall's wall. Venera was about to give some vapid reply (something on the or-der of "it's very nice") when she noticed what was happening near the doors.

"Excuse me." She sought out her husband, who was placidly sipping his fourth glass of wine next to Reiss. Gravity was taking its toll on them both. Venera leaned close and snapped, "They're lock-ing us in."

"Wonderful news, dear," said Reiss obliviously. "The government of Gehellen has agreed to grant shore leave to your shipmates. Why, I believe if we visit the postern window over there we might even be able to see them disembarking."

Chaison was staring over Venera's shoulder with a puzzled expres-sion on his face. "I do believe you're right, dear. And who are those people who just came in?"

Without glancing around, Venera said, "Compact, nondescript faces, no expressions, efficient movements, simple clothing?"

"Why yes, how did you—"

"Father bought a few of those from Falcon Formation, if I recall. They're secret policemen, love, you wouldn't recognize them be-cause of your appalling lack of education in certain areas." She kept the smile on her face—in truth, it was no more false now than it had been ten minutes ago. "We're about to be arrested, I believe, and our men are being herded off the ships."

Ambassador Reiss sputtered. "They can't do—"

"Think of something, fast," hissed Venera as she heard someone with slow confident steps approaching from behind. "Excuse me," said a voice that might have been stamped out of the same press as Carrier's.

Venera looked into Chaison's eyes, and saw something she'd never seen before—he was furious in some silent and calculated way that he'd never shown her. They had been separated during the battle with the pirates but she had heard he'd shot some men from the Rook's hangar. The leader who had done that was not the man she bickered with over dinner, who gave in so easily on domestic matters that it drove her to distraction. She'd hoped to meet that man someday, but under better circumstances.

Chaison Fanning was about to kill someone. Venera realized that it was time for her to get out of his way. She began to step to the side, saw his eyes widen, and felt a hand descend on her shoulder—

—And then a concussion sent her to her knees as stone and glass cascaded over her like water.

She looked up, blinking away dust, to see Chaison leaping over her as though she were a discarded chair in some bar brawl. A familiar roar filled the banquet hall, its presence here such a shocking violation of the order of things that it froze Venera in place for a moment. She whirled, one hand still on the grit-spalled floor, and saw indistinct figures struggling in a tunnel of spiraling dust. The stink of burning kerosene filled the air.

"Come on!" Hayden Griffin reached out of the cloud. His grim face and jacket's torn shoulder blazed into perfect clarity in a shaft of Candesce's light. Just as she moved to take his hand, however, he spun around and the sword in his other hand flashed a blur over her head. Someone screamed in the white opacity of dust that surrounded him.

"Officers to me!" That was Chaison's voice.

A pistol shot startled Venera into standing up. Aubri Mahallan appeared, smoking weapon in her hand. "Sir, it's a trap," Griffin was telling Chaison. "Dentius got here ahead of us. He must have cut a deal with Gehellen for part of the treasure."

"Details later," said Chaison. "Officers, to me! We have to get back to the ships!"

Venera looked up. There was a jagged hole in the wall where the intricate stone and stained-glass rose window had been. "Ah," she said to no one in particular. "But what—?"

Something in the corner was rolling around belching fire and heat and the cloying odor of kerosene. Suddenly Venera realized that it was the black racing bike she had Griffin flying, and everything came together for her.

"You came through the *window?*"

Mahallan grinned tightly. "It was his idea."

A chaos of screaming men and clashing swords surrounded her. Venera was standing at the pivot-point of an actual sword fight, not one of those staged duels from her father's house that ended in a scratched cheek. Men were dying. For some reason she was shaking, which hadn't happened even when she shot the captain of the *Rook*.

"How are we getting out of here?" she asked Mahallan. "Climb out the window and jump off the town? Then we're in the city, I guess we could fly back to the ships . . ." But Mahallan was shaking her head.

"We'd be easy targets in the open air," she said. "We have to get a vehicle."

"There." Venera pointed at the rattling, smoking bike.

"Not sure we can get it up to the window," said Mahallan, "and anyway, it'll only carry three."

Venera pressed her hand. "I'm sure you can hold them off long enough for Chaison and me to escape."

The armorer stared at her. "I'm going to assume that you're joking."

"Sometimes I don't know myself." Just then a wall of Rook officers reared into view out of the dust. They were being forced back by a mass of men pouring in from the opened doors at the far end of the ballroom. The Slipstreamers were already outnumbered three to one and it was just going to get worse.

"This is hopeless!" shouted the handsome one, Travis. His sword was bloody and his hair matted to his forehead. "There's a whole army coming the way we need to go."

"We need to clear that hallway," said Chaison. "Oh, for a rocket."

"How about a jet?" It was Hayden Griffin, appearing again out of the dust. This time his face was in shadow and he looked savage with his sword and ripped leathers.

He ran to the corner and dodged the angry lunges of the downed bike until he could grab its handlebars. Then he was in its saddle, feet skidding across the floor as he tried to manhandle it into submission. "Out of the way!" he screamed. Travis turned, yelled, and grabbed the shoulder of the man next to him. They hit the floor exposing several startled Gehellen swordsmen.

"Aerie!" That wasn't the battle cry Venera had expected but she didn't care—the vision of Griffin opening the throttle all the way and shooting across the ballroom in a shower of sparks would stay with her for the rest of her life. Men flew through the air but the bike continued to accelerate as it crossed the hall. Venera screamed something that was half cheer, half obscenity, and reached for an enemy sword that had fallen at her feet. Travis and the other Rook officers were also screaming as they poured into the breach Griffin had made in the enemy's line.

The building shook to a deep *whoomp!* and a flash of light pierced the corridor down which the bike had shot. Mahallan gave a shriek and Venera thought, *So much for my driver*. But no, when they entered the corridor in a knot of *Rook* officers it was to find Hayden Griffin lying among the soldiers he had knocked aside. He levered himself to his feet as Venera placed the tip of her sword against the throat of an enemy who had the temerity to try to do the same. "Stay there," she said to the man cheerfully.

"Jumped off the bike when it cleared the doors," Griffin was saying to Mahallan. "Come on." He limped ahead. Mahallan just stood there for a moment, hands to her face.

Venera clapped her on the shoulder. "Well, what are you waiting for? Let's kill some men."

To her surprise Mahallan laughed and readied her pistol. "Yes!" They ran after the officers.

The end of the corridor was a mass of flame; the bike's kerosene tank had burst. Behind the flames cursing soldiers waited. Several fired random shots and one of the Slipstreamers went down with a bullet to the neck. Meanwhile Travis was vigorously kicking down the paneled sidewall a few feet from the fire. "This way!"

They piled into what looked like a servants' corridor. Chaison indicated left with his sword. "But that's where the soldiers are coming from!" Venera objected.

"It's the way to the entrance," he said. "I'm not about to end the day with my back to a wall." He ran in that direction without waiting for an answer.

Startled servants jumped out of the way; they were almost comical with their stiltlike legs and frightened looks. Venera felt powerful and alive, galvanized by the knowledge that she was probably going to die here. For the moment, following her husband through shouting and screams, she didn't care.

————

HE ONLY HAD time for quick glances as they ran, but what Hayden saw of the Gehellen's servants' rooms was strange and disturbing. There were pulley systems that people raised gravity-free could use to glide from room to room. They passed one nine-foot man—who couldn't have weighed more than one hundred fifty pounds—dangling helplessly from one of these, weak feet scuffing the floor frantically as he tried to get out of the way. Nobody hurt him. There were lots of rolling carts, crutches and soft seats, and most of the side rooms had big tanks of water in which men and women floated, exhausted, during their infrequent duty breaks.

"It's like a fucking hospital," muttered Travis as they passed a group of servants who cowered on their cots.

Gunfire ripped at them from up ahead. "They've blocked us," said Fanning with no trace of surprise.

Somebody cursed colorfully. Hayden turned to see an elaborately dressed man with a wine-stain birthmark gesturing from a side door. "This way, you fools!"

Fanning raised an eyebrow. "Well, follow the man," he directed.

This man, a dignitary of some sort, had circled around through unknown means and now held open a door to the palace's formal spaces. Hayden found himself in a huge atrium with curving staircases sweeping up to either side. The portraits on the wall were double or triple life-sized. Fanciful beasts were carved into the banister posts. There was distant shouting, but so far no enemy feet had disturbed the deep red pile carpet. "Don't stand there gawking, up, up!" raged the dignitary. As he followed the mob of officers he added, "You might have thought to ask directions from the one man among you who's familiar with the layout of this place."

"Thought you were dead, Reiss," said Fanning with a shrug.

"In there!" Hayden allowed himself to be herded through a stout-framed door in the cavernous upstairs hallway. This brought him into a tall galleried library whose far wall was entirely composed of beveled-glass windows. There was only one other door and immediately some men ran to secure it. "Now where?" Fanning asked Reiss.

While the two talked and gestured, Hayden sought out Aubri. She was standing with Venera Fanning, who looked calm and composed as always. "Are you all right?"

Aubri nodded. "I honestly didn't think that window-crashing thing was going to work."

"I only did it because you didn't tell me not to. You're the technical one! I assumed you'd have said something."

"Oh."

Venera laughed. "You *have* to tell me how all of this came about."

Hayden was distracted by nearby shouting. Fanning was yelling at Reiss. "But we've got to keep moving!"

The ambassador stood his ground. "Admiral, sooner or later, we're going to have to jump off this town. There is no way to get to the docks. This library juts out from the edge of the wheel; it's the best jumping-off point."

"Trapped!" One of the men at the far door waved. "They're coming this way in force."

"This way too!"

"Well, that's just splendid," muttered Fanning.

"Richard, what is going on here?"

All conversation stopped for a moment. Two richly dressed women, unnoticed until now, stood with fans in their hands in the center of the room. When Reiss saw them he blanched (wine stain momentarily fading) and stammered, "L-Lady Dristow, what a surprise! I, I mean—"

The older of the pair strode forward, fan flicking above her robin's-egg-blue bodice. "We came here hoping to have a quiet conversation, Richard. Not to be burst in upon by a covey of hysterical barbarians with swords." She looked down her nose at Admiral Fanning. "You are disturbing the peace, sir."

"Secure the doors," said Fanning. "And tear down those curtains! They might come in handy." Then he turned to the women. "Our apologies, madam. Circumstances have forced us to commandeer your library for a few minutes. I suggest you leave before the shooting starts."

"We will do no such thing!" The matron pointed her fan at the admiral, stabbing it rhythmically at him as she spoke. "Richard, tell this man how out of his depth he is. He does not speak to one such as myself. You must leave this place, sir, not I!"

The crack of a gunshot made Hayden jump. Lady Dristow shrieked as the fan she was holding exploded in a thousand flinders.

Hayden turned. Venera Fanning stood with one hand behind her back, the pistol straight-armed and aimed at Lady Dristow's head. "Shut," she said slowly, "up."

Chaison Fanning seemed to be suppressing a smile. "Reiss, do these women have hostage value?"

"Do these . . . ?" Reiss seemed to have lost the use of his voice. He shook his head, fluttered his hands at the ends of his arms, and then hurried over to take the shredded remains of the fan from the matron's fingers.

"We'll look into that later," said Fanning with a sigh. "For now, put them up top. Build a fort around them using books, it might stop a few bullets."

"What have you done?" squeaked Reiss.

"If we do have to jump, those curtains will have to serve as parachutes," continued the admiral. "I have no desire to tour the city at two hundred miles per hour."

". . . Just like the dream," Venera was muttering, her eyes wide and fixed on nothing.

"What have you *done!*" Reiss's anger had caught like a reluctant engine. He reared back, seeming to grow an inch, and his birthmark flushed deep red. "Twenty years I've been here, serving my country loyally. Letters I've penned to the pilot, all this time—'Gehellen is a natural ally to Slipstream, we should increase trade connections'— slowly gaining these people's confidence and trust. Why, when I arrived they thought everyone outside of Candesce's light was a hopeless barbarian! It took two years just to set up my first cocktail party. And now you come sailing in here with a fleet of ships armed to the teeth, blow a hole in the palace wall and you ask me whether the dowager baroness of Cordia might make a good *hostage?*" He grabbed his hair and yanked it.

Venera shifted her aim and raised an eyebrow at her husband. Fanning pursed his lips and waggled a finger at her.

"Ambassador, if I even suspect that you led us in here in order to prevent us from escaping, I will shoot you myself," said Fanning quietly. Behind him, Travis was leading the matron and her cowering friend up the wrought-iron steps to the gallery.

"Admiral, I am loyal to Slipstream," raged Reiss. "Are you?"

"Unless I complete my mission, there will be no Slipstream," Fanning snapped. These words seemed to penetrate Reiss's fury. He crossed his arms and turned away.

"So, we may have to jump," said the admiral. He strolled over to the glittering windows. "We'd best line up our trajectory, then."

Venera jammed her pistol into the silk sash of her outfit. "You were going to tell me what led up to this," she said to Aubri. Behind her the air was assaulted by the sound of shattering glass as someone knocked out some windowpanes.

Aubri described how they had been followed by what turned out to be one of Dentius's pirates, and then had encountered the man himself. Venera's eyes widened at the mention of the name; Hayden could see muscles tightening under the scar on her jaw.

She didn't hide her disappointment when Hayden told of just missing Dentius's neck with his sword. "You'll have to do better than that next time, Griffin!"

"Aubri saw an open window and dived for it," he continued. "They chased us through the building—we were just a few feet ahead of them at one point." In the pandemonium the building's residents had swarmed out of their rooms, "And we thought we were done for. But they started throwing furniture and cutlery back at the police! They made enough chaos that we were able to get away."

Aubri shrugged. "I guess the people don't like their authorities very much."

"Well," said Venera with a shrug, "if they're deliberately kept without gravity then why would they? Ugh, I don't like the image you're conjuring—like a nest of bugs."

The image was indeed apt, Hayden thought. The residents had stuck out long and warped limbs, had thrown chamber pots and boxes, and cheered when Hayden and Aubri made it out a window on the far side of the place. "This put us in a cavity made by six or seven jammed-together buildings; the police bikes couldn't get in so we were able to jump to another building and escape into a crowded marketplace. From the market we made it back to the library and my bike."

"We knew the reception here was supposed to run into the evening," added Aubri, "and we couldn't get back to the docks because the police were blocking that direction."

"Did you at least do the charting I asked for while you were out?" asked Venera. Both Hayden and Aubri glared at her. "What?"

"The sky's packed with bikes," said an officer who'd stuck his head out the broken window. His hair was all tangled and his eyes were watering from the force of the wind. "They'll pick us off with no problem at all if we jump."

"Please, we have to negotiate!" Reiss was clasping his hands together in distress. "Give them the information they need, Admiral, and we stand a chance of getting home again."

"Unacceptable." Fanning was staring out the window. He

grabbed the man next to him and pointed at something. "Besides," he said, "there may be another way."

He ran over to the downed curtains and crouched atop them, gathering a handful and staring around at the other furnishings of the room. "Colors! I need the right color combination! And I need a man who knows semaphore like his own speech."

Travis leaned over the railing and waved. "I'm your man. What have you got in mind?"

"I can see several of our ships from here—the docks aren't that far away. There's people filing off them now, but I can't tell how many have disembarked. We need to get their attention and signal them. Are you up for it?"

"I'll need a bigger opening than that." Travis strode to the stairs, drawing his pistol. The gallery crossed the windows; methodically, Travis shot the panes out, showering leather armchairs and ancient side tables with glass. The wind from the palace's rotation tore at the leftover edges, growling and hissing like some monster trying to get in.

"Slipstreamers!" The voice came from the main hallway, beyond the barricade of stout tables and bookshelves that Fanning's officers were completing. "This doesn't have to end in bloodshed! You know the information we're after. It's ours by right, just as Leaf's Choir is ours. Give it up and I promise you'll be unharmed. You'll be escorted to the border and freed, along with your ships."

"You see," exclaimed Reiss. "Admiral, these are civilized people. They'll keep their word."

"Civilized people don't lay traps for visitors," said the admiral. "But tell him we're seriously considering his offer. It'll slow them down, and give you something to do." He turned to the others. "I want a salvo out that window. The sound has to carry to the ships, so every available man put his pistol outside."

They began firing, while Travis stood on the gallery overhead, waving makeshift flags as the wind tried to pull him out of the building. Meanwhile Reiss stood by the barricaded door and stammered out a wonderful string of vague promises and apologies; even Fanning had to smile at his tortuous negotiating style. "The man could buy us an hour at this rate," he said.

"Sir, something's happening at the docks." Fanning ran back to the window. "Everybody quiet! Listen." Travis stood stock-still, his hair fluttering in the wind. Faintly, through the constant roar of the air, Hayden could hear a distant, irregular pop-popping sound.

"Gunfire! And some sort of commotion by the ships. I think they're trying to cast off."

At that moment the dowager baroness of Cordia stood up and shrieked, "It's a trick! They're just trying to buy time, you dolts. You're letting them get away."

Venera spun and fired. The baroness fell back with a cry. Then the main door's barricade shuddered under an explosion that knocked paintings off the walls and books out of the shelves. The heavy tables that made up the barricade stepped forward several feet, knocking some of the defenders aside in a spray of smoke and splinters.

Fanning leveled his pistol and fired into the cloud. "Shore that up!" The Gehellens had misjudged the amount of powder it would take to blow the barricade, but next time they were likely to overcompensate. The door was going to open soon no matter what the Slipstreamers did.

"They're moving! The ships are moving!" A cheer went up at this announcement. The door defenders were back on their feet and using up the last of their ammunition to prevent anyone coming through as they shoved the smoking furniture back into the gap. It was too late, though—blades and bullets shot out of the smoke, taking down two of the officers.

Fanning stood on a central table and pointed with his saber. "Cut up those curtains. I want parachutes."

Men were smashing out the remaining panes of glass on the library's lower level. The wind now had free reign and it began sucking up everything—shards of glass, glowering portraits of Gehellen royalty, the buzzing pages of books. Gunfire ripped through both barricades, scattering the men there. Somebody screamed, "They're coming through!"

Suddenly the younger of the two Gehellen women leaped onto the gallery banister, wailing incoherently as she leveled a gun at the people below. The hand of the man left to guard her hung limply through the banister posts. She aimed at something over Hayden's head and fired, the recoil causing her to lose her footing. She fell off the gallery into the chaos of broken furniture and Hayden turned in time to see Travis, clutching his shoulder, stagger into the embrace of the wind and be snatched away by it.

Through the howl of the wind Hayden heard someone yell, "The Tormentor is coming," just as the barricades fell and armed men leapt into the room. Fanning leaped off his table and ran for the windows. "Junior officers first, get ready and line up your jump!" He handed large swatches of torn curtain to the young men then pushed them at the window. That was all Hayden had time to notice before he was faced with a grinning enemy with a sword and had to parry a cut to his throat.

The Gehellens were weak. It took long seconds for the fact to register with Hayden. As he cut and parried he realized that he outmatched his opponent in both strength and speed and that the same was true in the other duels being fought around him. Gravity was a precious commodity here, metered out unwillingly by the upper classes. These soldiers hadn't trained nearly enough in it.

He sent his opponent down with a slice to the ribs and turned to the next one. For a few seconds there was only the narrow world of slash-and-dodge; then someone screamed his name.

Glancing around, he saw Aubri holding one hand out to him.

She stood next to the window with several others; in one hand she clutched a crimson swath of curtain. Hayden cut madly at the man he fought, then dove back to take Aubri's hand. She pulled them both out the window, and the library, the palace, and the royal town of Gehellen swept up and away at awful speed.

17

SNARLING BIKES TRAILED banners of vapor through the city. Chaison Fanning expected bullets to strike him any second; he focused on holding on to the corners of the scarlet curtain that fought to leap out of his hands. This close to a town wheel, there was usually a zone of empty air for safety reasons; if only he didn't lose the sheet he might be able to slow down to a reasonable velocity before he plastered himself against some window in the weightless part of the city.

The riveted iron belly of the royal town wheel receded with alarming speed, but he could see no puffs of smoke to signify that his people were being fired upon. In fact, he heard no shots at all now, just the bikes and the juddering of the wind.

One bike slid across the air toward him. *Here comes the end,* he thought. But as the can-shaped jet closed the last few feet to run parallel with his fall, he saw the Slipstream crest on its side. Its rider leaned over and held out an open palm for him to catch.

Chaison let go of the recalcitrant cloth and grabbed at the offered hand. It took a while to make the catch but before he expected it he was astride the hot metal cylinder, hanging on with white knuckles while he tried to jam his feet into the passenger stirrups.

Everywhere he looked, bikes were picking up falling officers. He even spotted Venera by the color of her clothes as she wrapped her arms around the waist of her rescuer. In the middle distance—between the bikes and the tumbled shapes of the city—six battered cruisers were circling.

He clapped his driver on the shoulder. "The Rook, if you can."

"Yes, sir." The man hunched forward and they took off. "That's a mighty fine dress uniform if I do say so myself."

"One of the things they give you when you get to be admiral," yelled Chaison over the wind.

"Yeah? What else they give you?"

"Headaches!"

With a few seconds to spare, Chaison examined the tactical situation. A navy's worth of bikes, cutters, and strike boats was stitching just beyond the Slipstream ships. And at the naval shipyard, a dozen battleships at least were casting off their moorings. But so far, nobody had fired a shot.

"They're afraid we'll blow up their city," he said. Indeed, the Slipstreamers' rocket racks were all open and aimed, some at the palace.

Chaison began to smile.

The bike dropped him off at the familiar hangar; the hatch gang gawked at him as though he'd returned from the dead as they helped him inside. "Senior officers to the bridge as soon as they arrive," he said to them. "Prepare to get under way."

There was no way everyone had made it back on board. If the fight at the docks had gone the way it had looked, a sizeable knot of Slipstreamers might have been left behind when the ships lifted off. This presented Chaison with a bitter decision, and he considered it unhappily as he hand-walked up to the bridge.

"Admiral on the bridge!" He ignored the jubilant cries of the staffers and strapped himself into the command chair. He was sitting thus, glowering, when the wounded and adrenaline-fired officers began straggling in, laughing and shouting and embracing one another. To his astonishment, Travis was with them, pale and clutching his wounded arm, but otherwise intact.

Trailing them all came Ambassador Reiss, who appeared to be in a state of shock.

"Listen!" Chaison hammered the arm of the chair to get everyone's attention. "We have about one minute to make a major decision. We have a choice now. I understand that some of our men are still at the docks and may be scattered through the city if the bikes didn't get to them in time. We can recover all of them if we take a stand here and threaten to blow up the royal palace of Gehellen."

He had their full attention now. "Now, with luck and a little negotiation, we might then secure an escort to the border and escape this nest of traitors. But during all the talking and threatening, the Gehellens will have plenty of time to deploy their ships to best effect. We will have to give up any hope of reaching Leaf's Choir."

"Then they'll have won!" wailed a junior staffer.

"But we'll have our men."

They looked at one another unhappily. "On the other hand," continued Chaison, "if we abandon the stragglers, we can set a course directly for the Choir. The Gehellens will give chase and there may be a running battle, but at top speed the sargasso is only an hour or two away. Once in it we can hide—and hunt for our objective."

The door opened and Aubri Mahallan entered. Her harem pants had ballooned and ripped in the fall, her hair was a mad tangle, and her eyes were red—but she looked calm as she presented Chaison with a leather folder. "Best guess for the location of the treasure, based on the maps we found in the library," she said.

All eyes were on the folder as Chaison opened it. He noticed that, and half-smiled. "It seems," he said, "that we all know what we have to do. Perhaps later we can repatriate our men by offering the Gehellens some of their treasure back. Anyone here want to pledge a tithe to that purpose?"

Everyone shouted "Aye!" —Everyone, that is, except Richard Reiss, who merely hung his head.

"Good," Chaison said with satisfaction. "Make the same offer to the general crew, and get these ships under way! Maximum speed, use rockets to blow any obstacles out of the way—and prepare to lock down for sargasso running!"

In that small space, the cheer was almost deafening.

HAYDEN HELD THE handles next to a porthole and stared out at the dark. Candesce was fading as the Rook and its sisters lofted past the last pendant towers of the city. The mauve-and-rose-colored sky went on forever, its perfect symmetry broken by the glitter of countless home and town lights. The air was dense with rope highways and navigation beacons, vast and diffuse farm nets and weaving flocks of fish and birds. The ships did not slow down for any of these hazards; in fact, they accelerated into the dimming air, recklessly daring fatal collision with stone, water, or tree. The entire home guard of the Gehellen navy came screaming after them with only a little more caution.

Far in the distance, veiled by evening color, a vast black smudge polluted a full thirty degrees of sky. The sargasso of Leaf's Choir ate all the light shone at it, and cast an indigo shadow across hundreds of miles of air. Minor wars had been fought over the significant zone of winter caused by that shadow; among the principalities of Candesce a significant minority favored the idea of towing Leaf's Choir into a final incineration at the central sun. The majority was horrified at the prospect of smothering the Sun of Suns in that much ash, and predicted dire consequences from prolonged darkness, and as the purified residue fountained back up. Arguments about what to do with the Choir had seesawed for centuries.

No one had ever seriously suggested that the Choir be sent the other way, into the outer volumes of winter. To dispose of the sargasso among barbarians would sully the memory of one of the greatest nations of Candesce.

For all Chaison Fanning's intentions, there was no way that the expeditionary force could reach the Choir in only two hours. Darkness and the crowded air slowed them, forced detours and unpredictable maneuvers. Rockets began to appear from behind, red streaks zipping past in ominous silence as any second now an explosion might convulse the Rook; and yet you could only take so much fear. Hayden watched as long as he could, but eventually drowsed, and dreamed confused half-dreams of Aerie, his parents, and the destruction of their half-built sun.

The impressions stayed with him even as he woke to find someone shaking his shoulder. "Armorer wants you," said a crewman. Hayden grunted his thanks and levered himself away from the window. The thrum of the engines continued; apparently they weren't dead yet. But it was impossible to tell where they were or how long this chase would last.

As he made his way through the ship he saw men sealing portholes and cracks with thick gummy tar. Others were hooking hydrogen peroxide tanks to the engines and checking the air distribution hoses, preparing for sargasso running. There was little conversation, just a muted hum of urgency.

It all seemed reassuring, somehow. Without noticing, he had come to think of the Rook as his home—and it was hardly surprising. Hayden hadn't had a home in many years; certainly the various bug-ridden flats and one-room bachelor's nests he'd slept in hadn't counted. He had been alone for so long that he'd forgotten what it was like to be among friends. But the atmosphere of the Rook reminded him of Gavin Town. Ironic that it was a ship of the enemy.

He passed Martor, who slept strapped to a beam just behind the hangar. The boy looked younger than his fifteen years. A few hours before he had told Hayden about the fight at the Gehellen naval shipyard. The Gehellens had begun offloading the crews along a narrow metal scaffold, a barred cage with troops hanging in the air outside of it. It was a shooting gallery, really, had they all been in it when the shots from the palace had been heard. Luckily there were still men in the ships able to man the rocket racks, and they had blasted the troops who had tried to disengage the cage and sail it away to a nearby blockhouse. Men had spilled into the air and a fierce swordfight erupted. Martor had described this in his usual way, waving his arms and making stabbing motions. But his heart didn't seem in it; he'd known men who had died in this battle and he seemed to be beginning to realize what real death meant.

Hayden turned away from the boy, shaking his head. No—these people weren't the enemy, no matter what their homeland had done to his. Aerie deserved its freedom, and Slipstream as a nation deserved to be knocked down. But the people of Slipstream and the people of Aerie deserved equal respect and consideration. They were only human, even the loyal crewmen of the Slipstream navy whom he now counted as friends.

Somehow, he mused, there must be a way to separate the political from the personal. His bitterness over the past years seemed increasingly to have come from not believing that such a thing was possible.

He passed one other person on his way: the forlorn figure of Richard Reiss curled up next to a porthole, where he watched the skies in mourning for the life of luxury and prestige he had so suddenly lost.

Hayden rapped on the door to Aubri Mahallan's box-shaped workshop. The wooden panel squeaked open an inch, then widened, letting loose a fan of lamplight. He squeezed inside and the silhouetted shape of Aubri shut the door behind him.

And latched it.

"What can I do for you?" He reached out and somehow she had swirled closer and his outstretched fingers slid up her arm and onto her shoulder—which was bare.

He started to snatch his hand back but she held it, and now his fingers strayed onto the smooth soft skin of her pectoral. "You stuck with us through everything," Aubri murmured. "I thought you needed some sort of reward."

With the permission of her fingertips on his wrist, his own fingers slipped further onto the satin slope of her breast. With a simple scissoring motion Aubri reached around his waist with her legs and drew herself to him. His other hand reached down to cup her hip and encountered warm skin.

"Now we must be very, very quiet," she whispered. "Or we'll be the crew's main topic of conversation for days."

"Um," he said; but then she was kissing him, and he was spared having to think of any clever replies.

SPOTLIT BY SMOKING electric torches, men braced themselves in the hangar doors of the ships and waved flags at the dark silhouettes of their sister vessels. The flags fluttered and buzzed in the fearsome headwind, but the messages that flickered across the rushing air were clear and measured. Encoded status reports, inventories, updates to the chart numbers, all flowed steadily between the members of the force, routine and controlled.

—Until one message to the *Rook* caused the duty officer to curse under his breath. Reluctantly, he sent Martor to knock on the admiral's door.

Hayden Griffin was drifting in a timeless haze of pleasure in Aubri Mahallan's arms when the *Rook* shook from some sort of collision. They were both instantly awake. There was another bump and then the grating sound of hull-against-hull contact. Hayden heard shouting.

Aubri's eyes were wide. "We're being boarded!"

He shook his head. "No gunshots. Something's up, though." They both hastily dressed. "Stay here," he said. "It might be the Gehellens after all."

She shuddered. "If we really are being boarded, I'm going out the window this time."

He flipped out the doorway and closed the portal, immediately encountering Martor. "Come on!" shouted the boy. "We're taking on passengers." He bounded back toward the hangar.

The *Rook* and the *Unseen Hand* were lashed together, door to door. The ships bucked and strained against the ropes and wind whined through the gap. Men were leaping between the ships carrying boxes and rockets. The *Rook's* new boatswain yelled and pointed, face red and sweating, as crates and bedrolls bounced and tumbled through the air.

"What's going on?" Hayden asked one of the *Unseen Hand's* crewmen. The man grimaced and waved at his ship.

"Oxygen system's busted. We'll suffocate if we take the *Hand* into that place right now. Admiral ordered us to transfer over to the *Rook*, leave a skeleton crew on board. With fewer people breathing over there, they might stand a chance." He looked around at the crowded interior of the *Rook*. "Where can I strap my bedroll?"

"Martor, take care of him," said Hayden. He headed for the hangar doors, intending to help with the transfer. Glancing forward between the ships, he was startled to see nothing but blackness ahead of them. "Where are we?"

"Hard to say," said one of the hatch gang. "Word is that it's too dark for sighting and we don't know the local navigation beacons. The sargasso could be ten miles away, or we might be about to run into it at full speed."

Hayden spent a few minutes jumping back and forth between the ships carrying supplies—crates of food, coils of rope, and rolls of canvas for the braking sails. He was untying a barrel of hydrogen peroxide near the back of the *Hand* when the shouting in the hold took on a hysterical edge.

"Cast off! Cast off! Just cut it!" Hayden let go of the barrel and bounded up to the *Hand*'s hangar. Men were frantically slashing at the ropes that bound the two ships together. He opened his mouth to ask what he could do to help and was drowned out by the sound of both ships' collision horns going off. "Brace for impact!" someone screamed.

Something like a giant black claw swept through the narrow space between the ships. One crewman who had been jumping the gap was suddenly gone. At the same time, both ships lurched and a series of loud rattling bangs shook the *Hand*.

"We're in the trees!" They had reached Leaf's Choir; apparently the navigators had misjudged the distance after all. More bangs, rattles, and cracks signaled impacts with the charred branches of the former forest. The *Hand* shuddered and began to slow.

The gap between the ships suddenly expanded. Hayden realized he was holding tight to a beam aboard a vessel that had no oxygen supply. Everyone he knew was on board the *Rook*, including Aubri. In seconds they would be separated and he might never see her again.

He spun and put his feet against the beam. Looking up he saw the square of light that was *Rook*'s open hangar door. Men crowded there, but only one was looking in his direction. It was Carrier.

For a moment he and Venera's servant locked gazes. Hayden saw Carrier hesitate—just for a second—and then he extended his hand.

Hayden jumped. For a second he was in turbulent air, surrounded by lashing black branches and the scent of charcoal. Then Carrier had him by the wrist and was pulling him into the *Rook*. The hatch gang cheered.

Carrier let go and turned away. The boatswain pushed Hayden toward the inner door while shouting, "Shut the hatch! Tar it! Stand by for sargasso running."

Hayden looked back as the hatch closed. Carrier had disappeared. Through the closing hatch he could see the lights of the *Unseen Hand* flickering through a chaos of whipping branches. The *Hand* veered away, its light guttered and was lost; then the hatch slammed shut and the gang moved to seal it.

They had reached Leaf's Choir.

MOST OF THE Gehellen vessels fell back to circle the black forest in frustration, but some sargasso-equipped ships continued to follow the Slipstreamers. This made it risky for the *Rook* to slow down—but it was equally risky to continue at speed. The outermost layers of Leaf's Choir had been picked over by charcoal harvesters for centuries, and now consisted mostly of long spearlike trunks, denuded of branches, that wove and curved through the air for hundreds of feet at a time. These spears could puncture the hull of even an armored warship, if struck at high speed.

Each tree had originally been rooted to a small clump of asteroidal dirt. As they grew they wound branches around one another, like swimmers grasping for companions. With no sense of up or down, the trees had used Candesce and the local suns as their targets, sending threadlike stalks and branches through the empty air, spreading nets of leaves to catch light and passing moisture. Gradually, they had formed a vast and diffuse substance that made its own weather, caught drifting dust and stones and assimilated them, and greedily sucked up the carbon dioxide and smoke of the industries that thrived among them. Humans had woven the pliable branches into elaborate structures, entire cities of living green that went on, chamber by beautiful breathing chamber, for miles. Generations of gardeners cultivated their home trees, adding flowers and liana. Giant spheres and rods of water filled the central spaces, cupped by a thousand delicate fronds, in which fish and people swam. The people of Leaf's Choir had cleverly fashioned gigantic mirrors out of water—simply by stretching nets and wetting them until the water clinging to neighboring strands met and merged into a single surface—and used these to reflect the light of Candesce and their own two suns many miles into the forest.

All of it had burned. All was now black and sunless, the air replaced by stagnant smoke that never settled, merely eddied and spiraled around itself in an eternal dance of mourning.

The ships' navigators soon started cracking under the strain of finding their way through this gargantuan, mazelike tomb. They spent hours staring out at the advancing lines of black lit by the ships' headlights. Odd objects would appear in the light and slide by like hallucinations: window lintels, blackened shoes, spoons, and bedposts. The men began to swear they saw figures beckoning to them from the darkness beyond the branches.

And all the while, the Gehellens followed.

Chaison Fanning locked himself in the chart room with Gridde and Aubri Mahallan. They compared photographs of the measureless spaces and distant, branching buttresses of forest growth to the charts Aubri had found in the library. The precious treasure map from the tourist station waited in a glass case beneath the chart table. "It all hinges on finding the city of Carlinth," Gridde said over and over. "Find the city, we can find the rest of the way. If we don't . . ."

There were reports of men collapsing suddenly. Unless the air was kept moving, carbon dioxide, monoxides, and smoke from outside seeped in and pooled. You could put your head into an invisible cloud of death without knowing and just pass out. It was as though some unseen monster stalked the ship. Everybody watched everybody; nobody slept unless their face was near a fan.

Dangerous as it was, some men found themselves obsessively watching out the portholes. Hayden was one. He had no duties since the bikes were useless without oxygen. Though he hungered to be with her, Aubri was busy with the charts. The only way he could feel he was contributing was by maintaining some sense of where they were.

Of course he'd heard of sargassos. They happened whenever a forest became too large and caught fire. Normally, though, a sargasso didn't last long. Air moved through it chasing the smoke away. The charred raft of branches broke up or was taken apart and everything went back to normal. It was terrifying to think that a forest could become so large that its sargasso could never be healed. As he watched he thought about the fact that an entire civilization was entombed here in the dark: the Rook hummed past chalk-white stone house cubes and blackened town wheels where only ghosts now dwelt.

There were hints in the lines and buttresses of the forest that Leaf's Choir had once been a realm of grand sculptured bubbles made up of smaller bubbles, a fractal palace with living walls. At times the perspectives became dizzying. Miles-wide chambers and arches had walls made up of buildings—houses as bricks, towers as pillars, the city as building material. It was almost reassuring that their full extent was no longer visible; the grandeur and the feeling of loss that must go with seeing it would be unbearable.

At times it seemed as though the Rook had entered some other plane of existence. Home, friends, ordinary cares no longer existed. There was only the breathing of the pumps and the distant roar of the engines. Faces were side-lit or merely imagined on silhouetted figures passing between the active workstations of the ship. And maybe this otherworldliness was what caused the crew of the Tormentor to let down their guard.

Hayden didn't see the missile itself. The Tormentor was somewhere out of view on the other side of the Rook. He did see a row of distant house windows, previously black, light up in lurid reds one after another—a quick whipcrack motion from right to left—and then the ghostly network of dead branches was thrown into stark relief by a burst of white light.

The roll of thunder followed moments later.

The illusion of peace was shattered by shouts, warning horns, and furious activity. The porthole suddenly moved away from Hayden as the Rook began to roll over. "Running lights off!" the boatswain was shouting. "Headlight off!"

"What are we doing?" demanded the airman from the Unseen Hand who Hayden had spoken to earlier. "Aren't we going to stand and fight?"

The boatswain shook his head. "Admiral's orders. The others are going to draw them away while we make a run for the treasure. Don't worry. He planned for this."

"He plays fast and loose with our lives," muttered the crewman.

"Right here, right now," replied the boatswain, "caution'll get you killed."

Roars and rumbles could be heard through the hull for many minutes, but the light of battle faded behind quickly, and eventually the relentless silence of Leaf's Choir settled back over the ship—worse than before, if that were possible, because the Rook was barely moving now. The navigator and pilot sat with their noses to the bridge portholes, staring into the darkness until their eyes watered. Occasional thumps on the hull and the sharp snap of breaking branches signaled their mistakes. The ship would shudder at such times and slow, and the fire crew would rush around looking for broken seams, cracks, or punctures—anything that might let in the toxic mix that passed for air in this place. It was fully two hours before the admiral allowed the Rook's headlight to be lit again.

By that time, Hayden was certain they were lost.

———

CHAISON FANNING HAD begun to feel unpleasantly familiar with the back of Gridde's head. The old man had his eye glued to the periscope in the chart room and hadn't moved in ten minutes; Chaison suspected he was asleep. Would that Chaison could be.

He was hiding here, he had to admit. It was just too nerve-wracking to be on the bridge right now. After all, the entire mission—and possibly the future of Slipstream itself—was riding on the events of the next day. Or rather, no, it wasn't the direness of the situation that was keeping his nerves on edge. He'd already fought several battles to get here, and none had affected him like this interminable waiting. No, it was the prospect of being proven a fool that bothered him. In all likelihood there was no pirate treasure; the very phrase was an oxymoron, for pirates were outcasts, the poorest of the poor.

If it turned out that he had betrayed his men's trust by luring them halfway across the world on a bootless quest, Chaison would willingly step out of the *Rook*'s aft hatch without a gas helmet and make Leaf's Choir his tomb. Or give himself up to his men's wrath. It wouldn't matter which at that point.

"There it is!" Gridde had been awake after all. He said nothing else, until Chaison put a hand on his shoulder and said, "What, man? What do you see?"

"It's the city," the old man whispered. "Dead as a forgotten legend. "Your wife's map starts here. From here, I can find our way."

Chaison went to one of the portholes to look out. There had been nothing but relentless black out there for hours now as the *Rook* searched for landmarks in the open central cavity of the Choir. Once, two suns had lit this space, but it had shrunk until it was only fifteen miles across. Cities, farms, and palaces had soared through the luminous air. Now, any light you made was quickly eaten by the permanently drifting smoke.

Impatiently, he bounced over to a speaking tube and said, "I want flares, in all six directions. Air-free white." He waited impatiently by the porthole until the lights stuttered on.

And a ghostly image began to emerge from the frozen billows of smoke and killed air: the bone-white shape of a city, its arcs and curves embedded in shadows of perfect black.

This was Carlinth, once the second-largest city of Leaf's Choir. As Chaison examined it he realized he was looking at one of the legendary architectural forms of the principalities of Candesce. Carlinth was a geared town.

Six town wheels surrounded a seventh like the petals of a flower. Their rims touched and an elaborate scaffolding, shadowed behind them, indicated some fixed connection between them. When they turned, they would have turned in synchrony. You could step off one wheel and onto the rim of another—no cable cars for these people.

Each town wheel was twice the size of any of Rush's. They were crowded with mansions and minarets, and many more free-floating buildings hung in the surrounding dark. But it all looked unreal, like an ivory child's toy, because there was no color at all to the scene. Every object and structure was the same shade of purest white.

Gridde hissed as he squinted through his periscope. "It's ash, sir. Finer than smoke, it's like paint when it settles. The whole place is layered in it."

A shroud, thought Chaison with a shudder.

"But I can see the way," continued the chart master. He held up the long branchlike map Venera had taken from the tourist station. "I can navigate us from here."

The knot in Chaison's stomach began to unwind, just a bit.

The *Rook* slid silently past the dead town wheels. Just as the flares began to gutter Chaison began to catch glimpses of discolored areas on the motionless structures, places where objects had been removed, doors forced, and windows broken. Someone had come here to strip the dead city, but whoever it was had not come in force and hadn't stayed long.

Was it ghosts that had scared them away? Skittering sounds in the darkness, half-glimpsed movement down streets that had once thronged with people? Or was it just the silence, relentless and oppressive, that had made men begin by talking in whispers and end up not speaking at all? —Leaving, abandoning their ambitions of getting rich off the death here; shamed and uneasy, fleeing Leaf's Choir never to return?

Carlinth perched on the tip of a four-mile-long outthrust of foliage. As the beam of the Rook's headlamp grazed this bleached tangle it became clear that the fires had not reached the city. Perhaps through some heroic effort, the citizens of Carlinth had fended off the flames; if so, they had only postponed their fate as the air turned foul and smoke invaded from all directions, sliding under doors and through cracks until eventually everyone succumbed. He could only imagine the tragic tableaux that must still be on display in bedrooms and plazas throughout the city.

The unburnt forest was a porcelain filigree full of infinite detail; but Chaison was tired, and happy to leave the navigation to Gridde. He retired to his tiny cabin on the Rook's wheel to find Venera sprawled diagonally across the bed, snoring. When he tried to move her she awoke, grinned raffishly at him, and drew him down. Their lovemaking was passionate and fierce; all the words that stood between them during the day were erased by moments like this. They reaffirmed their loyalty to one another through caress and kiss, and said nothing.

When he awoke it seemed as though no time had passed. Venera was asleep. At least, he assumed it was sleep, and checked her pulse just in case. You never knew, with the pernicious gases that were lurking about.

The chart room stank of unwashed old man, and Gridde looked deathly ill, but he was still at his post. "Nearly there," he said hoarsely. His right hand clutched the end of a speaking tube and he alternated between sighting along the branchlike map and peering through the periscope. His eyes, when Chaison saw them, were hollow but burning with fierce intensity.

"The map works?" Chaison couldn't keep the surprise out of his voice.

Gridde laughed, a rattle like water through old pipes. "Get up to the bridge, boy. We can't be more than a half-hour away now."

Chaison grinned. He did feel like a boy, responsible to no one but himself. He was hungry—better get a meal sent up. He resisted the urge to laugh out loud. *It's working!*

On the way out of the chart room he paused to glance out the porthole, and gasped.

Color had returned to the world outside the *Rook*.

Here, the forest had not burned. Stifled and enmeshed in darkness, the trees had died slowly. It could be that one of the little suns had continued to burn for a time after the fire, because the myriad leaves now swirling past the *Rook* were all autumnal, like those of a forest that had strayed too far from its sun. They blazed red, shone gold, or were touched with delicate browns and tans. Little clouds of them danced in the vortex caused by the *Rook's* passage. The tunnel of foliage down which they were travelling was dappled in rich hues that burst into view as the headlight caught them, then faded to black as they slid past.

It was a mesmerizing sight; but he couldn't dally.

Chaison made sure he was well groomed and had a confident air as he entered the bridge. The bridge crew looked up blearily, then snapped to attention. "Sound general quarters," he said as he strapped himself into the captain's chair. "I want the excursion teams suited up and ready to go." He thought of sending someone to wake his wife, but an unfamiliar but pleasurable spitefulness stopped him. Let her sleep through the discovery. It would serve her right.

For a while he presided over the rousing of the ship. Ultimately he couldn't resist, though, and returned to a porthole to watch. And so he was one of the first to see it as they rounded a knee of forest that almost blocked the vast autumnal tunnel, and the fabled treasure of Anetene hove into view.

18

THE ANCIENT SHIP hung in the center of a cave of leaves six hundred feet in diameter. In the dancing light of lanterns waved by the gang of red-suited sargasso specialists, Venera could see occasional flashes of the ropes that suspended the old corsair like a fly in a spider's web.

"They're taking too long," she grated. "What's the holdup?"

Her husband rested his hand lightly on her shoulder and peered out the porthole. "They're testing for booby traps, dear. On my orders."

"And then we go over?"

"I go over. To find the box."

"*We* go. This expedition was my idea. The box was my discovery. You can't let me miss out on the final moment."

He sighed. "Have you ever worn a sargasso suit?"

"Have you?"

One of the little figures out there was waving its lantern in a strange pattern. The others were clustered around a dark opening in the side of the ship. The craft was smaller than the *Rook*, and unornamented; but the lines seemed archaic, even to Venera's untrained eye. "What's he doing?" She pointed.

"Signaling the all-clear. Apparently Anetene decided the sargasso was a big enough booby trap all by itself." The little figures began disappearing one by one into the dark hatch. Little glints of light on the hull revealed portholes hidden in shadow around the curve of the ship.

"It'll be there," she said confidently. Either that, or she'd have to find a new home. Rush would no longer be a suitable dwelling once Falcon Formation took over.

Venera tried to pretend that this would be a mere matter of convenience. But she kept imagining herself returning to her father's court with her exiled husband. They would eat him alive, those back-biting courtiers, the kohl-painted ladies with their poisoned hairpins, the gimlet-eyed men with their ready poniards. Chaison would be used as sport by the jaded or the marginalized, and he would have no one to defend him.

It would surely be a personal humiliation for her, if he were killed.

"Well, if it's safe, let's go then," she said, but a commotion from the chart room distracted Chaison. Venera scowled at him as he turned away.

"It's Gridde!" Travis was waving frantically at the admiral. "He's collapsed."

Chaison dove for the doorway. "Was it bad air?"

"I don't think so. Exhaustion, more like."

Venera followed the whole bridge staff back to the map room. This was a tiresome interruption, but she had to be supportive of her husband. She affected a look of concern as she entered the room. The air in here was close, stinking, but then so was the rest of the ship by now. Gridde hung limply in midair, tendrils of white hair haloing his head.

"I got you there," he whispered as Chaison moved to hold him by the shoulders. The old man's face quirked into a half-smile, though his eyes were half-closed. "Rest now."

"Slipstream will survive, because of you," said Chaison.

Gridde's head rose and his eyes focused on the admiral. He managed a weak laugh. "Don't give me platitudes, boy. Just make sure those damn fools in the academy hear about this. I proved it." He began to gasp. "Old ways—better than—gel charts . . ."

"Get the surgeon!" cried Chaison, but it was too late. Gridde shook and sighed, and then went still.

Some of the bridge staff began to weep. Venera crossed her arms impatiently, but there was nothing she could do but wait. The brief agony of military grief would burn itself out in a few minutes and then everyone would get back to work.

They had come too far to let one more death stop them now.

HER BREATH AND the suit pumps roared in Venera's ears. Every few minutes a loud bell sounded and she had to reach down to wind the clockwork mechanism that ran the pumps. She could barely see out the brass helmet's little window. The unfamiliar oil-cloth sack of the suit felt like prison walls against her skin, its chafing creating a subliminal anxiety that fed back with weightlessness and the dark to make her jaw throb.

She didn't care. Venera was in a state of rapture, gazing into the most wondrous place she had ever seen.

The others' bull's-eye lanterns sent visible shafts of blue light up and down, flicking from side to side—each darting motion lifting a cascade of sparkling reflections and refractions from the contents of Anetene's treasure trove.

Venera had seen clouds rub past one another and throw up a cyclone; at either end these looked like tubes full of turbulent snatches of vapor. The interior of the treasure ship was like that—except that here, it wasn't clouds that formed the spiral down which she gazed. It was jewelry, gold coin, faience, and ivory figurines by the thousand.

The nets that had once held the treasure to the walls had decayed over the centuries, and so every week or two a gem or coin would disengage from its neighbors and drift into the ship's central space. Once there, it would be caught up in the almost imperceptible rotation in which everything inside Virga participated. Something to do with orbits and tides, that was all she knew of that. But the vortex had grown and remained stable for centuries, the drift of its objects slower than a minute hand but inexorable. The spiral pattern, so delicate, was now being erased by the blundering passage of treasure seekers.

For the moment, though, garnets, emeralds, and rubies made in the fires of Candesce trailed in lines and arcs through the air. Here and there gleamed dry-amber from sargassos on the other side of the world; chains of diamond like runnels of light flashed in her lantern's beam. The currency of two dozen nations sat fixed in air as though in solid glass (the stamped profiles of pilots and kings layered into shadow like a history lesson) among clouds of platinum and buttons of silver. Beneath the ragged netting the hull was still plated with paintings, skyscapes half-covering formal portraits whose eyes awoke like a sleeping ghost's when her light touched them. One painting, only one, had broken free, and so it was that at the center of the cyclone stood a tall stern man in dark dress, his black eyes those of a contemptuous father gazing accusingly at the looters. Only the gilt frame surrounding him spoiled the illusion of reality. There was a fresh bullet hole in his chest, put there by the first man of Slipstream to enter the ship.

They'd be joking about that startled shot for weeks, she was sure.

Chaison had swam indifferently through the shining constellations and disappeared into the ship's bridge. Venera followed, not without plucking a few choice items from the air on the way.

Chaison's hand-light floated free in the air, slowly turning to illuminate the fixtures of the old-style, cramped bridge. Venera kept expecting to see skeletons, but there was no evidence of violence here; apparently Anetene had been compulsively neat. In the center of the room was a chart pedestal, and clipped to the top of this was an ivory box, its sides inlaid with fantastical scenes out of mythology: men and women under gravity, riding beasts she remembered were called horses. Chaison's hand hovered over the lid of the box.

"Oh, just open it!" Of course he couldn't hear her; even to herself, Venera's voice sounded muffled in the suit. She bounced over to grab the box just as Chaison reached down and flipped back the lid. Both of their lanterns lit the contents through the blue air.

The object was simple, a white cylinder a little longer than her hand with a single black band around its center, and a loop for grasping at one end. It was made of some translucent crystal that made it gather the light mistily. Chaison hesitated again, then grasped the handle and pulled it out.

He leaned his helmet against hers. "The key to Candesce," she heard, the distorted words barely audible through the metal. "Just as the old books described."

"Let's hope it works," she said.

"Candesce still works. Why shouldn't this?" He put it back in the case and closed it. Then he hung there in the air for a while, head down, as if praying.

Puzzled, Venera touched her helmet to his again. "What's wrong?"

Did she imagine the sigh or was it real? "I'm just trying to figure out what to do next," he said. "The Gehellens will be circling Leaf's Choir waiting for us to come out. How are we going to get to Candesce?"

"You're not one to live in the moment, are you?" she said. It was true she hadn't thought that far ahead, herself. Maybe she should have—for he was right, this was a problem.

A wide moat of empty air lay between the principalities of Candesce and the Sun of Suns itself. Venera knew they would have to cross two or three hundred miles of open space to reach the ancient sun. Candesce was so hot that no clouds could persist in this zone, and no living thing nor habitation within a hundred miles. As the battered ships of the expeditionary force crossed this span they would be easy targets for the Gehellen navy.

"If we send the others out as decoys again, and just take the Rook . . ."

His helmet grated against hers as he shook his head. "We'll be seen. Not even a bike could get to Candesce right now."

"We'll have to hide, then. Wait them out."

"But there's another problem," he said. "We're almost out of time."

"What?"

"That dreadnought . . . Based on the progress your photos showed, it'll be ready to fly by now. And in a few days the Slipstream fleet is going to be thoroughly entangled in the fight with Mavery. If Falcon Formation intends to invade Slipstream, they will be amassing their forces as we speak."

Venera scowled at the little box. Their original plan had been to visit Candesce during its night cycle and let Aubri Mahallan work the magic she swore she could perform with the Sun of Suns. Then they would take the most direct possible course at full speed to Falcon Formation, and the secret shipyard there. Mahallan claimed that she could set a timer on the mechanisms of Candesce that would trigger the correct action after a predetermined number of days and hours.

"Someone's going to have to stay behind," she said. "Wait until after our ships have left and the Gehellens have given chase. Then go into the sun."

"That's what I'm thinking," he said. "Mahallan, of course. And someone to keep her in line. Your man Carrier is the natural choice there."

"Me," she said quickly.

"No, dear, I absolutely—"

"Why? You think I'm going to be safer on board the *Rook* when you go into battle against Falcon? Besides, love, this is our plan, yours and mine. Who are we to trust to see it through, if not one another? When you go up against that dreadnought, you need to focus on the task at hand and not worry about whether Mahallan's done her job, or whether Lyle Carrier really is loyal. You need someone you can trust."

"And I can trust you."

"Why Chaison, that almost sounded like a question." She laughed and punched him in the arm. "It's the best plan, admit it."

He admitted it and they turned to go. As Chaison pulled the ivory box away from its moorings, something small tumbled out. He didn't notice. Venera waved her lamp around until the thing flashed; there it was, twirling away toward a forward porthole. She reached out and snatched it out of the air, then held it up between two fingers.

It was a ring, a signet made for a man's hand. The stone was opaque bloodred and the design was of a horse standing on its back legs. The horse had wings.

She slipped the ring over the bulky glove of her suit and followed her husband out of the bridge.

HOWLS OF DELIGHT echoed through the *Rook* as a spew of gold and jewelry flew from the wooden airlock door. Moments later a man in a red sargasso suit squeezed out waving his hands over his head. A muffled "unh, unh" sounded from inside his round brass helmet, but nobody was paying any attention to him. Crewmen and officers, the press-ganged and the volunteers, all abandoned civility and leaped on the ricocheting treasure. The man in the suit finally levered off his helmet and yelled, "This is just the dregs, boys! There's tons of it there! Tons!"

A light hand descended on Hayden's shoulder. "Hey," said Aubri in his ear. Hayden felt himself flushing, and his heart beat a bit faster.

"Admiral wants to see you," she continued. Peering past him, she said, "They look happy, don't they?"

He had to laugh at the absurd understatement. The men were weeping, fighting over trinkets, screaming, and bouncing off the walls.

Then her previous words penetrated his consciousness. "Fanning wants to see me?"

"Yes, he's in the chart room." She gave him a little push in the lower back and he began to glide through the center of the rioting crewmen.

He bounced off several people and ducked around the worst of the fighting—just in time, as the airlock opened again and another bag of gold was dumped into the air.

The forward section of the ship was relatively empty by the time Hayden reached the chart room. He knocked and Fanning's muffled voice said, "Come in."

The presence of numerous lanterns did nothing to brighten the can-shaped chambe. To Hayden's surprise, Fanning was alone, hovering with one foot in a strap near the map table. In the dim light he was a study in muted shades, his eyes and the folds of his uniform blended into shadow. He had his arms crossed and seemed to have acquired new lines of care around his eyes and mouth.

"I hear that you have gotten to know our armorer very well," said Fanning, his face deadpan.

How did he know? Was news of Hayden's tryst with Aubri all over the ship already? "Well enough," said Hayden cautiously. What did this mean?

"Maybe. Maybe well enough, for the task I've got in mind." Fanning waved him inside. "Shut the door, if you will." Hayden could still faintly hear the sounds of revelry through the walls after he did so; he glided over to a strap near the admiral's and stuck his foot through it. The two men faced one another over the glowing map table.

"I'm about to let my wife out of my sight for an extended period of time," said Fanning with a cryptic smile. "Months, probably. Do you know the details of our plan? —Why we're here?"

"No more than anybody else, sir."

"Hmm." Fanning stared off into the darkness for a moment. "What this is all about, Mr. Griffin, is defeating a numerically superior foe. When Venera first came to me and told me how she'd put together a collection of old clues and documents, and now believed that radar might be possible in Virga, I wasn't much interested. It's a technology that would have only marginal utility in a fair fight— in daylight, in clear air, I mean. But the evidence that Falcon Formation was about to invade changed everything. With no guidance from the Pilot, we were about to commit a strategic blunder and lose our nation."

"I can't much care about that, sir. I was born in Aerie." It was a half-hearted challenge, but he felt he had to make it.

To his surprise the admiral merely nodded at the revelation. "That explains some things about you, though by no means all. You're a good airman, Hayden, but I've been wondering if I could trust you. We fought side by side on the way out of Gehellen, but you know that proves little."

It was Hayden's turn to look away. "I considered you my enemy for many years," he said.

Fanning smiled. "Well, I probably still am your enemy, politically. But I don't feel like you're a personal enemy of mine, Griffin. And that makes a world of difference in the current situation. Tell me: what do you suppose will happen to Aerie if Falcon Formation conquers Slipstream?"

"It'll be as if we never existed," he replied. Fanning caught his eye and Hayden shrugged. "I know that you're the only hope for my people right now."

"And what do you think of my wife?"

Surprised, Hayden said, "Well, I like her well enough, if that's what you mean."

Fanning sighed. "In order to carry out our plan, I have to leave her here while we make a run for the Gehellen border," he said. "She needs to sneak by the locals, get into the Sun of Suns and turn a switch that will make it possible for us to use those radar units that Aubri Mahallan has constructed. Actually, Venera's not the one who has to throw the switch; she doesn't have the technical expertise. Aubri Mahallan does."

Into the Sun of Suns? And Aubri too? Hayden's face must have betrayed his surprise, because Fanning smiled.

"You understand. I'm not at all comfortable leaving my wife here, Griffin, but it was always her plan and one of us has to supervise Mahallan. Am I right in assuming that you'd feel just as uncomfortable leaving Aubri behind?"

Hayden chewed his lip. He'd been caught totally off guard by the notion that the expedition would be headed for Candesce. Old emotions and new questions were starting to boil up in him. Focusing on the matter at hand, he said, "I suppose. What are you getting at?"

"I want you to fly them into Candesce, and then find a way back to Slipstream when you're done," said Fanning earnestly. "I don't have anybody else I can trust to do the job. In fact, logic tells me you're the very last person on this expedition that I should trust. But I think I'm right about you, so I'm asking you straight up: can I trust you to do it?"

"You're not going to damage Candesce, are you? That would be—"

"Insane. Suicidal. Genocidal." Fanning shook his head. "I don't think we could damage Candesce, even if we wanted to. No, our change will be small, temporary, and unnoticed by anyone in Virga. If you agree to go, you have a chance to guarantee that yourself."

Hayden couldn't believe what he was hearing. Fanning trusted him! Surely he didn't deserve that trust, not with all that he'd planned and tried to do. There was no way he should accept an offer such as this; he was bound to betray it, by honor and the momentum of his long-held purpose.

Yet, Aubri would be going. She might need his protection. It was with a sinking feeling of guilt that he said, "Yes, I'll do it.

"I'll take them in," he said, unsure of whether he believed himself, "and I won't interfere with your plans. As long as Candesce remains safe."

And then, to shame Hayden even further, Fanning smiled at him. "I know I can count on you to bring them home safely," he said.

Hayden smiled, and nodded, but did not believe it of himself.

THE AIR IN the ship was stagnant and heavy by the time the Rook made its rendezvous with the other vessels. All six met under the empty gaze of Carlinth's windows. Huge nets full of treasure were towed to the partially repaired Tormentor and its sisters while in the Rook's chart room Admiral Fanning read reports of the skirmish with the Gehellens. The dangerous diversionary tactic had worked well and nobody had been killed, although two more ships had suffered hull breaches and their crews were only now able to take off the oxygen masks they had worn while they repaired them. They didn't care; there was jubilation over the treasure and cheers echoed through the sunless streets of Carlinth for the first time in centuries.

While Admiral Fanning shouted an inspirational speech through a bullhorn mounted into the hull of the Rook, Hayden camped out in the hangar. With the help of Martor, he was modifying one of the military bikes. Fanning's words came muffled through the walls; nearly everyone else on all the ships had their ears to their hulls and was listening intently.

"... *Falcon Formation will destroy* ..." Fanning was saying as Hayden held up an afterburner housing for Martor to see. "Designed for speed but built for reliability," said Hayden. "Typical military. These are tough bikes, but that extra armor and framing's gotta go."

"... *Only the most extraordinary measures can save* ..."

Martor was wiring two extra saddles onto the bike. "But the armor's insulation too, ain't it?" He tapped the outer shell of the cylinder. "I damn near burnt my foot off on your racer, and there was insulation on that."

"... *Up to us to do the job* ..."

Hayden shrugged. "Saddle, foot straps, and handlebars will be it. Touch the bike at any other point and it'll burn you. But it's the price we pay for decent speed with this baby."

"... *Not only rich, but heroes* ..."

Hayden reached out to flip a gold chain that looped around Martor's neck. "What are you going to do now that you're rich?" In the absence of gravity, the trinkets hung off the boy every which way, making an absurd tangled cloud in front of his face that he wiped to the side every few moments.

"I dunno," he said. "I always been navy. . . . Buy a ship, I guess. Explore."

Hayden grinned. "Hunt pirates?" But Martor shook his head.

"I didn't like the fighting, come right down to it," he said seriously. "Some things are great to talk about, but awful to see or do." He looked away shyly. "But, you know . . . talking about it was great fun. The lads loved my stories and they were easy to think up. I was thinking, maybe when we get back, I might try to learn to read and write."

"You, a storyteller?" Hayden nearly laughed, but he could see that the boy meant it. "That's a great idea," he said. "You'd be good at it. Uh, hand me that wrench, will you?"

"Hi." Hayden looked up as Aubri entered the hangar. She wore practical leather flying gear including an airman's cap with goggles. She swam over to the bike and stopped herself with one hand on it and one on Martor's shoulder. "How are you?" she asked the boy. Martor stammered something incoherent.

"You need to stay out of trouble while we're gone," she told him. "No fighting and no profiteering, you hear? We're going to check up on you when we get back."

Martor smiled at her shyly. "I'll survive—if only to see you again, Ms. Mahallan."

Aubri looked troubled for a moment, then smiled as well. "It's only ten days," she said. "That's how long it'll take for you to get to Falcon Formation, assuming you escape the Gehellen dragnet. And assuming you don't run into anything, and assuming that the navigation team can find your sun and you don't end up wandering around and around in winter til the end of time." She grinned at Martor's expression. "Don't worry. We've got it timed down to the minute."

"That's what worries me," muttered Hayden. This was the weakest part of the plan: Fanning would have to get back to Falcon Formation in time to attack the secret shipyard at an exactly predetermined moment. With all the vagaries of travel in Virga—navigation errors, collisions, breakdowns, fuel shortages, and piracy—it would be a miracle if they could do that in time. By contrast, Hayden's own part in the plan was simple.

Just fly straight into the Sun of Suns.

"And what are you gonna do after?" Martor asked suddenly. Hayden looked over; he'd been focused on his work and didn't know who the boy had asked. He opened his mouth and saw Aubri doing the same.

Hayden shrugged. "Haven't thought that far ahead." He avoided Aubri's gaze, though she also seemed to be looking elsewhere.

THE NIGHTWATCH WAS well under way when Hayden came back to the hangar. The *Rook* and its sisters were creeping toward the outskirts of Leaf's Choir, much more cautiously than when they'd entered. The hatch gang had left the hangar, but the place resounded to the snores of the various *Unseen Hand* crew members who'd been billeted here. Hayden wove in and out of the men who hung like pupae from the walls, floor, and ceiling, until he came to his bike. Then he eased the folded cargo net and heavy coil of cable off his shoulder and parked it in midair next to him. Unfolding his tool kit, he selected a wrench; he dug in his pocket for a moment and brought out some brackets and bolts. Quietly, so as not to wake the men, he proceeded to bolt the brackets onto the back of the bike, over the afterburner.

Hayden had been taken aback by Admiral Fanning's request that he shepherd Venera and Aubri to Candesce—so taken aback that for almost an hour afterward, he hadn't realized what doing that could mean. When he did, it was in the midst of a conversation with the new boatswain; Hayden had lost his train of thought in midsentence, and just stared slack-jawed at the dark hull until the boatswain said, "What's up? You having a stroke or something?"

He'd stammered some sort of reply and extricated himself from the conversation. Going to a porthole, he stared out at the blank nothingness of the sargasso, as an unfamiliar sense of lightness crept over him.

Words whispered in his mind; was he thinking them, or were they a memory of long ago? It might have been his father's voice saying, *"Candesce is the mother of all suns. If Aerie is to have a new sun, its core will come from there."*

No one had ever told Hayden how Candesce gave up its treasures; but he had heard that collecting them was easy. "Like picking fruit," one of the Resistance engineers had said.

Now as he worked as quietly as he could, he reflected upon the irony that Fanning himself would probably approve of what he was doing. If he got caught, he could in fact appeal to the admiral. Carrier was the one more likely to object, but Hayden wasn't afraid of Carrier. No, he was doing this in secret and on his own time not because he was afraid of being caught but because this particular task was his alone. It was personal.

He plucked out the stuffing of the bike's saddle and replaced it with the coiled cargo net. Little tufts of stuffing started floating away and he jammed them in his pockets. Then he reached around the bike's exhaust vent and began coiling the thin cable inside the bike's housing. He wired it in tightly and leaned back with a satisfied smile to admire his work.

Miles and his cronies in the Resistance had been right about one thing: it wasn't what you fought that mattered; the only thing that mattered was what you built. Hayden's own parents had known that, but he'd forgotten it for years after their deaths. Wasted years? —No, they had brought him here, now, to finish something that should have been done a long time ago.

He put away his tools, patted the bike, and headed for the ship's centrifuge to sleep under gravity for the last time in a long while.

19

CANDESCE BLAZED BENEATH Hayden's feet. Even here, hundreds of miles away, the heat from the Sun of Suns was almost intolerable. If he shielded his eyes and looked near the light, Hayden could just make out the bright tails of infalling lakes that were boiling away as they approached that point of incandescence. "They look like comets," Aubri had said when she first saw them.

Other things moved near Candesce. Ships from all the principalities hovered just outside its zone of heat, moving in after sunoff. Among the principalities it was common custom to consign the coffins of the dead to the Sun of Suns; Hayden imagined that they too must become comets at the last, never reaching their goal but evaporating back into the stuff of Virga to become places and people again. So must his mother have gone when Aerie's new sun exploded. His father would have become compost for some Slipstream farm.

Some of the ships hiding in Candesce's light would be funeral vessels. But some had another purpose.

"What are you doing?" Aubri looped an arm around his waist. "You'll burn your eyes out doing that. Come inside."

Hayden had been thinking about the ships that ventured close to Candesce during darkness. They were the harvesters—boats that scrounged the garbage cast out of the Sun of Suns. That garbage was Virga's chief source of sun components. His parents had used fusion-core pieces bought from the principalities to build Aerie's secret sun.

For now, Hayden would not let his speculations run away with him. He let Aubri draw him inside the charcoal-harvester's hut they had found on the outskirts of Leaf's Choir. It perched like an angular bug on the black branch of a tree whose roots lay miles away in darkness. Venera Fanning and Carrier had taken up residence in another harvester's hut some distance away; the bike was hidden there in a ball of sticks. Carrier would not trust Hayden to be its keeper.

He didn't care. It had been strange and wonderful this morning to wake to the first glow of Candesce coming through the one shuttered window of the hut, and find himself wrapped in Aubri's arms and in silence. He had slept with women before; he had never awoken the next morning to find one still with him. So he dwelt in this moment for a long time, breathing slowly and contentedly with her beside him.

The now-familiar hum of the Rook's engines was gone, and not even birdsong signaled dawn here. When Hayden pulled himself over to the window (sleeping Aubri coming along like she was tied to him) he looked out on an astonishing vista. It was as if he were a mite clinging to a giant's hair; for miles in every direction thin black trunks reached toward Candesce from a place of shadow and blackness. The giant's hairs twisted and intertwined as they strained toward the light; many still had branches though the harvesters were systematically stripping them. None had leaves, but life was not completely absent here. Wildflowers nestled in the crooked elbows of branches, and bright green bushes dotted many trunks. Aubri had discovered wild raspberries on this very tree, which might explain why the hut had been positioned here. It was too hot for fish, but a few birds cruised in the distance.

After an hour or two Hayden had started to wonder if there might be a beehive or wasps' nest hidden somewhere nearby, because he'd realized that it wasn't completely silent here. A deep basso thrum filled the air, faint but unwavering. He hadn't heard it last night.

When he mentioned it to Aubri she just shrugged and said, "It's Candesce. Up close it must be like a god singing."

He was in awe of Aubri's knowledge and said so. "You truly know how to control Candesce? You could make it your toy, like a bike?"

She shook her head. "Ride it like a rocket, more like. But Hayden, Candesce was designed before Virga existed. Those designs are still available to anyone willing to leave Virga to find them. I had them with me when I first came here."

That conversation had happened a few hours ago, and had trailed off into kissing and more personal intimations. But her words had stuck with Hayden, growing stranger and stranger the more he thought about them. Now, as they settled in the cooler shadow of the hut, he said, "Why would you have the plans for Candesce with you? Did you already know you were going to visit it?"

She frowned, just slightly, and looked around at the wicker walls. But when she met his gaze again she wore a carefree smile.

"I came here with every piece of information we'd ever collected on Virga," she said. She held up two fingers and pinched them close together. "All that data could be contained in something much smaller than a grain of sand, so why not carry all of it? Of course, when I got here, the memory store was disabled by Candesce's emissions. So I'll have to go on what little I remember when we get there. But I remember enough."

He nodded, still thinking about it. Suddenly Aubri grabbed his arm. "Look!"

Buzzing in the doorway was one of those odd little chrome insects that one saw sometimes. *Tankers*, Aubri had called them. Hayden reached out a hand. "Should I catch it?"

She shook her head. "I don't have my instruments with me, I couldn't study it now." The little tanker spun around and zipped off. A sudden cloud of similar bugs flicked past the window.

"You were right," Hayden said. "They're headed for Candesce."

"Carrying fuel," she said with a nod. "For the Farnsworth Fusors."

THEY FLOATED TOGETHER inside the hut, exhausted after making love, and were silent together. He was acutely aware that much had gone unspoken between him and Aubri.

At last he turned and laid his hand, gently, on her breastbone. "Does it listen?" he asked her. He had no need to say what it was.

She shrugged. "I need to be careful. But . . . it doesn't care. Not really. It's just a dumb mechanism."

He thought about that. Then he nodded to the window. "Was this your mission? To visit Candesce?"

She looked him in the eye and said, "No. In fact . . . it's the opposite. If there's anywhere in Virga where I might find a way to free myself from this . . ." She tapped her throat. "Then it would be there."

Hayden shook his head in confusion. "You don't need to be careful about telling me that?"

"No. The assassin-bug only cares whether I tell people what my real mission is. It's not able to care about anything else."

"Not even its own life?"

"It's not alive. So, no." She quirked a smile. "Look at it this way: some things trigger it, some don't. That's all."

"So . . ." He mused. "You think we might find a way to kill it in Candesce?"

"It's why I pushed the Fannings to do this. A selfish reason, maybe." She shrugged, grinning. "But it worked."

He laughed. "Can I help?"

She kissed him. "Just keep guard. I'll do the rest."

"You can help me too," he said seriously. Aubri cocked one eyebrow. "Both of us, really," he added. "Aubri . . . have you actually thought about what you'd do if you got free of that thing? Would you stay, or would you go?"

She hesitated. "Stay," she said finally. "I would stay."

Hayden sighed. He took a moment to compose his thoughts. "I have a reason for going into Candesce too," he told her. He felt his heart lifting as he described his plan to locate sun components in Candesce and return them to Aerie. "I want to finish my parents' work. Light a new sun on the edge of winter, that the people of Aerie can gather around. Let them leave Slipstream and the rest of Meridian behind. Save my people."

It would have sounded like an arrogant, impossible dream to Hayden—had not his mother and father confidently pursued that same dream.

"I'll need an engineer," he said. "You could be invaluable."

"Oh." She looked away. "Is that all you want me for? My engineering skills?"

"No!" He laughed and pulled her to him. "More. I want much more. We could found a new nation together, Aubri. Is that something you could want?"

She wrapped her arms around him and buried her face in his shoulder.

"More than anything," she murmured, "I would want that."

THEY BOTH AWOKE with a start. It was the middle of the night, and absolutely black inside the hut. Somewhere, far in the distance, something had screamed.

"Did you hear that?" Hayden asked. He felt rather than saw Aubri's nod. They both listened in perfect stillness for a while; then she relaxed against him.

"Maybe Venera's cohabitation with Carrier is not so chaste as we'd been led to think," she said.

"Ugh," he said. "Don't say that. I—" He stopped, as a long, ululating sound crept through the night to enwrap the hut.

They were both at the window a second later, peering out into the gloom. "That wasn't any person," said Aubri needlessly. There was nothing to see outside the hut, however—nothing at all, an extravagant blackness Hayden couldn't remember encountering even in winter. For a moment he wondered if the hut had somehow slid backward into the depths of Leaf's Choir. How would they know, before they suffocated?

The cry came again, and this time it was accompanied by the sound of branches shattering. The roar built—it seemed that entire trees were being thrown aside by something huge that approached through the darkness. The hut began to shake.

Then as quickly as it began, the roaring ended.

They stayed at the window for a long time, but nothing further happened. After an hour or so, a bobbing flashlight beam meandered up the trunk of the tree, and Carrier and Venera appeared. Both looked grim.

"Any ideas?" Carrier asked without preamble. Hayden shook his head.

"Maybe we should stick together tonight," he said. Then, with sudden urgency: "Where's the bike?"

Carrier waved a length of twine Hayden hadn't seen he was holding. It stretched off into the blackness. "I towed it over," he said. "Thought it best." Hayden nodded.

They all crowded into the little hut and sat there looking at one another for a while. "This is ridiculous," Venera said after the uncomfortable interlude had stretched on for fifteen minutes. "We have to do something. Talk, at least."

"I agree," said Aubri.

There was another long silence.

"Let's tell stories," said Venera brightly.

They all stared at her in the feeble glow of the flashlight. "Ghost stories," amended Venera; then she laughed. "Oh, come on. Can you think of a better time to do it?"

Everyone laughed, and a minute later, Hayden found himself relating the story of the black pirate suns, and of the strange monsters reputed to live in winter.

After his turn Venera spoke, and somehow Hayden wasn't surprised when it turned out that she knew lots of such stories, and relished telling them.

In one of Venera's stories, Candesce itself had gone roving one night; the sun had been hungry after shining for so many centuries, and it ate several of the neighboring principalities before being talked out of a further meal by a brash young farm boy. Venera tailored her description to the night's events: the unseen sun passing in majestic noise, a skyscape of sounds, no sign of what had caused its devastation after it returned to its station and lit again.

Aubri clapped her hands when the story ended. "You have hidden talents, Venera!"

The admiral's wife preened, examining her nails with ostentatious care. "I do, don't I?"

"I hope you don't mind my asking, but I've been wondering all along how you managed to convince Chaison to bring you on the expedition." Aubri looked genuinely puzzled. "During our planning sessions he seemed adamant about leaving you behind."

"Ah," said Venera with a smile, "but that was before I blackmailed him."

"Ah—what?" Aubri and Hayden both laughed nervously. Venera waved a hand dismissively.

"Back when he was a student, my Chaison wrote a few seditious pamphlets denouncing the pilot. Nobody knows that, of course— no one who would talk about it." She eyed Carrier, whose face was as wooden as always. "I found out about it from an old drinking companion of his, and I held it over his head to get him to take me along. That's all." She said this in a modest sort of way.

Hayden couldn't resist a grin. "Chaison Fanning . . . denounced the pilot?"

Carrier, however, was glaring at Venera. "You never told me about this," he said.

She shrugged. "Why should I?" Venera looked at him archly. "In any case, it's your turn, Lyle. Don't you have any ghost stories to share?"

Carrier stammered something, then looked down. After a moment, he met Venera's eye and said, "Ghost stories are for kids. Things that really happened are far more harrowing than any story."

Some line had been crossed, Hayden thought, but Venera didn't seem to have noticed. She pouted at Carrier and said, "For instance?"

"For instance," he grated, "take the story of a man who discovers that his son doesn't have the stomach for the things that need to be done to protect his people. The boy joins the Resistance of a conquered foe, and tries to convince his father to do it too."

Venera arched an eyebrow. "What's so horrible about that?"

Carrier took a deep breath. "The father plays along with it. In the end the Resistance comes to trust the boy, and of course he trusts his father—enough that one day he tells him the location of the new sun his friends are building. And the father," he said with a grim smile, "he does what any loyal man would do. He tells the pilot."

Belatedly, Venera was realizing how angry Carrier was. "Youthful zeal," she said. "They grow out of it."

"Only if they live," said Carrier. "Only if they live."

Aubri shifted, half-reaching out to Carrier. "What happened to your son?" she asked quietly.

"He died when the Aerie bastards blew up their new sun," said Carrier; his voice carried no emotion, no inflection at all. "But you know what? If I had to do it all again, I would. Because a loyal citizen of Slipstream will do nothing against the pilot; will do anything for his nation." Again, he was watching Venera as he said this.

The silence that followed was long and awkward. Aubri tried to salvage the mood by telling a humorous anecdote about her brief days in Rush, but her delivery was wooden and it fell flat.

The damage had been done; all they could do now was sit in silence and wait for dawn. This was just fine as far as Hayden was concerned; he didn't want to talk anymore. He just sat in the corner, nursing his shock.

The man he had sworn to kill sat next to him. For the moment, nothing else mattered.

But then a curious thing happened. As the hours dragged on, Hayden's anger lessened. When Candesce finally ignited in a stuttering dawn Hayden even allowed himself to exchange a wondering glance with Carrier as they gazed out at a vast gash that had opened up in the miles-long trunks of the dead forest.

"It's like some monster was *grazing* on the trees," said Aubri.

"Capital bug?" asked Carrier, but clearly he didn't believe it. Capital bugs were big, the way clouds were big, but they were not strong. Whatever had done this could eat whole cities.

"Candesce, walking," said Venera smugly. They all laughed, and the tension of the night broke.

Later, he watched Carrier and Venera fly back to their hut. Hayden felt curiously light, as if some huge responsibility had been lifted from his shoulders. Lyle Carrier was just a man, after all, and a sad one at that.

What had drained his anger? He wondered about that for a while, seeing Aubri, and Candesce burning at the center of the sky, there was really no doubt. Somehow in the past weeks Hayden had learned to look past yesterday and today. It was the possibility of a future that had changed him.

Maybe he could fulfil his promise to Chaison Fanning after all.

A SWARM OF bikes spiraled through winter. Each flyer had a large magnesium lamp mounted in front of his saddle and great spears of light pierced the gloom as they searched for safe passage. Behind them, recklessly fast, came the expeditionary force itself. Dew beaded on the sleek hulls of the ships and tumbled away in their wakes. Their contrails could have been followed by anyone who cared to pursue them; but the Gehellen navy had given up at the border. The chase had been half-hearted anyway, since the Slipstream ships had gone many miles under cover of night before they were spotted.

Giant multilimbed clouds reared out of the black, too big to circumnavigate. The bikers' flight leader leaned down to let off a sounding rocket and watched as its yellow eye receded into the mist. If it hit anything it would explode in a shower of phosphorous. He watched the contours of the cloud intently, heedless of the icy air tumbling past his limbs. After a moment he waved an all-clear and underscored the rocket's contrail with his own.

Some miles behind the bikes, Chaison Fanning climbed out a side hatch of the Rook and hooked his feet through a ring on the hull. He stared out across a hundred miles of cloud-dotted air at the hint of silver in the darkness that identified Mavery's sun. Faint flickers and flashes lit the sky far up and to one side of that silver area.

It could just be a lightning storm—but the colors were wrong. Some of those pinpricks were red, some vivid orange. The light came from the border between Mavery and winter. It was too far away for Chaison to hear the explosions, of course—but the battle must be huge, and fierce. He should be there.

After a while Travis clambered through the hatch with a blanket fluttering in his good hand. "Begging your pardon, Admiral, sir, but you'll freeze out here," he shouted as he tried to drape the blanket one-handed over Chaison's shoulders.

"Look at it," said Chaison. The tiny stars that signaled explosions had only been able to keep his attention for so long, despite what imagination and reason had told him must be happening there. His gaze had inevitably drifted forward and eventually he'd realized that framed by the cross-hatch lines of bike contrails was the collected light of nations. Half the sky was awash with luminescence in circles too broad to encompass with out-thrown arms. Their outer edges faded to dusk and black, their centers shone sky-blue and here and there a sun appeared for seconds at a time. There were a dozen such realms of light in the cluster of nations known as Meridian, but the farthest countries were hidden behind the nearer.

The pearlescent zone of sky next to Mavery was Slipstream—had been Aerie, once. Obscured behind the *Rook*'s hull was multisunned Falcon Formation. Chaison had climbed around the hull several times to look at it.

"The men want to go," said Travis, nodding at the sparkling battle. "They know we have another destination, but they're not happy."

Chaison sighed. "I'm not happy either. The fleet will be cursing my name that I'm not there. All of us—we've probably been branded traitors by now. If we don't bring back the figureheads of Falcon's flagship, the pilot will have me publicly flogged. At the very least."

He made sure his feet were anchored, then stood up into the *Rook*'s headwind. "That's where we go," he yelled, pointing to the vast span of light that was Falcon Formation. "And chances are we'll never see the light of Slipstream again. So enjoy the view while you can, Travis!"

"Come inside, sir!"

He shook his head. "When I'm good and ready. Leave me alone."
Travis retreated, a concerned frown on his face.

Chaison Fanning stood alone on the hull of his ship, feeling alone. Venera wasn't with him for the first time in many months, and he found the ache of missing her far more intense than expected. She was infuriating and inescapable; yet she made him smile as often as she outraged him.

They hadn't said good-bye as they parted; but the last of her he'd seen was a backward glance as she looked for him and spotted him watching from the hangar doorway. Her eyes had gone wide, and then she'd turned away again.

He smiled, as the wind tore salty droplets from his eyes and cast them into the vortex of the *Rook*'s contrail.

CANDESCE WAS FADING like an ember when the four travelers climbed into their saddles and Hayden lit the fan-jet's burners. Back became down, and they shot away from the threadlike trees of Leaf's Choir, seemingly straight up toward the sun. Hayden turned for a last look at the harvester's hut, and smiled. Then he adjusted the goggles on his nose and opened the throttle.

They weren't leaving a contrail, he'd noticed. That was probably due to the heat of the air near the Sun of Suns; whatever the reason, they would be less noticeable to the Gehellen cruisers that still patrolled the air here.

—Or so he was able to tell himself for the first ten minutes of the flight; then he saw Carrier's hand waving from the opposite side of the bike.

Hayden craned his neck around the metal cylinder and at first saw only the normal traffic of funeral ships and scroungers cautiously edging toward the sun. After a moment he saw what Carrier had spotted: eight sparks of light rising over the black furze of the sargasso. They were the color of the sun, their backdrop the mauve air of dusk.

Carrier leaned past Venera to shout, "Bigger than bikes!" But smaller than commercial vessels; Hayden nodded. These looked like catamarans—twin engined, with both pilot and gunner. They'd be fast, and they could reduce the bike and its riders to splinters in seconds if they got close enough.

Hayden tapped the throttle, feeling for the bike's response. Then he leaned in as close to the hot metal as he dared and kicked in the afterburner. The women on either side of him pressed their noses to the hull as well while the air began to thunder past and Candesce seemed to get perceptibly brighter.

For a few minutes, that is; then the Sun of Suns began to go out.

It didn't do so all at once. In fact, as Hayden squinted past the handlebars he began to make out structure to the radiance ahead. Candesce, he realized with a start, wasn't one sun but rather a cloud of them. He tried to count them, but they were guttering faster than he could keep up. Each one left a fading red spot and, in the eye, a lozenge of retinal overload.

But the heat remained. He could feel it first in the places where the wind didn't penetrate: in the hollow of his throat, along his calfs. As the minutes passed heat piled up against the bike as if they were pressing into a resilient surface made of exhaust and fire. They crossed fifty miles of air and were swaddled in it; a hundred miles and it was becoming hard to breathe. The commercial ships had fallen behind but the catamarans still followed, their gemlike highlights wavering in the rippling air.

Little flashes started to appear in the corner of Hayden's eye. He was alarmed—was he about to pass out?—and then saw the contrails that were sketching across the sky like meridian lines.

Venera waved frantically. When he caught her eye she held up her hand in a gun-shape. He nodded and began slaloming the bike from

side to side, gently at first so as not to shake off his passengers—
then more and more violently as bullets stitched the air to all sides.

After a minute the gunfire stopped. He glanced back to see their
pursuers close, but keeping a decent distance.

Hayden smiled. There was nowhere for him to go—or so those
men thought. They believed that if they hung on his tail long
enough he would have to give up. After all, there was no place to
hide here, and no way to get inside Candesce.

They were in for a surprise.

A LONG WING of shadow swept into winter behind Sargasso
44. The gnarled black fist of burnt forest, its outlines softened by
mist, wasn't much to look at after Leaf's Choir, but it was still a respectable three miles across. The Rook and its sisters crept up to the
hidden shipyard from its unlit side, their running lights off. Two
bikes jetted out of Chaison Fanning's modest flagship to reconnoiter
and he waited, not on the bridge but in the hangar, for their return.

Propriety be damned. He glanced at the ticking wall clock, then
at his men. Two hours until Falcon's suns dimmed into their night
cycle. In two hours the plan would succeed or fail. And everybody
knew it, but nobody would speak of it.

They'd installed the radar casting machines in the nose of each
ship and tried them. Of course they didn't work—there was only a
bright fuzz on the hand-blown cathode ray tubes bolted next to the
Rook's pilot station. But as each sister ship turned its own radar on
or off, the fuzz had brightened or dimmed. Some sort of invisible
energy was in play here. Chaison had been cheered by that tiny hint
of future success.

And the men . . . He looked at them again. They'd been running
drills for days now to perfect the art of firing blind according to orders from the bridge. The rocketeers looked confident.

He shook his head and laughed. "Men, I don't mean to be insulting, but you look like pirates." Some were wounded, others had hasty repairs to their uniforms to cover sword and bullet holes. It was the jewelry, though, that set them apart from any other crew Chaison had worked with. As battle approached the men had been sneaking off to their lockers to collect their treasures, as if the talismanic weight of future wealth would keep them alive through the coming battle.

It was so far from regulation that he could validly have any one of them whipped for it. Necklaces might get in the eye, or tangle a hand at a crucial moment.

Nobody was going to be disciplined, and they all knew it. Perversely, knowing they knew it pleased Chaison. He felt an affection for this crew he hadn't known for any other he'd worked with.

The bikes' contrails hit the side of the sargasso and vanished. Sargasso 44 was too small and old to have retained a toxic interior, especially with transport ships coming and going and all the industry happening inside it. Chaison had nonetheless insisted that the men on the bikes wear sargasso suits. It would be a fine irony if they were knocked out by fumes and sailed their bikes right into the shipyard.

"Now we wait," said Travis. Chaison shot him an amused look.

"We've been reduced to cliches, have we?" he said.

Travis stammered something but Chaison waved a hand in dismissal. "Don't mind me," he said. "I'm feeling free for the first time in weeks."

"Yes, sir." Then Travis pointed. "Sir? Look."

The bikes were returning already. Falcon's shipyard must lie closer to the sargasso's surface than he'd thought.

"All right." Chaison clapped his hands briskly. "Let's see where we stand."

HAYDEN HAD SEEN clouds bigger than these rising spires, but nothing else, not even the icebergs at Virga's skin could compare. On the outskirts of Candesce long arcing stanchions connected many glittering transparent spines, which soared into the surrounding air like the threads of the jellyfish that hid in winter clouds. These spines were miles long but they were not anchored to a single solid mass. Candesce, he was surprised to see, was not a thing, but a *region*. Hundreds of objects of all shapes and sizes gleamed within the sphere of air sketched by the giant spires. Candesce was an engine open to the outside world.

So what was Venera's key intended to unlock? They glided in between the outreaching arms at a sedate pace. The enemy catamarans were hanging back, confident in being able to catch the bike and curious to see what Hayden would do. The moment was strangely peaceful, or would have been if not for the savage heat that radiated from those needles of crystal.

"Are they glass?" he wondered aloud. Beside him, Aubri shook her head.

"Diamond," she said. "Re-radiators."

As they passed the spires dim orange glows from the dormant suns revealed traceries of intricate detail farther in: ribs and arching threads of cable, mirrored orbs the size of towns, and long meandering catwalk cages. With all the suns lit, internal reflection and refraction must double and redouble until it was impossible to separate real from mirage. Drowned in light, Candesce would disappear as a physical object. These spars and wires were like the crude ghost of something else that had no form. That something had left, for now— perhaps stalking the distant air to devour a principality or two. But it would return to its den come morning, and then this diamond and iron would give over to a greater reality, one made of light. Any person foolish enough to be here would disappear as well.

Venera and Carrier had raised their heads to stare too. Hayden breathed in little sips; the heat was making him dizzy. "Where?" he asked Aubri with renewed urgency.

She scanned the unlikely bauble of the Sun of Suns. "There." Where she pointed, a dark rectangle lay silhouetted by one of the suns. It was nestled against the diamond point at the base of one of the spines. "That should . . . should be the visitor's center."

Hayden barked a laugh and instantly regretted it as the air seared his throat. "Another tourist station?" But Aubri shook her head.

"This one"—she gasped spasmodically—"is for education and maintenance. No remote control. No tourists."

"Nobody waiting for us, I hope."

She shook her head. Hayden fired up the bike and they shot through the glittering clouds of machine and cable. Now, though, he heard the sound of other engines. The Gehellen catamarans were closing in.

He guided them down the curve of the spire, alert for anything familiar. The rectangle ahead slowly resolved into a boxy structure about thirty meters on a side, made of some white substance. The crystal spike pierced its side, and next to that spot was a small square on the box. Hayden blinked in the wavering air; was it real? Yes, it was there: a door.

Sleek blue spindles eased into sight on either side of the bike: the catamarans. They were like streamlined rockets with outrider jet engines and a cockpit on either side. Both cockpits had heavy machine guns mounted next to them; two of these now swivelled to aim at Hayden's bike. One of the Gehellens gestured for him to turn around.

He waved *yes*, and kept going.

The square door was only yards away when one of the Gehellens fired a warning shot. The bullet *pinged* off the diamond wall. Hayden took his hands off the bike's handles and raised them in surrender, while at the same time gripping the bike with his knees to steer it.

Another warning shot and this time Hayden looked down to see a puncture in the bike's cowling, inches from Aubri's face.

He reached to cut out the bike's engine and saw Carrier lean casually around the bike. There was a *bang!* loud in the sudden absence of engine noise, and then Carrier was off the bike and spinning in midair and firing again.

Both machine gunners were dead, with identical holes in the center of their foreheads. Carrier was yanking Venera off her saddle; he aimed her at the black outline of the door and pushed himself the other way into open air. Hayden yelled a warning and saw that Aubri was drifting off her own saddle, unconscious. Quickly he took one foot out of its stirrup and lunged for Carrier. They locked hands and he pulled the larger man back just as both catamarans rolled over—trailing spirals of blood—to expose their pilots, and the pilots' machine guns.

Venera had found an indentation in the wall and jammed in the white cylinder she'd been guarding. Both catamaran pilots opened up and bullets flew—sloppily as the recoil moved the gun platforms. A bullet hit Carrier's pistol and it shattered in his hand. He drew back, cursing.

Hayden grabbed Aubri's shirt with one hand and with the other, the bright edge of a suddenly opening door in the diamond wall. He hauled Aubri and the bike into dazzling light to the ear-shattering accompaniment of machine gunfire.

The sound cut off abruptly as the door shut and four humans and a bike tumbled onward into light.

"NOTHING? NOTHING AT all?" Chaison felt sick. The two bike pilots weren't looking much better; the crew had formed a half-dome around them, and were looking stricken as well.

"It's abandoned, sir. Shut down, except for one or two huts that look like security buildings. All the ships are gone—except the tugs, but . . ."

"They weren't just out of sight, hidden somewhere else in the sargasso?"

The two men looked at one another. They made identical shrugs. "Nowhere to put them, sir. We looked. Sir . . . sir, they're gone."

Gone. A Falcon Formation dreadnought and a fleet of new warships were on their way to Slipstream. Maybe they were there already. And Chaison Fanning had taken seven ships that might have helped defend his home, and frittered them away in a useless quest for an advantage that had now proven chimerical. He had lost.

"Sir? What do we do now?"

Chaison Fanning had no answer.

20

COOL AIR WASHED over Hayden's face. For a second he reveled in that, drawing in deep breaths and running his hands over his sweat-stained scalp. Then he turned to Aubri.

"She's not been shot." Carrier was already there, turning her over in midair like something he was inspecting at market. He was right, there was no blood.

Was it the assassin-bug she carried inside her? Had Aubri crossed some invisible line, or begun to say something that had triggered it? For a moment Hayden was sure that such a thing had happened, and that she was dead.

Then Carrier put his hand on her forehead. "Hot. Her pulse is a bit fast. She's not sweating; looks like she fainted from the heat."

Aubri coughed weakly and opened her eyes. "Oh, my head," she murmured. She looked around herself in confusion. "How did we get back to—oh." She pawed at the air, seeking something to hold on to. Hayden put out his hand and she took it, oriented herself upright with respect to the two men. "We're in Candesce."

"And we have a schedule to keep." Venera was waiting impatiently at a nearby doorway. The military bike hung in the air next to her, popping and pinging as it cooled. Hayden counted bullet holes as he pulled Aubri past it; there were at least twenty. A glance told him that the fuel tanks hadn't been punctured, but he wasn't sure about the burners or fan.

"Come on," said Venera. "Mahallan, are you awake enough to do your job?"

"Yes yes," said Aubri peevishly. But Carrier shook his head.

"She needs water and cold compresses," he said. "We don't want her making mistakes at a crucial moment."

Venera drew an ornate watch out of her silk tunic. "We have an hour," she said. "And I'm grudging you that."

They went to explore. It was easy for Hayden to tow Aubri, who seemed feverish and vague; if they'd been under gravity she might not have been able to walk.

"Familiar enough design," Venera said as they moved down a bright, white-walled corridor. The interior of what Aubri had called the visitor's center was divided into numerous chambers and corridors, but only in a loose sort of way by walls and floors that generally did not quite meet. Instead of the enclosed boxes one found under gravity, here were rectangles of pastel-colored material that were suspended in midair to suggest rooms and floors without limiting mobility. In many places you could slip over or under a "wall" into the next room, or glide through a gap in the floor into a room "below." Electric lights in many colors floated here and there, casting shadows that softened the edges of the space. This sort of plan was common in freefall houses and public institutions—but in those places you could always see the ropes or wires that kept the rectangles in place. Hayden could see no means of support for this place's walls.

The rooms were in turn subdivided by screens into different functional areas: eating and cooking alcoves, entertainment centers, even shadowed nooks for sleeping. It didn't take them long to find fresh cold water for Aubri. She splashed it over herself and began to look more alert.

"This place could house hundreds," said Carrier. "Are you sure no one ever comes here? It all looks a bit too well kept."

Aubri laughed. "After maintaining the suns of Candesce, taking care of this place must be light work."

"But light work for whom?"

"For what, you mean. Nothing we're likely to meet while we're here, Carrier. Nothing human."

He looked uneasy. "It's too empty in here. I don't like it."

Hayden searched the cupboards for something to help Aubri. To his surprise he found them well stocked, but the packages and boxes were lettered in an unfamiliar language.

Aubri was shrugging off any more help anyway. "I'm feeling better, Venera. Let's do what we came to do." She glided out of the kitchen alcove and slid through the loop of a large couch sling in the living area next door.

Venera frowned at Aubri. "Well then, what are you waiting for? Where's the . . . bridge, command center, or what have you?"

Aubri gestured at a blank picture frame that took up much of the ceiling. "It's wherever you want it to be, Venera. Watch." She spoke several words in a language Hayden had never heard before, and the picture frame swirled with sudden inner light. Then it seemed to open like a door or window, and Hayden found himself staring into the gleaming interior of Candesce.

Lit by some magical un-light, Candesce's interior teemed with motion like the little creatures Hayden had seen once when he looked through a teacher's microscope. The suns themselves resembled diatoms, spiky and iridescent; though they were quiescent, all around them things like metal flowers were opening. Their petals fanned like the hands of mannered dancers, hundreds of feet wide, to reveal complex buds of machinery that must have hibernated in tungsten cocoons during the day's heat. Bright things poured out of them like seeds from a pod—or bikes from a hangar.

Other things were moving too—long spindly gantries delicately picked crystalline cylinders out of the air and stuck them together end to end. Hayden glimpsed more machinery inside the cylinders.

"What are they doing?" he asked.

"Repairing," said Aubri in a distracted tone. "Rebuilding. Don't look at anything too closely, you could break it."

Hayden sent her a worried glance; he noticed Carrier squinting at her as well. But she looked more alert and lucid than she had a few minutes ago. Hayden decided to let her strange comment go.

"There!" Aubri pointed. Hayden squinted, and saw two catamarans peeling away from the awakening machinery. The Gehellens had been unable to follow their quarry into the Sun of Suns, and were giving up the chase. Maybe they intended to wait for morning outside Candesce's unnerving heart. Well, they would face that possibility when it came.

He turned his attention back to the unfurling non-life of Candesce. Hayden was looking for something, and after a few minutes he spotted it. One of the salvage ships from the principalities was nosing cautiously into the zone of mechanical activity. It flew a flag he'd never seen before, but he ignored that and its strange lines, and watched where it was going.

"Well?" Venera was asking impatiently. "Where are the controls, Mahallan? Hadn't you better get started?"

"Shush, Venera," said Aubri. "I've already started."

Hayden had heard that all the suns in Virga made use of discarded components of Candesce. He wasn't sure what he was expecting to see, but was still surprised when the principality ship swung in close to one of the big translucent cylinders as it was being hoisted near a sun. Some complex exchange had just taken place between the cylinder and one of the flowers; a door had opened in the crystal and swarms of metal insects swirled between it and the "flower." Now another hatch opened in the tesselated side of the sun, and another exchange began.

As it did, the hangar doors of the principality ship flew open and men in sargasso suits—star shapes at this distance—flung themselves into the stream of packages. They wrestled something away from its insectile courier; he could have sworn he'd seen the arcs and bands of that device before, in the half-constructed heart of his parents' new sun.

But wouldn't the metal bugs object? It seemed suicidal folly to try to steal from them. He waited for the swarm to turn and attack the men. After a long moment it began to happen: the remaining drones let go of their cargoes and turned toward the humans, who seemed oblivious to the threat.

Get away, get away, he willed them, even as the steel insects opened their claws and flung themselves at the men.

"Hayden, whatever you're doing, stop it," said Aubri. She was waving her hand in front of his eyes.

"Huh? I'm not doing—look at the ship, there!" He pointed.

Aubri turned and looked toward the principality ship. "Oh. You didn't, did you?" She sounded disappointed. "Let's stop that."

At the last second, the metal insects veered away from the men. "Hayden, stop it," said Aubri. "Look away, Hayden." She grabbed his shoulder and spun him around.

"What are you—"

"Hayden, we're looking into a command mirror. Don't you know what that is?" Aubri saw the blank looks on three faces and sighed. "No, you don't. Sorry. Listen, the command mirrors are the control system for Candesce. Whatever you look at in the mirror, that thing will do what you imagine it doing—insofar as it's capable of it and only inside Candesce. Hayden, you disrupted the movement of those cargo handlers by worrying whether they would stop what they were doing."

Venera laughed. "You made the bugs attack those men! You're meaner than I thought."

"Hey, I didn't mean to—"

"Command mirrors are sensitive," said Aubri. "Maybe it would be better if none of you looked into it for a while. I have to figure out which component of Candesce to switch off. It could take me a few minutes."

The three natives of Virga left the couch and returned to the food-preparation area. "How are we going to know if she's done the job or not?" whispered Carrier. Venera rolled her eyes.

"It's pretty late for you to worry about that. Chaison and I talked about it months ago. Mahallan's not the only person who knows something of old technologies; we had a professor at the University build this." She reached into her tunic and brought out a simple metal tube. It had a switch on its side and a single glass eye, like a bull's-eye lantern. "When I throw this switch, nothing happens. If Mahallan does her job, I'm told that a light will go on inside the tube when you switch it." She flipped the switch. Nothing happened.

"Does she know about this thing?" asked Carrier. Venera snorted derisively.

"No. Why would I tell her?" Idly, she turned the switch again. This time, the glass eye immediately glowed red. Venera yelped in surprise and let go of the rod, which tumbled slowly in the air between them. "Well," she said. "Well, well, well."

Hayden watched as the two of them hovered over the tube, talking excitedly. Venera's little indicator didn't impress him; he was thinking about his experience with the wish-mirror. The glass panels were scattered throughout this building; he tried to remember the words Aubri had used to light hers.

"Listen," he said, "the bike is full of bullet holes. If something's broken we need to know now, while there's still time to fix it. I'm not sure this place is going to still be safe for us once the suns start coming back on." Mother and Father had talked a lot about radiation; he remembered that. Even if it remained cool in here throughout the day, it might be lethally radioactive while the suns were operating.

Carrier was nodding. "Go check it out, then."

Hayden took one more look at Aubri. She was perched in midair, staring at the glowing images on the screen. Her face was masklike, expressionless.

Heart pounding, Hayden slipped under a wall and away from the plots of Slipstream.

"WHEN YOU'RE OUT of ideas, just give another order." Chaison Fanning recalled the cynical advice of one of his academy teachers as the helmsman moved to execute his latest command. The expeditionary force was sweeping the air around Sargasso 44 using sophisticated spiral search patterns. He had all the bikes out hunting for contrails. It was all he knew to do. Meanwhile he retained a mask of professional calm, as though he'd expected this and had a plan. He had no plan. There was nothing left but to run for home.

"Bike brigade sixteen reports no sightings, sir," reported the semaphore team. Chaison nodded. There was nothing but gray mist outside the forward portholes. The clouds on the edge of winter were to have been his greatest advantage if he'd succeeded in luring the Falcon Formation ships out of their den. Ironically, that dense pack of wraithlike mists was now obscuring any chance he had of finding where the enemy had gone.

The light outside the portholes was fading: night was coming to Falcon. The Formation synchronized its day and night cycle with Candesce, so the Sun of Suns must be going out now too. If Aubri Mahallan had done her job, in a few minutes the subtle distortions of space-time ringing out from Candesce would cease. This night, technologies long banned in Virga would become possible here again. Radar might now work.

The radar man Mahallan had trained was looking at him expectantly. Chaison gave a half-smile. Why not? "Begin radar sweep," he said, chin on his fist. It was nice to know that his voice was still calm, despite his desperate disappointment.

Even now the newly minted Falcon dreadnought might be bearing down on Rush. There was nothing in Slipstream that could stop it. The pilot richly deserved to be deposed—Chaison knew he would get no argument from his men on that score—but Falcon Formation would eat everything if it conquered Slipstream. They had done it before: art would be repainted according to the arbitrary standards of the bureaucracy, literature rewritten to match the ideology of the Collective. Architecture would be chipped away and eventually, even the language itself distorted to match Falcon's vision of a perfect world.

A horrible sick feeling filled Chaison. He wondered if the citizens of Aerie had felt that way when the pilot had uttered his ultimatum to them.

A younger Chaison Fanning would never have considered such a thing.

"It's working!" He shot the radar man an annoyed look. "Sorry, sir. I mean, we have a signal. The screen is clear! Look."

Despite himself Chaison was intrigued. Aubri Mahallan had made toy versions of the system that showed how things were supposed to look. Now as he unstrapped himself and glided over he saw little glowing smudges on the two green circles of the display, very similar to the ones Mahallan had displayed. She had drilled the bridge staff in the meanings of the various shapes, and so Chaison had no difficulty in recognizing the other ships of the expeditionary force as spindle-shaped lozenges of lighter green. The two screens showed the results from rotating beams that were at right angles to one another. Comparing them, you could roughly guess at the position of objects in three-dimensional space.

The bridge staff were all staring over his shoulder. Chaison ignored them. "What's that?" he asked, pointing at a broad smudge well behind the centerpoint that represented the Rook.

"I believe that's the sargasso, sir."

"Hmm." He stared at the display for a few seconds. "All right then," he said, "if these shapes are us," he pointed, "and that shape is the sargasso," he pointed again, "then what, exactly, is *that*?"

Right at the edge of the displays, a collection of tiny dots scintillated. One by one they were leaving the screen, which suggested they were moving very quickly.

Chaison and the radar man looked at one another. Then the admiral jumped back to his seat. "All hands! Prepare for maximum acceleration! Recall all bikes! Semaphore team, order all ships to activate their radar! Tell them, if you want to have a place to spend that treasure you're wearing, then follow us now!"

AFTER CHECKING OUT the bike and spending an hour or so repairing it, Hayden drifted back into the corridors of the station. He dithered over whether to look in on Aubri—but she had insisted that only she could find a way to excise the dark thing coiled in her throat. He didn't want to interrupt her in that crucial task. No, he had his own responsibility, and he had best fulfil it.

He found a small room far from the place where Aubri was working. It was dark here, but there was a command mirror on the wall. He strapped himself opposite it and tried to remember the words Aubri had spoken to activate hers.

It took several tries, but soon the rectangle began to glow. "Huh." Hayden couldn't believe he was actually here, in Candesce, doing something no one had ever told him was even possible. Controlling the Sun of Suns itself.

The twisting ballet of Candesce's night machines revealed itself to him and he scanned the air for the things he sought. It seemed like many years since he had played in the half-built sun while his mother ordered construction crews about. Not that long a time, in adult terms. He remembered the day the precious inner components had arrived, shipped at horrendous expense and in secret from the principalities of Candesce. The crates with their exotic stamps and lettering were more interesting to Hayden than their contents, but he remembered those as well. Now, he examined the interior of Candesce looking for similar mechanisms.

From what he'd seen earlier, Hayden had surmised that the crystalline cylinders were factories of a sort, manufacturing new pieces for the suns. Now as he examined them—the display zooming into fine focus if he wished it to, zooming out again just as easily—he began to understand the logic of the Sun of Suns. Those tiny glittering clouds spiraling into the cylinders, they were the bugs Aubri had called tankers, only here they swarmed by the million. They were bringing in supplies. Inside the cylinders and unfolded metal flowers, the metal foremen and laborers of Candesce forged new wicks for the sun, and when they were done they handed them off to other machines that installed them.

All that Hayden had to do was locate the pieces he wanted and then imagine them being brought here. *Park them outside the door,* he commanded. With mounting excitement he watched as his orders were obeyed.

No wonder no one was allowed in here! You could destroy Candesce on a whim from this place; and if Candesce went, so would go all of Virga.

The thought was disturbing. Hayden's excitement soured as he watched the slow parade of machines sidle through the air toward the visitor's center. This was too easy—there was too much power to be had here. It made him wonder what Venera Fanning would do once this episode was over. Or what the Pilot of Slipstream would do if he demanded and received the Candesce key from the Fannings.

After assuring himself that the machines were doing as he'd asked, Hayden left the little room. He flipped over and under walls, around floors, hurrying back to the entrance and his bike.

Double-check the bike to make sure it was flight-worthy. Tie the sun components he'd found into the cargo net and tie it to the back of the bike. And then . . . rehearse what he was going to say to the others when they saw what he'd acquired.

They would need convincing—particularly Carrier. His plan was to get to the man through his mistress, Venera. If he could convince her that these components were his just payment for his part in this adventure, then maybe she could restrain Carrier.

He flipped around a corner and spotted the entrance.

It was open.

Hayden slowed down and cautiously drew his sword. Had the Gehellens somehow managed to force the door? That didn't seem likely; why now, after so many centuries? Or maybe—the thought gave him a chill—maybe now that it was unlocked, anyone could get in here. He hadn't thought of that. Were the Gehellen airmen inside?

Hayden could see the first of the packages he'd ordered bobbing in the darkness outside. Despite his worry, the sight made him smile. He looked around the room. There was the bike, seemingly untouched. There was no one else in sight. He moved carefully toward the door.

Carrier swung in from outside to brace himself on the two sides of the entrance. Night was at his back. "So there you are," he said. "I wondered what exactly you were going to try. Of course, I had no doubt that you'd try something."

"This doesn't concern you," said Hayden.

"A new sun for Aerie does concern me."

Carrier drew his sword.

THE *ROOK* ROARED through blackness with exhilarating recklessness. Chaison imagined statutes and naval regulations fluttering in the ship's wake, centuries of rules about how fast to travel in cloud all broken in an instant. He pushed the Rook to one hundred miles an hour, then two hundred, and watched the dots of the Falcon Formation navy grow into circles, then distinct ship shapes.

The bridge crew were white-faced. Travis perched next to Chaison, his lips drawn thin while his fingers gripped the edge of the chair. Logic said they would run into something at this speed—but of everyone in the bridge, it was the radar man who was now the calmest. "Bear two degrees to port, five south," he would say, or "six degrees starboard right now." The pilot, flying blind, obeyed with frantic sweeps of the wheels.

"Getting secondary signals," said the radar man abruptly. "Just like she said."

"All right." Chaison smiled grimly. "You know what to do."

Falcon's fleet was creeping slowly through an ocean of cloud; nobody could tell how far the mist extended. He didn't need the cloud, of course, it was night anyway. But if they could strand the target vessels of the Falcon fleet in opaque fog they would still be vulnerable when daylight returned. —If the battle still raged at that point.

Meanwhile, he had to deny the enemy all their other assets. "Line up on those bikes," he said. "'Ware our other ships, they'll be doing the same. We're going to scrape the sentries off Falcon's fleet like old scabs."

The engines whined as they accelerated one more notch. There was a sudden dark flicker outside the portholes and then *bang!* The ship twitched to the impact, but ran on.

Chaison winced. They were running over the Falcon Formation's sentry bikes. As when the *Tormentor's* bikes had flown ahead to watch for obstacles—unsuccessfully, in that case—the Falcon fleet was feeling its way by sending them ahead and to the sides. Lacking radar, the bikes were its only means of safe travel through darkness and cloud.

Another crash against the hull, and another. On the radar Chaison could see the shapes of *Rook's* sister ships overtaking the dots of Falcon bikes, which simply vanished as they passed.

Ahead was the huge but indistinct blob that must be the new dreadnought—a weapon of terror no one from Slipstream had ever seen except in blurry photos. Ironically, they were unlikely to see it now. If all went well the men of Slipstream would never make visual contact with the enemy they were destroying.

The *Rook* swept out and around in a great circle. Chaison was reassured to see no clear air ahead as they came around for another pass. "Prepare to deploy mines," he said. Then, "Brake, brake!" He heard the flutter-chop of the braking sails being thrust out of the hull and then he was nose-down, Travis clinging to the back of the chair as the *Rook* groaned and began to decelerate. "Engines off!"

In sudden silence save for the rush of wind and the whuffing breath of the braking sails, the *Rook* slid past the invisible dreadnought and directly into its path.

"Deploy mines! Out out out now now now!"

There was the sound of wind in open hangar doors, and a distant rattle like some monster clearing its throat.

Then thunder.

21

A RIBBON OF Hayden's blood twisted in the center of the room, as if blindly trying to find him. Carrier had connected with a slash to his cheek.

"Wait!" Hayden backed away. The man's first lunge had taken him by surprise, but he had his own sword out now. Yes, it would be satisfying to counterattack Carrier, who had killed his family; so much more satisfying to change his mind.

"You still have a chance to save yourself," said Hayden as Carrier braced himself for another leap.

"Save myself?" Carrier laughed. "I'm the better swordsman by far!"

"That's not what I mean. I'm talking about your son."

Carrier's face went ashen white. "Wh—"

"You betrayed him! Betrayed him and had him killed. And it eats away at you. Your life has been barren since that moment, hasn't it? Anyone can see it in the way you walk, hear it in the tone of your voice. I just didn't know why, until the other night."

"My life's not your concern," grated Carrier. "Look to your own."

"You don't believe there's any way you could make up for what you did to him. I'm saying there is. Can you even imagine such a thing anymore? There is."

Carrier visibly fought to control himself. "No."

"How would your son feel if he knew that, in the end, you took back your choice? —That you let his project succeed?"

Now Carrier was silent, his eyes wide.

"Slipstream will leave Aerie in a few years. Why not leave a viable nation behind? That was all he wanted. Let me bring back the pieces of a new sun for my people; it won't be ready in time to be a threat to you. Why not? Your son's spirit will be reborn in that light. You'll have him back in that way. It's not too late."

Carrier lowered his sword, his face eloquently puzzled at a possibility he'd never even considered. Then, gradually, Hayden saw his features harden again, as if in the end his guilt were all he was really comfortable with.

"Nice try!" he shouted, and then he leaped again.

FOUR SLIPSTREAM CRUISERS glided silently through the dark. Horns and gunshots sounded in discontinuous bedlam, but in the impenetrable night it was impossible to put direction or distance to any of the sounds.

The courses of the cruisers began to diverge; observers on one ship watched the other silhouettes flicker and fade into the clouds. Now odd objects began twirling past, momentarily flame-lit: men, their limbs akimbo; smouldering flinders; the crumpled rings of military bikes. They shot by the ships with frightening speed, yet it was not they that moved, but the ships.

An order went out: brake! The cruiser strained and shook as the shuttlecock vanes of the braking sails tumbled into the airstream.

Next came the hardest thing. It was drilled into the minds and reflexes of naval gunnery teams never to fire a rocket blindly. Once loosed, ordnance just kept on going and in any military engagement in populated air, shots that missed the enemy would eventually hit another friendly ship—or civilians.

For weeks Admiral Fanning had tried to undo this training. Now the rocket teams waited tensely for the order, uneasily watching each other, the walls, the rocket racks—anything but the depthless black outside the square firing ports. When the order came it was a shock, however expected it had been. "Ten degrees by forty-three!" barked the officer at the speaking tube. The team cranked the racks around and up. "Fire!"

Sere lines of orange light leapt into the mist—five, ten, fifteen in less than a second. Backwashing fumes billowed over the team. Used to this, nobody coughed or moved. Mist swallowed the contrails.

The cruiser's engines whined into life; it was already turning by the time chattering bangs indicated a hit. By the time the enemy triangulated on the incoming rockets' contrails and fired back, the Rook would be gone.

Chaison Fanning looked up from the radar screens. Travis was staring at the glowing green circles, shaking his head minutely and muttering. Chaison caught his eye and smiled.

"Look at them all," said the officer. Travis had circles under his eyes; evidently his injured arm was giving him trouble but he hadn't complained, probably hadn't even noticed.

Look at them all. The navy of Falcon Formation spread away into in-determinacy in all directions; knots, clusters, and clouds of ships of all sizes and designations. The Rook was weaving recklessly through them at two hundred miles an hour, a falcon among pigeons. The enemy would see the glow of the cruiser's engines for seconds at a time as it lunged out of nothing and before they could train their weapons on it, it would be gone again.

"Admiral, sir!" He glanced back to see the boy Martor saluting him from the doorway. "Sir, we've had to restrain Slew."

"What? The head carpenter? What's he done?"

"Running around telling us to stop. Said it weren't natural to fight a battle this way." The old Martor would have smirked while he reported something like this; this new version, his side still taped up where Chaison had removed a bullet, looked very serious as he held his salute.

"Very good. Keep him out of our way until after the battle." He turned back to the radar.

"These vessels," said Chaison, indicating some boxy shapes on the edge of the screen. "They're troop carriers, aren't they?"

Travis nodded. "They've got the profile. No reason to send those on maneuvers. And they move like they're full."

The fleet had been driving in the direction of Slipstream. Venera's spies had been right, it was an invasion force. Of course, Chaison had known the spies' reports were accurate—or he would never have undertaken this mad escapade. Somehow, though, seeing the ships and their heading made him furious with Falcon Formation for the first time. As though he hadn't really known at all.

"More mines, sir. We can avoid the cloud this time, but they're going to disperse soon. It'll be harder to find a way around them next time."

"Hmmph." The dreadnought had not stopped when it realized Rook had mined the air ahead of it. To Chaison's astonishment and dismay, the huge vessel had simply plowed through the cloud, enduring a staccato barrage of explosions without apparent effect. It was not to be stopped that way; and if it kept going, sooner or later it would reach clear air, and Slipstream's advantage would diminish.

So Chaison was targeting its engines. He'd emptied barrage after barrage of rockets into them but so far the dreadnought hadn't slowed significantly. Having realized what was happening—if not how it was being done—Falcon was now mining the air around their ships. The mines were tuned to ignore impacts at less than fifty miles an hour, so the fleet continued to grind forward and maneuvering became harder and harder for Slipstream.

"I want to stop the dreadnought," said Chaison, "but I want

those troop carriers taken out as well. Without them there's no oc-cupying force." He gave the order to the semaphore team, who had reluctantly given up their flags and were cheerlessly using an elec-tromagnetic signaling technique called "radio telegraph" that was based on Mahallan's radar. It let the Slipstream ships communicate instantly, with no interference from clouds.

Travis glanced up at Chaison. "Bit of a surprise about Slew, isn't it?"

Both men smiled—and Chaison was about to say something witty when the green light of a thousand tumbling flares burst through the portholes. The Rook had entered clear air.

HAYDEN LEAPT TO the side careless of where he might end up. Free of doubt now, Venera's spymaster was relentless, econom-ical in his movements, and expressionless as he pursued Hayden around the room.

It didn't help that this place was so bare of ornament. The an-techamber where the bike had been left had only a few hand-straps on the walls, ceiling, and floor, as well as some cabinets and shelves that didn't make good purchase. The key to a gravity-free sword fight was never to let yourself become stranded in midair—and in this place, that was not so easy. As they circled one another Hayden tried to ensure that he had one hand or foot on a strap or piece of furniture at all times. With blank wall at your back, all you could do was jump straight out, and the enemy would know in advance where you were going. And when you dove at your enemy, you made your whole body a missile but you also could not stop until you'd made contact with something; your opponent would attempt to ensure that the something was his sword blade.

Carrier seemed unhurried. There was no indication that adrena-line powered him; it was more like he was going through a set of mechanical motions, cut, parry, dodge, cut. He would keep doing it until Hayden was dead.

Hayden dove for the door but Carrier anticipated him. They came together in the center of the room, thrusting with their sword-arms while reaching to try to catch sleeve or foot with the other hand. For frantic seconds they tumbled and then a thrust by Carrier took Hayden through the left bicep. He shouted at the jolt of pain.

Carrier gave a grunt of satisfaction. Hayden tried to pull back but Carrier fluidly moved with him, keeping the blade embedded in flesh as Hayden cursed.

Not so gracefully, Carrier flailed at a wall-strap with his other hand. He caught it—barely—and swung his sword, with Hayden attached, outward. Hayden knew he was seconds away from being placed motionless in midair, out of reach of the walls, at which point Carrier could bounce around and cut him to pieces at his leisure.

Desperately Hayden let go of his own sword, grabbed the blade of Carrier's, and pushed. The metal slid out of his skin, dotting the air with blood, and then Carrier yanked it out of his grasp, slicing Hayden's fingers open to the bone. Hayden writhed out of the way of the backhanded cut that followed. He tried to snatch his own sword out of the air but it had drifted too far away. He saw then that he really was stranded, two meters from the nearest handhold.

Carrier sneered and stood up from the wall-strap which he'd hooked with his foot. Hayden twisted around again and managed to kick the older man in the face. As Carrier cursed and spat blood, Hayden very slowly drifted across the room.

Carrier dove past him again with a vicious slash. Hayden did as Katcheran had drilled him to do: he rolled into a ball in the air and presented his feet to the blade. The sword chopped right through the tough leather but a cut foot wasn't going to kill him. And the pressure of the blow put him closer to the bike.

His sword twinkled as it turned on the far side of the room. Carrier perched at the inner door now, and was carefully lining up his next jump. This time he would thrust rather than cut, Hayden knew; there would be no evading the blow.

He stretched out, reaching for the bike. Carrier laughed. "Even if you can reach that what are you going to do?" he asked. "Throw it at me? Bounce somewhere? I'll never let you get your sword, you know."

Hayden's taut fingers brushed the curving metal of the bike. And Carrier jumped.

"FULL ABOUT!" CHAISON dove for the portholes, missed his grip, and banged his chin on the wall. He pressed his face up against the glass, staring out at vast sensual curves of green-lit cloud. He still had the advantage here, because the dozens of flares drifting out of the cloudbanks lit only a small volume; the plan had counted on the fact that there were many smaller clouds dotting the edge of winter. His ships could dive through them with impunity. But while the six battered, obsolete Slipstream vessels still had an advantage of speed and maneuverability here, it wouldn't be enough. Falcon simply had too many ships.

The Rook pivoted in midcourse, air tearing at its hull, and Chaison strained to catch a glimpse of what was behind her. Lurid tumbles of cloud; arms and arches of vapor. And emerging from it only one other ship, so far.

"All batteries, target that ship! Don't give it a chance to sound!"

Too late. Even as the first rockets lurched toward the distant cruiser, a faint echo of its clear-air signal came to Chaison's ears. He cursed. "Take it out!" The noise of battle would prevent most of the other vessels from hearing that lone horn—but if only one picked it up, it would repeat it, and so would every other one that heard.

Soon the clouds would be ringing with the signal that open air had been found.

He went back to the radar display. The shadow of Falcon Formation's giant ship still lay some miles inside the cloud, and it was slowing. "All ships: put everything into stopping the dreadnought. Release parachute nets ahead of it, mine the air—*anything!*"

—Hammering sound of bullets hitting the hull. Sudden flame of a missile veering past. He heard the Rook's own machine-gunners opening up at something. "Put us back in the cloud deck," Chaison commanded as he regained his chair.

The ship took a hit before they managed to escape into the mist. There was chaos over the speaking tube for about a minute, then an all-clear. Chaison frowned at the indiscipline, but most of his attention was on the radar.

They had arrived at this battle late. Daybreak was little more than an hour away. By the time Falcon's suns were glowing full, Venera would have had Mahallan switch Candesce's defensive systems back on.

During this long night of dark maneuvering, Slipstream had thrown the Falcon Formation fleet into disarray, had wiped out its bikes and smaller vessels, and scored crippling blows on a number of midsize ships. The troop carriers appeared damaged as well. But that was all—and it was nothing.

If they didn't score a decisive blow to Falcon's invasion plans in the next minutes, the whole mission would have been for nothing.

"Sir!" It was the radar man. "We—I think we've lost a ship."

Chaison looked where he was pointing. One of the fast-moving dots on the screens had broken in two pieces. As he watched the pieces subdivided and disintegrated. The dots dissolved into smudges on the screens.

"Any idea who that was?" Chaison asked into the sudden silence. He scowled at the display. *The damn fools flirted with a mine cloud.*

There was silence in the bridge; the men glanced at one another. "Back to the dreadnought," Chaison commanded. "I want the cutters packed with explosives—warheads, bullets, everything we've got. Rockets haven't had much effect on it, so we're going to ram something bigger down its throat."

And if those don't work, we'll make the Rook itself into a missile.

CARRIER JUMPED.

Hayden grabbed the seam of the bike's saddle and pulled as hard as he could.

The cargo net he'd stuffed under the saddle flowered into the air and he spun as best he could, throwing it at Carrier. The spymaster shouted and tried to evade it but he was in midleap now and there was nothing he could do. Tangled, swearing furiously, he bounced off the bike and back into the air.

Hayden planted both feet on the metal and pushed. The dive took him across the length of the room and he plucked his sword out of the air before spinning and kicking off from the far wall. Carrier was struggling to free his sword from the net; his awkward parry went bad and suddenly he was staring down at Hayden's sword which stuck out of his chest.

"Wh—" He tried to reach up; failed, and looked in Hayden's eyes. Carrier was trying to speak.

"Don't talk to me," said Hayden. "The one you need to explain yourself to isn't here. You'll see him soon enough." He let go of the sword, turned, and jumped back to the bike. Reaching around the exhaust vent, he caught a loop of the thin cable he'd stashed there before they had left the Rook. He pulled out the loop and began to unreel it.

When he was sure Lyle Carrier was dead he unwove the net from around him, and attached the cord to it. Then he moved to the door and looked for the first of the packages he'd ordered Candesce to provide.

AUBRI MAHALLAN WAS acting very nervous, and it was driving Venera crazy. After the tenth time that the woman bounced a circuit around the room, Venera said, "Is there something you need to do?"

Mahallan shook her head, becoming very still. "No. Nothing."

"Then settle down. It's not your husband who's in the middle of a battle right now. Your man's just down the hall."

"He's not my man," said Aubri quickly.

Venera raised an eyebrow. "Oh? He thinks he is."

Now Mahallan looked uncomfortable; as far as Venera was concerned, that was a definite improvement.

"You don't think the waiting gets to me?" continued Venera. She crossed her arms, glancing once at the indicator device she had stashed in her bag by one wall. It still glowed steadily. As long as it was on, Chaison retained his advantage; so in a sense, its light was her lifeline to him. But she would have to shut it down soon, when dawn came.

"I'm not you," said Aubri, scowling. "I've done a great deal for your little project, Venera. Have you ever asked yourself what I'm going to get out of all this?"

Venera shrugged. "You never asked for anything, did you? Which is odd, except that you're an exile for whom everywhere is the same. . . . But why not take Hayden Griffin? He's a fine catch for someone from the servant classes. Is that your problem with him? That he's not one of your own kind?"

"You wouldn't understand," said Mahallan.

Venera laughed. "On more than one occasion I've been told that my problem is that I do understand people, I just don't feel for them. Which is probably true. But you're right, I don't get it. We've completed our project, you're free and as rich as you want to be. In just a few minutes you can switch the sun's defenses back on, and then all you have to do is take your money and your man and go enjoy yourself. What could be simpler?"

Mahallan looked startled. "Is it time already?"

Venera checked her pocket watch. "Getting there."

"Okay." Aubri smiled; it seemed a bit forced to Venera. Mahallan glided over to the command mirror. "I'll get ready to shut it down, then," she said brightly.

"All right." Venera watched her, keeping her face neutral. As the strange outsider woman gazed into the mirror, Venera let herself drift over to her bag. She made sure that she could see the glow of her indicator, and Mahallan, without turning her head.

Just in case, she loosened the scabbard of her sword.

THE DREADNOUGHT WAS tangled in parachutes and trailed debris in a long smoking beard of rope and timber. Its engines were tangled knots of metal belching black smoke into the air. Its rudders were useless flags.

There were no significant holes in its hull.

The mist ahead of it was brightening as it approached open, flare-lit air. Just a few hundred yards and it would be free of the nightmarish disadvantage of the clouds. Its enemy would no longer be invisible. One shot from the rifled ten-inch guns mounted along its sides and the smaller ships would be matchwood. All it needed was the sight lines.

As the *Tormentor* slid into position to unloose a salvo, the dreadnought got its chance. The Slipstream ship had been relying on the veils of mist to let it do what it had done ten times already: stand off, hidden, and pummel the larger vessel before moving to another firing position. This time, though, the intervening clouds proved to be just a thin curtain and when it parted suddenly, the Tormentor was unluckily right in the way of a searchlight. The dreadnought's gunners had been waiting for this.

The first shell convulsed the cruiser with an internal explosion. The next broke it in half. Six more followed, pulverizing the twisting remains before the shockwave from the first blast had died out. The Tormentor and all its men were simply erased from the sky.

Rockets continued to rain on the dreadnought from other directions—but the gun crews were emboldened now and began firing wildly. If some of their own ships were close by, well, too bad; any sane Falcon Formation craft would be headed for that brightening in the clouds by now. Only the enemy would lurk in the darkness, and so into that darkness they fired.

A lucky shell clipped the Unseen Hand's stern and blew its engines off. Its crew bailed out, flapping away with foot-wings, but the Hand's captain was old, mean-tempered Hieronymous Flosk. He drew a pistol and aimed it at the bridge door. "Any man who tries to leave, dies!" he bellowed. "We're going in! Man your posts, you cowards! Make your lives count for something!"

The Hand still had steering and was doing over a hundred miles an hour. When it lunged out of the cloudbank the dreadnought's gunners had only a few seconds to fire and the one shell that hit bounced off the cruiser's streamlined hull. Then the Unseen Hand slammed into the side of the great ship and exploded.

In a zone of half-mist, where towering banks of cloud interspersed with pockets of clarity, the dreadnought shuddered and sighed to a stop.

"SIR." THE RADAR man sounded puzzled. Chaison looked up from trying to catch the flailing straps of his seat belt. The whole ship was rattling now as their airspeed peeled away planks behind the open wound of the hangar doors. They had to reduce their velocity, but a few bikes and cutters were still pursuing.

The radar man held up his chronometer. "Sir, it's daybreak in Falcon. The radar shouldn't be working anymore, but it's holding steady."

Chaison stared at him. What did this mean? Was Venera giving him a gift of extra time? Or had something gone wrong in Candesce?

He might have radar for as long as he needed it . . . or it might cut out at any second. It no longer mattered: daylight was here.

The clouds were an abyss of pearl dotted with instants of black—men, burnt-out flares, and wreckage only half-glimpsed as the Rook shot by them. And coalescing out of the writhing whiteness were the iron contours of the dreadnought. The great ship seemed determined to keep a pall of night around itself; it had drawn a cloak of smoke and debris around its hull. With each broadside it let loose, the smoke thickened.

"I bet they never thought of this," Travis said, shaking his head. "Rockets take their exhaust with them when they go. But guns . . . They're blinding themselves with smoke."

"It's a gift," said Chaison. "Let's take it while it's offered." He moved to the speaking tube. "Are the cutters loaded and ready? Good. Wait until I give the order and then let them fly."

The Rook spiraled around the motionless dreadnought just ahead of cannonades of deadly fire. Chaison stared through the portholes, looking for any vulnerable spot through the wavering lines of tracer rounds that subdivided the air. Enemy bikes shot past, snarling like hornets, and the Rook bucked to some sort of impact.

"Enemy closing from all directions, sir," said the radar man. "It looks like they've got another of ours boxed in too . . . I think it's the Arrest. I can't see the Severance, but they're still broadcasting."

"Bring us closer," Chaison told the pilot. He'd seen what he was looking for—a triangular dent, yards wide, in the hull of the dreadnought. The surrounding metal was scored and burnt; something bigger than a rocket had impacted there. He reached for the speaking tube—

—And everything spun and hit at him, walls furniture the men rebounding with the shock of a tremendous explosion. Half-deafened, Chaison shook himself and grabbed for a handhold, abstractly noticing that the bridge doors were twisted, half-ajar. *Slew's not going to fix this one*, he thought.

He struggled back to the commander's chair. The pilot was unconscious and Travis was shoving him aside to reach the controls. Chaison grabbed the speaking tube and shouted, "Report, report!"

A thin voice on the other end said, "They're dead."

"Who's dead?"

"The . . . everybody that was in the hangar, sir."

"Is this Martor? What about the cutters?"

"One's intact, sir." There was a pause. "I'll take it out, sir."

Chaison turned away for a moment, unable to speak. "Son," he said, "just aim it and jump clear. Make sure you've got a pair of wings and just get out of there. That's an order."

"Yes, sir."

Travis had the ship under control and was banking tightly to avoid a fusillade of shells from the dreadnought. "Sir, here comes the rest of Falcon," he said tightly. Chaison glanced at the portholes and saw a white sky crowded with ships. Just then a large shape obscured the view: the explosives-laden cutter had soared ahead of the *Rook* and was curving down toward the iron monstrosity.

Chaison couldn't look away. Tracer rounds and the shocked air of shell fire outlined the cutter; he saw pieces of its armor shattering and flying away. Then it was suddenly not there, and Chaison blinked away afterimages of a flash that must have been visible for miles.

The roar overtook the *Rook*, shaking the hull and starring another porthole. Chaison simply stared at the absence and coiling serpents of smoke. He felt a crush of grief and for a few moments was paralyzed, unable to think.

But everything rested on his decision. He shook off his feelings and turned to Travis.

"Prepare to scuttle the ship," he said.

22

HAYDEN TIED THE last of the sun components into the cargo net. His hands were shaking. As he fumbled with the cords, he noticed his shadow, hunched and vague, wavering against the gray wall of the visitor's station. He looked over in time to see the metal flowers of Candesce's strange garden closing. Silhouetting one of them was an orange glow that hadn't been there a minute ago.

"Oh no." He finished the knot hastily and climbed back along the cargo net's cables to the open entrance of the station. The bike was tethered there; it too had a shadow—no, two shadows. He looked down and saw that a second sun was opening its glowing eye.

He'd thrown Carrier's body into the open air. His story was going to be that the Gehellens had come back and there'd been a fight at the entrance. The attackers had been driven off but Carrier was killed. He had rehearsed his story over and over during the past hour, while he struggled against the pain of his wounds to fill the nets with sun parts. As he'd done so he'd found himself crying.

He no longer wondered at such tears. As he rehearsed the lie about the Gehellens, Hayden found himself wondering whether he was reluctant to tell the truth to Venera, or Aubri or himself. Either way, he felt no satisfaction at Carrier's death. The only thing he was proud of was his attempt to talk the man out of attacking him.

So in his head he began to rehearse a second story. This one would not be told until he was an old man, if he got things right. It began and ended with, "Carrier was the last man I killed, or ever wanted to kill."

Once inside the station he climbed quickly from strap to strap, heading for the inner chambers. "We have to go!" he called as he went. "Come on, the suns are waking up!"

Nobody answered. What were Venera and Aubri up to? From his own experience with the wish-mirror, he'd seen that once you set something in motion here, you could pretty much ignore it and go on about your business. Aubri shouldn't have had to nurse Candesce after shutting down its defenses against Artificial Nature.

"Aubri! Venera! Where are you? We have to leave, now!"

He heard a thump from somewhere ahead. Hayden ducked under and over walls, passing through several rooms that seemed familiar. Then, as he was gliding across a half-lit room filled with hammocks and rest nooks, he heard a woman's voice growl a single word:

"Bitch!"

More thumps and a gasp from the other side of this wall. Hayden perched there for a moment, blinking, then swung down to climb into the next room. He stopped, straddling the wall.

Aubri Mahallan and Venera Fanning clung to straps on opposite walls. Both women had swords in their hands, and those swords were pointed at one another. Venera's face was twisted into a rictus of fury, muscles jumping in her famous jaw.

"Turn it on!" Venera screamed. "Turn it back on!"

Aubri silently shook her head.

Hayden somersaulted into the room. "What's going on?" He made to join Aubri, but she dove out of his way.

"Stay back," she murmured.

"Stay . . . ? What's going on?" By now, he was too tired and in too much pain to catch her.

Venera pointed to where her special indicator lamp tumbled in midair, its light glowing steadily. "She won't turn it back on.

Candesce's defenses! She was willing to turn them off all right, but she won't bring them back. She's opened the gates to her friends from beyond Virga."

"Aubri?" He stared at her, but she wouldn't return his gaze.

He should have figured this out. He realized now that she had given him enough clues over the past week—but he'd been so consumed with the idea of finding components for a new Aerie sun that he hadn't thought through the things Aubri had told him. She had told him that she had not been sent to Virga to enter Candesce; but in the same breath she had told him that the assassin-thing coiled inside her was listening for any hint that she might reveal her true mission. Her denial should have tipped him off; but he hadn't been smart enough to see it.

"I'm sorry," she said in a low, shaking voice. "If I turn it back on, I'll die."

"You were sent to bring Artificial Nature to Virga," he said. "That's what you couldn't tell me." She nodded.

Hayden's thoughts were racing. Should he try to stop this? Or should he side with Aubri? "What happens now?" he asked her. "When you let them in . . . What are you letting in?"

Now she looked at him, her expressive features crumpled into sadness. "A trillion ghosts will come first," she said. "The disembodied AIs and post-humans will flood into Virga, make it their playground. They're hungry for resources. They'll transform everything they touch—and everybody. When that transformation happens, your reality will fade away. The walls of Virga will disappear. The suns, the darkness, the towns, and ships . . . They'll be erased by virtual realms. Glorious beauty, places like Heaven brought into being around every man, woman, and child. Whatever you imagine will come to pass. Everything and anything, except Virga itself. Everything you knew will be gone, replaced by fantasies made real."

Venera shuddered. "We won't survive it," she said.

Aubri shook her head. "Not as you are now," she said. "Whatever your hopes and dreams were, they're obsolete now. You'll need new ones. New reasons to live." Her mouth twisted in grief. "And that's the one thing the system can't make for you."

"No!" Venera launched herself across the room. Before Hayden could reach them the two women were twisting in the air, Venera slashing madly at Aubri who tried to parry. Hayden cried out as he saw Venera's sword slide into the muscle under Aubri's left shoulder.

Hayden's lover, the *Rook*'s armorer, tumbled backward streaming blood.

He screamed and jumped, too late, as Venera cursed and kicked off from Aubri's limp body. Venera reached a corner and ducked around the offset panels with one wide-eyed look back at Hayden.

He wrapped his arms around Aubri and turned so his own back took their impact on the far wall. She was jerking in his grasp, twists of blood reaching out of her with each breath.

"I'm—sorry," she gasped. "I was too afraid."

"Hush," he said, smoothing back her hair. "It's not your fault. It's theirs for making you and then condemning you for being who you are."

She closed her eyes and whimpered. "Hush," he said again, holding her close.

"No." She pushed against him. "No! Let me go. Get me to the, the command mirror." She pointed at a glassy rectangle on the ceiling.

"Stay still."

"No. Let—" She writhed in his arms, turning to glare at him.

"Let me beat them."

THE BRIDGE WAS full of drifting grit and the stench of smoke. Deafening explosions rattled the beams; all the portholes had shattered. Chaison clung to the arms of his chair and glared out into gleaming sunlight as the Rook came apart around him.

"Ready, sir!" Travis was holding onto a pipe with his toes, one-armed as he was with his hand in a sling; his free hand was poised over the scuttling console.

Chaison felt infinitely weary. It wasn't as though it mattered whether Falcon Formation got its hands on the radar sets. There wasn't anything they could do with them. Assuming, of course, that Aubri Mahallan did her job. The idea that she might not seemed distantly worrying, but he couldn't bring himself to focus on abstractions. Instead, he frowned past the jagged glass rimming the porthole, at the obstinately solid silhouette of the dreadnought that was even now turning to aim its biggest guns at the Rook.

All I wanted, he thought with an ironic smile, *was to get rid of that thing.*

As the dreadnought turned it exposed the dented portion of hull where something had collided with it. Sunlight angled around the dark hull and Chaison saw that the ship's armor had split at the bottom of that dent; there was a three-sided hole there.

"Wait a second, Travis," he said. Chaison frowned, then reached for the speaking tube.

"Rocket batteries one and two, are you there?" he shouted.

"Y-yes, sir. What do you want us to do, sir?"

"Don't bail out," he said. "You'll be shot to pieces in open air. I have a plan. Load the racks and get ready."

"Sir!"

He turned to Travis, who was watching him with a raised eyebrow. The radar man and the semaphore team were also staring. "Get to the helm," he told Travis. "We've still got power. We're going to ram her."

"Ah. I see." Travis looked faintly disappointed. Chaison had to laugh.

"No, you don't see," he said. "We're going to ram her *there*." He pointed. Travis began to smile.

The *Rook* ducked out of the path of the big guns, angling up and shooting straight at the line of Falcon Formation battleships that was bearing down on her. They were momentarily safe since the ships would not want to miss *Rook* and hit the dreadnought.

The *Rook* groaned as Travis spun them around and lined up on the dreadnought. "They're going to get at least one good shot at us, sir," he said.

Chaison shrugged. "Have you got a better idea?"

Travis didn't answer, but merely pushed the control levers forward. Chaison heard the distant engines whine toward full power.

"If you do want to bail out," he said to the semaphore team and the radar man, "now would be the time to do it."

Nobody moved.

"All right then."

Holed, dripping splinters and chunks of armor, the *Rook* accelerated for the last time. The air it crossed was layered with smoke and debris, the bodies of men and unexploded ordnance. Chaison watched it all pass in disgust. *How pointless.* He wasn't sure whether it was Falcon's invasion that he meant, or his own attempt to stop it.

"Brace for impact!" He strapped himself in and spun the chair around. It was designed to handle collisions like this; the *Rook*, like her sister ships, had a substantial ram on her prow. She was never intended to ram something as big as a town, though. This whole gambit might just provide a good laugh to the Falconers, if *Rook* simply splatted against the dreadnought's skin like a bug on a porthole.

He closed his eyes, and thought of the home he would never see again.

The impact, when it came, was surprisingly gentle. A vast grinding sound filled Chaison's ears and the ship shuddered and bucked.

Then it eased to a stop. In the swaying light of the gas lamp, he met Travis's eyes and grinned.

"Let's see where we are." The portholes were blocked by wreckage. Both men jumped over to the bridge doors and Travis flung them open. Chaison gasped at what he saw.

The Rook was holed in dozens of places. Its interior was in shambles, with dead men and parts of men, tangled coils of rope, broken bulkheads, and spars thrusting every which way. Way down past where the hangar had been, streams of sunlight made bluish shafts across the space. Nearer, the holes in the hull revealed only darkness.

"We're jammed inside it," Travis said wonderingly. "More than halfway."

Chaison nodded. "That's what I had in mind." He clambered through the wreckage, heading for the rocketeers who huddled next to their bent racks. "Ready to fire, men?" They stared at him.

Chaison laughed recklessly. "Come on!" he shouted. "This is the stuff of legends! We're going to rake this bastard of a ship with a barrage that'll tear it to pieces—and we're going to do it *from the inside!*"

Still they hesitated—and then a loud voice burst out, *"What are you waiting for?"*

It was Slew, smoke-stained and trailing a broken chain from his wrist as he flew up from the aft. Beside him, helping him maneuver past the wreckage, was Ambassador Reiss. Both men had swords in their hands; both looked grimly determined.

"You heard the admiral!" yelled Slew. The men looked at each other, then leaped to their posts. Already Chaison could hear gunshots, and just behind Slew soldiers in Falcon Formation uniforms began pushing their way through gaps in the hull. *The irate crew.* Well, they were too late.

"Reiss, Slew, behind you. You men—fire!"

The port and starboard racks unleashed their rockets and the Rook's hull tried to collapse as everything outside blew up. Some of the rockets must have found their way down long passageways, exploding hundreds of yards away. Some didn't get ten feet. But the dreadnought had never been designed to withstand this kind of attack. As the rocketeers cleared their tubes and made to load another round, the *Rook* was hammered by new explosions, much bigger than those they had caused. Now the hull really was collapsing, Travis grabbing at a stanchion, Reiss and Slew's faces lit with surprise and all of them disappearing into bright sunlight as the ship sheared in two and the sky filled with gouts of smoke and flying darkness.

Somehow, Chaison had caught a rope and found himself dangling over the infinite airs of Virga, watching while the aft half of the dreadnought fell away and wrenched itself to pieces with explosion after explosion. Mesmerized, he didn't look away from the sight until he felt the rope being tugged from the other end. He glanced up.

The shattered half-hull of the *Rook* still stuck out of the fore half of the dreadnought, right at the spot where the great ship had been torn in two. Smoke billowed out of the forward section but it hadn't exploded. Three Falcon airmen were hauling in the rope Chaison held, murder in their eyes. Of the rest of his crew, there was no sign.

"Gentlemen," Chaison said as he held out his hand, "meet the man who beat you."

VENERA WATCHED HAYDEN Griffin weep. A fluttering sense of disquiet plucked at her; she fought against it fiercely.

Aubri Mahallan moved feebly in the young man's arms, gesturing at the command mirror in front of which they floated. Venera clutched her sword in sweating hands and wondered why Lyle had not shown up yet.

The indicator light for Candesce's defenses still spun lazily in the air. Without fanfare, it suddenly went out. Venera frowned at it. Had its little battery died, or . . . She looked at Aubri Mahallan.

The woman's limbs drifted free now, and her head slowly tilted forward. Griffin gave one last wracking sob and then spun to look at the command mirror. It was a rectangle of white light now, all details washed away by the awakening suns.

Griffin turned again, and now he looked straight at Venera. Despite herself, she flinched from his glare. But all he said was, "We have to go."

The words made no sense at all; Venera could barely believe she'd heard them. "I killed your woman," she said. "If I come near you, you'll kill me."

"No," he said.

She sneered. "Oh? Where's Lyle?" Griffin looked away, and Venera's heart sank. "He's not coming, is he? You boys finally settled your little dispute, whatever it was?"

He gathered Mahallan's body in his arms again, and kicked off toward an open corner. "What choice did I have?" she called out after him. "You know what she tried to do!"

"Shut up," he said without looking back. "Just shut up."

Venera was furious and, yes, scared; but she wasn't going to back down. Not to this servant. "So strand me, or shoot me," she cried. "I did what I had to do."

Now, just before disappearing around the corner, he did look back. He looked sad, and puzzled. "Venera, I'm not going to kill you," he said. "There's room on the bike. Come with me."

"That would mean trusting you," she said.

"Yes."

Venera laughed, and hunkered down a little more in the shadows. "I've never done that in my life," she said. "I'm not about to start now."

"Suit yourself," he said with broken weariness. Then he was gone.

Venera remained where she was for long seconds. Outside, Candesce was rousing itself to full power. She couldn't feel the rain of invisible particles that Mahallan had said would flood this place during the day, but she imagined them like virulent poison seeping through the walls. Even if the heat didn't kill her . . .

But trust a man whose lover she had just killed? The idea was insane. Trust Griffin? Trust *anyone?* There were fools who did it and survived somehow. She could not be so lucky, she knew.

Venera fingered her jaw angrily. She would die here, miserable, abandoned.

When the bullet hit her and she lay moaning on the stone she had waited—waited for someone to come to her, to discover her in pain. She had waited for the cries of distress, the solicitations of her rescuers. Nobody came. There was no rescue for Venera Fanning. So in the end she had crawled, herself, unassisted, through the corridors and into the Admiralty. At the last second she had fainted, before knowing whether the ones who found her had cared enough to hold her as Griffin had held Mahallan, whether they wiped her drying tears and murmured that she would be all right. When Chaison tried, much later, it was too late.

Venera spat a curse, and uncoiled from her defensive knot. As quietly as she could, she crept after Hayden Griffin through the dimming rooms of the station.

HEAT AND INTOLERABLE light met Hayden at the entrance. The bike's handlebars were almost too hot to touch and he had to squint and grope for a loop of cable to wrap around Aubri.

He didn't have enough to tie her to the saddle, so he looked around for another solution. Put her in the cargo nets? Maybe—if he could get to them. The heat scored his face whenever he turned toward the suns; the very air was attacking his mouth and lungs.

He wasn't sure he could jump over to the nets and get back before the heat took him.

You've lost her already. Like he'd lost everyone else in his life. He should be used to this by now.

Heartsick, he gave her body the slightest of shoves, and she slipped through his fingers—waist, shoulders, finally one trailing hand smoothing his before the moment of separation. She seemed to be turning to look at him, face calm and lips parted as if to tell him it would be all right, while past her shoulder the mechanical flowers of Candesce curled behind their mirrored petals. As the eyes of the suns opened all around, Aubri Mahallan vanished into light.

Hayden turned and climbed onto the bike.

He spun up the fan and the burner started immediately. As the jet's whine escalated he clung to familiar routines, listening to it, judging the health of the machine. He jiggled it with his knees, estimating how much fuel was left. Hayden knew his machines, and this one still had some life in it. A few refuelings and it would get him back to Rush, he was sure of it.

And then . . . He fingered the pockets of his jacket, which were full of jewels and coins from the treasure of Anetene. He probably had enough to hire the artisans he'd need. The core components of Aerie's new sun were already in his possession. He might not even need the help of the Resistance to get it built.

Unsmiling, he opened the throttle and began to move away from the visitor's station. There was a lurch as the cable tautened and the nets fell in line behind the bike. That cargo would slow him down, of course.

He might meet the Gehellens on the way out. —What if they got into the visitor's center? Better close the door. He glanced back, and saw that the entrance to the visitor's station was already shut. Crouched beside it in a hurricane of radiance was Venera Fanning.

The cargo net was passing her, just a few yards away. Her eyes met his; there was no appeal in her gaze, just defiance. Hayden nodded once, then deliberately turned back to his piloting. After a moment he felt a slight jerk translate up the cable and through the bike as Venera caught and clung to the passing net.

He opened the throttle and the bike accelerated, but slowly, too slowly as the inferno of dawn welled out from the heart of Candesce. He imagined he could hear the familiar low hiss of the Sun of Suns, even over the scream of the bike. In minutes it became impossible to see; then he could no longer breathe except in shallow gasps; and then he started to tear at his clothing as it burned him wherever it touched. All the while, the air rushed past faster and faster. Before he completely lost his senses he stopped himself from throwing away his jacket and shirt. The light burned his bare skin as much as their touch had.

Gradually the agony abated. Candesce was reaching out to ignite hundreds of miles of air, but he was escaping it, barely.

Squinting ahead, he could see many long fingers of shadow reaching past him. Catamarans or bikes? He turned his head, trying to make out what they were.

Everywhere, the sky was full of shrouded human bodies, all gliding silently in toward Candesce. Joining Aubri. The faint specks of a hundred funeral ships receded into the distance, returning to their ports after unloading their cargoes.

When he was finally able to regain his flapping shirt and jacket, and look around himself, Hayden found that he had no idea where he was. Originally they had planned to navigate by keeping Leaf's Choir in view. They would head for one of Gehellen's neighbors, and from there return to Slipstream. Hayden could be going in the opposite direction now, for all he knew.

It didn't matter. He would find his way, eventually. He couldn't imagine spending the days and nights without Aubri beside him; it seemed impossible that he had done so before. But he had to try. He had responsibilities now.

A few minutes later he felt another vibration through the cable. He looked back, shielding his eyes with one hand.

Venera Fanning made a black cross against the Sun of Suns as she launched herself into the air. They were doing a good sixty or seventy miles an hour at that moment; she swept her arms ahead of her in a diving posture and arrowed away, clothes fluttering.

With luck she would make it to the principalities of Candesce. Though he wished achingly that it could be Aubri silhouetted in exuberance against that light, he hoped Venera would survive and find her way home.

Hayden turned back to his own task. He was done with fighting, done with brooding over the past. His nation and his life had been in shambles for too many years; it was time to rebuild.

He had too much to do to waste his time on resentment.

He settled into the bike's saddle, and opened the throttle wide.

an alteration. I was still there, but Harry was missing.

Whether Imogen or someone else had removed him, I did not know. Nor did I know whether the photograph had been cut or folded over. My owner was deeply distressed, and after his fifth swig and his eighth or ninth emergency cigarette he had revealed this other photograph and had come to the dismal conclusion that this meant Imogen no longer cared about him.

But I surmised that the photograph carried a message of hope. The crucial fact was that Imogen had displayed the photograph in such a prominent place in her new lodgings. Why keep it at all if it meant nothing to her? And though I was featured, it would have been that day that she remembered and the man who had stood beside me in the photo.

The clock on the microwave arrived at three a.m. and found a Labrador squirming in his corner while his profoundly drunk owner stared deep holes into the wall opposite his La-Z-Boy. Harry needed to know what I knew. Things might look bleak now, but I could at least temper some of his darker imaginings. The knowledge would diminish his pain and focus both of us on the next positive step. In the moments prior to the death of Imogen's mother, Iris, by

Grandfather Oswald's World War II–era-Colt .45 (and her subsequent plummet from the window onto the sidewalk below), Iris revealed several items. We already knew that she had killed several people, including Lyell Overton Minskoff-Hardy, literary light and cultural personage, and had been loved blindly by our friend Jackson for decades. But Iris added these points to our understanding: 1) Imogen was her daughter; 2) Imogen was slated to inherit an enormous Australian mining fortune if she survived to thirty and did not go crazy or prove herself homicidal; 3) Iris had confronted her with these two facts on the day that Imogen disappeared; and 4) there was a rugged Australian character tracking Imogen down for some as-yet-unknown purpose. These revelations, coupled with what I had learned from Imogen's journal and my own scent investigations (I had gotten a noseful when I pursued Imogen down the subway stairs), told me that my mistress had not simply moved on. I was certain, as only a dog can be, that Imogen was loyal. If anything, she was protecting us as she saw fit. Harry needed to know this now.

So here I was once again, ready to compose a message out of Alpha-Bits in the early-morning hours. My owner had ceased staring at the wall.

He had let the empty bottle slide to the floor and was now in a deep slumber. A movie ended on the television and an infomercial began. Dangerously tanned men and women with astoundingly white teeth and sculptured limbs held forth on the virtues of a plastic belt that they swore could build a Grecian physique in minutes a day. Yours Truly felt a momentary sense of relief that his girth is permanently clothed in stylish black, then got to work.

A box of Alpha-Bits stood open on the kitchen table. I lifted my paws and hefted myself up until I could snout-swipe it. The box tipped onto the table with a little bang. Harry stirred in the La-Z-Boy but did not wake. The Alpha-Bits box was empty but for four letters: *O-H-N-O*, which summed the situation up only too well.

THE MORNING SUN CUT through the living-room window and inched toward my whiskey-benumbed owner and his Labrador, curled at the base of the La-Z-Boy in guardian fashion. When a sliver of sun reached Harry's eyes, they began to twitch and finally to open at glacial pace. Then he groaned a deep cavernous groan that suggested emergence from the profound-est of hibernations. It was a bearish noise—the sound of a large mammal in sluggish agony. I too was feeling less than wonderful. My limbs were heavy, my paws were sore and the gray matter throbbed beneath the skull. We are sensitive creatures, and naturally I thought I was joining my owner's misery with a sympathetic hang-over. I had enjoyed none of the mental escape provided by Harry's stash of C_2H_5OH but would now endure all of the morning-after con-sequences. I could only hope that my owner's inevitable revulsion at the thought of breakfast did not translate into a missed meal for Yours Truly. I steeled myself against the possibility that Harry would forget to find something in our deeply troubled refrigerator to put in my bowl. I needed to communicate what I knew about Imogen before Detective Davis delivered any more bad news. An empty stomach would make this task very difficult.

Then my owner surprised me. He hopped to his feet. He stretched to the ceiling. He stooped to touch his toes. He did twenty jumping jacks and dropped to the floor for twice that many push-ups. When Harry regained his feet, he made an announcement.

"That's it, Randolph," he said. "I'm free. It's over. She's moved on and so have I. It feels good."

This moment of elation was not to last. A second later Harry was back in the La-Z-Boy and, for the second time in my life, had begun to sob. Human psychology certainly eludes my grasp, but I did what I could to comfort and sidled up to him. Soon, though, he was back on his feet and muttering about being late for a doctor's appointment.

Harry disappeared into the bedroom to get changed, passing his still-unfinished portrait of

Imogen in the corner and turning away from it with a pained expression and a scent that suggested a mother lode of sadness. I did not follow him but listened as drawers were opened and slammed shut again in frustration. Per usual, Harry had put off doing the laundry.

"I need clean socks," Harry said, and began to dig through the hamper that stood just inside his bedroom. "You can't go to the doctor's in dirty socks."

No doubt this conviction was the result of some boyhood programming by Harry's solid and practical midwestern mother. But amid the domestic ruin of our bachelor lives, the clean-socks-for-the-doctor mandate was a difficult one to observe. Once Imogen's presence had kept us males in line and compelled us to follow the basic tenets of the Geneva Convention. But without her we often contributed to each other's decline into barbarism. Lightbulbs went unchanged, plates were stacked in the sink and on every inch of kitchen counter, and newspapers were laid out like carpet over the floors to combat spills that had long ago evaporated. In many places, the newspapers were scratched to pieces during my more nervous and worry-heavy pacings. I had seen Harry commence this mad search for clean clothes many times before, and I knew how it would end.

"These aren't too bad," Harry said, and triumphantly emerged with a tartan pair that hadn't been worn since Christmas.

"I don't know why they're even in here," he continued, making reference to the well-known male theory that dirty clothes left long enough in a hamper actually clean themselves. But a second appraisal convinced my owner otherwise and that, where the hamper treatment had failed, the microwave treatment would not. He scrubbed the socks down in the sink, spun them around like the blades of a propeller and then put them in the microwave oven for five minutes on high. The microwave treatment was always a gamble. You could end up with dry socks or a fire condition. It all seemed to depend on where the items of clothing were placed on the revolving tray. Too far on the outside and they would stay damp. Too close to the center and combustion. But this time, my owner got it right. In no time he had slipped on his warm, dry and relatively clean socks and was headed out the door. I am not a pushy dog, but I could not allow the probability of breakfast to head out the door with him. I delivered an imperative whine.

"Of course you can come, Randolph," Harry said, completely misunderstanding me. I would have preferred to collect my thoughts on the sun-warmed floor of our apartment after an ample breakfast. Instead, he clipped the leash to my collar.

"Dr. Huggins loves dogs," he said, and with that we were out the door and making haste through the still-crisp early-spring air. I had heard of Dr. Christopher Huggins on several occasions. The first time was when the good doctor had prescribed extract of hemlock and barley water to aid in treating Harry's insomnia in those first sleepless months after Imogen went missing. If this sounds like a concoction left wisely unemployed by modern medicine, of course it is. Dr. Huggins liked his friends to call him *SparrowHawk* (the name he derived for himself from a hallucinogenic "spirit quest" in some southwestern desert that had not yet been turned into a theme park or gated community). Dr. Huggins was a practitioner of his own brand of alternative medicine, and while my owner resisted calling him by his spirit name, in a particularly unflattering loss of perspective he had once delivered this little chestnut about the good doctor: "He thinks so far outside the box that he'll probably win a Nobel Prize when the

world catches up and realizes how great he is."
His dog doubted this future turn of events and
watched with trepidation as Harry downed
murky potions to alleviate everything from in-
digestion to something called "psychic overload" from his so-called "ghost work" with Ivan
Manners, Harry's friend and a self-styled expert
on the paranormal. Ivan had managed to get
himself showcased on television, and his ghost-
hunting services were now constantly in demand. My owner has played his occasional
apprentice on fruitless expeditions to catch
some evidence of the supernatural with the fly-
paper of technology.

It is not that I am an uncritical fan of
the Western medical tradition or the cult of
the pharmaceutical industry that finds an ail-
ment for every pill, but I didn't think that
SparrowHawk's tinkering would lead to any
miracle cures in Harry, and I was right. I
breathed a sigh of relief when the hemlock
didn't put my owner to sleep like it did Socrates,
that great philosopher and gadfly of Athenian
society. Perhaps Socrates should have mixed his
poison with barley water.

Dr. Huggins operated out of a storefront in
the only dilapidated building on an otherwise
upscale block filled with handbag stores and

tapas restaurants. He shared space with a woman who read palms by appointment and a young man who sold vintage comic books and baseball cards. Neither was there at ten in the morning, but before we had a chance to dawdle on the stoop, the door swung open to reveal Dr. Huggins smoking a pipe filled with ginseng. He wore stained latex gloves sagging at the wrists. But with the exception of the gloves, longish sideburns and a large clay talisman hanging over his pressed oxford, he could have passed for an accountant.

"Harry," Dr. Huggins said. "Welcome, my peer and fellow journeyman."

"Hello, Dr. Huggins," Harry said. "Is it alright if my dog comes in?"

"Is he not a creature of the universe?" Dr. Huggins asked.

Oh Lordy, thought the creature of the universe.

"And please call me SparrowHawk, Harry. It is my true name," Dr. Huggins said as he led us across the threshold, down a hallway lined with questionable diplomas and into a small examination room. Dr. Huggins gestured for Harry to sit on the stainless-steel table. I rested on my haunches in the corner. Dr. Huggins tapped Harry's shoulders with his gloved hands, tweaked

my owner's earlobes, touched his index finger to
Harry's forehead, sighed and took a step back.

"Wheat allergy," Dr. Huggins announced. "I
can see it in your eyes."

Harry massaged his bloodshot, drink-addled
eyeballs with his palms.

"It was a rough night," Harry said. The weight
of those first hours of wrenching news and
horrific revelations about our mistress seemed
about to descend again. I detected glistening
drops of saline at the corners of his eyes, but my
owner fought them back.

"I can see that," Dr. Huggins said. "But what
I'm really seeing is deeper than the superficial
scrapes of a big night. You, my friend, are definitely allergic to wheat. Why are you here, by
the way?"

"We had an appointment," Harry said. "My
foot has been hurting."

"I could look at the foot if you want, but your
problem begins with wheat," Dr. Huggins said.
"You are extremely sensitive to wheat."

"Wheat could affect my foot?" Harry asked.

"Wheat could affect your everything. Your
foot. Your libido. Your general sense of happiness and well-being," Dr. Huggins confirmed.
"Wheat is one of the worst. As my teacher said

about diagnosis, when in doubt, think wheat. It's what we call a *general pernicious* in this biz."

"So what do I do?" Harry asked.

"Avoid wheat at all costs," Dr. Huggins said.

"You mean don't eat it?"

"Don't eat it, don't smell it, don't touch it, don't even look at it."

"I'm that allergic?"

"You're *that* allergic. I could not be more serious," Dr. Huggins averred with a solemn nod.

Then a look of worry, almost desperation, came over my owner.

"Does that include Alpha-Bits?"

"Do they have wheat in them?" asked Dr. Huggins, as if he had never entered a supermarket or watched a television.

"They're cereal."

"Can't eat. Don't eat. Throw out and use gloves with the box. Here's some lavender. It is an essential oil. Dab a little under each nostril before you get home. It counteracts the influence of wheat. Reapply as needed."

I had listened to most of the conversation with amusement, until my owner underscored just what the doctor's instructions would mean. Namely, the part about Alpha-Bits, at which point my amusement turned to deep disturbance. No Alpha-Bits meant that my bridge to Harry—my only avenue to communicate with my owner—was no more. I could only hope that the pure light of reason and good sense would descend once again on my owner, as it had done more regularly in our early days, and he would turn on his heel, walk out of the office and reject all of the nonsense advice. Needless to say, this did not happen.

"Thank you, Dr. Huggins," Harry said.

"It's SparrowHawk to my friends," Dr. Huggins said.

"Right," Harry said, not quite ready to make this leap.

Then Dr. Huggins asked Harry to take off his shoes so that he could examine his foot.

"Nice socks," he pronounced.

"Thanks," Harry said.

"They smell like popcorn."

The doctor twisted Harry's foot and my owner howled in pain.

"Just as I thought; once you stop the wheat, the foot will heal right up."

Harry nodded. Then his gaze turned to me.

"By the way, I know you're not a vet, but could you take a quick look at Randolph? He hasn't been himself lately."

A word on dog health. I am no trained expert,

but I do observe my body and I know what and how I have felt these last five and a half years. I have also communicated with enough of my kind to have a general notion of dog health as opposed to human health. This is my basic conclusion: we dogs don't get sick very much. A cold might annoy the sinuses or irritate the throat. A stomach virus might make our food lose some of its savor. But we soldier on.

That is why, as much as I hated to admit it, Harry was right. Something was wrong with me. I had been under the weather and I wasn't shaking it. I have never had a great deal of zest and have always avoided physical activity, but lately a powerful fatigue was causing me to sleep even longer than my typical Labrador quota and making even minor physical effort almost instantly exhausting. I had even found myself falling asleep over my books, something I had never done before. There were other complaints as well. Since the onset of middle age I have been susceptible to the occasional arthritic ache in the hindquarters on the foggy morning, but this was different—this felt very wrong. Hearing Harry recognize that something might be amiss with his charge was heartening, but realizing that his solution was to entrust me to the questionable

SparrowHawk made me contemplate an escape from the office — if only I had the energy to do it.

Dr. Huggins hefted me onto the examination table with an assist from my owner. Both men paused to catch their breath.

"He's a meaty one," Dr. Huggins panted. "This might be as simple a matter as weight loss."

Dr. Huggins neglected to follow standard hygienic procedures and was now examining me with the same gloves that he had worn for my owner and presumably every other patient who had preceded us. He ran his hand along the top of my snout. I tried to resist, but this dog only has so much willpower, and the effect of a snout rub (even one delivered by a quack wearing dirty gloves) is instantly intoxicating. The tail began to wag.

"You like that, boy," Dr. Huggins cooed in that the-dog-is-naturally-an-idiot voice that humans have reserved especially for us. "Sure, you like that. Good boy."

The glove ran down my back. Patted my generous sides and then — to my horror — attempted entry into Yours Truly's mouth. I resisted, of course, but to no avail. The other glove stunned me with a simultaneous snout rub, and soon my mouth was filled with who knows what kind of bacteria and an ample collection of my own fur.

Then Dr. Huggins turned to Harry.

"I'm not a vet, Harry, but I'd say that your dog has a thyroid condition."

"Oh no."

"I wouldn't worry too much about it. Plenty of Labs have it. It's hypothyroidism. That's what's making him sluggish."

"What do we do?"

For the first time that morning, Dr. Huggins delivered a responsible answer.

"Take him to a vet."

Harry paid the bill, which was something extravagant, thanked the doctor and we set off for home, my owner now limping more distinctly than ever. Harry took SparrowHawk's instructions for his own condition and we stopped at the Duane Reade on the corner of 90th and Columbus. He tied me to a fireplug (no doubt on the theory that no dognapper would want or could lift me) and disappeared inside. A few minutes later he emerged with a bag filled with cleaning supplies, rubber gloves and a face mask for the antiwheat crusade, along with a bulk supply of ginkgo biloba that must have required a whole virgin Amazon forest to produce.

"Ginkgo's good for the brain," Harry declared as he plunked his purchases down on the kitchen table that was soon to be rid of all traces of our favorite breakfast cereal.

Yes, I reflected, *we would be needing brain, and plenty of it.*

CLEANING OF ANY SORT IS a rare event in our apartment. I was not even sure if Harry would know what to do. But he threw himself into the work, and soon the place was mopped, scrubbed, deluged and purified of all traces of wheat and every other delightful, comforting, memory-evoking smell that had made this dog's nose at home. I have spoken of the profound power of the canine olfactories before, but I will mention it again here. Try to imagine if your nose was 100,000 times more powerful than it is. You would live in an utterly different reality. What is now a whiff that brings back a memory would seem to become the memory and assume all its comforting or discomforting dimensions. If you have noticed that I describe much of the action around me in terms of visual gestures, scenes and words—well, that is for your benefit, a kind of translation for the nose-deprived. My dog's eyes are surprisingly good, but my nose is like a psychologist and a lie detector. It is also the organ that orients me most in this world, and so when the carnage of cleaning fluids was over and Harry brought out the vacuum cleaner to finish the job, I retreated to the bedroom, looking for some trace of our former life, some trace of Imogen and lazy Sunday afternoons. I found it beneath the clothes dresser: a small tumbleweed of my fur and several years' accumulation of dust woven into it. I kept it close to my nose until Harry arrived and shooed me away and finally that memory too had vanished up the hose and into the vacuum's stomach.

Harry put the vacuum cleaner away and switched on the television, and Yours Truly curled up in the corner beneath the easel with the unfinished painting of Imogen and nursed his spinning brain.

Then the telephone rang and my disorientation grew worse. It was Zest Kilpatrick. This overly energized local-television news reporter had met my owner at the Pooch Palace a few months earlier and tried to force her way onto Harry's social calendar. This attempt failed despite the fact that my owner's social calendar was empty. They had not exchanged phone numbers, but she had left us with her business card. The telephone call proceeded as follows (Zest spoke so loudly that both sides of the conversation were quite audible):

"Harry," Zest said.

"Yes."

"This is Zest."

"Zest?"

"Zest Kilpatrick. Channel Eight. News on the Eight. I know this is forward but Ivan Manners suggested it. You know how involved he and Mr. Apples are with the bird cause. I'd like to invite you to come to the Lorikeet Rescue Fund annual dinner at the Discovery Society three days from now. I know it's short notice, but I figured, what the hell, he's cute. Ha-ha. I'm such an idiot. I did *not* just mean to say that. So what do you think? Can you make it? It's fine to say no. I understand. No pressure. Say no if you want."

"Yes," Harry said. "I'd like to come."

"I mean, it's for the birds," Zest said. "That doesn't sound right. I mean it's for a good cause. The birds."

"I understand," Harry said. "It would be fun. I'd like to see you."

The phone call concluded and this dog's brain reeled. Going to a dinner at which Ivan Manners and Mr. Apples, his Farsi-speaking rainbow lorikeet, were present was grim enough. But my owner's behavior was even more unwelcome. Savaging our apartment with the scent-wasting vacuum was minor compared to this gesture of openness to another woman, particularly *this* overly anxious, clock-ticking predator. The assessment was likely unfair, but I believed that Harry's loyalties lay with Imogen, no matter what he might have said that morning. For him to look elsewhere was a kind of desecration.

But I did not have long to contemplate this betrayal when the buzzer rang. It was Detective Davis. He was carrying a small shopping bag and wore a grim expression.

"Harry," Detective Davis said as he came into the apartment.

"Peter," Harry answered.

"What's wrong with your leg?"

"Wheat," Harry said.

Detective Davis shrugged. He had once been a Buddhist monk, and this training, combined with his tenure as a New York City police detective, had apparently given him the ability to hear the most absurd nonsense without betraying the slightest surprise.

"Wheat," he echoed. "I didn't know wheat could do that to you."

"I have an allergy," Harry explained. "Do you want to sit down?"

Detective Davis looked at his limited options and shook his head.

"Things are developing very fast, Harry. Imogen's DNA is all over that room and all over that parachute cord."

"You actually think she could have killed him?" Harry asked. "I can't believe it."

"I can't believe it either, Harry," Detective Davis said. "But she's in the crosshairs. There is one very puzzling detail, though. Remember I told you that the victim was probably drugged and we'd find evidence of that in the champagne glass?"

"Yes."

"Well, we did. He was drugged—toxicology showed us that overnight—but both champagne glasses have heavy traces of the drug chloral hydrate. Not just his glass; her DNA is all over the other glass. We have every reason to believe that she consumed it too. Not to be too clinical, but her saliva was in the champagne."

"Maybe she only had a sip."

Detective Davis shook his head.

"A sip would put a gorilla down. There's something else too. The dead man was a foreign national. He worked at the United Nations as a sous-chef in their international dining room."

"Oh?" Harry asked.

"He had several names and several passports. We don't even know what nationality he is. At the risk of sounding dramatic: there are bigger forces at work here. Maybe global forces. Imogen didn't disappear for nothing the first time, and she's running from more than just the NYPD now."

"You mean what Iris said could be true?" Harry asked. "That Imogen had some kind of fortune coming to her?"

"I can't say," Detective Davis said.

"But that story couldn't have been true. She was born in Akron, Ohio. She went to live with her grandmother in Kentucky after her parents divorced."

"Harry, Imogen wasn't born in Akron and she never attended school in Kentucky."

"But she went to Amherst."

"Yes, she did," Detective Davis said. "And their records show that she spent high school in Austria."

"How long have you known this?"

"Since this morning."

"I mean, shouldn't we have known this when she went missing the first time?"

"We should have," Detective Davis said. "But we didn't because, unbeknownst to me, one of my guys relied on computer records. This time I called Amherst myself and they went to the hard archives."

"Why were the computer records wrong?"

"I don't know."

Harry stared at the floor.

"So she's someone else," my owner muttered.

"I don't know about that," Detective Davis said. "She hid some things from you."

"Some things?" Harry said. "She hid her life."

"There's a lot that we don't know, Harry," Detective Davis said. "The fact that the victim's trail leads to the United Nations dining room makes things complicated. NYPD has to tread delicately in diplomatic circles. We can't push things. Already I'm getting resistance."

"This doesn't involve me anymore, does it?" Harry said. "Imogen's gone and she didn't want to take me with her. If she was in trouble, she could have told me."

"I can't speak to that, Harry," Detective Davis answered. "I've seen people disappear for the stupidest reasons. But it does involve you. If she contacts you, you need to contact me immediately."

"Why would she?" Harry said.

"*If* she does. It's guilty until proven innocent in this country, but you don't want to risk being seen as an accessory."

"Right," Harry said. "I'll call you. What's in the bag?"

"A little something for Randolph. Liverwurst," Detective Davis said. "My dogs used to go crazy for liverwurst."

PORK. PORK LIVER. COOKED goose. Goose fat. Goose liver. Salt.

These were the first six ingredients listed on the golden package that Detective Davis left with my owner for me. When Davis left, Harry tossed the liverwurst onto the floor, unopened, and sank into the La-Z-Boy.

"All yours, boy," Harry said. "Come and get it."

My head still spun from the loss of our apartment's familiar scents and the added burden of Detective Davis's revelations about Imogen, but a Lab's stomach is a powerful force and I was drawn to this new foodstuff. I had never encountered liverwurst before. It is a German delicacy seldom found on a dog's plate. I hesitate to admit even to myself what a slave I am to my lower natures. How even as I cringe at the antics of my kind at the dog run—the hindquarter sniffing, the indiscriminate urination, et cetera—I understand it all too well. And sometimes, restrained *Foliage-Finder* though I am, scent and the demands of the stomach can unite to overpower me. Such was the near-mystical power of the small golden package of liverwurst that rolled to a stop right beneath my nose.

In a blur of torn plastic casing, I soon found myself with large gobs of the stuff all over my mouth and stuck to my paws and snout. The smell was rich and transcendent. I believe I rolled across the floor. Possibly several times. Undoubtedly the tail was up to its wagging—this time completely justified—as the jaws chomped and the tongue moved and the throat swallowed the ambrosia down. To be a dog at times like this is to be perfectly in sync with some fundamental universal principle. It is to have found the key to life. From a hazy distance I heard Harry make some comment and then the package was being yanked away.

"Randolph," Harry said. "You can't eat the whole thing. Show some restraint. It's embarrassing."

As far as wolf-pack dynamics go, Imogen was my alpha figure, but Harry has some kind of alpha status and so his scolding cuts deep. The tail froze and sank, as did my head. The eyes looked up. I believe I even cowered.

"No, Randolph, it's my fault," Harry said. "How can I expect an animal to show restraint?"

I shook off the hereditary shame response and gave a loud snuffle, which does wonders to expel bad humor.

"At least we know another food that you like. Not that there's a limited number," Harry said. He took the remaining liverwurst, wrapped it in a scrap of aluminum foil he found under the sink and deposited it in our still deeply troubled refrigerator (Harry's cleaning binge had come to a dead stop before this wilderness). My eyes followed the disappearing golden package like it was a sacred relic.

"Now what are we going to do?" Harry asked. As the liverwurst-induced fog began to recede, I could sense that Harry was in a place he had not been in before. He was still forlorn, as he had been for so many months in the absence of Imogen, but now there was a kind of resolve building. It was the kind of resolve that appears after disillusionment. In other words, it was the wrong kind of resolve. It was a hardening. It was a rejection. It was a loss of faith. In an instant, I felt ashamed for a reason far beyond my little liverwurst bacchanalia. How could I have failed both of them so badly? Why had I hesitated to communicate to Harry what I knew about

Imogen when I had the power to do so? Now what could I do? The Alpha-Bits were gone. There was no bridge between species and no way for me to let him know that I believed Imogen had likely disappeared to protect us. And then, in a turn of events that frequently happens in novels but rarely in real life, my owner provided the answer: he decided to dust off his laptop computer and connect to the Internet.

The computer had been stowed on the bookcase since Imogen disappeared. One might have thought that Harry—desperate to hear some word from her—would never have put the computer away in the first place, but Harry and Imogen were a peculiar couple. They were technology-wary. They did not own cell phones, for example, and the laptop had been given to Harry by the midwestern patriarch, concerned that his son was falling behind the technology curve. Harry and Imogen had steered clear of e-mail, and all of their text-messaging was done with pen and paper. It was just their way.

"I've been out of the loop so long that I'm not even sure where the loop is," Harry announced, hitting the false I'm-an-old-fogy note as he flipped open the screen and powered up the device. "I'll see if I can get online."

Online... The word echoed with an almost mythic potential, like F. Scott Fitzgerald's *fresh, green breast of the new world*. I had read about the Internet with fascination, but as a lover of books and contemplation I still had my reservations. What did such instant communication and connection mean? Was being *online* something that would defeat the inborn reflectivness of the reader and thinker? Did *high speed* equal shallow, hasty and empty? Even so, the moment that Harry mentioned it, I saw a path out of the present incommunicative dilemma.

I sidled up to my owner and received a pat on the head while the laptop searched the vicinity for a connection. Fortunately, many of our neighbors had unsecured networks, and my owner was soon piggybacking on someone else's connection. These terms meant nothing to me, but I gathered the proper nomenclature from my owner's mutterings. I further learned that his e-mail account had long ago lapsed and that he was now opening a new one. I thought the address might come in handy and made a mental note of the ungainly and faintly embarrassing moniker: *Harryghostpainter2* (apparently *Harryghostpainter1* had already been taken).

Having set up an e-mail account, Harry commenced to surf. I rested my chin on the arm of the La-Z-Boy and soon was entranced by what I saw on the screen. The flowing virtual geome- tries of cyberspace, the images and the words, the many different fonts and shades: it was like television, but the viewer was at least partially in control. I watched Harry navigate from one page to the next. The word *navigate* itself evoked the heady possibilities of a journey across wide oceans. *Surf, navigate, wide oceans…* freedom. A world beyond the tyranny of the leash.

The first obstacle would be finding enough time alone with the machine to learn how to use it. I could only hope that Harry would leave the laptop open and accessible. Alpha-Bits had been snout-challenging, but the tiny keys of Harry's computer and the cursor-manipulating "touch" pad would demand still-untapped reserves in Yours Truly. Yes, there would be profound neck strain and nose angst in my near future. But even my newly diagnosed medical condition would not stop me from supplying my owner with the truth. Speaking of which, Harry, be- traying uncharacteristic efficiency, scheduled an appointment online for Yours Truly that very day at our local veterinary office. A small victory for responsible pet ownership.

Harry then found his way to Ivan Manners's site, which featured the rotund exhibitionist

urging all visitors to respect the paranormal, use
his ghost-hunting services and contribute to the
Lorikeet Rescue Fund. But before my owner
could linger there, the surf of the nonvirtual
world broke over us in the shape of a phone call
and swept us in an entirely new direction. It was
Jackson Temple, Harry's friend and benefactor.
He wanted to meet both of us in Midtown right
away.

HARRY PLACED THE LAP-
top on the kitchen table and picked
his jacket off the floor.

"Well, Randolph, this should be interesting," Harry sounded a dubious note. Jackson, after all, seldom saw us anywhere but in his cluttered suite at the Belvedere Hotel, where he had lived for decades among teetering stacks of books and the objets d'art of an eccentric collector. He was an independently wealthy man who was a well-regarded art historian. As I have mentioned, Jackson had loved Iris. He had also watched her die in that tense scene less than a month before. But he was a philosophical man and well bred—whatever pain he felt seldom reached the surface to mar his good manners. There was never any question of despising Harry because he had shot Iris before she finished the job by plummeting to the sidewalk. Jackson, it seemed, understood and forgave, if there was anything to forgive. But the call was strange, because Jackson wasn't spontaneous. A visit usually had some reason.

Harry hurried me along the sidewalk, rushing me through a thicket of scents. My nose brushed flower-bed rails and verdant sidewalk cracks. Spring was coming fast. It was pushing up through the thick stone crust that covered Manhattan's living earth, and it was in the air billowing down from the nascent buds and the temperate sky. I breathed it all deeply and let my four legs resist Harry's forward pull. But then we reached the curb and I looked up to see my owner hailing a taxi. New York taxis seldom take big dogs—I don't think they're allowed unless my kind is caged. But try enough times to convince someone to go along with almost anything in Manhattan and you'll succeed. After the fifth taxi had screamed by, an SUV hybrid decided to take a chance, and in fifteen minutes we found ourselves stepping out across the street from the United Nations. Midtown Manhattan is so much larger and more monumental than the Upper West Side. The coziness of our domain, with its narrow streets and residential buildings, seems far distant from the steel and glass austerities of consulates, corporations and NGOs—the workaday world of diplomats, businessmen and activists—but, in fact, our home is only a few miles distant. Even so, I had never seen the United Nations outside of photographs, and I was moved by the swooping roof of the main building and the general serenity of the place. At the same time I noticed how tired things looked. The tower—a modern wonder in its day—appeared worn and dated, its windows stained, unmatched and even peeling in places. It was as if I were looking at the visible evidence of the cost of humans trying to get along with one another. Harry interrupted these silent elegies with a brusque leash tug.

"Randolph, get out of the street," he commanded. This was followed by the blare of several taxis navigating around my hindquarters at dangerous speeds. Jackson waited on the sidewalk.

"It's good to see you," Jackson said, giving Harry a strong handshake. "You look good, but Mister Randolph seems a bit out of it."

"Mister Randolph has just been diagnosed with hypothyroidism," Harry said. "That's when the thyroid—"

"Doesn't produce enough thyroxine, I know," Jackson finished.

"How?"

"It's a common condition in Labs *and*

Guatemalan tree sloths, except in Guatemalan tree sloths it's essentially normal. If you treat it, you turn your sloth into a Hunter S. Thompson with fur—all wired for sound," Jackson said. Jackson knew of such things because he was the owner of Marlin, a sloth and a fine fellow, whose body traveled in laborious inches about his tree but whose mind moved with whip-smart speed.

"Come with me," Jackson said. He turned and led the way into a narrow building whose façade was clear blue glass. The ceiling of the lobby was high above us, and a large mobile composed of dangling hubcaps and tire irons was pushed in circles by a gentle current. The floor and the reception desk, behind which an ancient guard drowsed, were black marble polished to an astonishing shine.

"Austere but majestic," Jackson suggested.

"Where are we?"

"WAHA," Jackson said. "The World Artistic Heritage Association. It's a group of wealty duffers and starry-eyed Don Quixotes dedicated to the preservation of the visual arts and the community of world artists. I'm on the board. Our staff does good work when they're not at the pub frittering our money away on grog and loose women."

"That's a joke."

"Not really, I'm afraid."

As if on cue, the elevator door—polished to a gemlike shine—opened to disgorge what looked like a drunken elf smoking a pipe the size of a small croquet mallet.

"An artist?" Harry asked under his breath as the man hurried by without a glance at any of us.

"An administrative assistant. He manages the database," Jackson corrected. "Needless to say, the place does not run like a well-oiled machine. But at least it has character and spirit. Yes, lots of character and spirit."

Jackson gestured at the far wall between the two elevators.

"Something this place doesn't have is art. Not a scrap, unless you call that circling junkyard above our heads art. It's difficult, of course, to fit any art in, with all of this steel, glass and stone. The architect made sure of that. He didn't want anything to spoil his vision—you know, they've all tried to get away with the same nonsense since Frank Lloyd Wright. I understand it—they're making art too, and artists like absolute control—but there has to be a limit. In the end we battled the man back and we got that space with which we can do as we please. Thirty feet by ten feet, and we want a mosaic. And I want *you* to do it for us. Harry, this is the commission I spoke about at Christmas. Are you ready for it now?"

"A mosaic?" Harry asked. "Of what?"

"A mosaic that depicts WAHA's mission."

"But I haven't had much experience with mosaics."

"I believe in you. Besides, anything would be better than that goddamn mobile."

"Jackson, I'm honored. This is a big project," Harry said.

"It's a career-maker, Harry. If you do it right," Jackson said, "it could be a major work."

"I don't know."

"Think it over if you want, but I've managed to convince the board that you're the man for the job, even though there are others in line to do the work. Your résumé could use it; you're all bits and pieces right now—superbly done but nothing cohesive. I want something special on that wall. I want something that carries people walking through that door well beyond what they are used to. I want art—real art—the kind of work they say no one can do anymore because we're over it all, because we've moved on, grown cynical, don't or can't believe in anything. But I don't accept that view. Things are cyclical. Culture gets a body blow and shudders, and for fifty years no one can produce anything but crap; then the cultural body starts healing and we've got good work being done again. And good work is the kind of work you are capable of doing. I know that. I've supported you because of that—I like you too, Harry, you're a good guy, but you're an even better artist, and it's time that you started doing something about it. You know I'm usually not this emphatic—it's not a comfortable mode—but I can see the need in your face. You're at a critical juncture. There's either change in your life or hardening into something that can't change."

"There's news about Imogen," Harry said, and stared down at the floor. "Bad news."

"I'm sorry to hear that," Jackson said. I expected Jackson to stop and try to comfort my owner, but instead he became more strident. "But at the risk of sounding harsh and uncaring, whatever the news is, that wall is waiting. You have that gift of yours and you have that wall. No woman—especially not Imogen—would ever want you to stop that gift. No woman worth anything would stop you from spending your waking, working life doing exactly what you were meant to be doing. Bad news or good news can disrupt you, but it mustn't derail you."

I could tell my owner was stunned by Jackson's words. His benefactor and friend had never delivered anything but consolation where Imogen was concerned. For a moment I thought Harry would snap, but he didn't.

"I'll do it," he said. "I'd love to do it. You're right. It's time to move on."

"I hope you know I'm not saying this because of my disillusionment with Iris," Jackson said. "I'm not starting a chapter of the He-Man-Woman-Haters' Club, but whatever happens with Imogen, it is time to start working again."

"I know. I will," Harry said. "They think Imogen's alive."

"Thank God," Jackson said. "I admit to thinking the worst when Iris said that she had seen her on the day she disappeared."

It was Jackson's turn to fall silent.

"It's still painful, isn't it?" Harry asked.

"Yes," Jackson said. "It shouldn't be, but it is. We humans are a strange breed. We love all the wrong things."

"So what's involved?" Harry asked.

"This is something of an extraordinary commission in that there will be no oversight. You are free to create as you see fit. There is a budget, but it is flexible. There are only two requirements, but they're significant: one, whatever ends up on that wall must have something to reflect the essence of WAHA's mission—the notion of preservation and promotion of world art—and, two, you must show up for work every day, five days a week, until the work is done."

"I can do that, but the second condition is a little weird," Harry said.

"It's my requirement," Jackson said. "I think it's the best thing for you. There'll be days that you doubt doing this. There'll be days that you want to head back to the La-Z-Boy and stay there for the rest of your life, but you won't be-cause you have to be somewhere—you'll have to be here. Because if you aren't—even if it's just one day—you lose the commission and, as much as it pains me, you're going to lose my support too."

Once again I thought Harry would balk at Jackson. Harry is a quiet young man, but he is not the type of person to be pushed around. It was only a few months before that he had charged off to work at the mere reminder that Jackson paid our bills.

"I understand," Harry said. "Thank you."

"I hoped you'd take it that way," Jackson said.

"So when do I start?"

"Tomorrow," Jackson said. "Now, if you come with me, I want to show you one of the perks of the job."

Jackson nodded at the ancient guard, who

still dozed behind the black marble monolith that was reception despite Jackson's rousing speech that had rallied our promising young artist.

"WAHA's what they call a 'relaxed work environment,'" Jackson observed as he led the way down a corridor to a pair of double doors. "All of the administrative offices are upstairs and, if you're lucky, you'll never have to go up there."

"The domain of that tiny drunk man," Harry said.

"Yes, among others. Incredible the oddities that roll through the doors of a nonprofit and find permanent employment. As I said, if you're lucky you'll never have to go up there."

Jackson pushed both doors open in dramatic fashion to reveal a huge storage room with unfinished concrete-block walls, rows of fluorescent lights on the ceiling and a playing field of floor space.

"This will be your workshop. You can order any machines and supplies that you think you might need and keep them here. It isn't much..."

"I could build the Statue of Liberty in here," Harry said. "It's enormous."

My owner walked over to an object in the middle of the room. It was covered by a bright red tarp.

"What's this?"

"That is the perk," Jackson said, and smiled. "Take off the tarp."

Harry pulled at the covering and it dropped in a heap on the floor.

WHAT LAY BENEATH THE sheet was an object that has been labeled by others more knowledgeable than Yours Truly as the epitome of Italian design. It was a Vespa—specifically, a 150cc PX model with a Granturismo frame and large twelve-inch wheels. Harry instantly appreciated the device beneath the tarp.

"Beautiful," he pronounced.

A Vespa is indeed a beautiful machine. It was designed by an aeronautical engineer, Corradino D'Ascanio, who hated motorcycles and had been recruited in 1946 to create a scooter that would be revolutionary. It needed to carry both men and women, to carry a passenger and to protect anyone on board from the dirt and water of the road. The result was a vehicle that looked like a sculpture but could reach speeds in excess of eighty-five mph. The engine was mounted on the rear wheel, and the scooter featured a "pass-through leg area" so women wearing skirts and dresses could ride without inconvenience or embarrassment (apparently very important in Bella Italia). Yes, the vehicle was a triumph of engineering and design, but it also helped that popular culture was on its side—in the form of Audrey Hepburn and Gregory Peck speeding through *Roman Holiday* on the back of a Vespa. They were followed by legions of celebrities and fictional characters, including John Wayne and Salvador Dali (whose "surrealized" Vespa is now in a museum). The Mod youth of 1960s Britain made the Vespa a fixture of that country's roadways, but despite John Wayne's appreciation of the machine, it never caught on in the United States. The heavy rain and snow of the Northeast might explain why Vespa ridership was never particularly high in Manhattan, but a better reason was probably the soundness of our public transportation system and the fact that rushing on a small scooter through streets filled with drivers from every corner of the globe, each piloting large, carnivorous American vehicles, seemed unappealing to all but the most rugged. Of course, New York was changing—a new current of civility had swept across the cityscape with the turn of the century. In this gentler place, the artistic Vespa almost looked survivable.

"It's mine?" Harry asked.

"It's yours for the duration of the project," Jackson said. "I thought it would make sense. It'll get you here faster, especially with your foot. What's wrong, by the way—that's quite a bad limp."

"It's my wheat allergy," Harry said, sounding unconvinced himself, as he hobbled around the vehicle like a child surveying an astounding gift. "I'm happy it's silver. I've seen them in pink."

"And it's been adapted for your companion," Jackson said. With a sinking of the stomach and a weakness in the paws, I realized that Jackson meant me. "The seat behind the driver has been widened for Randolph, and there's a way to lock him in so he doesn't take a nasty tumble into the middle of Broadway or some such."

Indeed, the backseat had been amply widened and possessed padded sides that swung into place to create a sort of box where I was to sit.

Harry, who had knowledge of dogs riding aboard two-wheeled vehicles from his midwestern experience, admired the design but questioned the necessity.

"I've seen farm dogs ride on the back of

much narrower bikes, no problem," my owner said. "But, then again, we're speaking about Randolph."

"I doubt if a farm dog could stay on for long in a contest with a New York City pothole, or look sophisticated doing it," Jackson said.

I was about to snuffle in support but thought better of it lest I was understood. Once in puppyhood, the spareribs and plum sauce had arrived with a fortune cookie whose message I read and still value: *To be underestimated is to remain free.*

"Well, my boy, I have a lunch of academics to attend. Pray for me—there is nothing more frightening than sitting in a room filled with people who have tenure and know it."

"What about the bike?" Harry asked.

"By all means, ride it home," Jackson said.

"But I don't see a license plate," Harry muttered.

"That's the beauty of the thing. Check the storage compartment," Jackson said.

Harry lifted the seat and pulled out a small license plate.

"The license plate is on Velcro, so when you park on the sidewalk in front of your apartment—which I have been told is brazenly illegal—you simply remove the license plate from the back of the Vespa, stow it in the storage compartment and the ticketing authorities will be unable to issue a summons."

"Clever," Harry said.

"It was the elf's idea. He's very savvy when it comes to these things."

"So you think it's fine to break the law?"

"It's the spirit of the thing that matters," Jackson said. "With all this talk about fossil fuels and making New York air as fresh as a mountain glade, I suspect they'll welcome one more young man and his dog speeding about town on such a vehicle. Besides, if it gets towed, we'll let WAHA worry about it."

Then Jackson turned and fixed Harry with his eyes.

"I'm really very happy that you've agreed to do this, Harry. It is a very good thing indeed."

Harry looked mildly embarrassed, and Jackson passed through the double doors with a wave of his hand. Silence rushed in when his footsteps had finally disappeared and my owner and I were left alone to commune with the glistening machine. There is something about a new vehicle that can defeat (at least temporarily) the glummest of moods. I have spoken of the power of my dog's nose before and how even emotion and mental states are within its reach.

Harry was exuberant. I had not smelled exuberance in our house for a very long time. Its scent falls somewhere between a fine piece of steak grilling on a open flame for a summer barbecue and gunpowder. My owner might have been more of a motorcycle than a Vespa type, but he had had precious little experience with either. The smell, in this case, was closer to gunpowder.

"Well, Randolph," he said. "It looks like we've got a new ride. I guess I should practice, but how hard could it be? It's just a bicycle with a motor. Come on, let's go."

Harry pushed the vehicle out the double doors, through the lobby and past the ancient guard, who was still fast asleep.

When we were curbside, my owner rummaged through the storage compartment until he emerged with a helmet for himself. There would be no head protection for the dog's gray matter. Then he looked down at me.

My stomach shuddered once again and I instinctively dropped to the pavement.

"Oh no you don't, you big coward," Harry said. "You're riding in the back if I have to tie you there."

My owner reached down and heaved me up onto the seat. Then he raised the side panels and clicked them into place one by one.

"Now, how do you start this thing?" Harry asked as he slid into place in front of me. His dog only stared off to the side and tried to ignore the stream of fast-moving traffic speeding up First Avenue a dozen or so yards in front of us—a five-lane current that would soon digest us. Harry searched for a motorcycle kick-starter with his foot but could find none—one of the things D'Ascanio hated about motorcycles was the kick-starter, so no Vespa ever had one. After several minutes of this, a passing man dressed in an expensive-looking suit noticed Harry's problem and stopped. He addressed my owner in perfect English, with only the hint of an Italian accent, and explained that the Vespa was activated by a key, which he went on to point out was already conveniently located in the ignition.

"A real diplomat," Harry grumbled, as the man walked off in the direction of the United Nations. The machine hummed to life. The lack of a roar momentarily comforted me, but little did either of us know that we were aboard the GT250ie version equipped with the new QUASAR system (Quarter-liter Smooth Augmented Range). The fuel injection meant that our craft was capable of Labrador-unfriendly speeds. This fact was discovered when we squealed onto First Avenue in a miasma of burning rubber and jamming brakes.

"Now we're cooking with gas," Harry observed with unnecessary bravado as he wedged us between an uptown bus and a car ringed with purple lights and throbbing like a discotheque. By 60th Street, my central processing unit had failed before the vision of two or three near misses and an altercation with a bicycle messenger, who struck out at Harry's disappearing head (and his dog's most vulnerable back) with a cardboard tube marked *Priority—Architectural—The Children's Hospital.* I buried my nose in Harry's jacket and searched for some familiar scents that would ground me and help me regain my composure. But as we crossed 70th, my attitude changed. Our continued survival seemed likely, my owner had begun to tame the machine and drive sensibly and I recognized that there was a rich treasure of scents streaming past me—all of Manhattan was in the air. I straightened up and rested my chin on Harry's shoulder. Great gusts of New York City's essence streamed into my nostrils. Bagels and hot dogs. Falafels and Tastee Delite. Chinese and Indian. Tibetan and Italian. Ethiopian and McDonald's. The new life of budding trees and flowers mingled with the decay of restaurant refuse and gutter grit. This was heady stuff, well beyond the possibilities of a cracked window in a car. The scents, the rush of air, the speed, seemed to heighten my senses and freeze the city into a kind of *tableau vivant*—a living photograph, a fantastic spectacle of isolated images speeding toward me like a kaleidoscopic fantasy that liberated individuals from the collective blur. If New York is anything, it is its endless parade of characters. A man clomped along the sidewalk in a diving mask and a snorkel. Another man, in a linen suit with a shoestring tie, held aloft a book entitled *The Power of the Now.* He seemed about to proclaim something to an audience of turned backs and lowered heads. A young mother stared wonderstruck into the carriage she was pushing, as if she had just discovered Einstein's Unified Field Theory tangled among the blankets and plush toys instead of her baby. A traffic policeman waved her white gloves and, ignored by all, finally decided to light a cigarette.

"Having a good time, boy?" Harry shouted above the racing air. *Yes,* I would have replied, *a good time is one way of putting this transcendence.*

Then the light changed and we came to a stop. A well-groomed woman crossed the street in front of us, clutching a tiny animal to her chest with one hand and holding an expensive-looking handbag in the other. The animal appeared to be some kind of dog, but I could not immediately

pick the breed. It was ungainly, out of proportion, awkward. If it had been walking on its own
instead of being carried like a handbag, it would
have galumphed. Then I realized—in a moment
of horror tempered by amusement—that I was
looking at a walking oxymoron. I had heard rumors of this breed but had dismissed them as
mere myth. But, indeed, right before my eyes was
proof. It was a miniature Great Dane, the bonsai
tree of canines. The *Walk* signal vanished and the
Don't Walk signal began to flash. But the woman
did not hurry, and just as she passed in front of us,
the little fellow gave me a mournful look.

Naturally I was abashed and would have
promptly apologized for staring, but the light
changed. Harry once again set our GT250ie into
furious motion up the avenue, before making a
sudden turn onto 97th for the trip across the
park.

There would soon be the smell of trees and
acres of green earth filling the air, but the speed-
ball effect had fled. I felt a sudden heaviness
come over me. SparrowHawk would have as-
cribed it to the hypothyroidism. But I was certain that it came from my distinct sense of guilt
and failure. Even the most sophisticated and intelligent dog wants to please his human for reasons utterly beyond the scope of the conscious

mind. Primitive reasons they may be, but noble as well.

A young man was dead beneath a parachute. My mistress was a suspect and my owner was speeding away from her and the grief that kept them whole—and I was frolicking. I curled into a tight ball and sank low in my passenger basket, feeling every bump of the road.

Then, as if Yours Truly's mood could not become blacker, Harry muttered a name that brought back the blackest of my puppy memories: *Haddy McClay*.

Rising to my feet, I saw that we had reached our street and idling in front of our building was a familiar convertible, which, despite the early-spring chill, had its top down.

THE IDLING CONVERT-
ible contained Harry's sister, Iberia,
his brother-in-law, a Scottish banker
named Tony, and their daughter, Haddy McClay.
This eight-year-old child was the reason for the
creeping nerve tingle that had turned each folli-
cle of hair on my back into ice. The reader will
likely recognize how my kind is usually tenta-
tive, even skittish, around children. Part of this
is because on some primitive pack level we identify the so-called top dogs instantly, and children are never top dogs. The most forceful child
still lacks natural authority. But there is another,
more pressing reason: we don't trust the little
blighters. Even when their adults are watching
them, they don't hesitate to rough us up. Our
tails seem to fascinate them, possibly on the
theory that they are detachable. They also yank
our legs, squeeze our noses and pull our ears.
They try to make us walk on two legs or sit in

chairs. They wrap napkins around our heads and jam sunglasses over our eyes. One dog of my acquaintance was imprisoned in a hammock. Another painted purple to look like a grape. And when we don't play with them and scurry, tail at half mast, into the next room, then they complain to their elders and stern words are issued in our direction. I don't mean to sound uncharitable, but try, if you dare, to go through your day without your dynamic human hands and arms to defend yourself, and you will know of what I speak.

Fortunately, Haddy McClay and her family lived deep in the moneyed woods and manicured gardens of Fairfield County and led one of those hectic, self-absorbed modern lives that meant we rarely saw them. In fact, my deep fear and distrust of this little girl stemmed from a single visit one Christmas several years earlier when she fed me a box of saltines and I unwittingly ate them—not realizing that the diabolical child had also hidden my water bowl in the cabinet beneath the sink. Eventually, after an agonizing hour of resistance—and beaten down by a profound Saharan thirst—I succumbed, and she gleefully watched as Yours Truly plunged his head into the toilet bowl for a long drink.

"Harry, how *are* you, little brother?" Iberia said. The tight bun of his sister's high-strung hairdo whipped around in our direction and revealed the eyes of a suburban gladiator. Harry and Iberia were separated in age by only a few years, but they were generations and temperaments apart. Where Harry is gentle, considerate and slow-moving, Iberia is harsh, heedless of others and seldom at rest. She is also astoundingly selfish. The world, I suspect, is divided into those who take and those who give. Iberia was one of the former; Harry, one of the latter. And if you are the one who gives, you can never stay around someone who takes for very long or soon there will be nothing of yourself left. Harry had learned this lesson young with Iberia. Iberia had gone to California for college. Harry had gone in the opposite direction, arrived in Manhattan and never left. Even though Iberia married and settled within an hour of New York, our little island's natural defenses managed to keep her at bay. Imogen's presence had also helped (Iberia thought my mistress was aloof), but even after Imogen's disappearance and a perfunctory show of support in those first few terrible weeks, Iberia had stayed away. Until now. Now she was here to take, I thought. But I was wrong (at least technically). Iberia wasn't taking; she was giving Harry her daughter to look after while she and Tony jetted off to Paradise Island for a banking conference. For a week. And then another week while they went to a private resort on the Exumas for a "real" holiday.

"Haddy won't be any trouble, I swear," Iberia said as disbelief spread across her brother's face. I wondered which was more incredible: that Iberia had the temerity to appear on our doorstep and make such a request or that she actually believed that my unemployed, lovelorn, bohemian owner was capable of keeping her child in one piece for two weeks. Then again, I mused, perhaps she didn't care.

"Sorry for the short notice. Didn't you get my e-mail?"

"I don't have e-mail. Well, I didn't until this morning," Harry muttered. "I have a phone."

"Never mind. It doesn't matter now. You've got to stay in the loop, little brother. Nothing worse than not being in the loop. You never know what you're going to miss. Anyway, I'm sorry, but we don't have a choice at this point. Our plane's taking off in mere minutes and I've got nowhere else to kennel her."

Mention of a kennel brought dogs to Iberia's mind and her gaze turned to me, sitting upright and alert in the Vespa's custom passenger basket.

"Rudolph's gotten fat. Don't feed Haddy the same. Fish fingers twice a day. Peas for greens. Pizza on Fridays. One slice. One topping: pepperoni. And no soda."

She turned to Tony, who looked as if his mind was already poolside sipping a mojito on Paradise Island. He said something in his profoundly Scottish tongue that I believe was both a greeting for my owner and a joke of some kind, but I could not decipher it. I am a multispecies linguist, but Scots is well beyond my power. Iberia had already shifted her attention to Haddy McClay.

"Am I forgetting anything, baby?"

"Yes," Haddy said. "You're forgetting me. I don't want to stay here. What am I going to do for two weeks, play with the stupid dog?"

Tony said something that instantly calmed his offspring down.

"Really?" Haddy said. "Does he really mean it, Mom?"

"Whatever your father says," Iberia said. "God knows no price is too dear." She spoke this last part under her breath and well below the auditory abilities of the surrounding humans.

"But, Ibi," Harry objected. "I really don't know if I can do this."

"C'mon, Harry. It's not as if I ask you every day. In fact, I've never asked you. And besides, your calendar isn't busting at the seams with commitments these days, am I right? Bonding with your niece will do you some good. And it'll be good for Haddy. This has win–win written all over it. We're optimizing here."

Harry was obviously doubtful that anything was "optimizing," but resistance was futile. He had been defeated the moment he saw Iberia parked on 90th Street.

Haddy hugged her parents and stepped out onto the street. Her mother handed her an enormous bag, a teddy bear wearing sunglasses and an instrument case.

Tony revved the engine. Iberia closed the door. Their car began to roll away.

"Oh, and, Harry, don't forget to make Haddy practice."

"Practice what?" Harry asked the fast-disappearing Iberia.

"Her violin, of course," his sister shouted over her shoulder. "It's her ticket to the Ivies."

Harry looked Haddy up and down and sighed.

"My place isn't big like what you're used to in Connecticut," he said.

"I know. Remember, I've seen it. And Mom always calls it Harry's hovel to her friends."

"I guess you'll have to sleep in the bed."

"That's okay. I brought my own sheets."

"How did you know what size bed I've got?"

"I don't," Haddy said. "I've got a selection."

I jumped out of the Vespa and Harry rolled it up onto the sidewalk. He dropped the kickstand and removed the license plate from its Velcro housing.

"That's illegal, isn't it?" Haddy said.

"I have no idea," Harry said.

"You don't know a lot of stuff," Haddy said. "At least, Mom said you don't know a lot of stuff. I've got to make up my own mind about whether you know a lot of stuff or not. I've got to see for myself. I like to see everything for myself. I like to observe. Science is about observing. I like science. Do you have cable?"

Harry nodded.

"Good, I like TV."

Harry's sense of desperation seemed to ease a bit at these words.

"Can you watch a lot of TV?" Harry asked. "Like from morning until you go to bed at night?"

We had just reached our apartment and Harry was turning the key in the door.

"Mom never lets me watch that much TV. She says people who watch a lot of TV don't go to the Ivies. They go to second-tier schools and live second-tier lives, like you."

"Right," Harry said. "But you'd *like* to watch a lot of TV if you could?"

"You betcha," Haddy said, and, moving just short of the speed of light, she had clicked on the television, selected one of those twenty-four-hour child-friendly networks and was rocking back and forth on the La-Z-Boy.

This invasion of our domestic sanctuary was too much. My head spun, my paws felt even weaker than before. The situation seemed well beyond my Labrador's powers to correct. When would I have a moment alone to use the laptop to communicate with my owner and get him back on course if Haddy was to be planted in our midst?

I was about to make my way to my corner when Haddy took notice of me. I tried to scoot past her while shrinking my body as best I could into a smaller target. Alas, I failed, and soon both my ears were in her clammy little-girl hands. She tugged hard again, on the theory that, like my tail, they might also be detachable.

"Doggy," Haddy cooed. "Remember me?"

MY EARS—THOSE DELI-
cate, velvety minidrapes that cover
the sensitive auditory equipment—
were in desperate shape. I could not move for
fear that movement would only bring more
pain. I could not snap and snarl because it has
never been my way to give in to my lower beast-
like nature and certainly not on the first day of
our guest's fourteen-day stay. Haddy hid my eyes
with my ears. Children think this is particularly
amusing because they can't do the same with
their stiff cartilage. Then, just as Haddy was
about to attach a metal binder clip to Yours
Truly's left lobe, Harry—who had retreated to
the bedroom and was oblivious to the torture of
his animal—returned to interrupt her.

"Are you hungry?" Harry asked.

"Starved," Haddy said.

Harry peeked into our deeply troubled refrigerator and emerged with a foodstuff wrapped in clear plastic.

"How about a Ho Ho?" he asked.

The dog's ears were dropped, the Ho Hos received, ripped open and devoured.

"More," Haddy demanded.

"Sorry," Harry said. "That was the last one. I missed it cleaning. I'm allergic to wheat."

"I'm allergic to stuff too. Mom told them that I'm allergic to glue so I don't have to do crafts at school. Mom says people who do crafts don't get into the Ivies. They become craft people, and craft people don't make any money. Got anything else that's like Ho Hos? I really love Ho Hos."

Haddy stretched out in the La-Z-Boy.

"Chocolate anything would be good."

I glanced at Harry and he at me. For a moment there was profound—if silent—interspecies dialogue between us.

"Randolph needs to go for a walk," Harry said. "You'll be okay here, Had, won't you?"

"Can't I come?" Haddy objected. "It's so boring being alone."

I gave my owner a long, pleading stare and hoped it wouldn't be misinterpreted.

"Maybe another time," Harry said. "Randolph

is very shy. He doesn't even like going to the bath-room in front of other dogs."

"That's weird," Haddy editorialized. "Maybe he should see a dog shrink or something."

"Why?"

"For his problem," Haddy said. "Mom says if you have a problem, you fix it. People who don't fix their problems don't—"

"We know," Harry said, interrupting her. "But it's not a problem. It's just part of who Randolph is."

"I guess, but I bet there's a pill for it," Haddy said. "My daddy's on antidepressants."

"I bet," Harry muttered, and opened the door. I made haste to the landing with a kind of saunter (I try never to run), and for a moment it seemed that the problematic child would be left behind. But then the phone rang. It was Detective Davis. He wanted Harry to meet him at the scene of the murder again.

"I'm not staying here," Haddy announced. "There is no way."

I felt certain that Harry would recruit me as babysitter, but instead he looked at both of us and delivered this extraordinary line:

"We'll all ride down on the Vespa."

"Him too?"

"Him too."

"I'll need a helmet," Haddy said. "Motor-cycles are dangerous. Mom would kill me if I got brain-damaged."

"This isn't a motorcycle," Harry said. "It's a Vespa. It's a motorcycle dressed in a tuxedo and wearing comfortable slippers. Your brain will be fine. Anyway, you can wear my helmet."

"What will you wear?"

Harry emerged from the bedroom with his water-polo headgear from his college days. He had been a top varsity player.

"Don't be ridiculous, Uncle Harry," Haddy said.

Soon we were all aboard the Vespa and speed-ing (or, rather, proceeding at a moderate, child-safe clip) downtown.

"I'd exclaim 'whee' if I was the kind of person who exclaimed things like that, but I'm not," said Haddy, who was wedged between my owner and Yours Truly's custom compartment.

Traffic was with us, and even when it was not, our Vespa allowed us to cut through congestion like the proverbial hot knife through butter. Ah, butter. It is a favorite of this Lab's palate.

The yellow tape and police guard were gone when we pulled up in front of the boarding-house. Harry parked the Vespa at the base of the front steps and removed the license plate.

"Lucky I'm not a traffic cop," Detective Davis said, stepping out from behind the stairs. "I'd say you just committed a half dozen moving violations."

"Sorry, Detective, but you made it sound urgent and I wanted to get down here as fast as I could," Harry said.

"I want some Ho Hos," Haddy said.

"Who's the little girl?" Detective Davis asked.

"My niece. It's a long story."

"Let's go inside," the detective said. "It'll only take a minute. You can leave Randolph in the lobby. We're going back to the room."

"If it's okay with you, I'd prefer to take him with me," Harry said.

On the trip downtown, I had wondered why I wasn't left at the apartment. Now I suspected the answer. Harry wanted me to see what he saw. After all, it had only been a few weeks since he was instructed by the "other world" that I had been inspired. Perhaps he was regretting not bringing me on the first expedition.

The first thing I noticed about the lobby was its dizzying overload of scents. My olfactories reeled. I smelled the decades of decline, neglect, vagrancy, dissoluteness and crime. It was as if all the circles of Dante's *Inferno* had telescoped into a single foul-smelling place—a potpourri of despair. There was also—I began to recognize—another potent potpourri, of cinnamon, nutmeg and apple, emanating from dishes discreetly placed on either side of an old wooden clock on the mantelpiece. This potpourri was called "Country Kitchens" and stunned the noses of man and canine in bed-and-breakfasts across the country. This veneer of coziness, however, could not transform the essential nature of the place. Despite its upscale transformation and the utopian ideals of its proprietress, the boardinghouse was still a place of transience and disconnection—an urban way station filled with alien bodies in separate rooms. The coffee percolating on the sideboard, the scones cooling in a woven basket and the Currier & Ives originals could not change this fundamental reality. As if to emphasize the point, two men passed through the lobby, arguing about a missing shower cap, and casually stepped over a ragged-looking man sprawled on the braided rug.

"Goddamn it, Abe, that's what your room's for," one of the men said.

"It's the poetry," the other man said.

"It's the booze," the first man countered. "He's been drunk since the Beats."

Abe did not budge, and the two men disappeared down the stairs to the street.

"Is he okay?" Harry asked, stepping around the man.

"He's fine," Detective Davis said. "As I said, you can't take the Bowery out of the boarding-house."

A woman with a clear plastic bag filled with recyclable bottles and cans sat in a wingback easy chair and read *Vogue*.

"Let's go upstairs," Detective Davis said. "There's something else that I want you to see."

"Is it alright for Haddy?" my owner asked.

"Sure. Everything's been cleaned up."

There was one other scent that I could detect beneath the host of conflicting smells. It was Imogen, and as we climbed the stairs toward the room she had occupied for so many months, her scent grew stronger and stronger until, by the time we reached her floor, it was so distinct that I was able to detect scents within that one scent. Just like that moment on the subway stairs a few weeks earlier, there were the major characteristics—the mix of sandalwood, pear and cotton—the "essential" Imogen. And there were also the impermanent qualities—the state-of-mind or mood markers—that I had detected then: fear, deceit and a mother lode of sad-ness. But there was something else, two recent smells: terror and shock.

How could they be so strong and distinctly hers? I snuffled up deep swaths of carpet following this particular trail—entirely lost in the exercise—until my snout rammed the base of the banister and I was aware of something small and metallic sticking to my nose.

"Randolph, you big goober," Harry said. "What are you doing?"

Detective Davis was more circumspect and more observant.

"There's something stuck to his nose," the detective said. He reached down, removed the object and held it up to the light.

"It's an earring," he said. Detective Davis showed it to Harry.

"It's Imogen's," Harry said. "I bought it for her."

My owner stared at the object. It was a miniature Betty Boop, the bumptious cartoon icon from the 1930s.

"She loved kitsch," Harry said in hushed tones. "I found these at a vintage-clothing store for our first anniversary."

Even Haddy was momentarily respectful.

"Is that that girl you used to like, Uncle Harry?" Haddy asked. "Is that who you're talking about?"

"Yes, Haddy. That's the girl," Harry said.

"Mom didn't like her," Haddy continued. "She said she was stuck up and that she was a thinker, not an achiever."

"Thanks for that, Haddy," Harry said, and turned to Detective Davis. "I guess you folks missed this one—do you want it? I guess it could have dropped here anytime."

"Perhaps, but we found the other one in the victim's hand," Detective Davis said, and began walking toward the room. "I want your opinion on something."

Yellow police tape was strung across the entrance to the room. Detective Davis unlocked the door and ducked under the tape.

"Is it alright for Haddy to come in?" Harry asked. Though I could sense Harry's nerves bristling at seeing Imogen's room again, he did not forget his avuncular responsibility to his difficult niece.

"Sure," Detective Davis confirmed. "Forensics is done. It's like the room's never been lived in, except for this."

Detective Davis switched the ceiling light on, walked over to the window and lowered the blind. Then he herded everyone into the far corner of the room, shut the door and turned the ceiling light off.

"Wow," Harry said.

"Cool," Haddy echoed.

Hundreds of stars appeared on the ceiling—luminous green dots floating in the black.

"It looks like the night sky," Harry said. "It's very complex. Someone spent a lot of time doing this."

"I've got stars on my ceiling at home," Haddy offered. "Except it's the solar system, and now that Pluto's not a planet anymore, it kind of stinks because I like Pluto because it's purple, but it doesn't belong but still I don't want to get rid of it because, like I said, it's purple. I wish it was Mercury that wasn't a planet, not Pluto. But it's not."

"We think Imogen did this, Harry," Detective Davis said when Haddy finally came up for air.

"Why?"

"A few people on the floor remember," Detective Davis said. "Once or twice they walked past and she was standing on the desk sticking these things to the ceiling."

"Why would she have had her door open?" Harry asked.

"That's the way this place is," Detective Davis said. "It's like a dormitory."

"But I thought you said that Imogen and..."

Harry paused. It was difficult to connect our mistress to someone else.

"Yes?"

"I thought you said they didn't mix with the other people here. I mean, wouldn't it be unusual for her to keep the door open?"

"Maybe she wanted some air," Detective Davis said.

"I guess," Harry said. "It just sounds strange."

"You think she wanted people to see her?"

"It's just I know Imogen. I mean, I knew her, and the person I knew liked privacy. She wasn't somebody who kept her door open, especially in a place like this and especially if she was doing something that might draw attention to herself. She hated attention."

"Sounds like a different person," Detective Davis observed. "Don't get me wrong, she was aloof, but people here thought she was a party girl. A lot of comings and goings. All hours. Men asking for her. Waiting around out front. We'd like to talk to some of them, but they seem to have evaporated with the murder. There are two reasons I brought you here again. The first is that the picture that's emerging of Imogen is just not the one I've had, and I think you should be prepared to learn some hard truths about her ahead, Harry. But the second, and the cop-in-me reason, is these stars. I agree with you: I think Imogen wanted people to remember her doing this. Five people on five different occasions saw her doing this. Three of them asked her about it, and she closed the door in their faces without saying a word. And I can tell you from twenty years of police work that if you want somebody to remember something, make them angry or hurt. They'll remember it *and* they'll tell other people about it. For some reason she wanted witnesses to remember her standing on the desk sticking stars to the ceiling."

"But what is it?" Harry asked. "I mean, it's incredibly intricate, but it's as random as the night sky."

"Did she like astronomy?" Detective Davis asked.

"She told me that she had a telescope when she was a kid and used to look at the stars in her backyard in Ohio, but I guess that's not true."

"The geography might not be true," Detective Davis said, "but the details could be substantially the same. This is usually the case with people who want to conceal their origins. Someone said it's hard to be a good liar because you have to remember your lies—it's easier to remember the truth or some close version of it."

Had I the vocal power, I would have supplied Mark Twain as the "someone" Detective Davis meant.

"So it wasn't all made up," Harry said. There was pain close to the surface.

"No, it wasn't all made up," Detective Davis said.

"So what about these stars?"

"I think there's some message in this. It might not be for the NYPD or you, but there's something here."

I scrutinized the ceiling. The points of light wavered against the black background, appearing and disappearing, whole blocks of fluorescent dots turning as if caught in a gentle celestial vortex. It was difficult to focus or find anything like a pattern in this spill of stars. A row of half a dozen on the edge intersected another row of three. They seemed brighter than the rest. Could it be an *L*? Had Imogen built a message into the ceiling? Next to the *L* I thought I could just make out an *O*. But the more I stared, the more letters I saw and the less sense they made. There were no intelligible words beyond nonsense pairs. Perhaps, I thought, switching gears, the stars themselves added up to something, or the stars and the spaces between them served as some kind of Morse code. The dots could be the stars and the dashes the spaces. My musings were interrupted by little Haddy.

"This is so boring," Haddy said. "Mom said you'd be fun, Uncle Harry, but I knew she was lying. 'Cause before that she said you'd been a basket case since that girl left."

Detective Davis switched the lights back on.

"As I said, I think there's a message here, but it would take an army of cryptanalysts to figure this one out, and we don't have that. And we don't have much time either. Someone's moving in here today or tomorrow."

"That's fast," Harry said.

"Ms. Ramsey wanted it. She's the one who runs this place—the one I told you about. She's a saint but she's a character, and she has very strong opinions. Hopefully, we'll make our getaway without an encounter."

"You can't stop her?"

"Yes, but we won't. As I said, we've got all the forensics."

"But what about the stars?"

"We've got photographs. It's not the same

thing, but it should be enough. Anyway, we've requested that they not be removed from the ceiling for a month or so. But who knows? This is New York. Nothing stays the same for very long."

THE STARS PROVIDED A concrete link to my mistress and more proof that she was trying to communicate something essential. But to whom? Perhaps it was only to posterity or for her own sanity and sense of self. Preserving the photograph on the dresser but eliminating Harry so the context would not be identifiable might also be explained this way. But if it was just an act of memory or defiance, why allow witnesses?

My thoughts returned to Imogen's journal and its code. The code had been a simple cipher and spelled *Cymbeline*. Harry had ultimately cracked it after my analysis led nowhere, but only I had understood the connection to the action of the Shakespearean play *Cymbeline* and Imogen's namesake, a central character who feigns her own death to protect those she loves from malevolent forces. For a brief moment, I had the shocking idea that Imogen had intended me to be the audience and the code solver. To grasp this significance and somehow pass it on. But this made no sense. After all, I might be a loyal dog in her mind, but I was certainly still just a dog.

We left Detective Davis at the boarding-house and climbed aboard the Vespa for the trip home. I burrowed deep in my compartment so that I could sift through the scents I had gathered from the room. There wasn't much that was useful. Imogen's scent was strong, but it did not add much to what I already knew. I was certain of one thing, but this was no surprise: my mistress had not been romantically involved with the dead man. Nor had she slept in the room very often—at least not in recent months.

It was now even more urgent that I communicate what I knew to Harry, but the prospect of doing this in the near future looked unlikely because of the presence of Haddy McClay. But then I was granted a chance.

"I'm hungry," Haddy said as we turned onto the 90th Street home stretch. "I want fish sticks."

"I don't have any," Harry said.

"Well, we've got to get some. Fish sticks are basically all I eat. I adore fish sticks," Haddy

said. I suspected that someone had been reading a bit too much *Eloise* to our precocious
youngster. Harry, however, didn't seem to notice
the literary allusion and instead focused on how
to answer the demand without polluting our
newly wheat-free abode.

"I'm taking you out," he finally said. "We'll go
to the Gotham Diner on Broadway. You'll love
it. A real New York experience."

"They better have fish sticks," Haddy muttered.

"First, Randolph goes upstairs," Harry said.

"I'll stay right here," Haddy announced.

"No you won't," Harry said. "The last thing I
need to tell your mom is that I lost you."

"She wouldn't mind," Haddy said.

"Of course she would," Harry said.

"No, really, she wouldn't," Haddy maintained.
"She's always saying some women aren't cut out
to be mothers and that she's one of them."

Ten minutes later, Yours Truly was seated at
the kitchen table in the serene emptiness of
our apartment. Harry's computer had been
powered up with a snout-wipe. I had observed
Harry navigating the virtual environment, but
now that it was my turn, I knew this would be a

challenge. There is a part of any advanced animal that imagines itself free from the prison of
the body. Humans, unlike dogs, have ample dex-
terity. I had imagined using my paws like some
cartoon dog—tapping away at the keyboard
with my tongue a-wag. This was not to be. Like
cereal work, the computer would be a snout
job—painstaking and precise. Fortunately, the
keys were relatively large and the DELETE button
prominent.

The keyboard would matter most when I
had messages to write, and I wanted those messages to come from an outside source. I would
play on my owner's supernatural soft spot once
again—much as I disliked encouraging this bad
behavior—and send him e-mails from a spirit
guide. I had toyed with the idea of composing
the messages directly on his computer, but I
balked. Only recently had I watched a *National
Geographic* team on television sedate a harbor
seal for "its own good" and attach a camera to its
head. I didn't fancy becoming Exhibit B in the
dog-brain department at MIT, so it seemed
wise to cover my tracks in some way.

My damp nose skidded across the touch pad
(I tried not to think of the human germs festering there), and with laborious but steady
progress, I moved the digital arrow around the

desktop, imitating the actions Harry had taken
to get online. I was successful and soon had a
window open. This took me through the registration process for my e-mail account. I entered
the following:

> First Name: Randolph
> Last Name: Labrador
> Gender: Male
> Birth Date: 11/14/1970

The reader will note that I took some cre-
ative license with my birth date. I originally entered my calendar birth year but was informed
that I would need my parents' permission to
complete the registration. In any case, I told the
approximate truth in dog years.

A few clicks more and it was done.
Astudyinscarlet1887@hotmail.com was ready to
communicate. The name was a reference to
Conan Doyle's first Sherlock Holmes mystery,
published in *Beeton's Christmas Annual* in 1887,
and underscored the identity of a wise detective spirit guide—the same mastermind who
had employed Alpha-Bits so effectively. My own
identity would remain cloaked and known only
to the operators of the Web site, and what they
would know would be quite vague.

I heard footsteps on the stairs. Communication would have to wait. At first the footsteps sounded like Harry's, but then I realized that they were heavier and there was no little girl in tow. Perhaps it was some other occupant of our walk-up apartment, but they stopped at our door. The door handle jiggled. The door was pushed in and then pulled out. I closed the window and nosed the laptop's lid shut just as something metallic was thrust into the lock. The tool moved about inside the lock and manipulated the tumblers. *Click...click...click...*

I began to sweat between my toes. Our lock was supposed to be secure against such assaults, but one by one I heard the tumblers fail. I approached the door and produced a low growl, but the person on the other side did not pause or even slow the work. Another tumbler failed. I considered retreating to the bedroom, but before I could move, the lock turned and the front door swung open.

THE MENACING FIGURE
WATCHES TELEVISION

A LITTLE GIRL IS HARSHLY BUT
FAIRLY ASSESSED

"G'DAY, POOCH," AN ENORmous man wearing an Akubra hat said as he stepped into our apartment and shut the door behind him. "You must be Randolph. I've heard a lot about you from your mistress."

He reached down and gave my head a most agreeable tousle with his giant hand. The man spoke with a distinct Australian accent and I knew that this was the menacing figure from Christmas night the previous year. The scent matched. That night Harry and I had been returning from dinner at Jackson's and had—so it seemed at the time—only narrowly avoided a confrontation with this figure, who stalked us from the shadows on the desolate street and away from whom I finally managed to pull my owner. Now I also suspected that this man was the guardian of the fortune Iris had spoken about before she died. This guardian, she had told us, was an Australian lawyer entrusted with determining the worthiness of the fortune's inheritor and he would be coming to meet us soon. Nothing in his scent was threatening, and I wondered whether I had overreacted when my owner and I encountered him on Central Park West that dark night.

The man surveyed the apartment and his eyes settled on the La-Z-Boy.

"Think I'll wait for your young man in the rocker," he announced. "It looks like a ripper."

He lowered his monumental frame into the chair and let out a similarly monumental sigh — the kind of legendary exhalation that I imagined mythic figures might make. A Norse god sort of sigh.

A word seems necessary on dog territoriality. The reader might think it odd that I did not fly into a frenzy over this intrusion into our abode. But territoriality is a lot like nationalism in human beings: it occurs in varying degrees. Yours Truly, who naturally leans to the philosophical, considers the impermanence of our existence as the basic benchmark for his responses. As Detective Davis so aptly observed: in New York nothing stays the same for very long. Any apartment, including ours, is more temporary encampment than citadel. That said, when the man tried to put the footrest up, I growled a second time.

He laughed but desisted.

"Your master's sanctuary, huh, mate? I understand," he said, correctly grasping the purpose of my growl. "You don't mind if I watch telly, though?"

He smiled and turned on the television. A ghost-hunting program was on, and to my surprise—we had heard nothing of this project—Harry's friend Ivan Manners was leading a camera crew into a "haunted" mustard factory in Queens. Mr. Apples was perched on his shoulder and Ivan's mouth ran without stopping.

"Now, rumor has it that if you stand beneath Vat Number Three, where Orange B is added to the mustard mixture, you will hear—if you're really lucky—the spectral cries of one ill-fated Tobias H. Smith, who managed Vat Number Three until the day he plummeted to his death by drowning in its sticky contents..."

"What rubbish," the man said, and flipped through the channels until he found a twenty-four-hour news station. The anchor moved from a story on civil strife in the Congo to the exploits of a drunken former child star.

"There is no truth anymore, Randolph. Only hype and the power of your spin. And these daffy bastards call themselves journalists. Most of them aren't worth warm spit," he said.

I heard Harry and Haddy McClay on the stairs. Haddy was complaining about the fish sticks at the diner. I considered positioning myself at the front door and barking. The behavior would certainly alert Harry, but to what advantage? The enormous man in the La-Z-Boy gave me no indication that he posed a threat. Then another thought came to mind. What if Harry was carrying Grandfather Oswald's WWII–era .45? An image of my owner bursting through the doorway on the strength of his usually reticent Labrador's warning barks and shooting the Australian dead in the La-Z-Boy was sobering. It was also unwarranted, since a moment later I remembered that the NYPD had confiscated the weapon after Iris's death.

Harry fumbled with the keys. The Australian glanced at the door but did not budge from the La-Z-Boy. He seemed very relaxed.

The door swung open. Harry saw the man and froze.

"Harry, it's good to finally meet you," the man said, delivering a smile and a wave and turning the entire spirit of their meeting from criminal to pleasantly social merely by the strength of his personality.

"Who the hell are you?" Harry asked, instinctively pushing Haddy back into the hall. Then he looked down at me with a somewhat disparaging expression that suggested he was not happy to see me sitting next to this stranger in the La-Z-Boy.

"Randolph, come here, for God's sake."

"He's a special pup, that one," the man noted as he rose to his feet with some effort against the powerful gravity of the addictive La-Z-Boy.

"That chair's a ripper. I reckon you don't need a bed."

As tall as my owner is, the Australian had a few inches on him. He advanced with his arm outstretched for a handshake.

"My name's Malcolm Patterson, and I'm your new best friend," the man said. "Me friends call me Blinko."

"Why?"

"Because when I was a kid, I got hot ashes in my eye, and after I got my sight back I couldn't stop blinking. Aussies love their nicknames. Ha."

"Why are you in my apartment?" Harry asked. "How did you get into my apartment?"

"I picked the lock," Blinko explained.

"That's breaking and entering."

"Just entering... I didn't break a thing,"

Blinko said. "I'm always doing it back home with locking myself out and the like."

"We don't do that in America," Harry said. "At least not if we want to stay out of jail."

"Do you have any Ho Hos?" Haddy interjected, poking her head between Harry's arm and the door frame.

"Come inside," Blinko said. "It's no good standing out in the hall."

"This is crazy," Harry said, but came inside anyway.

"You should close the door," Blinko said.

"Not until I know what this is about."

"I told you," Blinko said. "I'm your new best friend. We need to team up. There are some dodgy forces at work."

"I don't even know what this is about," Harry said. But then he understood. "You're the keeper of the fortune. You're the one that Iris talked about."

"'The keeper of the fortune' sounds like bollocks. There isn't a myth here—only money. Money and power. The Great Game—the game that governments and corporations play with one another and sacrifice the little people doing it."

"So there is a fortune," Harry said. "Iris wasn't crazy."

"No, she was a genuine nutter, Harry. She just

got a few of the facts right. The word *fortune* makes it sound like a good thing when it's really a burden, an obligation, something that puts you on the spot when you'd rather be left alone. It's put your Imogen on the spot."

"What do you know?" Harry asked.

"Shut the door and I'll tell you, mate," Blinko said.

"I have a better idea," Harry said. "Let's go for a walk. Randolph needs to do his Numbers."

"I'd prefer to stay indoors," Blinko said. "Have you ever heard of a Heckler and Koch PSG-1?"

"It sounds like a gun," Harry said.

"It is a gun. One of the most accurate sniper rifles in the world. A shooter positioned on a building across the park could split an apple on the sidewalk in front of your building. Word has it that there are a number of PSG-1s floating about New York these days attached to characters with permission to use them. It's a good idea to avoid the open during the day."

"Are you suggesting that there is someone out there on top of a building somewhere ready to pop you off?" Harry asked. "New York isn't a war zone."

"Harry, there is always a war going on around

you; you've just grown up unaware of it," Blinko said.

Haddy pushed past both of them and turned on the television.

"This is boring," she said. "I want to watch TV."

"Only a miserable child would think that the prospect of having one's noggin turned to mush by a sniper's bullet was boring. I've seen blue-tongued skinks with more native curiosity."

Harry looked at Blinko.

"I don't know whether to call the police or buy you a drink," Harry said.

"Call the police if you like, but our problems are much bigger than the locals. They can't help us much now," Blinko said. "I'll go for the walk."

"But I thought you said it wasn't safe," Harry said.

"I just wanted to open your mind up to the hazards of your new life," Blinko said. "Besides, it's getting dark now."

HARRY ATTACHED MY leash and our strange, somewhat jumpy party headed to the bridle path that runs around the reservoir. Haddy McClay had been much chastened by Blinko's words and slunk behind the adults as we made our way toward Central Park. Harry was distracted and took three doggy disposal bags from the courtesy dispenser at the end of our block. New York suddenly seemed much less secure. People passing us on the street took on a suspicious cast. Two Yorkshire terriers bore down on me with almost militant fervor before their owner dragged them off in the opposite direction.

"Leave it," their owner commanded, using the rather offensive dog-training terminology that has now become ubiquitous on our island. I am not an "it," and few dogs are stupid enough to mistake me for a dropped hamburger or a dead bird. Yes, Yours Truly's nerves were on full alert. Blinko's theoretical sniper's bullet hung somewhere in the Manhattan air, stayed only mometarily from speeding toward its target.

We crossed Central Park West, dipped down the small path beside the 90th Street gate and then up and over the hillock and across the road until we were walking under the trees on a grass-covered trail to the bridle path. It was early evening and several dogs were out with their owners for the "after-work" walk, snuffling the rich soils beneath the trees and among the shrubbery and racing in lines and circles through the leaves and wood chips. Blinko was the kind of man who saw without seeming to look, and I could sense that whatever reluctance he had to coming outside had diminished in this crowd and he was now well at ease.

Harry let me off my leash.

"Go on, Randolph, do your business," Harry said. At his words, I noticed a certain bladder-based urgency that I had ignored, but I hesitated since I did not want to miss any of what Blinko might have to say to my owner while attending to my so-called business. Making matters more complicated, our party had stopped in the middle of the path, and as usual my *Foliage-Finder* nature prevented me from the public leg lift.

Needless to say, the *Squat-and-Drops* were out in full force and delivering seemingly endless quantities of "presents" for their owners to scurry at with doggy disposal bags worn like catcher's mitts. Of course, while the *Earth-Onlys*—the hippies of the canine world—were enjoying themselves in this narrow wilderness between road and reservoir, the *Asphalt-Onlys* were craving the nearest stretch of blacktop.

All dogs are compulsives to a greater or lesser extent. We have these requirements for our Numbers. And we have our odd dances, shakes and movements that are often habitual. One dog scuffs up the dirt with its hind legs after a Number 2; another rubs its right shoulder against the base of a tree or executes a half roll. Compulsivity might be classified as a neurosis in the human world, but in the dog world it is a form of sanity—after all, it is an attempt to repeat something in a universe that embraces the random and complete something in defiance of the perpetual loose end. When these habits are interrupted or threatened, a dog can lose its sense of proportion. Just as I was about to head off to the shrubbery—it seemed likely that I'd be back before Blinko had shared anything of import with my owner—an *Asphalt-Only*, shaky from blacktop deprivation, approached for the customary hindquarter sniff and information exchange. This sniff practice is revolting, a primitive holdover from pack days. It is also unnecessary, since the same information can be gleaned by a more thoughtful olfactory survey of the air, which doesn't require one dog's nose shoved into the other's rump. I pivoted away, deflecting the *Asphalt-Only*'s approaching snout. Unfortunately, the *Asphalt-Only* was a Maltese terrier–Chihuahua mix with a fierce Latin nature (the kind of temperament Thomas Mann spent pages puzzling over in his fictional works). The dog did not appreciate my maneuver and delivered a quick snarl and a yap-screech that stunned the ear. From a distance his owner cried out.

"Leave it, General Franco. Leave it."

But General Franco did not "leave it." Instead, he jumped into the air and clamped his little incisors into the side of my mouth. The pain was sharp and my reaction lamentable. My lower nature assumed command, and in an instant I was holding General Franco in my jaws like an oversized chew toy.

"Randolph, drop him," Harry said.

General Franco squirmed. Though trapped and his neck contorted, he did not surrender or release the side of my mouth. We were locked in a stalemate. His owner arrived seconds later, a generously proportioned woman wearing a T-shirt that proclaimed her status as *Disco Queen of New York*. Harry, Blinko and the Disco Queen stood mute before the image of her animal in my jaws. Haddy McClay alone made a comment.

"Cool," she said.

I frequently find that my philosophic disposition rescues me from the brutal reality playing out around me. Such was the case now as General Franco's incisors became the focus of a brief meditation on the subject of pain. At the core of the question of pain (and, indeed, its opposite, pleasure) is the idea of permanence. Pain fluctuates. It is not a constant. General Franco's incisors in the delicate skin of my mouth were initially a terrible thing. Now they were mere nuisance. But emotional pain—or, better, pain of the mind—has a different nature: it does not have such clear dimensions, such easily seen ebbs and flows. Imogen's disappearance was a chronic condition, and this dog knew neither Harry nor I would rest until we had one single good answer to all that had happened: a unified theory of loss. And, more important, until our mistress was back.

I dropped General Franco and focused my

mind on the excruciating, but limited, reality of his incisors digging a deep, raw trench into my mouth as he swung trapezelike onto the ground.

"Good boy," Harry said. He apologized to the Disco Queen, who insisted that General Franco was to blame.

"Wasn't he always," Blinko muttered under his breath, making pointed reference to the problematic historical figure without whom the world would never have been treated to Picasso's *Guernica*.

When the Disco Queen and her charge had vanished, Blinko bent down and gave my wound a quick look.

"She'll be apples, mate," he said, clapping me on the back while he dispensed the vigorous Australian idiom, which, roughly translated, means *As severe as things might appear, there is nothing to worry about, and if deadly infection sets in we'll take another look but won't be in any hurry about it.* Yes, they are a rugged people.

Sensing that any serious discussion was momentarily derailed, I hastened to the foliage on the opposite side of the path and found privacy behind a London plane tree. Afterward, I lingered for a moment to inhale the rich bouquet of an early-spring mushroom mingling with a clutch of crocus. I floated among these exquisite smells and gave a head-to-tail shake and stretch. I, like George Santayana, the notable Harvard professor and poet, had been late for my "appointment with spring." Thus, restored and with the pain of my wound diminishing—the clean environment of a dog's mouth is indeed curative—I returned to Harry and Blinko, who were beginning to discuss serious things.

"You did the right thing shooting Iris, you know," Blinko said, offering an assessment that the enormous man from the outback must have considered something of an icebreaker.

"I don't know," Harry said.

"She was a monster," Blinko said. "I knew her from the beginning. Not everyone you'll be meeting will be so cut and dry."

"She was cut and dry?" Harry asked.

"Once you knew the beast, yes, she was cut and dry: an evil nutter," Blinko said.

I noted how Blinko spoke with an almost prophetic hush at times, as if my owner was already on a mission whether he liked it or not. It was as if Blinko knew the course of the weeks and months ahead and was only the first of the many characters we were to meet in this strange new world that was opening up to us. My owner noticed this dimension as well and to my surprise addressed it directly.

"I don't know why you seem to think I am part of this," Harry said. "I'm not your new best friend. I'm at the end of this chapter of my life. Not at the beginning. Imogen has moved on and so have I. She's not the person I thought she was. She's involved in bad things. Maybe she's even done bad things."

Blinko was silent. Haddy McClay had run a few yards off and been momentarily adopted by a family playing a twilight game of catch. Finally, the enormous man spoke. It was like the door of a vault had been opened, carrying a rich cargo of knowledge up and out on a rush of air.

"She told me you'd be true blue," Blinko said. "And instead all I find is light blue, china blue, powder blue."

"She's the one who's not committed," Harry said. "She's the one who's been shacking up with someone else."

Blinko didn't answer this charge, although it was terribly clear that Harry wanted and needed it answered.

Instead, he waved his hand as if to dismiss my owner.

"No worries, mate," Blinko said. "I'll be on my way, and if you're lucky you'll get out of this with your life—but I wouldn't wager on it. You've been a bit too close to the flame for too long. And Imogen, of course, she'll be dead. That goes without saying. But you're over her, aren't you? She's not your responsibility anymore."

Harry drew the point of his shoe across the ground between them.

"She's not the woman that I thought she was," Harry said. "And for all I know you could be involved with what happened down at that boardinghouse. My God, you broke into my apartment. How legitimate is that? And if you care about her, what is stopping you from helping?"

Blinko sighed.

"I'm not sure I like you. I don't know if you're the right sort," he said. "But I'm short on options. I will tell you as much of the story as I know and I hope it is enough."

Harry nodded. I sat down on my haunches and listened.

"I'M A LAWYER BY TRAIN-
ing, but I'm a Jackaroo by inclina-
tion and upbringing," Blinko said.
"A Jackaroo is what you Yanks call a cowboy, but
without the guns. My home is the flats, the dry
expanses of Australia where the droughts are
measured in decades. Now, I had a good friend
and he was very wealthy because of his father's
pure luck."

"Iris told the story," Harry said. "Her grandfather was flying a plane and found the largest
reserve of uranium..."

"The largest in the world," Blinko said. "In all
of human history. And the bugger found it without even trying. His son was my friend, whose
daughter was Iris, the aforementioned nutter.
Iris's daughter was Imogen. Now, Imogen was
raised in secret to keep her safe from Iris—
that's why the past you probably thought you
knew was a bit exaggerated."

"More than exaggerated," Harry said. "A lie. Austria isn't Akron."

"Yep, a bit of a fibberoo, but it kept her alive," Blinko said.

"I would never have told anyone," Harry said.

Blinko nodded. "She was used to the other version."

"Why didn't your friend raise her himself like any normal grandfather would do?"

"I asked him that myself," Blinko said. "But Dolpho wasn't that normal either."

"Dolpho?" Harry said. "That's a funny name."

"Australians abbreviate everything and add an *O*," Blinko explained. "His full name was Randolph."

My ears instinctively pricked up at my name.

"Randolph?" Harry asked. "You mean she named Randolph after her grandfather?"

"That's right," Blinko said. "Understandable, since she never met him. If she had, she might have thought different. We always idealize what we don't know well. Randolph was a difficult man to get along with. I did because I had known him for yonks, since we were tots. Long story short: when Iris went bad, Dolpho was wounded, though he never said it. He struck out on the trail and followed his father's uranium lode from the south to the north. Then he walked it east to west. He did it solo. Searching out water. Searching out food. Becoming a creature of the bush. He was out there alone for the better part of a year, and when he came back he looked an utter wreck but that land was his. Australia's an ancient place, and it works on you if you let it. And it had worked on Dolpho. He had heard its voice about permanence and how small a man is. How insignificant. It warped him a bit the other way. He came back convinced it wasn't just dumb luck that his father found that uranium in a bloomin' airplane. It had his sweat all over it now. His hunger. His loneliness. The land had been his constant companion. It was his. That's what he told us. So one day I got a call. I was still a relatively young lawyer then. Dolpho asked whether it was possible to create a trust that would bypass Iris—whose whereabouts were unknown—and go to Imogen, who was a little girl now being raised by nannies in Paris. He didn't want *what had become his* precious uranium to go to anyone really, but he had limited options. And he wanted something extra built into the trust."

"He didn't want Imogen to have it until she was thirty," Harry said.

"Yes, Dolpho wanted to make sure that she wasn't a nutter too, and he wanted this to be a guarantee," Blinko said. "And being this man's friend, I agreed. Two decades later, Dolpho is long dead and I find myself stuck in this city assessing a young woman whose own grandfather never bothered to visit. But Dolpho's reach was long and my hands are tied. He kept me as a watcher. I can assess but I can't get directly involved, and if I do get involved I will be replaced by another trustee. At this point—for reasons I'm not at liberty to say—that would be disastrous."

"So Imogen can't inherit until she is thirty, and if she's crazy, the uranium..."

"Reverts to the government of Australia," Blinko said. "Not just if she's crazy, though. I think she's passed that test. She's not crazy like her mother. No, there is something more pressing right now. If she's arrested on suspicion of murder, that's it. As much as Dolpho loved that uranium, he was deeply ashamed of Iris and would rather have seen the government get it than let it support the life of another psychopath."

"It sounds like a complicated family," Harry said. "I'm surprised Imogen is so normal."

"She was raised far enough away," Blinko said. "All she had was the sense of loss instead of the up-close example of madness. She had love anyway. There were those nannies in France who raised her most of the way—they loved her and she loved them. One in particular. But that's another story. Right now I need you to help her and help us. As far as I can tell, when Imogen disappeared that day, she went underground. This worked for a while, but then things began to catch up with her. There was Iris, for one, thanks to Overton, whose reporting skills helped Iris find her daughter. But that was only part of it. Then the big boys entered. There are a dozen or so nations and/or large multinationals that would like to get their hands on what might be coming to Imogen. For many years, the uranium has gone unmined. The market has been weak, and digging it up and exporting it wasn't economical. There were also some very tough governmental controls. Both of those things have changed: the battle for energy sources and weapons fuel has driven the price through the roof, and the government has changed its tune. Needless to say, Imogen is a much-sought-after young lady. For a number of months Imogen managed to stay missing, but it seems then one or more of the big boys tracked her down and everything changed."

The enormous man drew a deep breath. Nothing in Blinko's scent suggested deceit.

Haddy McClay, playing catch in near dark, dropped the ball and loudly blamed the thrower. Harry traced another line in the dirt with his foot.

"These people will use anything at their disposal to coerce Imogen to turn over her rights to the uranium, and she has played them against one another."

"But what about the dead guy?" Harry asked. "Clearly she's had favorites."

"I don't know much about him," Blinko said. "My guess is that he knew something that the others didn't and she had to keep him especially close, but I don't know."

"But she's not in any danger," Harry said. "After all, if she's gone, then so are their chances of getting what they want."

"Yes, but I believe you might be in danger," Blinko said. "They learned about the details of the trust, and given that there are a limited number of copies of the document in secure locations, this was no mean feat. I am certain that the stakes have been raised in this game. One or more of the parties is no longer content to let Imogen play hard to get. They want to force her hand even if it means losing—but I am sure they are quite convinced they won't lose. Imogen didn't murder that bloke. They did—whoever they are. And now whatever control she had is overturned. She is on the run. The evidence might justify her arrest, and her arrest alone would put her claim to the fortune in jeopardy."

"But why would she care? Imogen was never materialistic," Harry asked.

"She'd still have this killing hanging over her. I'm sure she's going on instinct right now, and it's telling her to keep moving until she can get some clarity," Blinko said. "So she's on the run again and they hold her only way out. They could clear her. But, of course, they won't unless she agrees to their terms. And even then I'm not so sure."

"What do you mean?" Harry asked.

"Remember, this is a competition. There are different sides here. It's possible that some of them want the uranium turned over to the Australian government, because the government won't run it themselves. They'll sell the concession to someone who'll mine it for them—there's still a lot of money to be made that way. Of course, most of them would prefer to own it themselves, but business is business; it's just a question of better returns."

"My God, she's in deep," Harry said.

"She's quite a girl," Blinko said. "She's a little battler. But I've gone as far as I can. I know what the situation is, but if I try to track her down—not that I could, mind you—or I get involved, I'd be compromised. But *you* can do something."

"Get shot by some unseen sniper," Harry said.

"Oh, forget about that; I was just trying to get your attention. No one'll try to kill you—at least not yet," Blinko said.

"So what can I do?"

"You can solve the murder."

"How?" Harry asked.

"That boardinghouse is filled with characters, and some of them are players in this game. But there are four in particular, and one of those four buggers did the killing, I'm certain of it. They are agents for some country or some corporation. They were living there to keep track of Imogen. Everyone was angling to get near her, and they were the closest suitors."

"But she's gone now," Harry said. "Why aren't they?"

"It'd be too suspicious," Blinko said. "And, besides, you'll find that they have day jobs—all of them to the man are affiliated in some way with the United Nations—and the boardinghouse is near the six train, an easy commute to work. Even assassins can save taxi fare. They're all somewhere in the diplomatic food chain— mostly the lower rungs."

"And how am I supposed to get near them?" Harry asked. "You want me to move in?"

"No," Blinko said. "I want your dog to move in and I want you to visit often."

The Australian handed Harry a business card.

"Leopold Maranovsky," Harry read. "Who is Leopold Maranovsky?"

"Mr. Maranovsky is the agoraphobic press secretary for the small but cultured nation of Near Upper Pilasia."

"I've never heard of it," Harry said.

"You wouldn't have," Blinko said. "It is a small borderland nation whose chief exports are illuminated manuscripts and hot-water bottles. A place that is swallowed up a dozen times a century by its neighbors, only to reemerge as an autonomous nation again and again. This man is moving into Imogen's room at the boarding-house tomorrow. He is in desperate need of a therapy dog, and Randolph must provide that service. He is expecting a call from you. It is all organized."

A DOG JOINS THE TEMPORARY WORKFORCE AND RECEIVES A NOBLE ALIAS

BLINKO DISAPPEARED into the night, and Harry made the call to Mr. Leopold Maranovsky when we returned to our apartment. He arranged to meet Maranovsky at the boardinghouse early the next morning. Maranovsky explained that he had just arrived in the country but had been prevented from bringing his own dog to carry out the job of calming the diplomatic attaché. Then Harry remembered that in all the excitement we had missed the vet appointment that he had scheduled online.

"Oh well. I'll reschedule soon," Harry said to me. "It can't be too dire."

Haddy McClay went to sleep in the bedroom after Harry changed the sheets and turned on two of Imogen's Twelve Apostle night-lights, thinking that Haddy would welcome their comforting glow.

"I'm not into night-lights," Haddy said. "If it's not pitch black I can't sleep a wink."

"When I was your age," Harry said, "I couldn't stand the dark. I was afraid of it. It always felt like it was closing in. And there were monsters under the bed."

"Really?" Haddy said. "That's kind of pathetic. I'm special. I'm a child insomniac."

As if to emphasize this point, she donned eyeshades.

"Good night, Uncle Harry."

"Good night," Harry said. He closed the door and settled himself into the La-Z-Boy. In a few minutes he was asleep.

Only I stayed awake, puzzling through all that was said and smelled in the exchange between my owner and Blinko. Nothing in Blinko seemed dishonest. He might have been holding back parts of the truth, but, if he was, they weren't parts that mattered directly to us now. The light of the full moon spread slowly across the floor of my little corner. Blinko was what he seemed to be, I concluded, an old man who looked younger than his age, but still an old man who had become entangled in something because of friendship, loyalty and a basically good nature and now wanted to discharge his duties and go home without losing his integrity in the process. Blinko, Harry and I had a mess to clean up. A quotation from one of the greats, Edgar Allan Poe, came to mind: *The true genius shudders at incompleteness—and usually prefers silence to saying something which is not everything it should be.* Poe, when he wasn't worrying about being buried alive or losing money at cards, made sure to be complete in his work. He had poetry. Poetry makes it easy. Art you can finish. Life is different. Life drags on and defies resolution. Even geniuses struggle with life. The only geniuses at living life are those who—half asleep—can shape it into a kind of completeness and forget about all the loose ends. I drowsed in the shadow of these unpromising reflections.

The next morning, Harry, Haddy McClay and I arrived at the boardinghouse at a quarter to nine to meet my temporary charge, Leopold Maranovsky. Harry was going to leave me and continue on with his niece to his first day on the job of the mosaic commission at WAHA. We did not have to search for Maranovsky. A man in a poorly tailored suit sat on the steps of the boardinghouse with a large trunk at his feet. He had a jowly face and large brown eyes. He was a sad-looking man who gave the impression that he was about to sigh. When he saw us, he rose to his feet and suddenly looked happy, but he kept the trunk between himself and us like a shield.

"I was so afraid that you would not come. You are two minutes late. I was on the verge of panic," Maranovsky said.

"Sorry," Harry said.

"I would never manage to travel in one of those vehicles. Never," Maranovsky said. "They are so terribly open. My God, I would die. Just die."

Harry flicked the kick-stand and told Haddy McClay to stay on the bike.

"Here he is, Mr. Maranovsky," Harry said, shaking the press secretary's right hand and placing my leash in his left. "Randolph is particularly good at alleviating anxiety. He is my best dog."

Maranovsky scrutinized me.

"Near Upper Pilasian retrievers have flatter heads. He looks like Near Lower Pilasian or Near Middle Pilasian retriever. Yes, indeed, eyes are quite like Near Lower Pilasian," he decided with a classic Slavic disregard for the definite and indefinite articles of the English language.

"He's a Labrador," Harry clarified.

"Yes, yes, precisely. It is only matter of—what you say—semantics. He is calm dog?"

"A cool cucumber," Harry said.

"Good," Maranovsky said. "Because I am not very cool cucumber."

The press secretary laughed but gave my owner an embattled look.

"Everywhere I see danger," Maranovsky said. "The anxiety began when I was fifty, and, as I believe I said on telephone last night, only the presence of dog removes it from me. I may have him for two weeks, no?"

"Yes," Harry said, although I detected in his voice—or hope I detected—great reluctance to leave me with an utter stranger.

"Perfect," Maranovsky said. He bent down and affixed a purple ribbon to my collar that proclaimed me: *Therapy Dog.* "I shall move in, then. Would you mind carrying the trunk?"

Before Harry had a chance to respond, the press secretary had disappeared up the stairs and through the front door, with me in tow. Harry followed behind with Haddy McClay, whom he could not leave unattended on the city street. Harry pushed the case into the lobby with a grunt and said his good-byes lest he be recruited to carry it the remaining three flights.

"Good-bye, Mr. Maranovsky. Good-bye, Randolph," Harry said. "I'll be checking in regularly, and you have my phone."

I made eye contact with my owner. He

looked pained and uncertain about leaving me. Nevertheless, Harry managed to deliver a professional pat on the head, tell me to "do my job" and disappear through the door.

"It is just us now, my friend," Mr. Maranovsky said, and approached a small closetlike niche in the corner that resembled a coat check but served as a front desk. "Let us see about checking in. Ms. Ramsey is expecting us."

There was a small silver bell on the counter and the press secretary rang it several times in quick succession. As the rings receded, I heard two sounds. The first was the 150cc motor of Harry's Vespa revving to life and the vehicle speeding my owner and Haddy McClay away to points north on its twelve-inch wheels. The second sound was footsteps approaching us from down a long hall. They were light footsteps but distinct and swiftly moving, like a tidy flood. A woman turned the corner and approached, smoothing her apron and slowing almost imperceptibly to examine herself as she passed a mirror on the wall.

"Mr. Maranovsky," the woman said. "I am Ms. Ramsey. We are so pleased to be able to accommodate you. Was your trip pleasant?"

My temporary employer took Ms. Ramsey's extended hand in his own and delivered a kiss with exaggerated elegance, as if he were greeting royalty and not the proprietress of a once-seedy boardinghouse.

"Oh, Mr. Maranovsky. What lovely old-world manners," Ms. Ramsey tittered, as if *she* had just been reading a Jane Austen novel. New York is a city that plays against type. The taxi driver is a Joyce scholar. The academic-looking man will hit you with a tire iron and run off with your wallet. It is also a city of second and third chances, glorious reinvention and magical holes in the wall that one could never predict. Some version of Narnia's wardrobe hides behind every doorway or flight of stairs. I am not sure what I expected in the proprietress of this establishment, but it wasn't Ms. Ramsey. She stepped through a low door and behind the desk.

"I see you have brought your pet," Ms. Ramsey said. "He will be most welcome. In addition to afternoon tea for our human guests, we have an animal smorgasbord on the sunporch. My father was a zoologist, you see, and he fostered in me a deep love and respect for our animal brethren. He was convinced of their intelligence and their infinite goodness. Not all of them, of course—he couldn't brook squirrels, but that was because of a traumatic experience in his childhood."

"I love animals also," the gentle and courtly Leopold responded. "It is my human colleagues whom I find hard to love."

"Oh, Mr. Maranovsky, you must look for the good and you will find it."

Ms. Ramsey smiled and jotted something down.

"This is wonderful place," Leopold said. "It feels like home."

"It is a home," Ms. Ramsey said. "I was raised here and I have never left. My father bought it as an investment when he was at the university. Then there were his controversial experiments. He was a man ahead of his time, Mr. Maranovsky."

"Leopold, please."

"Leopold, my father was a genius, and if a genius does not have the good fortune of escaping the gravity of this world's standards—like Einstein and others escaped to the divine above—then they are slowly crushed by the mundane and the unimaginative. This happened to my father. But he was such an optimist until the end, poor soul. And a lover of animals. Our home—this place—was filled with animals of all sorts, including seven of us children. They all fled—the children—my brothers and sisters, that is. The animals were eventually taken by the city—not all of them, mind you, just the ones that violated the health code. And then Daddy and Mommy died. But I stayed and kept the place running through those terrible years—the 1970s—when New York almost gave up on herself. Now New York is back, and we are here to celebrate it and extend welcome to wonderful people from all around the world, like you, Mr. Maranovsky."

"Leopold. Would you like lozenge?"

"Oh no thank you. I never eat hard candies."

"Very well," Leopold said, and put one in his mouth.

"Leopold. Yes. That is a lovely name," Ms. Ramsey said, allowing her gaze to rest approvingly on the press secretary of Near Upper Pilasia. The proprietress ran through a short list of house guidelines designed to enable the guests to live in "good and cheerful convenience" with one another. Then she rang another bell, and a young man came to collect Leopold's trunk and take it upstairs to his new room.

Before we left Ms. Ramsey, she singled me out, staring deeply into my eyes for a long moment.

"He looks so familiar," Ms. Ramsey said.

"It is possible that you have seen him,"

Leopold said. "He is New York dog. I am borrowing him for my stay."

"I have known many, many dogs, and this one is special," Ms. Ramsey said.

"Yes, he is particularly calm."

"That too," Ms. Ramsey said. "But clearly very intelligent. He seems to be taking it all in. What is his name?"

Leopold looked momentarily embarrassed.

"To tell truth, I have forgotten," the press secretary said. "I think it begins with *R*."

"Let's call him Rembrandt, then," Ms. Ramsey said. "He has the same soulful, sad eyes as the painter of Rijn."

"Rembrandt it is," Leopold said. "Come on, Rembrandt. Let's get settled."

I paused, hesitant to accept the new moniker.

"I'm not sure he likes it," Leopold said.

"He will," Ms. Ramsey said. "Just say it with a bit more force."

Leopold did, and strange as it was to heed a different name, I decided that it was best to follow. There was much to be learned upstairs.

I WAS NOT WELL AC-quainted with the culture and manners of Near Upper Pilasia but learned several things about one native within five minutes of arriving at our new room (which had been Imogen's for so many months). Leopold was: 1) very fond of highly polished black shoes (his trunk contained a dozen pairs); 2) very fond of bow ties, in a variety of colors and widths; and 3) equipped with a large selection of very sophisticated electronic equipment in addition to a laptop computer. While Leopold busied himself putting away his shoes and hanging his bow ties, I tried to make sense of the electronics. I am no expert on such things, but the proliferation of antennae, satellite dishes and one very expensive-looking shotgun microphone made me conclude that Leopold—as is the case with so many embassy attachés—had a clandestine role in addition to whatever services he provided Near Upper Pilasia as a press secretary. Blinko had already set my mind in this direction with his suggestion that a good number of the boarders were, in fact, agents of some power or another, and Leopold's equipment seemed to confirm it. I imagined there must be a waiting list of foreign agents for a place at Ms. Ramsey's boarding-house.

A great fatigue swept over me, and I remembered SparrowHawk's diagnosis of hypothyroidism. Quack though he was, I was certain he was on to something. I had been trying to ignore my condition, but several times over the last day I had been laid flat by a profound tiredness. It was only the excitement of events (and my fear of Haddy McClay's problematic hands) that had kept me awake with a rush of adrenaline. Now this condition and my Labrador nature's twelve-hour sleep requirement overwhelmed me, and I sprawled on the floor. I hoped that Harry would remember to reschedule that veterinary appointment.

"Tired pup," Leopold said between bars of "The Blue Danube Waltz," which he was humming as he arranged his things in the dresser. "Have good nap. You're already earning your keep."

And so I rested but did so productively, by lying on my back with my four paws in the air. This enabled me a full view of the stars on the ceiling, which I could now examine in the light of day. They were plastic adhesives and looked small and cheap. I was surprised that Ms. Ramsey had not noticed them and prevented Imogen's ongoing work. Perhaps she had tried. I was curious to learn more about how my mistress had been perceived in the seemingly close-knit community of the boardinghouse. How I was to do this would be the challenge. But for now I surveyed the ceiling for some pattern that would have been invisible the night before. At first, nothing stood out, but then I noticed a pencil trace along the farthest edge of the stars. I followed the pencil mark and soon realized that there were dozens across the ceiling. There were even more erasures, where Imogen—I assumed it was my mistress—had tried to eliminate the pencil marks, many of which seemed to have been made with a straightedge. But my observations stalled as my eyelids grew heavier and heavier.

Somewhere in the distance, I heard Leopold sit down at the desk and begin to type. Then there was the sound of electronic equipment being shuffled about and assembled. Wires were plugged into outlets. Dials were adjusted. Antennae and satellite dishes moved about the room. Then my ears closed to the sound of the world around me and I began to dream. I dreamed of Imogen. The room was so suffused with her smell—it was the nearest I had been to my mistress in so many months. The subway encounter was nothing compared to this prolonged olfactory contact. My dreams, usually so abstract, were unusually clear. Imogen was standing above me in the room, looking down at me. She was smiling, but her eyes were narrowed just slightly at the corners, as they did whenever she was a little worried. She stooped to pat my belly and scratch me under the chin.

"Randolph," she said, "you've got to carry us all now. But I know you can. Keep Harry safe. Watch out for friends. Friends can be enemies. And don't forget the stars."

Then I dropped out of the dream into a deeper, blacker sleep. The next thing I knew, my leash, which had never been removed, was being tugged.

"Get up, my friend," Leopold said. "You are quite a sleeper and talker. Barking and whining. If I spoke dog, I would have known all of your secrets. Now, though, it is time for you to really earn keep. We must meet neighbors. We are late for early-afternoon tea. And I am very nervous. I am not so good with most humans as I am with your kind."

Leopold gave my head a good rub and we went downstairs. As we approached the landing on the first floor, I heard the clatter of china, the sound of conversation and the smell of many delectables rising from the ground floor. Leopold paused. I could feel his nervousness in the tight grip he held on my leash and the scent of fear. I sat down and looked up at him. His face was a pale green. His breathing had become rapid, shallow and wheezy.

"No, I don't think I will go down to tea now," Leopold said. "I'll get newspaper and read in room, and perhaps Ms. Ramsey can send something up later."

Action was required if I was to deserve my title as a therapy dog. I began to descend the stairs, and to enforce the sense of necessity, I gave a short whine. I hoped that if he focused on me, it would help him escape from his anxieties. It worked. Leopold steadied himself and followed.

"Ah, but we couldn't deprive you of goodies," Leopold said. At the base of the stairs we turned right and proceeded down the long hallway from which Ms. Ramsey had earlier emerged.

The sounds and smells grew closer, and at the end of the hall we found ourselves in a large room with a long wooden table covered with sunflower place mats. Twelve or so people sat around the table, and from what I could smell— I could not see too far above the table—there was an abundance of lemon-poppy muffins, a freshly baked chocolate cake, roast beef and ham sandwiches and a particularly sharp ched- dar. There were also urns of fresh coffee and three kinds of juices: apple, pear and pomegran- ate. Ms. Ramsey sat at the head of the table. The apron was gone and she wore a high-necked white dress that looked like it had come from Merchant Ivory's *A Room with a View*.

"Rembrandt can go to the sunporch with the other animals if you'd like, Mr. Maranovsky," Ms. Ramsey said.

"Leopold, please," the press secretary said. "If it is all same to you, could Rembrandt remain here with me?"

"Of course, Leopold," Ms. Ramsey said. "Dean Perkins is always with us as well."

Ms. Ramsey gestured at an obese bird perched on the sideboard beside the windows. So inert was the animal that at first I thought it was stuffed. Although its features were dis- torted by excessive feeding, Dean Perkins was clearly a rainbow lorikeet. At the mention of his name, Dean Perkins spoke.

"I'm sorry, Mr. Ramsey," Dean Perkins said. "I'm sorry, Mr. Ramsey."

Ms. Ramsey nodded and tossed him a piece of lemon-poppy muffin, which the bird snagged out of the air with a flick of his head.

"That is extraordinary name for bird, Ms. Ramsey," Leopold said. "And why—may I ask—does he say, 'I'm sorry, *Mr.* Ramsey'?"

"Dean Perkins was the name of the troglodyte at the university who fired my father," Ms. Ramsey said. "This Dean Perkins is doing the hard work of repentance."

"I see," Leopold said, and we proceeded to the sunporch attached to the end of the dining room, where a large number of cats and dogs and the odd reptile were partaking in their own tea, with surprisingly good manners. It seemed that Ms. Ramsey's powerful vision of tranquility and civility had influenced everyone in the house. All the animals, even the ones (unlike Yours Truly) who operated mainly in their lower natures, were peacefully at work on petits fours and tuna briquettes. Leopold found a plate and assembled a healthy selection of the treats for me, then we returned to the dining room. Ms. Ramsey indicated that he take a seat at the

corner so that I could sit beside him. He placed
the food on the floor beside me and let my leash
drop. I had a robust appetite after my nap and
ate with gusto, while retaining an acute reporto-
rial sense of the goings-on above table.

Ms. Ramsey introduced Leopold to the other
guests. The woman whom we had seen counting
recyclables in the lobby on our first visit was
there, as was the poet whom we had stepped
over in the entranceway. His name was Abraham
Pollop, and when Ms. Ramsey noted this man's
proficiency at spoken verse—"a king in the oral
tradition of the word"—Mr. Pollop, apparently
discomfited by such high praise, let fly a string
of profanity that stunned the room, especially
Dean Perkins.

"I'm sorry, Mr. Ramsey," the rainbow lorikeet
said. "I'm sorry, Mr. Ramsey."

"Language, Mr. Pollop," Ms. Ramsey said.
"Language. You've disturbed Dean Perkins."

The proprietress threw the bird another
piece of lemon-poppy muffin and continued
working her way around the table. Four people
stood out at once. Despite the rich and beguil-
ing smells rising up from the tuna briquettes
and wafting down to me from the delectables on
the table, I detected a great deal of anxiety and
deception from these four. Leopold's own anxi-

ety, I sensed, was connected to their presence, and their anxiety was connected to him and one another. The deception was a presence in the nature of each of them, a kind of permanent scent or one that through years of inhabiting and promoting lies had become permanent. Deception has a kind of varnishlike smell—distractingly strong, but, like varnish, ultimately just a cover-up for what lies beneath. I assumed these were the diplomats and/or spies Blinko had suggested.

The four sat scattered among the other guests but seemed far apart.

"It has always been my dream to make this place a welcome mat for all nations," Ms. Ramsey said. "It was Daddy's belief that if humans could only learn about one another and transcend the limits of our individual cultures, so many problems would be solved."

Several of the boarders nodded their heads vigorously. Mr. Pollop, the rhetorically inclined bard, seemed ready to launch another barrage of profanity but instead cut himself a monumental hunk of the cheddar, which he buried in his mouth. The four diplomat/spies stared at the wall. Only Leopold responded to Ms. Ramsey.

"We have saying in Near Upper Pilasia that I think you will find apt, Ms. Ramsey," the press secretary intoned. "It is difficult to translate into English, but I will try: though we in Near Upper Pilasia are above Near Lower Pilasia, we must never think ourselves superior."

"That is very enlightened, Leopold," Ms. Ramsey said.

"Yes, it was spoken by our Philosopher-King Egon prior to his glorious slaughter of entire Near Lower Pilasian army in 1585," Leopold said through a mouth full of roast beef.

One of the diplomat/agents coughed. His name was Ponce. I had missed his last name because I was exploring the layers of my last petit four, but I gathered he was of South American origin and did something culinary at the United Nations.

"Ha," Ponce said. "Lower Pilasia came back to defeat your country a decade later in one of the most legendary routs in military history and Egon lost his head."

Leopold bristled but remained silent.

"Ponce, please, remember the house rule against inflammatory statements," Ms. Ramsey cautioned. "Leopold was merely taking the ideal sentiment of human brotherhood and rescuing it from the sordid march of history."

I had caught the full names of the three other men: Otis Cheng, Max de Tocqueville and Lindmar Wingman (pronounced Wing-en). These men were not as forceful as Ponce, but they were clearly interested in Leopold. They also all seemed to be cut from a similar mold. Their native accents were indistinct. Their pronunciation of English smooth and generic. Their manners schooled and scrupulous, but in a way that struck me as being learned in adulthood rather than in youth. I also had the sense that all five of the men had met one another before and concluded that perhaps the world of international espionage was a smaller one than I had thought.

"Why have you come to New York, Mr. Press Secretary?" Lindmar asked Leopold.

"For conference," Leopold replied.

"Which conference? There are thirty currently ongoing at the United Nations," Max de Tocqueville said. "It isn't, by chance, the Forum on the Exploration of Norms and Standards for Nonrenewable Energy for Developing Nations?"

"Oh no," Leopold said. "We in Near Upper Pilasia have little interest in such things. Nor do we have manpower. We are modest country with modest means in world of giants."

"What are you here for, then?" Otis Cheng asked.

"The Forum for Linguistic Goals for a New

Century," Leopold said. "We in Near Upper Pilasia believe that building language bridges between cultures will someday achieve those noble goals that Ms. Ramsey has articulated and result in true connectedness of our species."

"Isn't that amazing," Ms. Ramsey said. "All five of you are attending the same meeting. The United Nations is so wonderful. That is why I keep places open for those who work for that wonderful institution. Leopold, these four aren't just here for this forum, they are my very honored near-permanent guests. They all arrived together or, at least, within days of one another. I was so pleased. What has it been, Mr. Cheng? A year?"

"Something like that," Mr. Cheng said, tapping his teaspoon on the edge of his coffee cup. "I have enjoyed it greatly. Your hospitality knows no bounds, Ms. Ramsey."

Mr. Cheng was about to say something else, but he was interrupted by events. Three things seemed to occur simultaneously. One of the windows cracked and glass spilled onto the carpet. Dean Perkins, a large piece of lemon-poppy muffin in his beak, squawked and hopped into the air as several of his feathers were separated from his body. And the poet, Abraham Pollop, slumped facefirst into the remains of his roast beef sandwich and large slice of chocolate cake. Then several other things happened in quick succession. Otis Cheng, Max de Tocqueville and Lindmar Wingman rolled onto the floor and crawled for cover. Leopold fainted and slid off his chair. And Ms. Ramsey screamed while the rest of the residents remained stunned and unmoving. A halo of bright red blood spilled over the poet's roast beef and chocolate cake and flowed in all directions across the table, turning the sunflower place mats brown on contact.

"Abraham," the recyclables lady pleaded, nudging the man. "Abraham, wake up."

"He's dead," Max de Tocqueville announced. "The exit wound took off most of his face."

All three men were already back on their feet.

"It was a sniper," de Tocqueville continued. "He is gone now, but he shot from that rooftop over there."

De Tocqueville pointed at a building down the street with a roof garden.

"It was a difficult angle," de Tocqueville said appreciatively. "He must be an expert."

Ms. Ramsey had regained herself and began issuing orders. Abraham Pollop was lain on the floor and emergency resuscitation was attempted, but de Tocqueville's judgment was confirmed. Pollop was quite dead. Within minutes an emergency-services crew had arrived. They moved leisurely. There was no hurry with a corpse. A few minutes after this, Detective Davis arrived.

The room had cleared of all the diners except for Ms. Ramsey, the four diplomat/spies and Leopold, whom the emergency-services crew had revived and moved to a corner of the room. Now he lay with his head on a pillow and his feet up. He refused to be taken to the hospital.

Detective Davis stood over the poet's body.

"What a shame," he said.

"He was a great oral poet," Ms. Ramsey said. "I hope the tradition does not die with him."

"He was also a witness. He saw Imogen flee," Detective Davis observed. "Ms. Ramsey, I am going to need to seal off this room for the next few hours while we remove the body and gather forensic evidence. Afterward, I will want to speak with whomever was present in this room at the time of the shooting. I'm sorry, but it seems like you're getting used to the routine."

The detective walked over to the window and looked out.

De Tocqueville pointed at the rooftop he had indicated to us minutes earlier.

"The shot came from there," de Tocqueville now told the detective.

Detective Davis looked de Tocqueville up and down as if trying to place him. Then he followed the invisible line the man was indicating with his finger above the parked cars and across the street.

"That is quite a shot," Detective Davis said. "And you say you heard only one?"

"We didn't hear any," Ms. Ramsey said. "Just the glass breaking, Dean Perkins—that's the bird—squawking and poor, poor Mr. Pollop falling dead."

"A silencer," Detective Davis murmured. "But still one shot. At least, no one was aware of any others."

"Just the single round," de Tocqueville agreed. "Yes, he was quite a shot."

"He?" Detective Davis said.

Then the police officer asked for the room to be cleared. Leopold was helped to his feet, and as his senses returned so did his anxiety. I had remained near the corner of the table, observing the commotion, and Leopold now approached to reclaim me.

"Whose dog is that?" Detective Davis asked.

"It is mine, Detective," Leopold answered.

"He looks like a dog I know," Detective Davis said.

"Come with us, Rembrandt," Ms. Ramsey said, taking Leopold's arm and leading both of us from the room.

"Dogs are wonderful, aren't they?" Detective Davis observed, the odd sliver of transcendent joy breaking through the grim reality of his job.

Ms. Ramsey paused and took one last look at her dead boarder.

"Indeed they are," Ms. Ramsey said. "They do not shoot guns. Daddy was convinced that they were smarter and kinder than we could ever be."

MANY OF THE BOARDERS had congregated in the lobby, much the way I imagine they did on the night when Harry had arrived to find Detective Davis and receive the news that his missing love was suspected of murder. Ms. Ramsey moved among them, offering food and drink.

"The best response to shock is to stay well fed and well hydrated. Daddy used to say drink plenty of liquids in times of stress," Ms. Ramsey said as she handed the woman with the recyclables a donut and a large glass of lemonade, which she had secured from the kitchen before the forensics team arrived and declared it off limits.

"It is so, so terrible," the woman with the recyclables moaned as tears ran down her nose and into her lemonade. "He was very gifted."

"He was just an old drunk," a man muttered. I recognized him as one of the two men who had stepped around Abraham Pollop when he lay in the lobby the previous day.

"We all have our demons," Ms. Ramsey said. "No one deserves such a fate, and on the sunflower place mats. What a tragedy."

Leopold sighed. Color was gradually returning to his face. The four diplomat/spies were nowhere to be seen, and the crowd in the lobby was going in endless circles of speculation. The general consensus seemed to be that it was a random act, one of those bizarre urban occurrences that claim the occasional life. And even though the boarders were initially afraid for their own lives, soon—as is the human way once danger seems to have passed—a kind of normalcy returned. Abraham Pollop was the sacrifice to death and no other victims were immediately required. Death's appetite had been sated. I was doubtful of this. If anything, death's appetite was growing.

Leopold turned to go out the door, but Ms. Ramsey stopped him.

"Mr. Maranovsky, I don't think you should leave. I am so sorry for this terrible turn of events on your first day with us, but the detective explicitly said that he wants all the people who were in the dining room at the time of Mr. Pollop's demise to stay put. I think he will be interviewing everyone. That is what he did last time."

"There was last time?" Leopold asked.

"Oh yes, we have had more than our share of worries recently," Ms. Ramsey said, and busied herself in her office before my temporary master could pose a follow-up question.

Leopold sighed again, and we began to weave our way upstairs past two men seated on the bottom steps, dressed as women and speaking in self-conscious *Cage aux Folles* fashion. But just as we reached the top of the first flight, Detective Davis entered the lobby and stopped us.

"Excuse me," he said, addressing the room and trying to be heard above the noise of several different conversations. "If you don't mind, I need a moment of your time. Anyone who was in the dining room when the victim was killed, I'd like to speak with you now. We'll try to be as orderly as possible and take as little of your time as possible. I know it's been a sad day for all of you. Forensics is still at work, so I'd like to see each of you, individually, in the kitchen."

Leopold continued to climb the stairs.

"Sir, if you don't mind, I'd like to start with you," Detective Davis called after him.

We arrived in the kitchen. It was a surprisingly tiny space, given Ms. Ramsey's endless supply line of food. Detective Davis was eating a lemon–poppy seed muffin, drinking a cup of coffee and looking at a black sniper rifle. He motioned to a chair pushed up against the two-burner stove.

"Is that murder weapon?" Leopold asked.

"We believe so," Detective Davis said. "It was fired once and then discarded."

"So Frenchman was right," Leopold asked.

"Is that what he is?" Detective Davis said. "It's hard to tell—it's the United Nations around here."

"Yes, Ms. Ramsey keeps rooms available for diplomatic attachés and the like," Leopold said. "In fact, technically I'm not required to speak with you."

"I'm aware of that, Mr. . . . ."

"Mr. Maranovsky. I am rotating press secretary for Near Upper Pilasia. You can call me Leopold."

"I'm aware of that, Leopold, and speaking on behalf of the New York City Police Department, we appreciate your cooperation."

"May I ask what you think has gone on here? Are we in any danger? That is very sophisticated-looking gun."

For all of my temporary master's seeming softness, there was a savvy worldliness right beneath the surface, quite used to things like guns and assassination.

"It is a very sophisticated gun," Detective Davis said. "It is Heckler and Koch PSG-1—one of the most highly regarded short-range urban sniper rifles in the world. This one's been equipped with a sight worth tens of thousands of dollars and a state-of-the-art sound muffler. It certainly explains how the shooter was able to make the kill. What doesn't make sense is why the gun would have been left on a rooftop of an empty building. And even if the gun couldn't be disassembled and needed to be left, why not take the sight and the muffler?"

"This is all Greek to me, as you Americans say," Leopold said. "I am chiefly interested in linguistics, not guns and death. We Near Upper Pilasians are peaceful people. From what little I witnessed at tea table, this poet was foul-mouthed and I doubt possessed much in way of literary merit, but he did not deserve to die. Alas, *the moving finger writes and, having writ, moves on. Not all your piety nor wit shall lure it back to cancel half a line. Nor all your tears wash out a word of it.*"

Detective Davis shrugged, apparently not

recognizing the reference to the poetic quatrain of the *Rubaiyat of Omar Khayyam*—any fatalist's favorite, since it speaks of the brutal power of time and events to break the strongest of hopes and wills.

"As I said, I appreciate your cooperation and I won't take too much of your time," Detective Davis said. "Ms. Ramsey said you've just arrived."

"Yes, I'm in town for United Nations conference."

"A tough thing to arrive to," Detective Davis said. "Can you describe how it happened?"

"Yes, we were eating around table and poor fellow dropped dead in his chocolate cake."

"Do you remember what you were talking about?" Detective Davis said.

"No, Detective, I'm afraid I don't," Leopold said. "Wait a moment: we were speaking about how long one of boarders—Asian man—had been living here. Then window cracked, bird squawked and, as I've mentioned, poet dropped into chocolate cake."

"Did you notice who was sitting next to the poet?" Detective Davis asked.

"A funny little woman with enormous bag of cans and bottles sat to his right, and chair to his left was empty."

Detective Davis furrowed his brow.

"The backs of those chairs are pretty high, aren't they?"

"Yes, they're unusual chairs."

"But the poet was a tall man, so his head was well above the back? It cleared it by several inches?"

"I suppose it would have, Detective," Leopold said.

"Do you know whether he usually sat there?" Detective Davis asked.

"As you yourself said, Detective, I have only just arrived. I am not familiar with customs of house yet," Leopold said. I detected a slight uptick in his anxiety through both his scent and the heel of his highly polished black shoe, which he pressed back into the floor.

"So seating was casual," Detective Davis continued.

"It seems."

"Well, that's about it, Leopold," Detective Davis said.

"May I ask again? What do you think has gone on here? And are we in any danger?"

Detective Davis looked out the window.

"It's an almost philosophical question. Almost a spiritual question. The world is on fire," the policeman said, revealing his roots as a

Buddhist monk. "I guess we are always in danger from something, but in terms of a specific threat to you or most of the residents of this boardinghouse from a high-caliber, hollow-point nine-mm round—nope, the chances are very good that you're safe. This was a specific killing. Someone wanted Abraham Pollop dead. They could have killed anyone or everyone else in the room, but they didn't. They chose him and they put him down."

"So it was professional job, as they say?"

"I'm not sure of that," Detective Davis said. "These rifles and that sight could be used fairly effectively by almost anyone. It's user-friendly—not that it's in most people's price range."

"So Frenchman is wrong about it being difficult shot?"

"No. It was difficult. It just wasn't that difficult," Detective Davis said.

Leopold began to move toward the door.

"One last thing, Mr. Maranovsky. Did you happen to notice anyone make any particular gestures before Pollop was killed?"

"Gesture? What do you mean, Detective?"

"Something that could be interpreted as pointing out Pollop to the shooter?"

Leopold paused. I could remember no such gesture, but my view of the table was partially impeded by the height and angle. But my temporary master apparently was trying hard to remember, so hard that in the end he made something up — he began to reek of deceit (a terrible smell, as I've suggested).

"Now that you mention it, I did," Leopold said, dropping his voice to a confidential hush. "What I tell you is strictly for your ears, yes, Detective?"

Detective Davis nodded.

"Both Asian and Frenchman did things with their utensils that could be interpreted in this way. The Asian seemed to point his coffee spoon subtly but like compass needle in poor man's direction, and Frenchman did same with his butter knife."

I could not attest to what de Tocqueville had done with his utensil, but I clearly remember that while Otis Cheng tapped his saucer with his coffee spoon, he did not point it at anyone. Leopold seemed to want to muddy the waters for his diplomatic peers.

"Interesting," Detective Davis said. "I will be speaking with them."

"But you will not mention this," Leopold said.

"I will not mention that *you* said this," Detective Davis assured him.

A young police officer entered the room, holding a piece of paper.

"There were no prints on the gun, Detective Davis," he reported. "But we've run a mobile DNA test on the hair in the firing mechanism and..."

The young man paused as if for dramatic effect.

"We're not on some New York police show, Jim," Detective Davis said. "Who is it?"

"It's Imogen. She's our shooter."

I couldn't believe the name I heard. How could this be true? Not only did I refuse to believe that my mistress was a killer, I knew she despised firearms (Harry had received his grandfather Oswald's World War II–era .45 only after she disappeared—the gun would have been an unfathomable possession in a house shared with Imogen). Detective Davis did not readily accept the news either. For the first time in my acquaintance with him, I noticed him lose his color—albeit only slightly. But he responded to his colleague in a measured and educational fashion.

"Jim, you have to observe the way you think. You are saying two separate things: one, you found a certain person's DNA on the murder weapon, or at least what we believe at this moment—three-forty-seven on a Wednesday afternoon—is the murder weapon, and, two, that she is the shooter because of this presence of DNA. The trick is to keep them separate in your mind until it becomes absolutely clear that the facts are not separate at all but lead to the same conclusion. Our calling is about building evidence until we reach this point. As we build, there is no point to jump ahead."

"Right, sir, but I think it's still pretty much a slam dunk," the young detective said.

Detective Davis shrugged. "There is no such thing as a slam dunk anywhere off the basketball court," he said. "I'm sorry, Mr. Maranovsky. You can leave now. Thank you."

Leopold bowed and we left the room. As we passed the entrance to the dining room, I saw that all the sunflower place mats had been collected and sealed into clear-plastic evidence bags, and a technician was in the process of removing a small bright metal object from a lemon–poppy seed muffin with a pair of tweezers.

"Got it," he said, as the tweezers came free. He held the object up to the light.

It was a bullet.

The crowd in the lobby had thinned. Those who remained had grown quiet, as if the reality of the situation had settled in about them like a cold fog. The four diplomat/spies were present, as were the other occupants of the table. Ms. Ramsey was still moving among her "guests" but much slower than before. Leopold passed through the room with a nod, and as we mounted the stairs to our room, the stretcher carrying the oral poet's body passed through the lobby and out the door to the coroner's wagon waiting on the street.

"Can you imagine," Ms. Ramsey observed softly. "When poor Abraham walked into the dining room, he did not know that he would be carried out dead."

Then the stalwart proprietress sank into the overstuffed cushions of one of the sofas and began to sob. But in a muffled, discreet sort of way.

Each step up the stairs was a struggle for me. My fatigue seemed to have gotten worse despite my long nap earlier that day. When we reached our room, I curled up next to the bed. Leopold settled in at his desk and began tapping away on the laptop. I fell into another sleep. This time, though, my dreams were a chaos of terrible images. From a dark stage, Mr. Pollop delivered an obscenity-laced poem on sudden death. He sipped from a glass of thick red pomegranate juice, but, instead of having his thirst quenched, his mouth only became drier and drier. In a rage he hissed his lines, until his tongue cleaved and he could no longer speak at all. Then a second spotlight appeared on the dark stage and Imogen approached the podium, wearing her bright red party dress and carrying a silver platter with a beautifully shaped lemon–poppy seed muffin. She offered the delectable to the poet, and as she did I awoke with a low whine.

"Chasing rabbits?" Leopold asked. "It's alright, boy."

I turned onto my back. The meaning of the dream was painfully obvious. Pomegranate juice, after all, was what Hades, the Greek god of the Underworld, gave to Persephone to bring her down to the land of death. Whatever art was on our poet's foul-mouthed tongue would stay there, and Imogen's troubles were grave indeed. Through half-opened eyes I scanned the dots on the ceiling for some message and, still drowsy, I made connections where there were none. One cluster formed a *G,* another a *U,* another an *I,* and so forth, until the word was spelled: *GUILTY.* I shook sleep off and the word disappeared into the meaningless jumble of stars.

"It is time to get ready for banquet, my friend," Leopold said, getting up from the desk and rubbing my belly with his foot. "Tonight you will earn your keep. There is formal diplomatic gala at headquarters of United Nations to inaugurate our weeklong linguistics conference. You must keep me very calm. Though I am experienced in these matters of state, I am still—somewhere deep inside—only little Leo from the tiny village of Moot in Near Upper Pilasia, easily flustered by speed and manners of modern world. First, nice long shower."

The pudgy diplomat took a fresh towel folded on the end of the bed and disappeared down the hall to the shower. My head spun and I felt quite groggy, but I hopped up onto the desk chair and examined the laptop. To my surprise, my temporary master had left the device powered up and still connected to the Internet. I hoped his shower would be long, since I wanted to compose my first message to Harry from my new e-mail account. It was not that I had anything specific to report. He would learn soon enough through other channels of that day's murder and Imogen's suspected role, but perhaps I could reestablish a bridge to him that would support him as he went forward. I knew from his conversation with Blinko that Harry would be visiting the boardinghouse frequently and use my cover as a therapy dog to try to discover who really murdered the young man beneath the parachute. Communicating by e-mail would give us a direct line of communication about things only I could learn.

Leopold's laptop had a pointing device, which was difficult to manipulate with my snout. Just as I was about to navigate to my e-mail account, my nose slipped and suddenly I found myself in an entirely different place, a magical place, an extraordinarily wonderful place. Somehow I had stumbled upon an online bookstore. With a few more snout strokes and keypad jabs, I made my way to a specific screen where, floating on the screen in near three-dimensionality, I found *The Inferno of Dante* (the Pinsky translation). As I have mentioned, our copy was still under the daybed in the living room, with little hope of salvage. Not only was the Dante for sale, but it had been paired with a second title that I longed to read, Joyce's *Ulysses* (I had devoured his *Dubliners* and *A Portrait of the Artist as a Young Man,* courtesy of Imogen's college collection). For a substantial discount a purchaser could get both books and a tote bag with Virginia Woolf's profile emblazoned on both sides. Not since my encounter with the bewitching sidewalk pâté of Central Park West had I experienced such a sense of transcendence (in fact, I had the sudden urge to roll). A dog—as you have likely gathered—is given to more moments of this kind of escape than a human, moments when we seem lifted off our four legs and beyond the confines of our limited bodies and thrust into the glorious hurly-burly of life and living. These are the moments when most dogs race around the kitchen table or jump into the pool. Typically, my rational mind keeps these moments to a minimum, but when they occur I am powerless to resist.

Lost in the moment, I added the two books (and the complimentary tote bag) to my shopping cart and, putting aside any ethical concerns, I hurriedly entered Harry's credit-card number—which I easily recalled from the many times he had spoken it aloud when ordering food delivery. Then I typed in our address on 90th Street and selected *Priority Delivery*. My dog's life had known only dependency: dependency on my owner for walks and food and a general dependency on human society to continue to find my kind useful or lovable. Online shopping was a kind of empowerment, and it was also—sad to say—a comfort in the face of the gruesome death in the dining room.

I heard a door down the hallway open and

shut and Leopold's feet coming down the hall. I closed the screen with the books and hopped back onto the floor. When he entered, I delivered a look of doe-eyed innocence that generally earns a pat and a biscuit if one is on hand.

"What good guard dog," Leopold said. He shut the door behind him and removed a tuxedo shirt from a hanger in the closet.

He whistled "Blue Danube" as he dressed and I curled up at the base of the bed, warmed by the excitement of my recent purchase. I could not wait for my books and complimentary tote bag to arrive.

JUST AS YOURS TRULY began to recognize that he had once again been less than noble and loyal in his behavior, there was a knock on the door. Leopold, dressed only in shirttails and with what remained of his hair still in need of combing, opened it without hesitation.

Ponce, the diplomat/spy of vague South American origin, stood in the doorway, pointing a blunt object at Leopold.

"Here's the toothbrush you needed," Ponce said.

"Come in," Leopold said, and in classic Hollywood cloak-and-dagger fashion poked his pudgy face into the hallway to determine whether there was anyone following Ponce. Determining that there was not, he closed the door. Ponce sat down on the bed.

"I'm not an amateur, Leopold," Ponce said.

Leopold gave a short apologetic bow.

"I am getting bit ridiculous in my old age, Ponce," Leopold said.

"Why the dog?"

"Ah, I am bundle of nerves. Dogs, it seems, are only cure. I have tried all manner of sedatives, but they dull me bit too much for our sensitive line of work."

"A shame about the poet," Ponce said casually, as if a man were shot over tea every day.

"Are you sure it wasn't meant for one of us?"

Ponce shrugged.

"I can't believe that you fainted," Ponce said.

"It was humiliating but effective," Leopold said, examining the knot of his bow tie in the mirror. "The detective could hardly be bothered with me."

"I threatened him with diplomatic immunity," Ponce said.

"Why?"

"Because I can."

"You always were hothead," Leopold said, as if he hadn't done almost the same thing himself. "And that idiotic Frenchman..."

"De Tocqueville is Swiss," Ponce corrected.

"Talking like he was military expert right out of gate."

"I thought you fainted."

"It was light faint."

"You are a tricky one," Ponce said. "Strange that you showed up today of all days."

"A coincidence and damn nuisance. Of course, Home Office won't be pleased. They don't like our people being near anything that might become media event."

"This won't," Ponce said confidently. "They've already quashed it at the highest levels."

"Yes?"

"I got advance word that this won't be going anywhere," Ponce said. "And when I was speaking with the detective, a representative from some government agency arrived and had a few choice words for the lieutenant. After that his tone was quite different. Defeat had crept in. Not that he seemed to be on to anything."

"What have you boys been up to?" Leopold asked. "Two murders in a week. If Near Upper Pilasia were playing, I'd be furious. Six months spent trying to secure rights to reserve, and then violence and empty hands. What farce."

"I have never met a more clever woman than Imogen," Ponce said. "Nor a more elegant one."

"You sound like you are in love," Leopold said. He was now entirely clothed in his evening attire.

"She is a woman worthy of being loved,"

Ponce said in a voice that was free of his usual dose of cynicism and world-weariness.

"I think she played you all and now she is gone and none of you has what you wanted. Even major players were fooled on this one. Otis Cheng and his lot have been left with nothing."

"Of course, Near Upper Pilasia isn't interested in the outcome at all," Ponce said.

"Only in entertainment value," Leopold said. "We have never been ones to get into Great Game. Oh yes, in old days we subcontracted for major players, but now we are happy with scraps that fall from table. As I said, I am here for linguistics conference."

"If you are, then you are the only one."

"My question is why?" Leopold mused, sitting down at the desk and giving me another belly rub with his foot.

"You mean, why has someone framed her," Ponce said.

"Indeed. Clearly she is not murderer, and this was wet operation. But by killing witness who implicated Imogen, it only makes her look more guilty. It makes no sense."

"So you do know more about the case," Ponce said.

"I like to keep abreast of current events, and

this maneuver confuses me. What is to be gained by turning her into suspect? If she is apprehended, then she loses all value because she loses claim to resource. She will be disinherited, no? If she is not arrested, then she might retain claim, but she cannot inherit it unless she is cleared. But *if* she is cleared, then real killer will be compromised—which will presumably involve turning in trained member of one's team. It makes no sense."

"This is deep play," Ponce said. "It wasn't us—I'm sure you'd like to know. Professional courtesy permits me to tell you that much and also deliver a toothbrush. Do you really need it, by the way?"

"Actually, I do. Those damn poppy seeds get stuck in every crack and crevice," Leopold said, taking the implement. "Of all the things to forget to pack. So it wasn't you? Do you think it was Cheng? De Tocqueville?"

"I could not say," Ponce said. "But it was one of them or an operative—and my sense is that they would not have done it themselves. All of us were in the final stages of our operations. It was frustrating, but there seemed to be movement—and it was fair. But someone wanted to change the rules, I think. They got tired of Imogen playing Holly Golightly. They wanted a forced marriage."

"Good luck to them," Leopold said. "But this simply wasn't done in old days."

"Things are more desperate now," Ponce said. "The resource is valuable and the need is great. There is a scramble on for raw materials and energy. I wouldn't be surprised if it all ends in a global war."

"Let's hope not. Things have been desperate before," Leopold said. "As long as we have United Nations and dear, daffy Ms. Ramsey and all useful players flitting about in shadows, things should not derail. You are young yet, Ponce. I've seen it cycle around several times now."

"So it can keep going like this?" Ponce asked. For a moment he sounded like a student.

"When everyone is dead Great Game is finished. Not before," Leopold said, without mentioning that the pithy statement came from Rudyard Kipling's novel *Kim*.

"Well, I've got to go," Ponce said. "I'm taking an adult-education class at the Learning Center."

"Really?" Leopold asked. "What about?"

"They've got two lectures on. It'll either be

Buying Your First Home at Foreclosure or
Designing the Perfect Gift Basket."

"Fascinating," Leopold said. "It is good to
hear that you have outside interests. You will
need that if you wish to be in this business for
long haul. Thank you for toothbrush."

Ponce nodded and left after Leopold had
taken his usual precaution of checking the hallway. Then Leopold looked at his watch.

"We must go or we'll miss cocktails," he said.

I would not have time to reflect upon all of
the extraordinary things that I had just heard.
Blinko seemed right. The boardinghouse was a
hotbed of spies and agents, all engaged in trying
to gain rights to the fortune—"resource," they
had called it—that would soon belong to my
mistress by law. The casualness of the two men
surprised me, but perhaps it should not have.
After all, every profession I have ever encountered has its casual, workaday side. Man seems
inclined to be "normal" even in the most abnor-
mal occupations. Leopold and Ponce were no
exception. The world might hang in the balance, but there was always the need for a toothbrush or a lecture on the Perfect Gift Basket to
put things in some kind of perspective.

Leopold hurried me downstairs. The lobby
was deserted and the police were gone. When

we reached 5th Street, he hailed a taxi. The
driver did not object to my presence. Traffic was
light on First Avenue and we were at the United
Nations in ten minutes.

"Oh no," Leopold said when we stepped from
the vehicle. "You will need to be walked."

My little island is remarkable for many
things, not the least of which is the millions of
dollars' worth of real estate given over to the
recreation of its canine noncitizens. Ah, the dog
run. I am not a social creature by nature and
would rather curl up with my own thoughts
than interact with another dog. Nevertheless,
the dog run is a welcome place because of its
role in the accomplishment of my Numbers and
for entertainment value. Prior to Leopold, my
experience with dog runs had been limited to
the Bull Moose and a few others. Nothing in
those places could have prepared me for what I
was to encounter at the dog run adjacent to the
United Nations complex. As we passed through
a series of four gates to gain entrance, a sign
identified the space as the *Dag Hammarskjöld
World Pet Unity Area.* There was a second sign
written in a dozen languages and tiny print that
outlined the exclusion of cats, ferrets and ven-
omous animals as well as pointing out several
key behaviors (for the human owners) that

would ensure utmost cooperation and goodwill within the dusty pen surrounded by a chain-link fence.

"This is where secretary general brings Flowers and Puppet," Leopold noted as he struggled to open the last gate.

Then he bent down to unhook my leash.

"Be gentle if you see them, Rembrandt. Puppet is recovering from hernia surgery and Flowers is paranoid."

But Puppet and Flowers were nowhere in sight, and my first aim was to navigate across the dog run unscathed. I had spotted a discreet location for a Number 2 on the opposite side behind a bronze statue of Winston Churchill, which was mercifully bottom-heavy and provided good cover for a *Foliage-Finder.* The more diminutive Mahatma Gandhi on the near side was insufficient. Though I admire him, the vegetarian ascetic was no match for the whiskey-guzzling carnivore prime minister's bulk. Unfortunately, several large animals from the Icelandic legation were menacing the yard. There are times when having a generous belly insulates one from the indignity of dog power politics. The Icelandic horde bypassed me but targeted a Yorkie playing with a small orange ball. Soon they had surrounded him. His flustered owner, a striking

African man in a multicolored full-length gown, swept across the space, yelling at the pack, which utterly disregarded him. Fortunately, a Polish Tatra sheepdog—one of the largest specimens I had ever seen, a brute upward of 150 pounds—took up the Yorkie's cause. Falling into rather typical instinctual behavior, he began to growl and herd the Icelandic horde into the base of the Gandhi statue. The Yorkie was picked up by its owner and peace was momentarily restored. I took the opportunity to saunter across to Churchill. Leopold followed, bag in hand, and disposed of the Number 2 with an elegance that complemented his tuxedo-clad persona. A few well-tailored yards of cloth had turned him into a sleek international figure.

In all my observations of humankind, this question of clothing's transformative power stands out. How many people go into debt buying clothes? How many pairs of shoes are really necessary? But still humans seem obsessed with clothes. Many fine thinkers have weighed in on the question and caught up, I suspect, in romantic overexuberance have leaned toward nudism (though it is doubtful that they practiced it themselves). The novelist Katherine Mansfield observed this about clothing: *How idiotic civilization is! Why be given a body if you have to keep it shut up in a case like a rare, rare fiddle!* And Mark Twain offered: *Indecency, vulgarity, obscenity— these are strictly confined to man; he invented them. Among the higher animals there is no trace of them. They hide nothing; they are not ashamed.* Perhaps, Mr. Twain, this does apply to most "higher animals," but we are clothed, after all, in our own fashion and by our own fabric—and even so there are *Foliage-Finders* among my kind and *Phantom-Dumpers,* who do their business without ever being seen. No, I think Montaigne, the father of the essay, is closest to the mark on the human-clothing question: *Man is the sole animal whose nudities offend his own companions, and the only one who, in his natural actions, withdraws and hides himself from his own kind.* As noted, I am always dressed in fashionable black. While a dog's body can be fat or skinny, it can rarely be strange, distorted or grotesque. There are natural limits to how odd we can look. Not so with human beings. Leopold Maranovsky, fresh from showering and minus a towel, presented a very different picture from Leopold Maranovsky, sleek and elegant in an expensive tuxedo. I, for one, applaud the invention of human clothing. May the Churchills, Gandhis and Leopolds of the world long embrace the practice.

After Leopold had disposed of my business,

he reattached my leash and together we left the dog run. As we walked away, the Icelandic pack had resumed their harassment. This time they were left unchecked by the Polish Tatra, who was canoodling with an Irish wolfhound in the shade of a ginkgo tree.

"Damn," Leopold said, looking down at his shoe. He had stepped in the rogue Number 2 of another dog. "People who do not pick up after their animals are barbarians."

He scuffed off the offending matter on the stones, and we hurried along beneath a long line of flagpoles and onto a wide stone pavilion. I suddenly felt very privileged to be entering this legendary institution. The sordid realities of power politics aside, somewhere contained within the United Nations complex was an enlivening and liberating ideal, and sometimes idealism is one's only defense in dark times. Peace and freedom are ideals for which Yours Truly will always be willing to make a fool out of himself.

Leopold flashed an identification badge, and we were whisked by a guard past the creeping line of tourists waiting to pass through the metal detectors for a glimpse of the General Assembly. Even so, we were subjected to a metal detector, both of us were given pat-downs and my collar was removed and put into a bomb-sniffing machine.

"Gentlemen, gentlemen," Leopold protested. "My dog is not bomb."

The guards only nodded, and put the leash into the machine as well.

When this was over, we walked across the monumental lobby, ascended two escalators and arrived in a ballroom filled with people in evening wear. There was much laughter, the occasional hushed tones of shared confidence and the light clatter of glasses and plates heavy with hors d'oeuvres.

I could sense Leopold's anxiety growing with each step until, only a few feet inside the room, he froze. My tail gave an encouraging wag. When this didn't work, I sat down next to him, allowing my generous Labrador girth to lean against his right leg. Cynics might see this maneuver as a pathetic bid for food, and given the urgencies of a Lab's stomach this could sometimes be true, but at this moment it was my best way of reminding my charge that I was there to support him. Leopold noticed, bent down and patted me.

"How are you doing, boy?" Leopold asked, and as if this act of reaching out and the sound of his own voice had steadied him, he rose to his feet and proceeded to the bar to get a cocktail.

"A Manhattan," Leopold said to the bartender in a moderately steady voice. He was still in a state of near panic even after the first few sips of his beverage, so I directed him to a cozy spot along the wall from which he could gather his strength and we could both survey the room.

Ponce's words had made me expect to see a place teeming with diplomat/spies, a virtual cavalcade of cloak-and-dagger types using "professional courtesy" in intricate plays for the upper hand. Of course, in the real world things are rarely so obvious or so interesting. The diplomat/spy is the aging academic or the bespectacled tax accountant behaving bureaucratically even where death and extortion are involved. A poster board at the ballroom's entrance had welcomed all comers to something called *A Night of Linguistics.* If any of the occupants of the room were interested in anything but the stated subject, I could not tell. None of the four diplomat/spies from the boardinghouse was present. I began to believe that Leopold was likely here for the cocktails and the free meal even if it meant putting his anxiety to the test. Leopold, like Yours Truly, seemed to understand the value of the stomach.

Leopold polished off two more Manhattans before everyone was ushered into an adjoining dining room. Dinner passed amid a din of academic gossip. Leopold had little to contribute and didn't seem to know any of the people at the table. He ate his filet mignon, baby carrots and whipped potatoes with vigor and in silence and sucked down great quantities of Bulgarian red wine. From time to time he noticed—to my embarrassment but also relief—that I was drooling and delivered a few choice pieces of the beef below table.

"This is a very conventional meal for the United Nations kitchen," one of our table companions complained. "Typically, the fare is much more wide-reaching and representative. I cannot even remember all of the delicacies at the End Global Hunger Dinner last week. Needless to say, we all stuffed ourselves silly."

Memories of that fine meal did not prevent him from cramming a heaping forkful of beef into his mouth as he continued to speak.

"Even the staff cafeteria downstairs is filled with the most unique specialties from around the world. Once I actually saw Near Upper Pilasian goats' ears in jellied blood among the sushi and yogurts."

Leopold winced.

"That is savage delicacy and bastardized import from Near *Lower* Pilasia," the press secretary growled. "If I had kopek for every time some idiotnik made mistake about goat ear, I would be wealthy man."

Leopold's undiplomatic response did not deter his table companion.

"I apologize for any offense, but goats' ears are most certainly a Near Upper Pilasian delicacy," the man insisted. "But that's beside the point. I was merely saying that the kitchen staff at the United Nations is extraordinary and constantly pushing the limits of our culinary prison to include all of the edible wonders of the world."

Leopold drained his wineglass and motioned to the waiter for a refill, which he immediately lifted to his lips. I had thought that Harry was a robust drinker, but the press secretary from Near Upper Pilasia had a monumental capacity. Before I could reflect on human drunkenness (for which I would have referred to Rabelais), a woman with a clipboard addressed the crowd from the dais at the front of the room, and a screen began to lower behind her.

"Ah, the keynote presentation with diagrams. Wonderful," the man said. "I am so eager to hear Professor Kretchmar's insights into the idioms of the Mati Mati tribe of the Amazon tributaries."

"God help us," Leopold grunted. I half expected him to leap to his feet, but instead his multitiered chin dropped to his chest and he began to snore.

Having an active interest in almost all areas of academic inquiry, Yours Truly listened with genuine enthusiasm to the lecture. But as the idioms of the Mati Mati tribe were dissected by the keynote speaker, a great and irresistible fatigue again descended over me and soon I too was fast asleep on the banquet-hall floor.

THE NEXT DAY LEOPOLD awoke with the dawn. Yours Truly could have slept until noon, but the press secretary insisted on rising for breakfast. We had managed to find our way home despite the late hour and my temporary master's extreme inebriation. Ms. Ramsey had been awake when Leopold stumbled home, and she informed him that Harry had stopped by to "check up on things." I suspected he was following Blinko's advice and using my presence at the boardinghouse as a pretense to visit often. Ms. Ramsey also mentioned that Harry had left word about a vet appointment rescheduled for the morning, but Leopold had not paid much attention.

This was unfortunate, because now my head spun and my body was heavy, a sensation that seemed to have become permanent. I remained stretched in a warm sliver of sunlight as Leopold moved about the small room, getting ready for the day. He checked his e-mails. Seeing him do this, I knew that I should feel an urgency to communicate with Harry, but I didn't.

The halls were empty when we left the room and began to make our way downstairs. Extraordinary aromas were wafting upstairs from the kitchen: bacon and home fries, eggs and pancakes, banana bread. I took a deep snout sample and momentarily felt the heaviness lift from my bones. Thus distracted, I did not immediately notice another smell beneath the cooking as we approached the second landing. Alas, it was a smell that I had become all too familiar with in recent months: death.

Leopold was about to proceed down the stairs to the lobby when I pulled him up.

"Rembrandt," Leopold said. "Come, boy. Breakfast is waiting."

But the smell was potent and fresh and coming from around the corner and down the hallway. It was an imperative smell. A smell that demanded action. I began pulling the press secretary toward it. At first he resisted, but I was insistent and he relented. When we rounded the corner, we saw her slumped at the end of the corridor beneath a window with red-and-white farmhouse curtains.

"Oh my," Leopold said, stopping us while we were some twenty feet distant.

The recyclables lady's corpse seemed peaceful, but her face was distorted by a twenty-ounce bottle of soda that had been crammed into her mouth base-first, with the neck and mouth pointing upward at a sharp angle to the ceiling. The effect was to make her head look like a grotesque fountain spout. Her large clear-plastic bag of recyclables was beside her body on the floor, and her left arm was draped over it as if she were posing for a photograph with a good friend.

"Quite terrible," Leopold observed. "She was only stupid, innocent woman. This is *not* done."

The diplomat/spy did not move any closer, but I knew that I must. As distasteful as it was, it was critical that I perform a full snout stamp on the poor woman. If, as I suspected, one of the people in the house was responsible, then I would know. I gave a heave forward and pulled my leash from Leopold's hand.

"Rembrandt, no," Leopold shouted. Even the most casual observer of dogs will recognize the snout stamp. A dog approaches the leg of a human and nudges his or her nose into the calf or shin. This is the snout stamp. In normal situations the snout stamp serves two purposes: it gives the dog all the identifying scents of that person, and it leaves a trace of the dog's own scent as an easy way to identify that human in the future. It is more discreet than marking them with that other leg-lifting behavior and certainly more hygienic. But since the recyclables lady would sadly be on her way to the city morgue and points beyond, I needed only to retrieve scent, not leave a mark. In a moment I was done and had already begun to back away from the corpse when Leopold picked up my leash and gave a sharp yank.

"Bad dog," Leopold said. "Very bad dog."

The commotion had awoken several of the boarders and they now appeared in the hallway, in various states of undress. A scream went up from a female impersonator and soon Ms. Ramsey had arrived, puffing up the stairs with a spatula in hand that glistened with bacon grease.

"Rembrandt found her," Leopold said. "I believe she is dead."

"Oh no," Ms. Ramsey said. "Not again. Sweet Miss Dunbar and all her cans and bottles. Just last night she told me she was going to finally redeem them. All of them. They had gotten so heavy for her. She would have been free."

"She's free now," Leopold said.

One of the boarders, a large man wearing overalls and a hard hat, took Ms. Ramsey in his arms just as the proprietress was about to faint. The female impersonator inched toward the body.

"My God, she's been skewered," the female impersonator said.

In my hurry to perform my snout stamp, I had missed the apparent cause of death: a long metal skewer protruded from Miss Dunbar's chest, as if she were a kabob.

"And what's she holding?" another boarder asked. After the initial shock of discovering the body, everyone had grown bolder, and the boarders now formed a semicircle around the body.

"It looks like jewelry," the female impersonator said. Indeed, it was jewelry, and with a spirit of near despair I was prepared to recognize it as some kitschy icon from Imogen's collection, but it wasn't. Instead, it was a small lapis lazuli stone in a simple metal housing with a clasp that suggested it was meant to be connected to a necklace.

"Tasteless," the female impersonator declared. *But not kitsch, per se,* I thought.

Soon the police arrived, and Detective Davis was looking more beleaguered than I had ever seen him. Ms. Ramsey attempted to distract the house with breakfast, declaring it a "two-egg day if there ever was one." With the exception of Leopold, whose appetite seemed unaffected by events, the boarders picked at their breakfasts. Detective Davis appeared downstairs and again spoke with the boarders individually, but this time he held his investigations in a corner of the lobby, since the kitchen and dining room were busy. Leopold went first and related how he had found Miss Dunbar, but I could tell Detective Davis—while always the professional—felt constrained by something. His scent was strong with frustration and annoyance. Apparently Ponce was right and Detective Davis had been hamstrung in his detective work by higher authorities. At one point the frustration seemed to come to the surface in a surprising exchange.

"Tell me, Mr. Maranovsky, aren't you the least bit surprised by any of this?" Detective Davis said. "After all, you've been here two days and two people have died. Does this usually happen when you visit New York?"

"You have asked me two questions, sir," Leopold replied. "Second question and its preceding implication is patently absurd and possibly offensive. First one is reasonable. Yes, I am surprised. Laws of probability are surely against this kind of thing happening."

"You diplomatic types seem awfully cool about death," Detective Davis said.

"Perhaps. A diplomat dies thousand deaths, Detective," Leopold said. "Every day we must compromise. We watch our dreams of agreement and peace get quashed by compromise and must call it victory. We call lack of courage, imagination and simple mediocrity success and achievement. Physical death is nothing compared to thousand little cuts of compromise. Compromise is death to soul. A good diplomat is already dead. Though I at present feel quite unnerved."

Detective Davis shook his head.

"I swear I must be wearing a kick-me, I'm-an-idiot sign. I haven't heard this much nonsense since graduate school," he said. His voice raised. His face flushed. The former Buddhist monk was clearly close to losing his temper. "You people are too much. You come to my city with your diplomatic immunity and satellite-high view of the human condition—empathy for the idea of man and no clue about caring for the individual directly in front of you. I have a poor little old lady who collected cans and bottles because it made her feel safe with a metal skewer through her chest and a bottle stuck out of her mouth for no good reason, and for once I'd like to hear that one of your kind cared. It would give me some hope for the world."

"I understand exactly how frustrated you must feel, Detective," Leopold said. "I do care, personally, you must understand—but so many do not. Yes, I know you must have your hands full with this lot, and whatever I can help you with I will be most willing."

Leopold's voice dropped into a confidential hush.

"Remember, I did deliver that little bit of information on the gestures yesterday. That must count for something, Detective," the press secretary said. "And I promise to keep my eyes open. But you must excuse me now; I have morning session up at United Nations that I must attend."

Detective Davis gave a defeated shrug.

"That poor woman was our other witness," he muttered.

Leopold delivered a bow and we left Davis in the lobby as we made our way to the street. Once on the sidewalk, we had to cut through a thicket of police officers and a small group of ragged-looking men and women holding burning candles against the bright sunlight of the morning. They were reciting poetry laced with colorful language.

One of the men was carrying a large photo of Abraham Pollop, the dead oral poet. A sign identified the group as the *Friends of Abraham Pollop*. A woman pushed a photocopied sheet into Leopold's hands.

"Don't let his poetry fall on deaf ears," she implored. "Keep the tradition alive."

The press secretary bowed. When we had turned the corner, Leopold crumpled up the piece of paper about the poet without reading it and tossed it onto First Avenue. Five minutes later we were once again headed uptown in a taxi.

Traffic was terrible because of overflow from the Midtown Tunnel, and when we arrived at the United Nations building, Leopold jumped out of the taxi and raced us inside. This time the guards recognized him and waved us through. We were apparently on our way to another conference. Fortunately, I had been fortified by several slices of bacon and a generous dollop of Ms. Ramsey's home fries.

We passed a room with a sign out front that read *Language: Our Common Bond*. The occupants and even the lecturer were in varying stages of a midmorning snooze. Leopold took us down one long corridor, then another, then through a set of fire doors, down a flight of stairs, down another corridor, up another flight of stairs until, finally, we arrived at an enormous kitchen. A sous chef glared at us from behind the long stainless-steel counter where he was chopping thousands of walnuts.

"The dog can't come in here," he said. "Unless he's been skinned."

"Ha," Leopold said. "Talk about diversity."

"It's the United Nations, pal," the sous chef said. "Today I'm stuffing a hundred goats' ears with walnuts. God knows what's on the menu tomorrow."

"I need to speak with Ponce," Leopold said. "It is important. Would you mind getting him?"

He flashed a twenty-dollar bill in the sous chef's direction, but the man waved it off.

"Are you kidding me? Not with this week's anticorruption initiative, I won't," the sous chef said, and disappeared in search of Ponce.

He returned a minute later and resumed his walnut-chopping.

"He'll be with you in a sec," the sous chef said. "He's deep-frying Mars Bars for the Scots."

Soon Ponce appeared, his face covered with

sweat and his apron with flour, egg and chocolate.

"You look terrible," Leopold said.

"It is hell over that deep fryer," Ponce said.
"Let's go out onto the loading dock. You don't
want Milo Paz to get a look at that dog. He's doing the menu for the Security Council next
week and he's promised them yak. But he can't
get his hands on it, and apparently dog is *the* yak
substitute."

"You can't be serious?" Leopold said. "He
can't possibly think that he can get away with
cooking dog in this day and age."

"With enough sauce, people will eat anything," Ponce said. "That's my motto. So what's
going on? This is very unconventional to meet
like this, Leopold."

We had reached the loading dock. Ponce lit a
cigarette and flopped down onto a large crate
of cabbage. Leopold remained standing, with an
almost military uprightness, and I stood beside
him.

"You've heard about events of morning at Ms.
Ramsey's?" Leopold asked.

Ponce nodded.

"In my thirty-plus years of service, I have
never seen such brazen behavior," Leopold said.

"It is like there is goddamn hunt going on. Tell me, Ponce, what is really happening?"

"The stakes are high, Leo," Ponce said. He had a nonchalance that seemed calculated to annoy the older man. It is sometimes considered a weakness of my kind that we can develop feelings of loyalty very quickly. Often the object of this loyalty might seem unworthy (the curmudgeon who rarely showers or the young woman with a princess complex), but we see beyond these failings and look for the best in the individual. We believe when all others have stopped believing, and we—not the doubters and the critics—are typically right. It is the possibility of goodness, kindness and soulful vulnerability that really matters, and we find these things in our masters and drag them out into the light. Leopold might have been an aging spy. He might have done many less-than-reputable things in his life. But at that moment, faced with the insolent Ponce on the loading deck, he seemed like a tired, decent man who thought that something was going wrong and ought to stop.

"Someone higher up is going to intervene," Leopold said. "They always do if things go too far, and I have never seen them go this far. Discreet poisoning, stabbing during a 'robbery attempt'—those kinds of killings were the limit. But sniping in broad daylight and then this grotesque slaughter before breakfast..."

"I'm sure they're *not* going to intervene," Ponce said. "In fact, I'm sure they're the ones calling the shots. There's a rumor going around that the poet and the recyclables lady weren't killed only to frame Imogen. They were killed because they had seen someone else leave that room after Imogen and they were threatening not to stay quiet any longer. Did you know those two old birds were a couple?"

Leopold shook his head.

"Did that silly detective ask after me?" Ponce asked.

"No," Leopold said. "He's sick of all of us. But you're right, I can tell he has his hands tied. But they won't be tied for long if more bodies keep piling up."

"So is that all you wanted to say—that this is outrageous by the standards of the old days?" Ponce asked. "As I said, things are different now. The stakes are higher."

"And still no sense of where girl might be?" Leopold asked.

"One of us knows, but it isn't me," Ponce said. "And if it was me, I wouldn't tell you."

"But sniping was an outside job," Leopold said.

"Sure, one of the guys in the house had support do it," Ponce said. "That's not surprising."

"That's fine," Leopold said. "But what about killing this woman inside house this morning? That could have been any one of you four. It isn't easy to sneak into place. Ms. Ramsey is an insomniac and the halls are seldom empty. There is always someone wandering about. No, I'm quite sure that it was one of you four."

"It wasn't me," Ponce said. "I've been chopping walnuts since six."

"I'm sure nobody knows exactly when she was killed yet," Leopold said.

"Well, I'm on that floor, and the bottle lady wasn't lying there dead when I left for work this morning. And there are witnesses who saw me walk down that hall leaving for work."

Ponce put his cigarette out on the loading dock.

"I don't really get you, Leo," Ponce said. "Why does this matter? You're in town for a conference. Maybe. Maybe not. But whatever it is—you're not at the high-stakes table anymore. This isn't your game, is it? You're an old man now. Things are winding down."

"When you have played game long enough,"

Leo said, "you'll get bit of respect for it and protocol will matter. Style and proportion will matter. It's dirty game, but there are rules and
dignity. Little people, innocent people being
bounced off to tighten the noose on target is
just not done."

"I've got to get back to work," Ponce said.

"Do you want lozenge?" Leopold asked, offering Ponce a shiny yellow candy from the top
of the roll. "They're ginger and lemon. Excellent
for smoker's throat."

"Sure, thanks."

Ponce took one from the pack and so did
Leo. Then we followed him back inside. When
we reached the kitchen, he looked down at me
and then up at Leopold.

"I'm serious about the dog. He has *main course*
written all over him. Good and fat," Ponce said.
"Milo's a dimwit, but he's determined. He's living at the house too. I'm surprised you haven't
met him. He's from your neck of the woods:
Near *Lower* Pilasia. Oh no, there he is. Hide
the dog."

But it was too late. A smiling man with a
large white chef's hat came around the corner.
He bore more than a passing resemblance to
Leopold—same jowly look and pale skin. My

temporary owner started to back out the door, but I could not move out of his way fast enough. He stumbled over me and leaned heavily into the wall.

"Nice dog," Milo said, sharpening the meat cleaver he was holding, like a cartoon figure. "How much? I'm in market for yak substitute."

"He's not for sale," Ponce explained.

"He's therapy dog," Leopold said.

"Nice dog," Milo said. "Good fat belly. Big brain. Thick tail. I pay one hundred dollars."

Recently I had watched a commercial on television in which an ergonomic office chair was said to fetch $625 and a puppy $100. Although I am an admirer of Milton Friedman, the relative values of the human marketplace can boggle the mind. I doubt if this world will know either peace or be free from lower-back pain until things can be genuinely valued and a dog never fetch less than an ergonomic office chair.

"He's not for sale, Milo," Ponce repeated.

"Ah, but he's perfect," Milo said. "I convince you. You see."

The determined chef put his meat cleaver on the adjacent counter and reached down to give me a pat.

"Friends?" he asked.

He did not reach within three feet. I backed up and delivered an undiplomatic growl.

Milo laughed. "You'll see. Milo convince you," he said, picking up his meat cleaver and disappearing into the walk-in refrigerator a few paces away.

A DOG REVIEWS HIS MISSION

A DONUT FALLS FROM THE
TABLE OF JOY

SEVERAL FULL-BODY, head-to-toe shakes were needed to exorcise the prospect of serving as Milo Paz's entrée for the Security Council. Even so, I reflected on Ponce's statement that the dog-focused chef lived in the boardinghouse and, given Leopold's carelessness with locking our door, my mission had suddenly become much more perilous. It is rules and respect for rules that keeps this planet from falling to pieces. A man driven like Milo was a dangerous man indeed. Leopold arrived at the linguistics lecture after the break had fortified the participants with coffee and donuts and part two of five had begun.

And what was my mission exactly? Harry and Imogen were well out of their depth. They were little people, after all, facing international powers. Anyone is little when looking out for one's own interests, one's own happiness, against the interests of some vast government machine. I was more sure than I had been before that Imogen had fled to protect us. She had chosen to become the target, and only a publicized disappearance and rejection of her life could achieve that. Harry had been safe as long as the powers that be thought he had been left. She burned the bridges before anyone else could use them to cross to her treasure (or, at least, this was my belief—and a dog's conviction must count for something). But what could Harry and I do? Where was Imogen? She had fled the young man dead beneath the parachute. She had consumed the same chemical that had rendered him unconscious, but she had somehow not succumbed. My experience with Leopold and the four diplomat/spies (after learning Ponce's job, at least one could be classified as a sous chef/spy) only confirmed what Blinko thought: someone wanted to put pressure on Imogen, but it was certainly an extreme and uncertain way of doing it. One could almost say desperate. And what of my snout stamp from the recyclables lady? Ponce wasn't lying. He hadn't killed the woman. It was not his scent on the victim. That left the other three. If one of these three was guilty, then we would be getting somewhere. I could identify the killer, communicate that fact to Harry and he could pass this information on to Detective Davis, along with other evidence that I could attempt to assemble. Of course, there was the question of the sniper, but Ponce was probably correct on that score as well: it was an assistant of some kind. I did not know how these types operated or how powerful their networks were, but it wasn't too hard to imagine a professional killer lurking in the wings to support one of the boardinghouse operatives. No, the mission was daunting, but it wasn't futile. The murder of the recyclables lady was a tragedy indeed, but it was also a major misstep. If someone could be found guilty of this one killing, then more connections could be made and the chains of suspicion that bound our Imogen would be broken. She would be free (at least from this immediate threat).

The lecturer droned on, drawing no wisdom or insight from the literary masters whom I valued and instead subjecting language to the kind of analysis better suited for diagnosing a knock in a car's transmission or a geriatric's rheumatism. Surely Dante—that great bridge builder— would have something to say about the topic: *Language: Our Common Bond.* James Joyce, whom Virginia Woolf wrongly called a pimply-faced schoolboy, would have obliterated the academic with his potent word music. The poet Auden would have taken an analeptic swig from his hip flask, lit a cigarette and cried eloquent, untechnocratic fire down on humanity's collective head. Yes, my thoughts were darkly inclined, since the better angels of my nature knew the great virtues of linguistic study. Perhaps it was low blood sugar. I *was* feeling a bit *eleven o'clock-ish,* as Pooh Bear might say. As if in answer to my stomach's need, a woman wearing Coke-bottle glasses knocked a crème-filled donut onto the floor right beside me. As Langston Hughes put it: *Sometimes a crumb falls/From the tables of joy . . .*

I downed the delectable in a single satisfying gulp and, thus sated, fell fast asleep.

"REMBRANDT," LEOPOLD'S voice fell toward me like the sound of ashes feathering down a long dark chimney. "Rembrandt, wake up."

A tremendous heaviness was upon me, worse than any of my previous mornings. My paws and every joint ached. My eyelids were sandpaper on the inside.

"Rembrandt," Leopold said. His voice was full of worry and I struggled to move my body. At last I managed to open my left eye. The light streamed in like boiling water, and I shut it promptly. I apologize up front for sounding dramatic, but it is the only way to express the rottenness of Yours Truly's physical condition. Other voices joined Leopold's. Someone poked a toe into my ribs, and I stirred against it by pawing the air. Then I heard Leopold's sharp rebuke.

"Don't do that," Leopold said. "Can you not see he's unwell?"

My brain struggled to reconstitute itself and begin to function. I was on the floor of the lecture hall. I had fallen asleep. I had eaten something before I fell asleep. A donut. A crème-filled donut. A chocolate-glazed donut. Chocolate? How could I have been so stupid? My kind is not supposed to eat chocolate for some reason—a missing digestive enzyme or some such. And now I was useless to anyone and perhaps dying of chocolate poisoning. My appetite had finally been my death sentence.

I slipped back into a painful, semiconscious darkness. From far away I heard Leopold make a phone call. Sometime later I smelled a welcome scent and a familiar voice. It was Harry.

"I'm here, boy," Harry said, and gave me a belly rub. My owner's arrival lifted my spirits, and I managed to raise myself up and look at him. I could scent that he was worried and felt guilty—no doubt for dallying on the visit to the veterinarian. Though it is not my usual way, I gave him an encouraging lick on his shoulder. Then I saw that Haddy McClay stood behind him, which tempered my spirits.

"Is he gonna die, Uncle Harry?" Haddy said.

"I doubt it," Harry said. "He's a tank."

My owner bent down and took me firmly in his arms. With a grunt he lifted me up and carried me out of the room. At least there was one bright spot: I did not have to stay for the rest of the lecture.

Leopold followed us out.

"I'm so sorry," he said. "There is veterinarian on premises. He takes care of secretary general's dogs. I have already called ahead and they are expecting you. We can use motorized cart if you like. I will contact guard."

"How far is it?" Harry asked.

"A hundred yards or so."

"I'll be fine," Harry said. Though I noticed that his breathing had become labored and he strained a bit to keep me aloft.

"When you're all better, buddy, you and I are going to start running in the park," Harry said.

I was not worried. He had made these threats before.

The veterinarian's offices were small and clean. There was a great deal of bleach and ammonia but little richness or diversity of smell. In fact, they were so clean that I could not detect the scent of a single animal. Typically, the veterinary office is a heady place that sends the most levelheaded animal into either euphoria or a fit of nerves, mostly nerves. The smells of hundreds of animals layered upon one another drives the dachshund's blood pressure to dangerous heights and the great bull mastiff into territorial red alert—after all, the dog's most powerful sense is telling them that somehow these invisible dogs are still present (hiding, perhaps, just behind the water cooler or under the end table with the magazines and the pet-insurance forms). But no such reaction could happen in this sanitized place.

Harry was about to put me down on the floor, but a young man in a white medical jacket appeared. He motioned all of us through another door into an even smaller room with a large metal table.

"You can put him here," said the vet, who introduced himself as Calvin Smiley. Harry did as Dr. Smiley directed, and his dog received the shock of freezing metal on his belly.

"Not feeling too great, huh, pup," Dr. Smiley said. Doctors diagnosing humans can usually rely on their patient's ability to express some important facts about the condition. Of course, a vet does not have this advantage, and so Dr. Smiley poked and prodded, kneaded my pliable flesh, plucked at my tongue, dug into my ears and, in a particularly strenuous trial, pulled on each of my four legs.

"He ate chocolate," Leopold said. "A lady told me her donut fell on floor and he gobbled it up before she could stop him."

Dr. Smiley fixed Leopold in a stern gaze.

"Where were you?"

"Asleep," the press secretary said.

"How much chocolate?" Dr. Smiley asked.

"A bit of glaze on a donut."

"I wouldn't worry about it."

"I was told he might have hypothyroidism," Harry interjected, just before it seemed Dr. Smiley might begin another round of leg pulling.

"You've been told he might have hypothyroidism," Dr. Smiley repeated. "Interesting. Has he been sluggish lately?"

"Yes," Harry said. "Very sluggish. It's not that he's the most active dog."

"I can see that," Dr. Smiley said. "You're working on your Buddha belly, aren't ya, boy?"

"He doesn't like to run," Harry explained.

"Not the first lazy Lab," Dr. Smiley said. "I need blood. Lots of it."

A needle was brought out. A very long needle. I could endure the leg pulling and the misguided insult about my work ethic, but, unfortunately, the needle proved my limit. I suffer from *try-panophobia,* or fear of needles, and at the mere sight of that three-inch sharp I once again fainted.

This was merciful because, when I awakened, I saw that the good doctor had several vials of my burgundy in his hand and the needle had been stowed away.

"Very good patient," Dr. Smiley said, apparently unaware that I had lapsed into unconsciousness.

"So what do we do now?" Harry asked.

"I'd like to keep him here overnight," Dr. Smiley said. "We have modest kenneling facilities. He will be able to rest and we will be able to monitor him. In the morning we'll have the results of the blood test, and my sense is that it will probably be hypothyroidism, which is easily treated with regular tablets of thyroxine. But we will know more then."

I tried to catch Harry's eye. If only he could be made to understand that his dog was not to be left in a building that housed a dog-cooking chef. Feeling a bit stronger, I lifted myself unsteadily into a standing position.

"Whoa, boy," Dr. Smiley said. "Take it easy. We have a nice bed all ready for you."

My options were few. I whined, but Harry just rubbed me under the chin and looked resolved to leave me. I was regaining my senses and noticed that my owner wore old jeans and a black T-shirt—his work clothes—and these were covered in dust, paint and drying concrete. His work on the mosaic, I reasoned, must already be well under way. At least he would be across the street for most of the day. Leopold, though, seemed reluctant to leave me. Like most people who suffer from anxiety, he could not help his fear from occasionally getting the best of him.

"Perhaps it would be better, Doctor, if Rembrandt came home with me," Leopold said. "I will be very vigilant. Yes, I think he will do very well indeed in my care."

Harry looked puzzled at my new name but said nothing.

"I couldn't advise it," Dr. Smiley said. "I don't think this is serious, but it's better for him to stay put. He is obviously very weak."

At the doctor's confirmation of my symptoms, I felt a new wave of fatigue break over me, and as if on cue I slumped onto the table despite my best intentions, where I lay utterly unable to move.

"See," Dr. Smiley said. His point resoundingly delivered by Yours Truly. "I can meet both of you here tomorrow morning. I have the owner's phone number? Yes?"

Harry nodded. Apparently he had filled out the paperwork while my trypanophobia had kept me senseless.

I could sense that this outcome did not please Leopold, but he stayed silent.

"Uncle Harry, are they going to put him down?" Haddy McClay asked. "That's what they did with Garbanzo, our cat, when Garbanzo's liver stopped working. They put her down. They said it wasn't serious and then she was dead. Are they going to put him down too? If they are, can we stay and watch? That's what we did with Garbanzo—we watched, and it was really sad but educational too. Mom is always telling Dad to put her down if she ever gets like her mom when she gets old."

Harry shook his head and gave me a gratifying ear rub. I thought I could detect a glistening at the corner of each of his eyes. It did me good to see this.

"And don't you worry," Dr. Smiley said as the trio exited. "There's no more dog-friendly place than the United Nations. He'll sleep like a baby."

When they were gone, Dr. Smiley summoned a large man named Bruce to carry me into a cage in another room. Bruce wore a dark blue jumpsuit and smelled of sardines and cigarettes. I expected to be manhandled but was not. The bottom of the cage was smooth, hard and as cold as the table in the examination room. Bruce noticed this and found a thick blanket to cushion the interior. A water bowl was placed in the corner but no food provided (I couldn't have eaten anyway). I had lost all track of time. I seemed to exist in a timeless place, a limbo with no consequences, and had only the faintest sense that there was a goal or change of circum-stances in the works. All of this was because of the fatigue that had exhausted every part of my being. How strange that so much of our experi-ence is dependent on how our bodies feel. I drowsed on and off throughout what I believed was the afternoon. No one visited me, and the fluorescent light in the ceiling panel, with its in-cessant hum, burned into my eyes even with the lids closed. At some point, Dr. Smiley poked his head into the room, saw that I was still breath-ing and extinguished the light. I was grateful for the rest this gave my eyes—before realizing that it meant he was leaving for the day. The outer door to the office shut and I was left all alone.

This was very unpleasant. It was more than unpleasant, because, since awakening, I had be-come more conscious of my situation. I was lonely and frightened and quite sad. I wished very much that I was at home in our apartment, with whatever familiar scents were left after Harry's recent cleanup and settled in among my books and the unfinished canvases of my corner. I write in a way that would suggest that I am "all grown up" and "quite independent." But, really, I am not. Writing is the craft of the illusionist. A writer frames and reframes reality, and soon this mirror trick becomes the world. Language makes me old, but I am only five and a half. At this point canine middle age might be fast approaching, but I'm still saddled with many of the longings of a chronological youth not much past infancy. Home matters, perhaps more than it should. I scratched into the blanket and burrowed my nose in its folds.

Then the outer door opened and the light went on. The good doctor had returned. True to his name, he flashed an extravagant smile. He opened my cage, gave my head a rub and dropped a piece of clothing next to me.

"There's a good boy," Dr. Smiley said. "This'll make you feel more at home. Your owner dropped it off."

It was one of Harry's T-shirts. Most comforting.

I RECENTLY CAME ACROSS a newspaper article that surprised me. The writer maintained that study after study has shown that many humans are afraid of big black dogs. I confess to being afraid of many types of dogs (particularly those trigger-happy nerve baskets that have lashed out at Yours Truly like steroidal cobras in the past), but I find big black dogs amiable. I go by the eyes, which is where a dog's character is to be found. But how many humans go by the eyes? Eyes are a subtle quality. Soulful eyes can be missed by the crude or callous. Intelligent eyes, unremarked. Pleading eyes go unnoticed. We hope to communicate something of ourselves through our eyes, but the world is blind to the projections we cast upon these two-way screens. I have mentioned my difficulty before, but it is worth mentioning again to convey just what it is like to be kept prisoner in a small cage in a dark room in a giant building shared by at least one person who would fancy you for a main ingredient. To be conscious in a dog's body is the equivalent of being constrained in a full body cast with only the eyes showing. I have no facial muscles and my body has a limited range. An owner who is fond of you can make this reality bearable, even pleasant. But a dog on his own is a different matter. A dog on his own is like a desert island far beyond the shipping lanes. A dog on his own cannot pick up a phone and call for emergency assistance.

Harry's T-shirt had been enough to permit me to doze, but sometime in the night I awoke with a start. The outer door had opened and someone was crossing the lobby. The examination-room door opened and the footsteps drew closer. Then the door to my room opened. Milo Paz flicked the light and the fluorescent bulb crackled and hummed to life. The chef was dressed in street clothes and wore a baseball cap. The cap and a broad grin made him look like a child about to do something morally questionable but fun. I edged back into the cage, but Milo had his eyes fixed on me. I had recovered some of my strength, but I doubted whether I could stand and, even if I could, whether I would be able to walk more than a few feet. Running was not possible. He put a hand on my cage and began fumbling with the lock. There was a handle on a spring that had to be depressed at the same moment a latch had to be lifted. Milo had just figured this out when there was a rattling of the outer door. Then a key slipped into the lock and the outer door opened.

"Hello," a voice called out. "Dr. Smiley, are you here?"

Milo stopped fiddling with my cage and flattened himself behind the open door. Footsteps approached. I heard the whine and static of a walkie-talkie, and then a tall security guard, going soft in the middle and bald on top, stepped into the room. He glanced to his right and left. He looked at me, and I, with my lack of facial musculature and vocal cords, could communicate nothing. I decided to bark, and for the first time since the misdirected emotion of my puppyhood I let loose with a raucous volley.

"Shut up," the guard said. "I ain't feeding you."

Then he flicked off the lights and left the veterinary office. His key turned in the dead-bolt lock of the outer door with a decisive sound. *Clunk.* Milo emerged. He flicked the light on, and, as if he had figured out how to open my cage while standing in the dark for those few seconds, he came over to my cage and opened the door with ease.

"Milo is good friend," the chef said. "You see. I convince."

He muttered on like this in a mixture of English and a language unfamiliar to me. Then he donned plastic gloves that had an overwhelming latex smell, which prevented me from detecting any scent beneath them, hefted me into the air and dropped me into a rolling laundry hamper that he had wheeled into the examination room. I was too unwell to resist and lay on my back in a mound of dishrags with my paws in the air. He rolled the hamper out of the veterinary offices and down one long hall and then another. We rode one elevator. And then another. We descended a ramp and ascended a ramp. We rounded a sharp corner, and the hamper listed but did not flip over. And then we were in a kitchen. Not the kitchen that Leopold and I had visited earlier. The smells were not the same, and neither was the ceiling and décor passing by above me. The décor seemed older and dilapidated and there were different spices in the air and the smell of mineral oil from kitchen machinery being worked heavily. I thought I heard several meat slicers operating around me with enthusiastic whirrings of their blades. Thomas Stearns Eliot crowbarred into Yours Truly's consciousness: *I should have been a pair of ragged claws/Scuttling across the floors of silent seas.* Or, at the very least, I shouldn't have eaten chocolate or been a Labrador retriever.

The hamper came to a stop beside one of the slicers. Instead of lifting me out, Milo dumped the hamper like a trash bucket onto the floor, and I rolled to a stop flat on my back among the dish towels. My panic-numbed mind and fatigue-numbed body came to strange, incoherent conclusions. The mad chef would have to skin me first before feeding me to the slicer. No, he would opt to put an apple in my mouth and stick me in the roasting oven hair and all. There are always shortcuts in the kitchen and, like easy-cook lasagna in which one does not boil the noodles first but softens them in the baking process, Milo might simply trust that 450 degrees Fahrenheit would burn off my hair and save him the trouble of skinning. Of course, there would be a lot of smoke and the smell would be awful. In moments of great stress, my mind is prone to take a holiday, stepping away from the hideous probabilities and looking at them with a critical distance that ignores that I am the one about to be scooped into the roasting pan. I also turn to literature. I think of the great scribblers. Their art and, in fact, their lives are like a hedge against the utter senselessness of death. But tonight only Eliot's line ran through my head, alternating with a suffocating sense of this dog's limitations and a craving for home, Harry and Imogen.

A radio in the background played Sinatra. The signal went in and out and the singer's legendary phrasing sounded strained as he worked his way through that tribute to the metastatic ego: "My Way." I have always been most fond of his work in *Guys and Dolls* and, now delirious, wondered if "Luck Be a Lady" would be the backdrop to my demise and whether I would be offered a cigarette, like the condemned in an old black-and-white movie about the French Foreign Legion. But, of course, those who become poultry and pork loins are afforded no such option at their exit, so why should a Labrador? Was I a white meat? Would I taste like chicken or yak? The night, the city, seemed so far away. The threat of one's own death destroys the romantic dream, and each nook and corner of civility, each small joy and peaceful habit becomes a mockery buried beneath the sudden details of biological terror—the details of an extinction that suddenly seems so intimate and so inevitable. Milo had chosen the easy-cook option. He returned with the largest roasting pan I have ever seen. Soon I was being garnished, Sinatra was off and the radio had gone into a commercial for Tempur-Pedic brand mattresses.

I had closed my eyes tight and was looking for some corner of escape deep within myself when suddenly Milo stopped. He dropped his knife. Raw onions burned my nose and I could not smell the chef's emotions, so I opened my eyes again. To my great surprise he was staring at Blinko, who stood in the doorway.

"A dog's not for eatin', mate," Blinko said. Nothing in the massive Australian's voice hinted at it being the least unusual that a Labrador was occupying a roasting pan, which was now ringed with garlic cloves, onions and bell peppers.

His great breadth filled the doorway and loomed, even though his voice had nothing of the looming or threatening quality in it. His was a fresh, clear voice simply making a statement that was not to be questioned, second-guessed or objected to in any way. Milo stood up and wiped his hands on his apron.

"For photographs. My hobby is photography," Milo said. "Dog as food. Food as dog. A meditation."

"That's a pearler, mate. So where's the camera?" Blinko said. "You were going to cook the beast and I've caught you like a barramundi."

Milo nodded.

"We had no yak," he confessed, and backed away from me. "Sorry."

"That's stealing too," Blinko said. "But I'll let you go on that count. You must be a crazy bastard trying a stunt like this. Put the dog back in the hamper and we'll leave it at that. Your next dish is vegetarian."

Milo did as Blinko told him. I was heaved up again and dropped into the hamper. An armful of dishcloths followed and then the hamper was pushed in Blinko's direction. Nothing else was said, and I cannot report with accuracy what gestures and expressions occurred outside my limited vista in the hamper since once again my four legs were awkwardly positioned and my neck was twisted in such a way that I could see little above me.

Soon the hamper was moving and we retraced the path to the veterinary offices. Blinko did something to the outer door when we arrived and we slipped inside. The giant Australian seemed to have little sensitivity to the concept of trespass and a preternatural ability to move around presumably restricted places. I was grateful for it.

When I was back in my cage, Blinko spoke to me.

"You're a special dog, Randolph," he said. "*I* know you're special and *you* know you're special. You might not think anyone knows how special you are, but you need to know that I do. Don't forget it. You keep your eyes open, mate. You keep involved. There's a light at the end of this tunnel, and when you get there, things will be clearer than they are now. I'll do my part, but like I told your owner, I've got to stay at a distance. Tonight was a one-off. I had a sense that you'd be in trouble. I could feel it in me guts. You can't count on me always being around to save the day. You have to get better at looking out for yourself. Things are dangerous and you're in the middle of it. Being dependent is no good. Being sick is no excuse."

And thus having delivered words that left me with the impression that Blinko could see through walls, he gave me a vigorous head rub, rose to his feet and walked out the door, leaving me with one last consolation.

"You'll be apples, mate."

I SPENT THE REST OF THE night confident that my ordeal with Milo would not be repeated and instead focused on Blinko's strange words. Humans can speak to my kind in many different ways. The most common is the patronizing tone that they also employ against five-year-olds or telephone representatives on the other end of a customer-service line. This tone is characterized by an emphasis on the last syllable and a lilt toward a higher register that turns every statement into a question. As in *Go for a walk.* The question is completed by a word—usually made silly and embarrassing—that suggests that the dog will understand only a childish version of the actual word. In the case of *walk*, this word is *walkie*. Another common tone used by humans is the strange *You-Are-a-Fellow-Sentient-Creature-Even-Though-I-Know-You're-Not-Really-and-I'm-Oddly-Aware-that-I'm-Talking-to-Myself.*

This is employed by both the busy and the businesslike, who cope with the potential embarrassment of a dog's less respectable behaviors by pretending as if they were delivering orders and reasons to a subordinate. As in *Puffins, eating shoes is not acceptable. When we reach the park I will let you off your leash. Let's wait here for the light to change and then we will cross. I can't be late for the meeting, Puffins.* Needless to say, Puffins would soon be a traffic fatality if a leash were not used (I have said that I am unusual among dogs for the cogency of my thought).

But Blinko spoke to me as if he knew I understood. He had called me *special.* My ego was flattered less by this one word than by the fact that it seemed the man wouldn't have been surprised if I had spoken back. What could this mean? It was possible that I was unfamiliar with Australians and thus culturally at a disadvantage. Perhaps all antipodeans spoke to their animals with this kind of respect (though I doubted it, having once read an article about how Australians regularly slaughter their kangaroos even though the animal is featured on their currency—the equivalent of the American going on a hunt for the bald eagle). No, clearly there was more. Blinko seemed to be instructing me but also expecting something out of me.

It was this last part that baffled me the most. Why would anyone expect anything out of me? To outside eyes I was a faithful and amiable dog. I could be counted on to be regular where habits counted. I did not tear up the furniture because of separation anxiety or do unspeakable things to people's legs. But worthy of responsibility? Suddenly the mystery of the young man beneath the parachute, the wealth in the Outback, Imogen's flight, the subsequent murders in the boardinghouse, the Great Game of nations were joined by Blinko's odd assertion and belief. And suddenly, somehow, I began to sense that a thread—only now barely discernible—ran between all of these things, connecting them, and if the right thinking was done and the right facts were learned, that thread would draw them all tightly into one.

"Hound, behold your cure," Dr. Smiley stood outside my cage and boomed. His command wrenched me from a sleep that could neither cure the acid trauma of the previous night's brush with death by roasting nor answer the questions raised by Blinko's strange words. Dreams of Yours Truly being fed like so much pastrami into a gleaming slicer were replaced by image of the good doctor holding my test results in one hand and a bowl of food in another.

Into this bowl he dropped a hot-pink pill and mixed.

He opened my cage and pushed the bowl under my nose. I ate with gusto, and only after I had swallowed the last of the food—dry, tasteless and undoubtedly healthy nuggets—did I note a certain bitter residue lingering at the back of the mouth. This, I assumed, must be the medication that would bring the cure.

"Excellent patient," Dr. Smiley said. "Your humans will be along in a few hours. You'll be standing by then. Drink some water."

I did as instructed.

"It's great when things go easy. You're definitely one of the good ones. I actually feel like I could love animals again," he said.

Then, as if the universe wanted to emphasize that ease was the exception, not the rule, and that loving animals might entail saintly resolve for Dr. Smiley, there was a commotion outside. The vet disappeared through the door and I could hear several people talking at once. Dr. Smiley moved the crowd into the examination room adjacent to my area and I heard everything very clearly.

"Whatever you do, don't call the secretary general yet," one man said.

"What can you do?" a second man demanded

of Dr. Smiley. "There's got to be something that you can do."

"Puppet is dead," Dr. Smiley said. "I've been trying to prepare the secretary general for this day."

"What do you mean, *this day?*" another man said. "For God's sake, you can't die from a hernia."

"It wasn't a hernia that we operated on," Dr. Smiley said. "It was cancer. The secretary general didn't seem to grasp this for some reason. Maybe he didn't want to know. I guess he's a complicated man."

"SG loves his dogs," the second man said. The second man spoke with a kind of authority that the other man didn't possess. "This couldn't be happening at a worse time. SG is brokering a border agreement. It's huge. Front-page news. Make the UN cutting edge again and not some Burt Bacharach, asbestos-ceilinged laughingstock filled with long-lunching public servants. But the parties are at each others' throats, and, well, you know, SG, Doc, he loves Puppet more than his own kid. He's an emotional man. He *feels* everything. This will be too much for him. He'll be stymied. He'll be flattened. He'll mope for months. Is there any way we can keep the dog alive—at least for the next few days during the negotiations? If we don't, it's gonna be a train wreck."

Dr. Smiley sounded worried that his message wasn't reaching the secretary general's advisers.

"I'm sorry," he said. "But Puppet is dead."

"There's no shot to get him back on his feet? Steroids? Adrenaline?" the man in charge said. "Just for a few days. Then he can die."

"How often does the secretary general see Puppet when he is busy?" Dr. Smiley asked.

"Not much. Maybe at night if he doesn't have an official dinner."

"Did he just say the dog is dead? I'm not getting this," one of the other men said. He was apparently sending messages via his cell phone and had misunderstood the plight of the dog on the examination table.

"Yes, dead. Quite dead. Dead for several hours, in fact," Dr. Smiley said for the third time. "How much contact does the secretary general have with his dogs at times like this? I mean, does he play with them? Does he bring them to the park?"

"No, we do that."

"We can keep Puppet here, then, and tell the secretary general later."

"Impossible. He needs to pet them each once before he goes to bed or he can't fall asleep."

"Once?"

"Once."

"Does he look at them?"

"No," the man in charge said. "He's always reading. Do you know how many briefs, resolutions, memoranda and meeting points the press office produces every day?"

"I can only imagine."

"Reams of paper. None of it matters or actually accomplishes anything—I sometimes think that the United Nations only retains its authority by remaining irrelevant—but SG is very studious, and it's easier for him to read a document than to talk to a human being."

"Allow me to outline the facts," Dr. Smiley said. "The secretary general's dog is dead. You cannot allow him to learn about this until certain negotiations are complete. He has little contact with his dogs but needs to pet them at least once a day before bedtime. He does not look up from his reading material to do so."

"Right."

"Well, then, gentlemen, I think I have your solution," Dr. Smiley said, as if he were about to outline the plans for the next Great Train Robbery.

"Terrific. What is it?"

"Use a surrogate dog, a stand-in," Dr. Smiley

said. "I was going to suggest a taxidermist, but no one does it in twenty-four hours. Besides, Puppet is a common-enough-looking dog. Large and black. Labradoodle. He should be easy to replace—at least for our purposes. In fact, I think, I have the perfect candidate."

"You do?" The man in charge sounded nearly ecstatic.

"I do. He's the therapy dog for the press secretary from somewhere called Near Upper Pilasia."

"Not those backwater savages," the first man said. "They eat stuffed goats' ears."

"This guy seems alright—overrefined, if anything—and his dog is terrific. Actually, his dog is on loan, I think. Look, the owners are getting here in an hour or so. I'll talk to them. I don't see why they'd object. I bet someone from Near Upper Pilasia would welcome the chance to do a favor for the secretary general."

"But what if SG finds out?" the man in charge said.

"He's a professional, isn't he?" Dr. Smiley asked.

"Sure. Except for the crying jags and the manic temper, he's as steady as they come."

"Then he'll understand that you did it for the common good."

"Terrific," the man in charge said.

Clearly both man and beast were dispensable pawns in the great contest of nations. Puppet was removed to cold storage without a single tear, and the man in charge of the SG's entourage poked his head into the room to assess me.

"He'll do," the man pronounced, and consulted a clipboard he was carrying. "We need him at ten tonight when SG has snacktime in the study of his auxiliary apartment on the thirtieth floor."

An hour later, as predicted by the good doctor, I was feeling much stronger. The heaviness of so many days was lifting and I began to realize that at least part of my recent melancholy was the result of this problem in my blood. The idea that a shortage of thyroxine could give me such bleak, Lincolnian thoughts would have been saddening in itself if I wasn't feeling so much better. But sometimes the body buoys the brain, and if sprinting was the kind of thing I liked to do, my legs would be ready to oblige.

I felt so good that I began to pace about my cage. It was this picture of health that Harry and Leopold discovered a short time later. Haddy McClay, after a trial period as artist's helper, had been deposited in the United

Nations nursery. If it was anything like their dog run, Haddy would likely end in tears.

"There's a good boy," Harry said when I jumped up and put my front paws on his stomach, something that I had never done before.

Dr. Smiley instructed them on my medication regime and then introduced the possibility that I serve the ends of world peace by keeping the secretary general in ignorance about the fate of his pet.

Leopold reacted strangely to this request. The press secretary from Near Upper Pilasia began to reek of fear and look visibly nervous. His right hand even began to shake.

"I'm afraid that I will not be able to accompany Rembrandt on humanitarian mission. My conference is hosting smorgasbord at the Pierre tonight," Leopold said. "And, indeed, it would be unseemly for me to be involved in deception of any kind, particularly at such high levels."

Leopold was not being honest himself. He reeked of deception.

"I'll bring him," Harry said. "I'll be in the neighborhood. Is that okay with you, Leopold?"

The press secretary was reluctant.

"I can't be without Rembrandt for long, you know," he said. "My nerves have been particularly bad with the mishaps of late. Yesterday and last night were very difficult without him. The replacement wasn't the same. I have never seen a dog move so little, and he destroyed the curtains with his incessant climbing. Ms. Ramsey was not pleased."

"I'm sorry about that," Harry said. "It was very last minute. I promise you'll have him back for good soon."

A compromise was arranged. Leopold would keep me for the rest of the day while Harry worked across the street at WAHA on his mosaic. Then Harry would pick me up and retrieve Haddy McClay from day care.

I spent the day in another series of lectures on language, wondering how Leopold could possibly have mistaken Jackson's curtain-climbing Guatemalan tree sloth, Marlin, for a dog.

THE EVENTS OF THE PRE-
vious week and the discombobu-
lation of leaving home only to be
shuttled from boardinghouse to kennel had
made me forget Ivan Manners's Lorikeet
Rescue Fund annual dinner. Tonight was the
event, and Harry was scheduled to attend in formal dress and as the date of Zest Kilpatrick.
The local-television news reporter, perky and
brash in the extreme, had asked my owner in a
weak moment. While I knew that Harry had
not recovered from the blow of learning that his
love had shared such close quarters with the opposite sex, I doubted whether he was ready to
"move on." Of course, my owner is a gentleman
and would never think of backing out. His table
manners may be Stanley Kowalski's, but he is a
Mr. Knightly when he doesn't have Chinese
takeout in his hands.

Harry picked me up from Leopold later that

afternoon. The press secretary surrendered me at the Dag Hammarskjöld World Pet Unity Area, where we watched two dog walkers deliver sharp blows to each other with pooper-scoopers after a disputed Number 2 went uncollected. A police cruiser arrived to cart them both away.

"Animals," Leopold remarked.

Soon Harry, Haddy and I were aboard the Vespa and speeding crosstown. When we reached the Plaza, Harry turned into Central Park and we whipped up and around the Loop north. Even a few days had made a difference in the foliage, and most of the trees showed signs of new life. And the idea of going home—even if it was only for a few hours—lifted my spirits.

"Whee," Haddy McClay screamed into the wind. I seconded the motion.

When we arrived home, a parcel awaited us. It had been left in the foyer for any New Yorker to steal, like all of our packages.

"What's this?" Harry wondered as we climbed the stairs and he tore open the cardboard box.

"I didn't order Dante and Joyce. I don't need a tote bag with Virginia Woolf's face on it."

I had forgotten my impulse purchase. Fortunately, Harry had too much on his mind to pursue the matter, and the parcel was thrown down next to the bookcase, where I would be able to explore the books and tote bag in a free moment. Harry searched through the closets for a tuxedo he believed he had once owned, until he remembered that Imogen had donated it to Goodwill. This left him with either his business suit or Grandfather Oswald's polka-band outfit (Grandfather Oswald was a talented accordionist, who had toured Michigan and Illinois on weekends after his service in the war). If this was the movie version of our story, Harry would have been forced to choose the polka-band outfit, which would have offered a funny shot or two of my owner speeding through the streets of New York on his Vespa, looking ridiculous, and then arriving at the black-tie affair looking even more ridiculous. Thankfully, no matter how strained it seems at times, this is reality, Harry is not insane or beyond embarrassment, and he chose the business suit.

Unfortunately, reality also dictated that young Haddy McClay must practice her violin per Iberia's instructions. For a half hour, Harry's niece scraped away on her instrument, inflicting grievous harm to my sensitive Lab eardrums. Then Harry said it was time to go. Apparently all of us were invited to Ivan Manners's Lorikeet Rescue Fund annual dinner.

The phone rang. It was Zest Kilpatrick. I suspected that she was not pleased to learn that she would have to find her own way to the dinner and we would meet her there.

"I'm sorry, Zest," Harry explained. "There's just no room on the Vespa with Randolph and my niece. I'm thinking of installing a sidecar."

But when we arrived, Zest stood on the curb looking utterly composed and, by human standards, stunning. Her television good looks had been amplified by strategic use of makeup. A facial made her skin shine and countless hours at the gym ensured that she was both muscularly sound and aglow with aerobic health. To underscore the "aha" effect, she wore a profoundly red gown that hung from her shoulder like a celebrity in search of the paparazzi. If a certain critical shrillness has entered my description, I apologize. I was merely thrown on the defensive by Zest Kilpatrick's pincer movement on my owner's vulnerable male front.

I needn't have been. Harry was more interested in fixing the kickstand on the Vespa, which was sticking in its housing.

"Hi, Zest. I'll be there in a minute," Harry

said, reaching for a wrench in the Vespa's tool kit.

While Harry attended to our vehicle, Zest occupied herself speaking on her cell phone about a breaking news story that she apparently now wished she was covering.

"Get the widow to say what you need, Caroline. You can do it. You didn't get hired in a number-one market for nothing," Zest said. "Tell her that you totally understand what she's going through. You know, the usual. Lay it on her. Get her to talk about their vacations. Their kids. Their first kiss. Whatever. And if that doesn't work, do the public-needs-to-know stuff. That usually works. People think they have to be noble when someone croaks. Don't get me wrong. The story's decent television without the widow, but decent isn't good enough for Channel Eight."

"Are you ready?" Harry asked, having fixed the kick-stand and gathered his charges in respectable order for entrance into the dinner.

"I'm sorry for that. I guess I can't help talking shop," Zest said, her voice sliding down the register from hard-edged newswoman to soft, fuzzy and approachable.

"That's okay," Harry said. "I've been wanting to fix that kick-stand since I got this thing."

Many of the attendees of the Lorikeet Rescue

Fund annual dinner had brought their birds and were making their way up the magnificent marble staircase that rises from the entrance hall of New York City's Discovery Society. Bird and man ascended beneath crystal chandeliers that evoked great nets and alongside tapestries showing famous discoverers past. These discoverers included Teddy Roosevelt emerging from behind a palm, holding a dead armadillo, and Sir Isaac Newton stirring a cauldron.

"I don't think this is going to be your average black tie," Zest said. "And by the way, I notice my date isn't, strictly speaking, black tie. More business formal."

Harry smiled.

"It was this or my grandfather Oswald's polka outfit."

"Wise choice," Zest said.

Due to my owner's chronic lateness, we had missed the reception and the stuffed mushrooms and baked brie (though I managed to Hoover a good number of wayward appetizers off the carpet). My appetizer maneuver reminded Harry that it was time for my medication, and another hot-pink pill was thrust between my jaws. Not even the strong quince paste in the baked brie could diminish the bitterness of the medicine. I searched for water

but there was none in sight. Zest seemed to notice my dilemma but charged ahead to the assigned table.

"This is us," Zest said. A small flag declaring
the table Channel 8's rose from the center.
Although there were eight places, only two were
occupied by a couple who gave Zest a wave and
then began to fork their salads as if they were
loading silos.

"We paid ten thousand bucks for this table.
Our CEO is a bird freak but he couldn't make
it," Zest whispered to Harry and gestured at the
two. "Be nice to them. They do makeup. They're
geniuses, but if they hate you they can make you
look like death."

They took their seats, and I sat on the floor
between Harry and Zest and assumed a watchful posture. Harry supplied Haddy McClay with
some paper and crayons and she began to draw.

"You're a good daddy," Zest said, a sudden
maternal appetite opening like a deep New York
pothole between them. Zest blushed. "I meant
uncle. Uncle. Uncle. Uncle. I'm an idiot."

I could see how her vulnerable persona could
be disarming and even appealing, if one was not
aware of the steely character that lay beneath it.
Fortunately, Harry seemed only too aware.

A waiter arrived and we learned that there

was a choice of Dover sole or filet mignon. I
wondered what would happen to the three
meals that had been destined for the unoccu-
pied places at our table. With the treatment of
my thyroid deficiency, my appetite was even
more robust than usual.

Harry ordered filet mignon for himself, a special order of fish fingers for Haddy, but nothing
for his dog. After the waiters had taken all the orders, Ivan Manners gave a speech that seemed to
equate the plight of rainbow lorikeets with the
deficiencies of the American educational system
and the nuclear arms race. Then he pointed to
the band and invited everyone to dance.

"Thank you," Ivan said. "Remember, a bird
without seed is a bird in need."

"Want to dance?" Zest asked Harry. Harry
was digging into his salad as if the emergency
exit to the evening might be found there.

My owner nodded, said that he'd like to and
then escorted Zest onto the dance floor, where
they danced through two fast songs (during
which Yours Truly's ears suffered high-decibel
torture), one slow song and another fast. At first
Harry looked awkward, but during the slow
song he seemed to relax, and when they returned to their seats (Zest making quite a show
of being out of breath as if she were on a soap

opera), I detected a distinct change between them. Harry was warmer and more open than I would have expected. That strange telescoping effect that happens between two humans in romantic situations was suggested in the way that Harry turned his chair toward hers and Zest turned her head, supported on her palm, toward his head. I had been present when he and Imogen began dating and, being a much-interested observer, noted many of the details of human courtship: the conspiratorial quality that enters the voice, the lingering eye contact, and the moment of self-revelation followed by a short explosive laugh. It all said the same thing to me: how the distance between very different people is bridged by the mysterious processes of the blood. Harry and Imogen were very different people indeed, but their physical attraction was matched not by a specific affinity of tastes—they were quite far apart—but by an affinity of spirit. But human attraction is such that physical attraction can mask the kind of differences that should doom a relationship from the start. I was prejudiced in Zest's case, but I could not imagine that the woman capable of squeezing a story out of a widow for the evening news had the kind of sensibility that could match Harry's more compassionate and artistic depths. But dinner passed with familiarity growing between them. They shared each other's main courses, and when dessert arrived, Harry split his crème brûlée (Imogen's favorite) with the television reporter, who admitted that she was watching her weight but "absolutely loved" crème brûlée.

"It's been hard ... this past year or so," Harry offered after the dessert was gone and they had returned from a second slow dance to a table from which the insular makeup artists had fled and beneath which Haddy McClay had curled up to sleep. Yours Truly remained between the couple, despite several attempts by Zest (when Harry wasn't looking) to be bribed away from his station by food held beneath the table on her far side. The candles burned down into their holders.

"It's been hard since she left," Harry said.

"You mean your girlfriend?" Zest said.

"Girlfriend," Harry said, testing the word. "*Girlfriend* sounds so casual. I never think of her that way. We would have been engaged the next day."

"One of my best friends has been engaged five times," Zest said. "It happens. Trial and error. Mainly error, I guess. I'm sorry, that was a stupid thing to say. I am always saying the wrong thing."

"No, I'm sorry," Harry said. "I don't know how we started talking about this."

"Because it matters to you. And if something matters to you, I'm interested," Zest said, perhaps on the wings of one red wine too many. She edged her chair closer to my owner and tried to push my substantial flank out of the way with her heel but was unsuccessful.

"Look, Harry, I really, really like you. I'm not usually this forward, but I think you're great. I'm not a psycho, I'm just someone who has always seen what I want and gone for it."

I could sense Harry weakening. The loneliness and doubt of so many months without confirmation of Imogen's side of things had accumulated into a heavy load that was crushing him. He had been a guard at the shrine to their memory until the shrine was shown to be a sham. He had lived for more than a year alone. Without enough solitude a man loses himself, but too much solitude makes him vulnerable—even when he denies it—to another's touch and some outside confirmation that the universe isn't just a reflection of his limited self. Solitude provides perspective, only to strip you of it, if you indulge solitude too much. As one wag has put it: if you stare into the abyss long enough, it starts staring back. I could not stand between these two forever. A physically attractive, charismatic media personality had targeted my owner. Powerful forces of attraction were at work. I should have made a greater effort to communicate with Harry what I knew about Imogen while I had the chance. What had I been doing? Ordering books on a stolen credit-card number, snuffling food scraps off the floors of New York and getting sick and almost eaten?

"I've got a confession to make," Zest said with a choreographed flip of the hair and an intense use of her left eye. "I noticed you when you were on TV and they were interviewing you about your girlfriend. I thought you were adorable, so adorable. And then when I saw you at that dog spa..."

Harry leaned in toward Zest. I thought of averting my eyes. I thought of intervening. I could give Zest a kiss on the lips like some proactive cartoon dog taking one for his master, but something other than my pride and the thought of Zest's lipsticked petri dish held me back. This was Harry's moment, and he would have to decide its outcome on his own.

Zest fluttered her eyes and she repeated herself.

"I just really, really like you."

"Zest, you're a lovely girl. But I would be lying if I said that this can go anywhere. It can't. I can't. Maybe I'm like that widow for you. Someone who's attractive because they're showing they can be hurt. I'm not that goddamn widow."

"Harry, that's not it at all. I'm coming on too strong. Let's just stop. I'm all work, and when it comes to this kind of stuff, I never know what to say. I guess I just think that you probably need closure."

My owner put his head in his hands. At first I thought Harry might cry, but instead he steadied himself.

"I'm not that widow."

"I know," Zest said.

"No, you don't know," Harry said. "Seeing you tonight has changed things for me. It's made things clear. I was slipping. Now I'm not. You're very attractive. You're successful."

"Whatever that means," Zest said.

"You are successful by any usual measure," Harry insisted. "And you're not the kind of woman that a man would walk away from. But I can't forget Imogen. And even if I could forget her, I don't want to. And it doesn't matter where she is. Or who she's with. It doesn't matter if I'm an idiot to think this way, because it's my choice. And it wouldn't matter if she was here and told me to forget her. Because I wouldn't. I wouldn't forget her smell or the way she says certain words or is nervous in crowds or breathes when she's asleep or holds a pen or a photograph or a book. I've made up my mind. I know what I believe, and it doesn't matter what she believes or what she doesn't believe. I knew her at her best, and that's the person I know she is. And I believe that there's no such thing as closure, because if I don't see her again, and hold her again and get one more chance to spend a Sunday afternoon doing absolutely nothing with her again... I've said enough, Zest. I'm sorry."

Harry woke Haddy up, and with one cranky child and a saddened television news reporter in tow, we left the the Discovery Society, descending the grand staircase in silence beneath the ever jolly Roosevelt with his dead armadillo. At the curb, my owner hailed a cab for Zest, and in cinematic fashion she turned to him as she slid into the backseat.

"Good-bye, Harry," Zest said. "I only wish someone says those things about me someday. Too bad it couldn't be you. Imogen is a lucky woman. I hope she knows it."

IN GRAPPLING WITH THE important truth of his love for Imogen and sparing Yours Truly a disturbing scene in which my vision of a happy family was wounded by the amorous Zest Kilpatrick, Harry had forgotten what time it was. As Zest's taxi disappeared into the night and my owner began to rev the Vespa, it occurred to him to ask the Discovery Society's doorman the hour. Neither Harry nor Imogen ever wore watches.

The answer was sobering.

"Ten-thirty," Harry shouted. "We're late."

We squealed off toward the United Nations, treating all manner of street signs and traffic indicators as mere suggestions rather than law. Ten minutes later my owner had parked the Vespa outside the tower's entrance, removed the license plate and hustled all of us through security.

"I'm bored," Haddy McClay said. "*And* I'm tired *and* I don't think you're being a very good role model."

"You'll survive, chestnut," Harry said.

The elevator creaked skyward, and when it stopped at the appointed floor several minutes later, we were met by the man in charge from Dr. Smiley's office.

"Lucky—you caught the fast one. People have gone mad in Shaft Three."

He was an unlikely-looking aide to a high-level diplomat. He had a boxer's forearms and giant, rock-breaking hands that looked a bit ridiculous holding a glass of milk and a plate of chocolate-covered marshmallows.

"You're just in time," he said.

"I thought we were late."

"Technically, but nothing runs on time at the United Nations. I'm just bringing SG his bedtime snack now. If you can wait in that room for the next ten minutes, then everything will be just fine."

The aide pointed at a large conference room walled off by glass from the corridor. It was filled with people who were screaming at one another.

"Are you sure?" Harry asked.

"Oh, you mean them," the aide said. "They've

been in there so long, I'd almost forgotten about them. They're not SG's problem, but he lets them use the conference room. They've been haggling over water rights for a decade. Every so often the negotiators rotate out. This is the fresh crew. They're very animated, but after a week of this they tire. There's coffee in the corner and juice in the fridge. I'll be back in a moment."

We slipped into the room and sat as far from the arguing horde as we could. Haddy McClay resumed her nap. Harry drank a cup of coffee and then turned the Styrofoam cup into a miniature sculpture with a plastic spoon. I watched the dozen or so men and women clustered over a map. At some point, the entire group departed the room. I took the opportunity to examine the matter over which they were arguing. I was already familiar with the dispute, since it had been covered in a feature article in *The New York Times* some months earlier.

As the aide to the secretary general had suggested, these two nations had wrangled over this issue for nearly a decade, and the dispute had produced more than a few fistfights as well as several marriages. The dispute was not really about water at all but about drilling and fishing in a river that ran between the two countries. One of the more colorful aspects of the article (and the reason I think the *Times* ran the story in the first place) was the map itself. As the wrangling had progressed, the map became littered with small plastic pieces that represented various aspects of the dispute. There were tiny drilling platforms and fishing boats peppered all about an enlarged map of the river. These pieces had been in movement over the years as the terms of future propositions were presented and, inevitably, rejected by the delegates. Although I frequently find journalists to be sloppy with their facts (too eager, perhaps, to escape the wrath of a deadline-focused editor and not concerned enough with the eternal posterity of truth), as I hovered over the map I found the writer to be quite accurate in his description. The little pieces were there jostling for position: red for one country, green for the other. There were even deep tracks in the map where a piece had been moved back and forth several times along the same path. The whole idea of these negotiations struck me as ridiculous, because neither country had ever had very much luck feeding its citizens and yet here their pampered delegates were, arguing themselves hysterical over game pieces that in most cases represented only theoretical rights. The stress of recent days had accumulated to dangerous levels within me, and now, looking down on this absurd game board that represented millions of lives, I felt like that god/giant that Voltaire described in one of his more subversive writings on the human condition. I had read the passage only once before Imogen plucked it away and returned it to the library, but I vividly remember the concept of a giant coming to earth and making a mockery of various human conventions of church, state and tradition. He was a massive, universal figure. The kind of creature whose very existence makes man look very small indeed and reminds him of how large and indifferent is the cosmos that surrounds him. The giant could gulp down Lake Geneva or straighten Italy's boot.

Harry's head was in his hands. Haddy McClay was snoring. The delegates were nowhere about. I began to move their pieces around with my snout. I was that giant fiddling with absurd human conventions. To one side, I gave all the drilling platforms. To the other, all the fisheries. Let there be commerce between them. Let them trade each for each. A simple solution heedless of the true marketplace perhaps, but a solution nonetheless for these technocrats who could come up with no solution while their people went hungry. If there were Alpha-Bits present, I would have laid out more-complex instructions or perhaps drafted an entire treaty. But this would have to do. I suspected that my tinkering would only cause more arguments and accusations of dirty tricks in the matter of the little plastic pieces, but Yours Truly could not be bothered. I had taken a mental holiday—the whole exercise was a bit like the roll with the liverwurst.

I had just hopped down when the aide to the secretary general returned.

"He's ready for the dog," he said. "I'll take him. You two can stay here. It'll only be five minutes."

The aide led me down the hallway and into the anteroom of what looked to be a private apartment. There we met Flowers, the deceased Puppet's companion. Puppet's death had only served to make the already paranoid Flowers even more acutely so. *Paranoid*, the word that had been used by Leopold to describe the secretary general's dog, was not strictly speaking correct. Flowers was a hypochondriacal compulsive, a nerve basket in grave fear of doing anything not habitual. The condition was so serious that Flowers ignored me completely, not even attempting the customary glandular hindquarter sniff or the off-to-the-side non-threatening glance. I was grateful for the absence of the hindquarter sniff but offended by Flowers's utter disregard of my presence. After observing her for a moment, I realized that this wasn't rudeness but that she, like so many with her condition, was trapped within a mental prison of fear. For every two steps forward, Flowers would scratch the floor three times, as if not to do so would cause her sudden death. If she turned her head to the right, then the next move would have to be a sharp turn to the left. She seemed spastic, and all of her movements, except her tail, were strictly controlled.

"Flowers, you stay here," the aide said as he pulled me past the other dog and we passed down another short corridor. "You've already gone in."

The walls of the corridor were white and lined with photographs of the secretary general meeting various people, including the pope and someone dressed as a Hershey bar. The career diplomat wore the same practiced smile in each picture: a sensitively designed expression of empathy that could be interpreted as either pain or joy.

The aide pushed open the door to the library.

The man himself sat at the other end of the long, book-lined room in a plush green chair that swiveled with a squeak because it was old or needed oil.

"Mr. Secretary," the aide said. "Here's Puppet."

The secretary general looked up and delivered his practiced smile to no one in particular. There was an enormous stack of documents on his lap and another one on the floor beside his chair. An empty glass and plate sat beside the stack of papers, and at the corner of the secretary general's mouth were two dark smudges from the chocolate marshmallows.

"You can leave the dog," the secretary general said. "And go home. It's late."

"But Mr. Secretary," the aide said. His voice was measured, but he reeked of nervousness. Clearly SG was going against habit.

"You shouldn't be too surprised, Bertie. They're my dogs, after all. Though you wouldn't know it because I never see them."

"Would you like Flowers?" the aide asked.

"Definitely not," the secretary general said. "Things are tough enough without me needing to be reminded of my nerves. Just watching that dog makes me worried. Check her out, by the way."

"I'll bring her to Dr. Smiley in the morning," Bertie said. "Perhaps I should bring both of them then, sir. I don't mind waiting tonight. It will be easier in the morning."

But the secretary general returned to his papers and did not answer, and Bertie was left to unhook my leash and hope for the best.

I decided that the soundest approach would be to get as close to the secretary general as possible so that he would be least likely to recognize that I was not Puppet. Bertie left the room, and without warning the secretary general launched into a monologue.

"Puppet," the secretary general sighed. "I am tired of this life. You know this. How many times have I shared my secrets with you?"

Apparently, Puppet served as confidant to the secretary general. I wondered what burdens the loyal black dog had borne for his master that led to an early grave. Cancer is a funny thing. I have sometimes wondered if it is a rebellion of the body against the excesses of the soul.

The secretary general did not wait for any gesture on my part to acknowledge just how many secrets had been shared with his dog but launched into a sweeping statement on his day and its challenges. He complained that the shock absorbers on his official car needed to be replaced.

He fretted that he had eaten too many beans at lunch and would "pay for it" the next day. He spoke ill of the Brazilian representative for a minor indiscretion but praised the Austrian emissary for his taste in clothes. The secretary general was a complex man whose scent is best compared to a ripe cheese. It was not a bad smell. It was not a good smell. He was neither sharp nor mild, but there were layers of sophistication tempered by time and experience. The experience had made him interesting, but he had paid a price to get to a place few men ever reached. Yes, he was a complex cheese just on the cusp of spoilage. His monologue confirmed it. He stretched out his long corduroy-clad legs and smoothed his forehead with his palm.

"Puppet, things are getting worse. The world had stabilized there for a while with the two superpowers, but we're past all that now. It's a brave new world that looks a lot like it did before the First World War. Alliances faltering. Competition for resources. But there are differences that make the moral picture even more troubling. Overconsumption and starvation. Millions of rich and billions of poor. A modern self-absorption that makes concerted social action unlikely. We've always been a sounding board at the United Nations, but now it seems that nobody is listening. A war is coming, I'm certain of it. But that's not what bothers me anymore, Puppet. I'm starting to think about all the victims of our compromises...of my compromises.

"Today I remembered something that I had forgotten for so many years. It happened when I was a young man. I had just passed the civil-service exam and was stationed in Cuba—the Cuba of Batista. His regime was reaching its end. Castro's forces were squeezing its legitimacy on all sides. I was representing my government at the dedication of a school in the countryside. A demonstration was organized by middle-class women protesting the policies of the Batista government. The army was called and began to use billy clubs on the crowd. Women fell. There was blood and screams. Even though I had no authority, I demanded that they stop attacking the protesters. They did. But when I returned to the embassy, my superior was furious with me. He told me that it was undiplomatic. He told me that in the future—if there was going to be a future for me as a diplomat—I was to turn my back. That is what a diplomat did."

The secretary general sighed and scratched his ear. I thought his story sounded vaguely similar to something I had read by Graham Greene.

"I've been turning my back ever since, Puppet."

He shuffled his papers.

"And now I am being asked to turn my back again. Or, more accurately, not turn toward something against which I have kept my back turned for too long. The United Nations has always tried to stay above the dirty games that nations and corporations play. We say that we maintain our credibility by taking the so-called high road. But we have been used and now it has gone too far. Diplomacy and the games of nations are big games. We measure human lives in percentages and probabilities. Cost and benefits are not about individuals but about a portion of the population pie. Fifty thousand live or die because seat belts have been required by law or not or because war has been declared or not. We never think that little man living in that little village will never see his wife again because we spent another month dawdling over lunches and cocktail parties and not resolving the dispute that will cost his life. If we thought that, I suppose, we could never see enough of the big picture to get anything done. We smile for the photographers and shake hands and things happen in the dark of night and the women scream and the children disappear or they don't.

But somehow all of this stays abstract, because we're drunk on the big picture. If we can reach such-and-such number or a certain projection, then those things that happen to those individuals might not happen."

The secretary general sighed again.

"Puppet, I can't turn away anymore. The credibility of the United Nations—whatever credibility we still have—is at stake. The nations and the corporations have been practicing their dirty games all along and I've known about it. We all have. But now they are so much more blatant and so much more destructive. I know that the knives are out because of what they are willing to do in our backyard. This uranium situation, for example, and this innocent girl."

I had been mulling over the secretary general's hard-earned observations on statecraft, but mention of uranium and an innocent girl made me snap to attention. What did the secretary general know? Was this what Ponce meant when he spoke of those at the highest levels being aware of what had gone on at the boarding-house?

"This has never happened before, Puppet. One murder. Then a second. Then a third. Three murders. Unprecedented. And all three certainly connected in some way to our institution. There has always been cloak-and-dagger work and agents at the UN, but this is so brazen. All the authority of the United Nations is being called upon to protect the guilty and chase down the innocent. I am sick of it. I am being called upon to put our credibility and decency in the balance by quashing this investigation. Yes, I'm being asked to keep my back turned while one of the big players makes off with one of the little people's rightful fortune. I'm sick to death of myself, because up until tonight I wouldn't have thought twice of letting this happen. But something's changed. We need to have a housecleaning. We need to throw the dirty parties out. We need to stop this. Of course, everyone denies knowledge of who did the killings. Honor among thieves. They're all afraid that if they stop playing by the winner-takes-all rule and start behaving honestly, their pasts will catch up with them. And they're right, of course."

The secretary general sighed again.

"What am I supposed to do, Puppet? The United Nations will suffer if I act, but if I allow it to serve as cover for this kind of outrageous criminality and intrigue it will suffer even more. Perhaps this time I won't turn my back. Then again, perhaps I will."

The secretary general seemed to have exhausted himself. He fell silent and returned to his stack of documents. A few minutes later Bertie appeared at the library door.

"Are you still here?" the secretary general asked.

"If I could take the dog, sir."

The secretary general nodded.

"I'm done," he said.

Bertie escorted me from the room. He met Harry in the conference room, where the feuding delegates had once again assembled over their maps. The debate seemed more heated than before and I suspected they had discovered my intervention. But we left before I could learn more.

"Same time tomorrow night?" Bertie asked Harry at the elevator.

"I don't think it's a problem," my owner said. "The other guy will be bringing him."

Leopold surprised us by picking me up downstairs at UN headquarters. He seemed more nervous than usual.

"It has been a difficult night without Rembrandt," Leopold said. "I am very shaky."

I did not want to leave Harry, but the secretary general's admission had emboldened me. There was more to learn at Ms. Ramsey's boardinghouse.

ACCUSATIONS ARE MADE

———

A DOG GETS TOO LITTLE SLEEP

THE LOBBY OF THE BOARD-inghouse was quiet when Leopold and I arrived. A lamp burned in the corner and the plug-in fireplace was aglow. Leopold had begun to lead me up the stairs when someone behind us cleared his throat. The press secretary snapped his head around and seemed about to jump into the air. But then he saw it was Ponce.

"Oh, it's you," Leopold said. "What do you want?"

"We need to talk," Ponce said.

"Not now. I am exhausted."

Leopold turned to go.

"Yes, now," Ponce insisted. "Or I will tell the Near Upper Pilasian government who you really work for."

Leopold's scent suddenly changed from a defiant nervousness to a genuine fear. But neither his voice nor his body betrayed this change.

"Ponce, you're a jackass. A young idiot. At best this is stuff of pulpy espionage movie— creeping up on me like this with your accusations. What does it matter who I work for?"

"It would matter to the Near Upper Pilasians, since you are traveling under your country's diplomatic protection but working for a foreign government and doing things that will be destructive to us all."

"What do you know?"

"More than a few things."

"Name one."

"You are involved just like the rest of us in the uranium matter."

"That's ridiculous. I just arrived."

"Perhaps. Although our people believe you have been in the United States longer than you say. But that isn't the point. You are a handler. We're not sure who you're handling, but you are part of this mess, and now the secretary general himself is considering getting involved and cleaning house."

"The secretary general," Leopold said. "That is extraordinary. But really, Ponce, this is stupid. Even if I was involved, what would it matter? There are a number of players in this house."

"It would matter because your operative has made serious blunders that have jeopardized us all. Someone has to be held responsible or all of us will be."

"Have you spoken to anyone else about this?"

"Only my side," Ponce said.

"Not Otis Cheng, Max de Tocqueville or Lindmar Wingman?"

"Of course not," Ponce said. "Any one of them might be your operative."

"So this crusade to clean house is crusade of one man—you—and one country?" Leopold asked. "Or perhaps it isn't even one country at all. Perhaps it is only matter of one man looking for little something extra. You are wise to be interested in real estate. It will be good to have such things set aside for your retirement. So you would like me to pay you something to stay silent?"

Ponce nodded.

"Very well," Leopold said. "I will see what can be done."

We began to climb the stairs.

"I need to know in twenty-four hours. No less than a million euros."

"It isn't ideal, but I will make arrangements," Leopold said.

When we reached our room, Leopold made a phone call.

"You must stop," he said into the phone.

"This is well beyond what I signed on for. This is simply not the way things are done. Enough is enough. People are aware of my involvement. The secretary general is going to be taking action. Hello? Do not hang up on me. Hello?"

Leopold redialed the number but no one answered. He was worried now. Very worried. But this did not stop him from changing into his pajamas and brushing his teeth. Perhaps, when one lives the stressful life of the diplomat/spy, one becomes equipped to handle even crises without disturbing routine. In a very short while, Leopold was settling into bed beneath Imogen's stars, aglow and as indecipherable as ever.

"Rembrandt, go to sleep, for God's sake," Leopold said. I must have been pacing. I curled up and for a short while I managed to fall into a light sleep. Sometime after midnight, though, I was awoken by the sound of voices down the corridor. It was Max de Tocqueville, Otis Cheng and Lindmar Wingman. They seemed to have paused on the landing and were discussing something in hushed tones that would have been out of the reach of all but my dog's ears.

"He obviously did it," Cheng said.

"I'm sure you're right," de Tocqueville said. "But he could not have done the first one."

"That's right," Wingman said. "Then it was one of us."

"Us or Ponce," Cheng said. "But who are we kidding? None of our governments would endorse such lunacy."

"The stakes are high," de Tocqueville said. "Things are not the same. The game has gotten very dirty. I heard that the secretary general is considering intervening."

"There's no question that someone is going to have to be sacrificed before all this is done," Wingman said.

"But the girl will get away from all of us," Cheng objected.

"She'll resurface and we'll all have another chance. But this cannot go any further," de Tocqueville said. "Or all of us will be finished here. And I, for one, love New York."

"So what do we do? And how can I really be sure that neither of you bumped off the last one?" Lindmar Wingman said. They continued to climb the stairs and their voices dropped out of range.

Blinko had been confident that there were four diplomat/spies involved. Leopold made five. But Leopold had been speaking to someone on the phone whom I presumed was neither Ponce, de Tocqueville, Cheng or Wingman.

And these last three were speaking about someone as well. They could have been speaking
about Leopold. *He could not have done the first one,*
de Tocqueville had said. But certainly none of
the three could suspect that Leopold was behind the killing of the poet at tea. There was a
sixth figure then.

Leopold continued to snore. I needed to
learn more. At the very least, I needed to get a
snout stamp from each of them. Fortunately,
per usual, Leopold had neglected to lock the
door. Although numerous movie dogs drive au-
tomobiles, pick locks, and the like, Yours Truly
is not paw-capable. I have never attempted to
twist a doorknob, knowing only too well how
unresponsive my rigid limbs and floppy paws
are. However, this door was different. Instead of
a knob, Ms. Ramsey had opted for the homier
and snout-friendly latch lever. In a moment, I
was out in the hallway and proceeding with
haste toward the men.

They had just arrived at the next floor when I
reached them.

"Hi, doggy," Lindmar Wingman said, and
reached down for a pat. One sniff and I knew
that Wingman was not the recyclables lady's
killer. Otis Cheng was equally friendly and

equally not the killer. Only de Tocqueville remained, but he threatened to disappear.

"Good night. I trust we're on the same page,"
de Tocqueville said as he opened his door. But
not before I was able to deliver a solid snout
stamp to his right calf and get a good sample.

"Get away," de Tocqueville snarled. "Now I'll
have to wash these."

De Tocqueville, though terminally snobbish
and Labrador-hostile, had not killed the recyclables lady either. The three men disappeared
into their rooms and I was left standing in the
empty hallway. There was no doubt now. I could
not be certain who had killed the young man under the parachute or the oral poet, but I did
know that neither Leopold, Ponce or these
three had killed the recyclables lady. The killer
was someone else.

I had begun to saunter back to our room
when another door opened and things became
decidedly worse.

MILO STOOD BEHIND ME. This was unwelcome. Particularly since he still wore his chef's apron. "Friends with Milo now?" asked the zealous chef with exotic tastes as he knelt down beside me. But I was already moving toward the stairs. Unfortunately, despite being on the heavy side, Milo was remarkably quick. He put me in a headlock. I struggled. I tried to bark, but he was pressing very hard on my throat and I could make no sound. Then he pulled me into his room and closed the door. He held me in place with one arm, and with the other he began searching for something on his desk. The lamp caught something shiny: the point of a needle. My trypanophobia was drowned out by terror of Milo and his culinary designs. I needed to stay conscious. I needed to fight. But he was so much stronger, and a moment later I felt a sharp pain in my hindquarter as the needle punctured the skin and its contents were injected into my body. The mystery was over for me now. The search for Imogen done. Harry would face the loss of another creature he loved and I would join the ranks of "the disappeared." The light seemed to brighten, then fade. There was a trickling sound in my ears. But as my eyes became unfocused and I slipped into darkness, I gained one last concrete revelation through my nose: Milo had killed the recyclables lady. He was the sixth man. Then all went black.

"Rembrandt, you lazy dog."

Once again, Leopold's voice fell down toward me like ash down a high chimney. He was somewhere far above me.

"A lazy and fat dog," he continued. "There are countries where lying around like that would get you a one-way ticket to the dinner table."

I felt a nudge in my ribs (I still had ribs) and sun—late-afternoon sun—stung my eyes. This was good news. Tremendous news. My spirit wanted to race around the room and knock over all the furniture. I was alive. My body was less responsive.

"Come on, Rembrandt," Leopold said. "It is time to get up now. You have been asleep all day. Here, Ms. Ramsey has prepared you special dish, and I have added your medicine."

A large bowl of food was placed beneath my snout. I was lying sprawled across the floor of our room and apparently had been lying there for some time. I managed to open my eyes and saw that, indeed, it was late afternoon. The sun was already bathing the façade of the building opposite in golden yellow light.

"Eat, eat," Leopold said. "Your incapacity has left me incapacitated, my friend. I have barely ventured out all day. I missed several lectures because of you, but we won't tell the ministry, will we?"

Whatever drug Milo had pumped into my system wore off quickly, and I ate the food Leopold presented with gusto. I assumed it must be the next day. Leopold sat at his desk, typing on his laptop.

"Remember, I must drop you at secretary general's tonight," Leopold said. I lay on my back and stared straight up. The message of the ceiling still eluded me. I began to search for letters and assemble words from the letters I could find. I realized I must still be groggy when I formed the sentence: *I AM IMOGEN.* But the sound of Leopold's fingers on the laptop keyboard soon drove this less urgent puzzle from my mind. After all, I knew that Milo had killed the recyclables lady. I also had reason to believe that Milo had been the poet's shooter. And if Milo had killed both witnesses to the first murder, then he had probably killed the young man under the parachute as well.

I needed to relay this information to Harry and through Harry to Detective Davis. Certainly if the police arrested Milo, they would find evidence that would connect him to the crime. And if the secretary general was no longer going to tolerate international espionage in his house, nothing would stand in the way of prosecuting the guilty and clearing my innocent mistress. Perhaps this was too simplistic, but it was a start.

Leopold looked at his watch, muttered and hurried off to shower down the hall. Fortunately, he kept his computer open and online. I climbed up onto the chair and got to work. This time I moved faster through the virtual environment (I bypassed several book offers, including a strange one that combined the collected works of Kafka with the memoir of a celebrity chef). I composed a message to Harry that read:

Investigate Milo, resident at Ms. Ramsey's boardinghouse and cook at United Nations. He is responsible for recent killings. Pass on to Detective Davis.

—Holmes

I used the name Holmes to remind Harry of the spirit detective who had guided him through our last misadventure with strategic use of Alpha-Bits cereal.

Just as I pressed SEND, I became aware of a weight around my neck. The screen briefly turned black and I saw my reflection. My therapy-dog ribbon was now attached to a new collar. A collar is never completely comfortable, but this collar was quite heavy and it was uniformly thick, a bit like a black garden hose with a leash clip at my nape. Who had placed this new collar on, and why? I shook and noticed that the underside of the collar seemed to have small protrusions that scraped against my skin, and one segment was slightly warm, as if it was generating heat. Then there was a smell. It was quite distinct and familiar, but at first I couldn't place it. I heard Leopold coming down the hall. What was that smell? Somehow this was important, I thought. Somehow this was something I needed to convey to Harry.

Leopold stopped in the hallway. He had dropped something. I heard him strain to pick it up. He fumbled it. He strained again. Then I recognized the smell. It was similar to the smell of gunpowder—a gritty, salty smell (I had smelled gunpowder when Harry discharged

Grandfather Oswald's .45). It was an explosive
of some kind.

Leopold picked up the object and kept moving. And just as he reached our door, everything
came together and I understood. Out of my dark
and woozy memory I felt the collar being secured
around my neck and heard Milo's accompany-
ing mumbles: *ten o'clock...damned secretary general...the only way...* Milo wanted to use me
to blow up the secretary general of the United
Nations. As impaired as my memory of the previous night was and as outlandish as this conclusion
seemed, I was certain that it was correct. The
secretary general was threatening to take action
that would likely end in Milo's arrest. Milo was
taking the opportunity to frame Leopold, another diplomat/spy (why else would he have
passed up the chance to roast Yours Truly?). The
two protrusions were part of some kind of triggering device, and tonight, at or about ten p.m.,
the secretary general and I would be blown to
pieces together with his milk, chocolate-covered
marshmallows and stacks of documents. I needed
to get this second message to Harry, but already
the door handle was turning. I closed my e-mail
and hopped back down onto the floor.

Quite aware of the heaviness around my
neck.

WE REACHED THE UNITED Nations just before eight o'clock. Despite having an acid bath of nervousness and terror sloshing about my belly, I was also quite in need of a Number 1 and 2. My mind was racing. If Harry had chanced to read his e-mail, the authorities might already be racing into action against Milo. But that was unlikely. Even though it was Saturday, he was planning to spend the day at work on his art commission and away from his computer. And as far as he was concerned, I was in Leopold's care for nearly another week. The other night had been an exception because of my medical condition. Now that this condition was stabilized, I was once again on my own.

Fortunately, though Leopold had not seemed to notice my new collar, he did sense that a visit to the Dag Hammarskjöld World Pet Unity Area was in order. We slipped through the gate.

Night had fallen. Only a few dogs wandered about in the dark while their owners huddled in the circles of lamplight near the entrance. Tonight, the standout canine was an exquisitely refined yet spirited dachshund named Dulcie. Dulcie stayed near her owner and from time to time added a welcome English accent to the culture of the dog run.

Leopold sat down on a bench and sucked on a lozenge.

Clearly whatever I was carrying around my neck could not be so sensitive that it would simply explode. There must be some triggering device. And it could not be a timer, since my visit to the secretary general could be delayed again as it had been the night before. No, Milo would need to be near enough to know that I was at the target.

I shuffled among the wood chips on the opposite side of the dog run and delivered my Numbers. Somehow between now and then, I needed to get this collar off my neck. Then I saw him, beckoning to me from across the yard: Mahatma Gandhi. The great Indian statesman stood frozen in advancing stride, his loincloth miraculously held aloft while his two arms were outstretched at waist level in a gesture of welcome and peace. The index finger of his right hand was independent of the rest. It was longer and gleamed in the lamplight because it had been burnished by people rubbing it over the years. It was this index finger that offered Yours Truly the hope of salvation.

I hurried to the base of the statue. Leopold was distracted by an Alsatian, which was standing on the bench and attempting to steal a second lozenge that the press secretary was trying to deposit on his tongue. I jumped at the index finger but missed and fell back down on my paws. Then I jumped again, and this time the finger slid between the collar and my neck, just as I had hoped. For a moment I thought I might accidentally hang myself, but then the collar began to stretch and my neck and head slid backward out of it. I fell back to the ground for a second time, but this time the bomb collar was left dangling from Gandhi's finger.

Leopold had driven off the Alsatian and was ready to leave.

"Come on, boy. I want to be especially early for secretary general," Leopold said, stressing for any interested diplomatic ears the fact of his high-level meeting. When we reached the sidewalk he muttered what I thought must be an expletive in his native tongue.

"Where on earth is your collar?" he asked, but

quickly dealt with the problem by fashioning a temporary collar from a plastic bag he found on the sidewalk and hooking my leash to it.

The guards at the entrance to the General Assembly waved us through. They were no longer interested in determining whether the press secretary's dog was a bomb. Had I not disposed of the device myself, this would have been the wrong night for them to come to this conclusion.

Bertie, the secretary general's aide, met us at the elevator as he had the night before. But this time the conference room Bertie took us to was entirely empty of arguing delegates. Leopold seemed to be aware of the long-running dispute over fisheries and oil rights and asked Bertie where they were.

"Haven't you heard?" Bertie asked. "They've settled their dispute. Some visionary rejiggered the board while no one was looking, and the resulting terrain was pleasing to all involved. The formal settlement will be signed within days. It is a great victory for the United Nations. If you can just wait here, I will bring the secretary general his bedtime snack and then the dog can visit. He did a beautiful job last night. The secretary general was much soothed."

At fifteen minutes to ten, Bertie appeared

and said it was time. He led me down the corridor toward the secretary general's quarters. Several of the conference rooms that lined the hall had people milling about in them, hunched over papers, listening to speakers, and just outside the room closest to the secretary general's quarters, sitting in a comfortable chair, I saw Milo. He was dressed in a tailored suit and equipped with an attaché and a sheaf of documents that he seemed to be poring over with great intensity. Anyone would have mistaken him for a delegate gathering his thoughts and studying his notes before making a case in one of the busy conference rooms, and they would have missed that his right hand was plunged into a pocket, waiting expectantly for the right moment to push a button.

Bertie and I passed in front of Milo, but the aide stood between us and blocked Milo's view of my neck as we entered the secretary general's quarters. Milo did not notice that the collar had been removed.

The secretary general was in no mood for a monologue on the challenges of his work, and Bertie never left us alone. I received a pat on the head and a quick ear rub and was quickly escorted out of the room. The entire exchange took less than a minute. We emerged to find

Milo looking visibly shaken. Bertie led me down the corridor toward Leopold, and Milo followed.

"Thanks," Bertie said. "SG wasn't into him tonight. One more night is all we need and then we'll break it to him about Puppet. Can you do it?"

Leopold nodded and smiled, but his smile vanished when Milo stepped into the room after Bertie bade the press secretary good night.

"What do you think you are doing?" Leopold asked. "Are you mad, you Near Lower Pilasian ass? We can't be seen together like this. That day in the kitchen was bad enough."

Milo shut the door behind him and, as Leopold attempted to stand, shoved the older man back into his seat.

"You sit," Milo said. "And you listen."

Milo was not only imperative in his tone, the Slavic rockiness of his English had disappeared and he spoke like an Oxford don, as did Leopold now.

"This is unacceptable," Leopold said. "I am your handler. Not the other way around. How dare you push me down like that? Your superiors will be hearing about this."

"You killed the young man," Milo said. "And you had me cover your tracks because you knew that it would only be a matter of time before those two old fogies revealed that you had passed them in the hallway before you were ever supposed to arrive. They weren't just witnesses to the girl leaving the room. They were witnesses to you leaving that room earlier in the day. And you could never pay them enough to keep them quiet. All of that was fair enough."

"Just part of the game," Leopold said.

"Part of the game," Milo echoed. "But you were going to sell Near Lower Pilasia out, you Near Upper Pilasian bastard. You were using us."

"Indeed, I still am," Leopold said. "In a short while the police will be arriving to arrest you for the murder of Abraham Pollop and the poor old lady who liked her recyclables. They will also be arresting you for the murder of the young man. And possibly even the attempted murder of the secretary general, which would have implicated me had Rembrandt not been so clever to remove your primitive bomb collar. Of course, had he not done so, I would have. Did you really think I wouldn't have noticed? Why would you try to kill the secretary general? This sort of stuff is madness. You and your people can't take our game to this level. It ruins it for everyone."

Milo looked stunned.

"I don't believe you," he said. "The police

aren't coming. Why would you call them? I would only turn you in. Oh no, we're going to leave here and we will figure out a way to get the girl into our good graces. You will get us our uranium and then both our countries will have a fine bargaining chip to use with the great powers. King Bougainvillea's fifteenth-century vision of harmony between our two lands will finally be realized."

"You're right," Leopold said. "Of course you're right. Why would I call the police?"

Leopold took out his lozenges and put one in his mouth.

"Would you like one?"

Milo nodded. Leopold gave him a lozenge—this one was orange, not yellow, like the others.

Milo put it in his mouth.

"I'd like to be friends," Leopold said. "We have been too long at war, and this recent alliance must not fail."

But his dog knew that the press secretary was lying, and a moment later Milo knew as well. There was a commotion in the hall. Police officers led by Detective Davis charged toward the conference room. Finding the door locked, two of the policemen shattered the glass and stepped through the hole. Their guns were drawn and pointed at Milo. But the man only stared at them. Then, before anyone could re-act, he fell dead at their feet.

"Are you alright?" Detective Davis asked Leopold.

"It wasn't ideal," Leopold said.

"Gandhi lost half his arm," Detective Davis said. "The man was a maniac."

"He put something in his mouth," Leopold said. "I think he might have poisoned himself."

A HALF HOUR LATER, Harry and I were walking away from the United Nations and toward the Vespa. My owner was taking me home. Leopold had decided quite suddenly that he no longer needed a therapy dog. Milo's revelations prior to his death were disturbing. Leopold, the real murderer of the young man, was free. I would not make a good diplomat, because my concept of right and wrong is not so shaded or ambiguous. This could not stand, but I would need to have access to the computer or some other message medium to get this point across to my owner, and then what... It was hard to imagine how someone like Leopold— whom I now knew was as crafty and wicked as they come—would not somehow escape justice.

Harry took the Velcro license plate out of the pocket of his Driza-Bone rain gear (a light drizzle had begun to fall) and reattached it to our

vehicle. He had just straddled the bike and begun rolling it backward onto the street when I
heard a whistle. My mistress had rejected the
use of silly dog names in favor of a set of distinct
whistles. There was the whistle that meant
"stop." The whistle that meant "come." The
whistle that meant "sit." There was even the
whistle that prompted me to roll over.

Now, beneath the gentle sound of rain and
the distant rush of traffic up First Avenue, I
heard the whistle that meant "come." This time
I saw my mistress before I could smell her. She
was standing some fifty yards away, next to a
taxicab double-parked at the First Avenue entranceway to the FDR. She was dressed in a long
black cloak and her face was concealed under a
hood, but there was no mistake. She whistled
"come" a second time.

And I did.

"Randolph," Harry shouted. But I was running as fast as I could toward my mistress. I
sprinted across the drive and then up onto the
sidewalk opposite and down the hill. Harry was
somewhere far behind me. And then I reached
her. I had imagined this moment so many times,
but the proximity to my mistress overwhelmed
any dream.

"Good boy," Imogen said, and knelt down beside me. She put a warm hand to my cheek. Such a warm hand. And in the sliver of lamplight and the luminescence of the falling rain, her eyes flashed and looked with such deep love and kindness into my own eyes. And her scent. It was Imogen: authentic and lovely, but so heavy with desperation and loneliness. She could not conceive of a way out. That is what her scent told me, and it made me instantly very sad.

"Now hold this and don't let it go except for him," she instructed me, and thrust an envelope into my mouth. Then I noticed that she was looking up at something behind me, and I realized that Harry was approaching and that my mistress was fighting the urge to stay. She almost lost, but instead she put her other hand on my cheek, clasped my head firmly and repeated her words.

"Good boy."

Then she got into the cab and it sped away. Harry was indeed approaching, but not on foot. The Vespa pulled up just as Imogen's taxi turned onto the FDR heading south. I knew he had seen her.

"Give me that," Harry said, snatching the letter from my mouth. "Get on."

I jumped onto the back of the Vespa. Harry snapped up the sides of my box and soon we were on the FDR, searching for her taxi. The rain battered our faces, and buckets of water sprayed over us from passing cars. Then, just when it seemed that we would never catch her, Harry spotted her taxi. He kept on its tail even though a fog began to develop as we reached the southern tip of Manhattan Island. Then the taxi stopped, and she jumped out and began running toward the Staten Island Ferry. A boat was getting ready to depart and Imogen raced toward the ground-level loading ramp. We abandoned the Vespa and gave chase. As the deckhands began to lower the gates, Imogen weaved among the stragglers and disappeared into the crowd. Harry and I got on board a moment before the ferry jerked free of the dock and began to throb its way out into the channel and the frigid early-spring waters of the harbor.

"What do you think you're doing?" a deckhand cried out at our backs, but we had already run inside and were tracking her down the side of the boat, past drowsing Staten Islanders heading home. Imogen pushed through the far doors onto the forward deck, and a few seconds later we did as well.

The rain was falling heavily now. The fog was thick but was being driven about by a building wind. Only a few dozen feet of the water ahead of the ferry was visible. It roiled like tar, and occasionally the ferry would strike a wave the wrong way and a sheet of foam would spray up onto the deck. And all the while the giant boat throbbed forward on the strength of its massive engines, crashing through the fog and the rain because it had somewhere to get to.

There was no one on the forward deck except for Imogen. She had climbed over the protective rail that separated the passenger deck from the semicircular iron wedge that extended over the water and the frothing bow.

Harry and I raced to join her, but then her eyes met Harry's and we stopped and she took a step back.

"Everything's in the letter," Imogen said. "And everything's also in the stars."

Then, as if she had been practicing the maneuver from infancy, she turned her back toward us, gave herself a short running start and dove off the boat and into the water.

Without any hesitation, Harry jumped the rail and threw himself into the water after her. I followed. Hitting the water was like falling into a mound of hard-packed snow, and despite my ample water-dog coat, the freezing liquid immediately began to suck life from me. Before I even made it to the churning surface, my limbs had grown heavy and seemed almost incapable of keeping me afloat. My head broke into the air but was just as suddenly pushed back under by a heavy wave. When I broke to the surface again, I saw Harry struggling in the water and realized that the back of the ferry had passed us, its lights being dimmed to black by the fog. Then the ferry and the throbbing of its motors were gone and we were left with the driving rain, the fog and the waves. Harry kept shouting out Imogen's name, but there was no response. Water-polo player though he was, I could tell that my owner was losing strength. We were both losing strength. We treaded water for several minutes, and then I knew he was slipping. His head dipped beneath the water for a moment, so I swam under his arm to buoy him up. But he was heavy, and besides the waves and the sound of the rain, everything else was black and silent.

THE CALLER WHO RE-
ported a man and a dog overboard
on the Staten Island Ferry remained
unidentified. But he was prompt. In fact, he was
so prompt that, against the odds, the New York
City Police Department Harbor Rescue Unit
managed to pluck the two out of the water.

They did so just as Harry and I began to sink,
rigid and limb-frozen, into the deep. At first I
thought the helicopter's spotlight was a cold-
induced hallucination, a trick of the eye before
the final curtain. Then someone was beside us
in the water, and Harry was lifted up into the air
to the helicopter that beat heavily just above
the fog. Soon I was being hoisted skyward as
well. I don't remember much of what happened
next. Harry managed to tell them about Imogen
being in the water, but he was in worse shape
than me, and the rescuers worked hard to raise
his core body temperature with warm liquids,

blankets and vigorous rubbing. I was left to shiver my own way back to normalcy on the floor of the helicopter.

The helicopter trolled back and forth over the waters, panning the satin swells with its powerful spot and coordinating the search with two boats below. The diver who had rescued us seemed ready to throw himself back in the water at any sign of life, but there was no sign of life. At one point, he gave me a pat and pinched my generous belly.

"You're a living flotation device, aren't you, buddy," he said. "Without you, your owner would have been a goner."

He smelled strongly of rubber from the gaskets of his dry suit, the sealed outfit that protected him from the frigid waters. It was a powerful smell and familiar, but in my still-diminished state I could not place it.

After twenty minutes, the helicopter turned to home. Harry, who was regaining his strength and his senses, began to get agitated, but the crew told him that the boats were still searching.

"Imogen," Harry moaned. "Imogen."

And then my owner put his head into his hands and cried.

Two hours later we were back at our 90th

Street abode. Harry had improved so much after the cold-water shock that a hospital stay was deemed unnecessary. Detective Davis had met the helicopter at the ER, and after a great deal of debate and gentle coercion had convinced Harry that going to his own home to wait for any news was the best idea. They hadn't rescued anyone else from the water and it was very unlikely that they would. Imogen was gone—at least, gone beyond the reach of the New York Police Department Harbor Rescue Unit.

Detective Davis understood that he needed to focus Harry's mind on the concrete. How had Imogen looked as she jumped? What had Imogen said? What was in the letter? As battered and as pained by the emotional tumult of the evening as my owner was, Detective Davis needed him to focus, and so sitting in our apartment, Harry summoned great reserves of strength and did just that.

Together, detective and artist pored over the letter, or what was left of the letter. There wasn't much. But what had survived changed everything.

> *Harry, I don't know what you know. What you don't know. I'm not my mother. I'm not a murderer. I didn't kill Richard. Maranovsky*

did. He drugged him. He drugged me. He
thought

All the rest was ink stains and meaningless fragments, with the exception of this compelling snippet near the end:

At the risk of sounding melodramatic—you
can find me in the stars.

Detective Davis began to smile.

The clock on the microwave said that it was three in the morning. The apartment was silent. Haddy McClay was asleep in the bedroom, having been entertained by a babysitter all day and evening while my owner worked on his mosaic. Harry shook his head. "Why are you smiling?"

"This confirms what we already suspected."

"What do you mean?"

"I've been earning my salary, Harry," Detective Davis said. "The young man beneath the parachute had a name."

"Yeah, I know, Richard," Harry said with bitterness.

"Richard Camier," Detective Davis said.

"Imogen's boyfriend."

"Hardly. Richard Camier was the son of Madame Camier. Madame Camier was the nanny who raised Imogen. Richard and Imogen were like brother and sister. Madame Camier lives in France. Or, rather, lived in France. She seems to have disappeared."

"What?"

"We believe Richard was trying to protect Imogen when he was killed."

"And you believe Imogen's letter—that she didn't kill him?"

"We do," Detective Davis said. "You know we found equal amounts of chloral hydrate in both drinks."

"You mean the knockout drug?"

Detective Davis nodded.

"When we found traces in both glasses, things began to make less sense to me. Why would Imogen knock herself out? And if she had planned the killing, why would she have run away, leaving all the evidence? So we hit the streets and the bars of the East Village. There were several descriptions of a woman who matched Imogen, disoriented and lapsing in and out of consciousness. Some good samaritan even called the police, but by the time they arrived she had disappeared."

"But why was Richard wearing a parachute?"

"He was a BASE jumper. In fact, he was quite well known around Europe for jumping from dangerous heights in heart-print boxers. He had bought the parachute that day. I guess he was just trying it all on together."

"So you should grab Leopold."

"Mr. Maranovsky is under surveillance. He's at the boardinghouse tonight and we've got two cops on him," Detective Davis said.

"How did you know before the letter?"

"I didn't," Detective Davis said. "But I never trusted that guy and I made sure my bases were covered. I've just texted my guys to bring him in."

Detective Davis's phone rang.

"I see," he said. His voice was suddenly subdued. "I'll be right there."

Detective Davis hung up the phone.

"What's wrong?" Harry asked.

"The murderer has murdered himself. Leopold Maranovsky just swallowed an orange lozenge and croaked."

A FEW DAYS LATER, HARRY took me to work at WAHA. After hearing about the harbor swim, Iberia had promptly removed Haddy McClay from our midst. Jackson had offered to give Harry a week off without penalty in light of recent traumatic circumstances and the great progress my owner had already made on the mosaic, but Harry was determined to keep working. What he had accomplished in his first week on the job was impressive. A female eye dominated the piece—an enlarged version from the still-unfinished portrait of Imogen in our living-room corner.

We passed through the lobby and into his workshop in the back.

"There will be stars," Harry muttered, stepping over enlarged photos of the stars on the ceiling that he had taped to the floor as a kind of model.

We had copies of the same photographs at home and I had lingered over them for a long time over the last few days, trying to puzzle things out, but to no avail.

Now Harry stopped above these photos. As he stared, a change came over him.

"I know where I've seen these before," he said. "She showed me a photograph of a night sky. It was on Curaçao."

My owner was elated.

"My God, that's where she's going."

Then he was sad again. Detective Davis had already suggested that Imogen might still be alive and on the run, but the improbability of her survival in the water that night baffled them both.

"But how? How could she have gotten out of the water? It almost killed me and I'm a swimmer."

Then his dog filled in the blank with a scent memory. I remembered the strong and distinctive rubber smell of the rescuer's drysuit gasket. I had smelled it beneath all of Imogen's other smells when she stooped to put her hand on my jowl. My mistress had been wearing a drysuit. She had expected us to follow her onto the ferry. She had wanted us (and perhaps others) to see her plunge into the harbor. It is not lack of swimming skill that kills most cold-water drowning victims, it's hypothermia.

I needed to communicate with Harry and ready us for the next step. As soon as I was able, I would e-mail this revelation to my owner. Perhaps I would even be so bold as to purchase tickets to the Caribbean and buy appropriate travel guides and other reading material for the journey (Graham Greene's *Our Man in Havana* or Hemingway from his Cuba and Key West periods). Complimentary tote bags might even be necessary.

Harry and I would soon be leaving Manhattan and traveling south.

About the Author

J. F. Englert, a writer of fiction and nonfiction for both book and screen, lives in Manhattan with his wife, P. Englert; daughter, C. Englert; and dog, R. Englert.

DON'T MISS

J. F. ENGLERT'S

other charming
Bull Moose Dog Run Mystery,
A DOG ABOUT TOWN

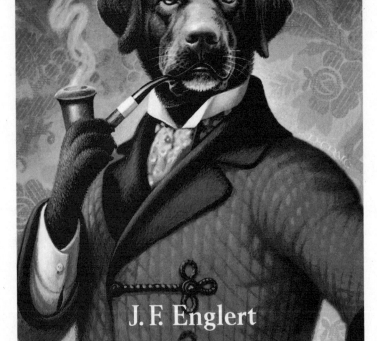

A **DOG**
ABOUT TOWN

MEET RANDOLPH.
A DOG LIKE ANY OTHER DOG—
BUT WITH A NOSE FOR MURDER...

J. F. Englert

LYELL OVERTON MINSKOFF-Hardy, literary light and cultural personage, perished a few days before Christmas beneath a stainless steel toilet on the Upper West Side of Manhattan. With his fly open. Harry, my owner, prone to accept all explanations involving the paranormal, believed the death had a supernatural flourish. Almost from the start I thought Harry quite mistaken. Overton's death had nothing to do with ghosts, spirits or the occult and everything to do with science, human nastiness and greed.

I first learned of Overton's death upon the return of my owner to our humble walk-up apartment. I had been rereading Robert Pinsky's excellent translation *The Inferno of Dante*, an artifact from Imogen's time in our lives, when I heard the familiar clump-clump on the stairs and the jangle and click of locks being opened—notably more urgent than usual. I did not have time to close the book or even move too far away from it. I imagined my owner's imminent surprise. The book would be the first thing he would notice, no doubt. The reading light that had been off when he departed would be the second.

I was wrong. Harry was in such a distracted state that he noticed nothing out of the ordinary. Rain dripped from his Driza-Bone jacket and pooled on the kitchen floor. My owner is a broad-shouldered, strapping fellow, standing almost six foot three, and you would never guess that his regular regimen of physical fitness had long been derailed by frequent retreats to the La-Z-Boy recliner with buckets of fried chicken and takeout Chinese.

"A great man is dead tonight, Randolph," he pronounced.

I could think of several great men who were dead that night. Dante Alighieri, Florentine poet, first among them; Sir Winston Churchill, a close second, but I did not so much as growl a qualifier.

"A famous man," Harry emphasized.

He crammed what looked like a Maryland crab cake into our deeply troubled refrigerator, the interior of which had remained a shadow-land of petrified broccoli and pizza since the bulb burned out months before.

"Lyell Overton Minskoff-Hardy." Harry spoke the dead man's name with a kind of reverence.

It is a point of pride that I remain well acquainted with the biographies of luminaries past and present. I do this chiefly through newspapers and magazines. There is much truth to be gleaned from the gossip columns. Rich treasures of it. I had already assembled a full mental file of notes on the man Harry named and I drew from it now.

Lyell Overton Minskoff-Hardy was two men really. There was the patrician figure, Lyell Overton, whose name evoked English estates and private libraries where wolfhounds stretch before the sputtering hearth and leather-bound volumes lie open awaiting the return of some tousle-haired savant from Oxford. An appropriate image, I think, for he was tall and graceful in that insouciant, underclassman way—a perennial student and college man, his torso forever sheathed in the invisible, but palpable, entitlement of the varsity letter sweater.

The Minskoff-Hardy contribution was gritty, ethnic and glamorous in a hard-won sort of way. It was Broadway via Ellis Island and the Five Points—vintage New York. Minskoff-Hardy could be urbane and world-wise, but also, as are so many native New Yorkers, hopelessly parochial, predisposed to view with suspicion anything not found or imported to their narrow island. Minskoff-Hardy was brash and full of colic, demanding and impatient. But more than anything, Minskoff-Hardy was ambitious and his ambition had wounded, scarred and made an army of permanent enemies along the way.

Both men inhabiting the hyphenated identity died that night with their flys open, their eyelids slightly ajar and their last bon mot left unspoken.

These matters of temper and temperament are now locked in his dead heart, but his death—and this moment with Harry in our cramped but cozy Upper West Side abode— would bring out that inner being in Yours Truly concerned with the murderous significance of details and the disastrous consequences that stem from small gestures. All such questions of the heart and the character are my concern because the detective is the last true humanist, standing at that lonely intersection where observation and reason meet emotion and intuition revealing the secrets that measure our fragile, inconstant, but extraordinary beings. How ironic, then, that I am not even human.

Yes, that is correct. I am *not* human.

You see, I am a dog—not a scoundrel, a cad, a rascal—no, not a dog in that sense, but an actual dog, *Canis familiaris*. One of the most familiar and lovable (I only repeat the general perception): a Labrador retriever. A Labrador retriever is defined by Merriam-Webster as "any of a breed of compact, strongly built retrievers largely developed in England from stock originating in Newfoundland and having a short dense black, yellow, or chocolate coat...called also *Lab, Labrador*." Faithful to that definition, I am indeed compact and strongly built (though bulging at the midsection from my owner's generous feedings) and black but for a wisp of premature white on my chin that serves to impart a sort of sage-like impression.

I am also sentient. I can think. I can remember. I can understand that as the teller of this tale I had best get most of this explanatory material over with at the beginning. Like the reader, I compare the past and the present. I strategize and calculate. This is not a possibility entertained by the Merriam-Webster definition. The competent editors of that publication are not to blame for the oversight. Most dogs certainly do not behave in ways that would suggest sentience (though I might also add that most humans do not either as is apparent from the hastiest of glances at the newspapers). Moreover, there is at present no way to penetrate my species' muteness. Science is unable to plumb the depths of our cerebral cortices and discern the life of our minds.

Even so, among my brothers and sisters, I am unique. Where other dogs babble, I sing. Where they follow tangents like they are darting from scent to scent, my thoughts are precision-guided. If you could speak our language, you would understand. It is a challenge to extract a single relevant word from one of my brethren let alone a competent sentence and forget reasonable analysis altogether. It's all myth, rumor and constant distraction with them. What makes my kind endearing to humans makes them difficult for me to endure. It is a mystery why I am different. Genetic mutation, something in the water my mother drank during her pregnancy, my rearing, who knows? I came to consciousness, I suspect, in much the same way a human child does: sticky scraps of reality gradually collaged into a bigger picture within which an identity was assumed.

"Randolph, tonight was unbelievable," Harry said finally. "It's going to be all over the papers tomorrow."

He forced the refrigerator closed with a grunt. I had the momentary sense that something might try to escape.

"One minute Overton was at the table telling stories: a taxi ride with Truman Capote; strip poker with Kerouac; arm wrestling with Fidel Castro..."

Harry reached behind the toaster for his emergency cigarettes. He shook one free from the pack, lit it and put the rest into his pocket.

"Halfway through dinner, Overton gets up, walks down the hall, then there's a sort of yelp. I expected that he would burst out into the dining room with a joke; instead he was dying on the bathroom floor in a pool of urine. A woman found him. I think she owned the apartment. At least, she acted like she did, but I don't think she is the one who invited me."

Harry had been invited to assist at a séance that night. The invitation had come through the mail with no return address. Harry wasn't too sure who had invited him, but he accepted anyway—lately he had become vulnerable to the promises of the paranormal and immersed himself in that otherworldly network of charlatans and misty-eyed believers. It was a fascination that was trying my patience even though I understood the tragedy that had caused it—a tragedy that had crippled me as well and made it impossible to act with any decisiveness for many months.

"She acted like she owned Overton too, because she kept nagging him. When she found him, she screamed. We didn't even get to the real part of the séance. Overton wanted us to contact his first wife. She had died on their wedding night. He said she was his true love ..."

Harry's voice trailed off, leaving only the hollow, tinny sound of rainwater down our drainpipe and his crisp inhale. I knew he was thinking of Imogen; talk of true love always had this effect on him. Imogen was *our* tragedy.

Less than a year earlier Imogen had left our apartment for an evening walk. She was going to Zabar's to buy some bread. She often made this trip on the nights she returned home early from her work as an archivist at the Morgan Library—that fabulous New York institution endowed long ago by the solitaire-playing tycoon J. P. Morgan. Imogen liked to buy bread at the end of the day. It was usually marked down, but more than this, the idea of getting bread daily appealed to her romantic nature. She told Harry that it made her feel like we were living in Paris and she had ducked down to the *boulangerie* for a baguette.

But that night she didn't return. Harry launched a massive search. He enlisted the police. He rallied friends. He chased down every lead he received and spent hours in excruciating vigil by the phone. Weeks passed. The police finally found her red beret under a bench in Riverside Park. The assumption was that she had somehow fallen into the water and drowned. At least that was one assumption, but darker visions of my mistress's fate haunted me. Her body was not found and she remained a missing person.

Harry and I had been living a sort of half-life of false starts and impossible expectations ever since in the same apartment to which we three had all moved so happily, filled with future promise. Harry and Imogen had met at a party downtown—a party that she frequently liked to remind him she had almost skipped because her Labrador puppy had a cold that night.

Harry took another long, reflective drag of his cigarette. I tried to keep my body motionless but the involuntary canine trembling that many humans mistake for excitement made my collar tinkle.

Harry mistook the sound for bladder-based urgency. He took my leash down from the hook beside the door and clapped his big hands together.

"Want to go for a walk, boy?"

Harry employed the singsong voice reserved for inducing the delivery of a swift Number 1 or 2 by Yours Truly.

I sat down and let him snap the leash to my collar. I am fortunate in this important regard: he is sensitive to my need for walks, seldom inflicting a marathon of waiting that might force me to test my house-trained credentials.

It was well past midnight and our street was empty. It had stopped raining, but the sidewalk still glistened. Young Harry remained silent. He sucked the life out of his cigarette and lit a second. Together we exhaled great clouds of steam and smoke into the cold night air as we trotted toward Central Park. We crossed the avenue, passed through the park gate and down the tree-lined path. The ground was hard beneath my paws, but a little spongy in places from the rain. Indeed, it felt like December—winter but not quite.

My nose filled with an inexplicably rich array of winter smells. Smells are a central fact of my universe. I will do my best to share them with you despite the extreme differences in our noses which, to make a wine-tasting parallel, will reduce the finest vintage for you to a third-rate beer for me. What a marvelous organ! A Labrador's sense of smell is 100,000 times more acute than that of man. Imagine what the world would be like if humans could smell with the same complexity. Humans would have at their disposal a rich vocabulary that could illuminate nuance and shed truth. But more on that later.

Even in the absence of need, I never forget to pull Harry toward the little hill that has been designated for my Number 1s. I think if I act a bit Pavlovian it reinforces the importance of regular walks in my owner's mind. That night, I lifted my right leg and as usual felt embarrassed even though there was no one else about.

Not that Harry was paying me the slightest bit of attention. He was off with the pixies—sad and brokenhearted pixies.

"Sometimes," Harry said, "the spirits will call to us so strongly that our bodies just let us go. Maybe that's what happened to Overton. Maybe his first wife was calling from the beyond."

Malarkey, of course, but I couldn't blame Harry. Imogen had left us both quite alone, forced to pick up the fragments as best we could and lick wounds that showed no sign of healing. Harry had responded to her absence by opening himself up to people and ideas that Imogen would have promptly dismissed as fools and absurdities—and Harry would have felt the same confident disdain in happier times.

If Imogen's disappearance had taught me anything it was this: men need to be loved or they will slowly and invariably go bad. A perfectly adequate male in his twenties will become, in little more than a decade—if unloved—a strange creature statistically prone to die of an ingrown toenail in an apartment crammed with hoarded newspapers and unwashed cereal bowls.

Harry wasn't the only male that could use Imogen's help. I was also slipping without her. She had been my mistress long before she had been Harry's. My mind scrolled backward five years.

"Aren't you a wise little dog?" Imogen had said, lifting my puppy body high in the air and gently flicking my chin, white even then. That very day she had whisked me away from the pet store clods, the sawdust and the poking children to my first home: a little studio in the East Village.

Imogen had made better males of us both and yet the anatomy of my dog's eyes would never permit me to shed a single tear for my vanished mistress.